BT2 1/22

Twitter: @Samantha KingBooks
Instagram: @samanthakingauthor
Facebook: @SamanthaKingBooks

The Secret Keeper's Daughter

SAMANTHA KING

ONE PLACE. MANY STORIES

HQ
An imprint of HarperCollins*Publishers* Ltd
1 London Bridge Street
London SE1 9GF

www.harpercollins.co.uk

HarperCollins*Publishers*
1st Floor, Watermarque Building, Ringsend Road
Dublin 4, Ireland

This paperback edition 2021

1

First published in Great Britain by
HQ, an imprint of HarperCollins*Publishers* Ltd 2021

Copyright © Samantha King 2021

Samantha King asserts the moral right to be
identified as the author of this work.
A catalogue record for this book is
available from the British Library.

ISBN: 9780008471439

MIX
Paper from
responsible sources
FSC™ C007454

This book is produced from independently certified FSC™ paper
to ensure responsible forest management.

For more information visit: www.harpercollins.co.uk/green

Printed and bound in the UK using 100% renewable
electricity at CPI Group (UK) Ltd

*For every parent who's ever wondered
what's going on inside their child's head . . .*

Present fears are less than horrible imaginings.
WILLIAM SHAKESPEARE, *Macbeth*, Act 1, Scene 3

Prologue

The North Sea was my mum's final resting place, but even before then I found a strange sort of comfort living so close to it. Dad always hated it, of course, complaining about its 'bleakness', its 'savage unpredictability'. But that's why I loved it. Dirty, gunmetal grey one moment, then ethereal silver the next, somehow it gave me hope that all my troubles would eventually pass over too, like the changing currents and ever-shifting clouds.

The eager rush of its waves breaking on the shingle beach of our little stretch of the Heritage Coastline was also my favourite noise. As a child, I would lie in bed at Sea View, eyes tightly closed, letting the crashing roar drown out the worries in my head. And when I grew up and had a home of my own, I still relied on the sea to lull me to sleep, even though by then I spent each night safely wrapped in Jordan's arms.

Then we had you, Marley, and I fell in love with a new sound. *Your voice.*

*

1

You were such a noisy baby, and you grew up into the chattiest, most inquisitive child. As we picked our way across tide-sculpted drifts of gritty sand each morning, you would fill your little bucket with stones and your mind with facts: about the incongruously mystical white orb of Sizewell Power Station that seemed to hover, UFO-like, in the distance; about the famous Scallop sculpture facing impassively out to sea, its hinged steel shell spread wide in stoic defiance of the buffeting winds and furiously pounding waves.

You fired endless questions at me, about the hovering gulls that kept plaintive company with us overhead, the fishing boats with their tangled nets strewn out to dry, enticing us with the salty whiff of adventures. Sometimes I conjured up imaginary ones for us, and when you were old enough, you dreamed up even more colourful stories of your own.

Your inventiveness astonished me; you were like a little magpie, collecting new words like pretty shells. Then, one day, a few weeks ago, everything changed. We still walked along the beach before school each day, but you asked no questions; you told no tales. In fact, you began to speak so rarely that when you did, I wanted to scoop up each and every word and hoard them like diamonds in a treasure chest. A worry box, as it turned out.

I can't take my eyes off it – that jewel-spangled box on the kitchen dresser. Here I am, flat on my back on a paramedic's stretcher, half-blinded by pain and a dark curtain of hot, sticky blood, while my chest is rhythmically, urgently pumped – and all I can think about is the words buried inside a glittery old shoe box. No precious gems, in fact, just sharp pebbles of fear. If I close my eyes, I can picture them: five little words; one devastating secret.

I wish you'd told me sooner. No, that sounds as though I blame you. I don't, darling. All I mean to say is that I wish I'd realised what you were worrying about, before it was too late. Before you were snatched away from me; before your baby brother was wrenched so brutally from my arms. I can't stop thinking about

2

that, too. His little pink face all crumpled, blue eyes searching frantically for me. Then the world went black.

That's not your fault, either. I've got a hole in my heart, you see. One of nature's cruel little quirks. *Atrial septal defect*. ASD. That's what the doctors call it. Mostly, it's fine. Medication helps, and when it doesn't . . . well, sometimes, when I'm stressed or frightened, when my heart wants to beat faster and finds it can't, then it simply . . . stops.

This time, I think it might be for good; I can feel that my battered body wants to let go. Only the weaker it becomes, the fiercer my brain rages. *Why has this happened? Why? Why?* That small yet frighteningly enormous word. It's eating away at me, hungry for answers. If it's the last thing I do, I need to find them. Find *you*.

But memory is my only guide, and the only clues I have are the seven notes you left for me. It's been just one terrifying hour since your last one, and seven traumatic days since the first. Since we made that wretched worry box together . . .

Chapter 1

SUNDAY – SEVEN DAYS BEFORE

'Now *this* is perfect. Look, Marley. What do you think?' I smiled, but I could barely breathe as I strolled back into our kitchen and saw you sitting bolt upright at the table, exactly as I'd left you ten minutes earlier. You hadn't moved an inch while I searched the cottage. Or, to be honest, sat on my bed tearing my hair out, wondering what on earth was going on with you.

I didn't tell you that, of course. I told you I was looking for something we could turn into a treasure chest. 'Half-term's over. It's school tomorrow. Last chance for us to get messy and have fun!' I'd coaxed, hoping the idea might excite you. You didn't even look up.

'What do you reckon, love?' I prompted again, holding out the box like I was still a teacher prepping for the afternoon art lesson – only not to a class of lively primary school kids, this time, but to one unnaturally quiet, scared-looking seven-year-old. 'I found it under my bed. No idea how long it's been there. Or what used to be in it.'

That was the first lie I'd ever told you, but my problems could wait; yours couldn't. It wouldn't help you to know what *really* happened to the contents of that glossy white cardboard box, or how it had haunted me for so many years.

Even now, dazzled by the fluorescent glare of hospital lights, I can picture it; even as anaesthetic pumps through my veins, my fingers tingle as I imagine touching its smoothness. Doctors crowd around me, but it's other faces I see – other voices from the past that clamour accusingly in my head. Yours. Your daddy's. My parents'. *Amy's*.

'It looks new.' At last you spoke, your little hand reaching out to hover, butterfly fretful, over the pristine box. 'Isn't it bad to spoil it?'

'No, love, it's fine. It's empty. See?' I shook the box nonchalantly, trying not to remember the last time I'd held it – the angry words and shocked sense of betrayal.

Tentatively, you plunged your hands inside it, and when they emerged, they were filled with frothy almond-white tulle. *My bridal veil*. I genuinely *had* forgotten about that, and I shivered as I watched you crown yourself with the gauzy silk, wishing for the thousandth time that my own mum could have watched me do the same eight years ago.

'Can I keep this?' you lisped.

'Of course, sweetheart.' I took off the veil and tucked it inside the chest pocket of your dungarees, where it couldn't taunt me with reminders. 'As long as I get to keep you.'

'Forever-together-whatever?'

'Till the seas run dry.' I leaned forward to seal what was usually our bedtime promise with a kiss on your forehead.

'Just you and me?'

'Well, we mustn't forget about—'

'Daddy.' Your voice was a squeak. 'And *him*.' Your dangling foot nudged repeatedly against the smart red carry-cot tucked, as usual, under the kitchen table.

'Hmm. We'll have to start calling your baby brother by his name, don't you think?'

'Benjamin.' You chewed it over in your mouth like a sour sweet.

'Don't you like it? Daddy chose it. It's *his* daddy's name. Isn't it, Benji Boy?' I cooed, stooping to pick up your squirming baby brother. He let out a soft, milky burp, and I laughed, turning to smile at you. But your face was blank, your eyes shadowed.

'Can we call him BB instead?' you whispered.

'BB? Oh, I see. Benji Boy.' It hit me that I should have asked you to help choose his name, to make you feel more involved. Maybe that was the simple explanation for your recent mood change: jealousy of all the attention on your new brother; resentment at having to share it with him. I knew how *that* felt. 'Yes, darling. We can call him BB, if you like.'

'Will Daddy be cross?'

'Cross? Why would that make him cross?'

You shrugged. 'For not doing what he says.'

'Well, *we* have a say in things around here too, don't we?' I teased, but you didn't smile. I sighed, frustrated that I had no more clue now about what was bothering you than I'd had for the entire half-term break; all I knew for certain was that you weren't yourself. I tried again to cheer you up. 'Look, I know it's all a bit new, having such a little person around. But it doesn't have to stop us playing *our* games, does it?'

'I don't like games.'

'Really?' I recognised the lie and felt my stomach flip. *What else weren't you telling me?* 'Hmm, I bet I can think of a good one.'

I looked around, determined to find something to entertain you. Only as my gaze trawled our small, bright but messy kitchen, all I could see was boxes of nappies stacked in one corner, a wicker basket near the Aga piled high with freshly washed baby clothes. Bibs and baby toys spilled off the blue-painted rocking chair you used to pretend was a sailing ship, before it became the place where I fed and rocked BB to sleep.

I groaned inwardly, knowing the same scene was repeated in every room of our tiny, two-bedroom fisherman's cottage, wedged in the middle of a pastel terrace fifty metres from the beach. Guiltily, I wondered if the mess, the chaos, was bringing you down.

'OK, how about a silly-rhymes contest?' That *always* got you giggling. I settled BB back in his carry-cot, then leaned on the kitchen table, pretending to think. 'Right, let me see. The pig, who was eating a fig . . . jumped on the sofa to chew Grandma's wig!'

'Did Grandma Olivia have a *wig*?'

'Oh. Well, she . . .' Torn between reluctance to talk about my mum and relief that *something* had finally piqued your interest, I decided to roll with it. 'She had beautiful hair, actually. At least, before she got ill. It was like a river of silk, my dad used to say.'

'A river?' Your eyes widened. 'Like the one where Daddy goes fishing?'

'Sorry?' Jordan always had the daily catch delivered to the restaurant kitchen at the country club where he was head chef; I'd never known him to go fishing himself. He loved sailing and spent half his life on the sea, but . . . 'Has Daddy ever taken *you* fishing, Marley?'

You shook your head, clamming up again.

I couldn't let it go. 'Has he taken you out on his boat at *all*?'

'I wish I had hair like Grandma. I hate my curls.'

I registered the deliberate change of subject, but let it pass. 'I felt the same about mine when I was your age. But I love them now. You will too, one day. My hair's chocolate-brown like Grandma's, but yours is just like your daddy's. Like pockets of sunshine. It's *beautiful*.'

'It's not. It's messy.' You tugged angrily at it. 'Leah called me Mop Head.'

'She called you *what*?' My heart jumped at the nickname, a memory hammering in my head, distracting me from niggles about Jordan. 'Well, that wasn't very kind, was it? Nor is it true.' I reached out, scrunching your soft, golden ponytail between my hands.

You shrugged. 'I don't care.'

'Are you sure, love?' I searched your eyes for the truth. 'I know Leah's your best friend, but . . . has she been teasing you? Is that why you've been a bit quiet lately?'

Another shrug.

'Best friends do fall out sometimes,' I said brightly. 'Look at me and Aunty Amy. I've known her my whole life, and we still have squabbles.' More memories roiled; I pushed them away. 'They blow over, though. That's what friendships are like.' I lowered my voice. 'You can tell me, you know? If you've been worrying about Leah. Or . . .' Breathlessly, I brooded over your question about whether Daddy would be cross. 'Someone *else*?'

This time, you shook your head until your hair spilled out of its ponytail, half covering your face. Selecting a matted strand, you chewed the end.

'OK,' I relented, not wanting to push too hard and scare you off. 'Well, try not to pay any attention to what Leah said. *I* love your curls. And so does your daddy.'

'He doesn't! He said they're a nuisance. My hair got tangled at the beach, and—'

'The beach?' I grabbed your hands, looking you straight in the eye. As far as I was aware, you hadn't left the house all day. 'When was this, darling?'

Your eyes filled with tears. 'I wasn't supposed to say, Mummy! I didn't mean to!'

'You weren't supposed to say *what*, Marley?' I asked, and my faulty heart beat faster.

Chapter 2

By the time I'd bundled BB into his buggy and helped you with your jacket and boots, before slipping into my own, we'd both calmed down. I grabbed some stale, leftover bread for the seagulls, then ushered you out of the back door, bumping the buggy down the step. 'OK, sweetheart? Here, you can push BB for me. You mustn't worry, Marley. Everything's fine.'

I'd managed to cajole out of you that Jordan had taken you to the beach early that morning – 'for a walk'. I hoped a stroll with *me* might help you to relax and say more; we'd always had our best chats wandering along the pebble beach.

'Are you upset, Mummy?'

'Why would I be upset, love?'

'Daddy said it was a secret. I was to be quiet and not say a word.'

I paused, key still in the back door. 'He said that?' I turned to look at you over my shoulder, but you'd already hurried through our small back garden, disappearing into the alley beyond. 'Wait, Marley! Don't run off!' I called out, concerned at how easily you'd managed to unlock the gate; I hadn't even realised you knew the security code.

'I'll push BB, Mummy.' You manoeuvred yourself in front of me as soon I caught up with you, angling yourself between me and the buggy. 'You *said* I was to push him.'

'So I did. Although the buggy's a bit heavy, and I'd forgotten how bumpy this path is.' I pushed harder to roll the sturdy pushchair along the pebbly path leading straight to the beach, trying not to feel bad about the subtle manipulation: taking you back there to see if it would prompt further confessions about that morning.

Returning to the scene of the crime, I tried not to think, surreptitiously glancing at the spot where Jordan secured his motorbike on days off. You'd refused to say if he'd taken you out on his boat; I wondered if he'd ever secretly given you a ride on his bike . . .

'Can we go home, Mummy? I don't want to go.'

'Come on, nearly there. The fresh air will help BB nod off.' I knew that would please you. 'Oh, Marley, careful!' I exclaimed as you tripped, slipping between me and the buggy.

'I told you! We need to go *home. Now*, Mummy!'

Your face flushed scarlet, and I had a strong feeling that you'd deliberately engineered the fall, to force me to turn back. But *why*? You'd always loved the beach . . . what could possibly have put you off going there? The burst of anger was so completely unlike you that I crouched down, cupping your face in my hands. 'Are you OK? Are you hurt?'

You pulled back, wrapping your arms around yourself, knees hunched.

'Sweetheart, let me see.' I brushed your hands gently aside, gasping when I saw purple, tender-looking bruises. They were recent, but not fresh; they couldn't possibly have been caused by your trip just now. 'Marley, how did you get these?' I asked quietly.

'The ground was really hard,' you mumbled. 'The stones hurt.'

'When? Just now? Or . . . this morning?' I tried to keep my tone even, not to yell in panic, but I couldn't entirely contain my frustration. 'What on earth were you *doing*?'

'Daddy said it was just our little game.'

I don't like games, I heard echo in my head. 'What sort of game?'

11

'But I got sand all in my hair. I tried to get it out, Mummy. I'm sorry.' You leaned your head on your knees, burying your face.

'Silly bean, you don't have to apologise. That's what half-term is for, isn't it? Getting messy and having fun.' I smiled, even as I continued to puzzle over what 'game' you'd been playing, and why Jordan had taken you out without telling me. He *never* did that. 'So?' I asked casually. '*Did* you have fun?'

Your body hunched even tighter, as though you were trying to disappear into yourself.

I watched you for a few moments, then glanced along the narrow path leading to the beach, racking my brains to think of any possible reason for going there so early, before I was even awake. 'OK, well, let's get you home. I'll speak to Daddy later.' I forced myself to breathe slowly, feeling a fluttery pain in my chest as my heart started to thump.

You looked up at me, eyes wide, pupils narrowing to pinpricks in the bright October sunshine. 'No. Don't tell. Please.'

'But . . .' I didn't want to make a promise I knew I wouldn't keep. 'OK, don't worry. I know, why don't we stop by the café and pick up something nice for lunch, then home for a bath? I'll sort those sandy tangles out in no time.'

Not even pizza from The Kitchen café, followed by a browse around The Thorpeness Emporium afterwards, could cheer you up. Usually, you loved exploring the shelves packed with old curiosities and colourful bric-a-brac – it had always been your favourite thing to do with my dad, who loved antiques – but you practically ran out of the shop, refusing to look. I lost my appetite completely, and neither of us spoke as we wandered home.

After bathing BB, I filled the tub for you, kneeling down to shampoo your hair. 'That better?' I soothed, working my fingers slowly through your knotty, sandy curls.

You nodded, scrubbing at your face as tears rolled down your flushed cheeks.

12

'Marley, love. Please, talk to me.' I stared at your bruised knees, my heart aching. But not even a bubble-blowing competition could coax any joy, and afterwards we skipped our usual hairdryer game of pretending we were caught in a tornado. In silence, I helped you fasten your dungarees, and we made our way downstairs to the kitchen.

The first thing I saw was the box, still sitting in the middle of the table. I lifted the lid, wishing I could look inside your mind so easily. 'We were going to make a treasure chest, weren't we? Or maybe . . . this would make a great post box, don't you think? Our own special, private one. Shall we decorate it?'

I stood up and took two strides to the kitchen dresser, throwing open the cream-painted pine doors and taking out the big craft box holding all my old classroom supplies: stickers, buttons and gems. Sparkly bits of material. After setting it on the table, I hunted in the dresser drawer, pulling out a pad and pen.

'I hate writing,' you protested, but I saw your eyes fix on the little notebook.

'You don't have to write much,' I encouraged, without pointing out that, usually, you loved writing. 'Anything that's made you smile. Or feel sad. Or angry. Scared, even.' I paused, waiting, hoping you'd say something. *Anything*. 'Or you could draw a picture.' I sat down at the table again, doodling a heart with your name inside it. 'Then fold it up and post it in here. See?' I flapped the lid again, a white flag of surrender.

The idea for the worry box had come to me in the middle of yet another sleepless night. I'd used one many times before – in the classroom. But that had always been anonymous: a chance for any child to get things off their chest without stepping out of the shadows where they felt safe. I had no idea if a sparkly box at home would work the same magic; all I knew was that it felt like my last chance to find out what was troubling you.

If it failed, I was going to find a counsellor. For reasons I couldn't fathom then, Jordan was dead set against the idea, and in truth I wanted you to talk to *me*, just like you used to, chatting on the way home from school, in the bath and at the beach. Your withdrawal frightened me. I knew you were hiding something; I just didn't know what it was.

'Post it how?' Head tilted to one side, you sized up the box.

'Well, let me see.' I reached over to the craft box and took out my scissors, eyeing the blades dubiously. Half-blunt from years hacking away at egg boxes and milk cartons, the paraphernalia of endless school projects, I wasn't sure they'd be sharp enough. 'I might need to use a knife,' I mused. 'Oh! Sweetheart, mind your fingers!'

The scissors were too big for your tiny hands, and blood rushed dizzyingly to my head as you grabbed them, lifting them high before stabbing those half-blunt blades through the cardboard lid, as fiercely as though you were thrusting them deep into someone's heart.

I never guessed whose face you were imagining – who, in your terrified, traumatised mind, you were fighting off. I saw only sparkly red shoes, a stranger's suitcase in the hall at Sea View. I remembered being a child myself, the same age as you are now . . . and I remembered Amy Jackson's smile, the day she accidentally came to live with us.

Chapter 3

AUGUST 1998

'Holly? We've got a visitor, love. Where are you?'

My mum's soft, singsong voice was a siren call to me. Even when she called up to me in my bedroom at the top of our four-storey townhouse, or summoned me in from the garden for tea, she barely raised her voice. But I always heard her.

'HOLLY! You've got ten seconds to get down here, or I'll come and find you!'

Dad, on the other hand, was always loud. Even as a young man – and he was in his early thirties then – he reminded me of the new prime minister he loved criticising on the news. Animated. Edgy. Like he had too much energy and nowhere for it to go.

'Coming!' I yelled back that afternoon, dashing out of my room and down the spiral staircase, trying to think of anything that might warrant a double summons.

As I reached the first-floor landing and peered down into the stone-flagged hall below, I could see nothing heralding an emergency. Sunshine dazzled through the stained-glass front door of our converted former church, and Mum's favourite Tiffany lamp sparkled reassuringly, projecting ruby and emerald

15

shards of colour onto the white walls. Next to it, the antique globe my dad was forever lecturing me was 'not a toy' was still intact.

But something was different. Unusually, both my parents were waiting for me, along with a skinny, pale-faced girl with long dark hair and the bluest eyes I'd ever seen. She looked as wary as I felt.

'Ah, there you are.' Mum beckoned me with a gentle wave. 'Come, sweetheart. Your father would like you to meet someone. This is Amy. The daughter of an old friend.'

'Not just any old friend – my best man,' Dad pronounced as I continued to loiter uncertainly. 'Amy's daddy and I go way back. We're old partners in crime.' He bent towards the girl, adding conspiratorially close to her ear: 'But I expect he's told you that, yes?'

'No.' The girl scowled, backing away.

'Really? I thought he'd have given away *all* my secrets.' Dad grinned as he straightened up, running a hand across his short, dark hair, and I tried to remember when I'd last seen him so amused, so *happy*. It made his eyes seem bluer, his teeth white against his tan. 'Ha. Most of them made up. Born storyteller, Luke Jackson. Isn't that right, Olivia?'

'He certainly has a way with words,' Mum replied. But she didn't laugh along, or even smile. She untied her apron and pulled it over her head, carefully, so as not to dislodge her usual neat bun. Then she rolled the apron up so tightly, I saw her knuckles turn white.

'He sure does,' Dad agreed. 'No wonder he made it to barrister, while I got stuck lecturing law. He let slip that he's writing a book, too. You've got one clever daddy, Amy.'

'He's just writing the words.' Her scowl deepened. 'Mummy's doing the pictures.'

'Pictures? Is it a children's book, then?'

The girl shrugged, looking bored now.

'Well, whatever it is, I'm sure the illustrations will be the best

16

bit.' Dad rested a hand on her shoulder. 'Your mum's an incredible artist, Amy. I've never met anyone so creative.'

'She makes all her own clothes.' The scowl finally evaporated. 'And mine.'

'So does *my* mum,' I said, pleased to discover I had something in common with this sulky but interesting stranger. Although, as I finally stepped off the last stair and crossed the hall, I noticed that her plum jersey dress was far more stylish than my brown pinafore, and her ears were pierced with tiny gold hoops I instantly envied. I wondered about the clothes her mum made, whether they were flowery dresses like the ones my mum always wore.

'They're an insanely talented couple,' Dad said, chuckling. 'Far too glamorous for their own good. They haven't changed a bit, either. I spotted them immediately this morning. What a lucky coincidence, hey? I never go into Cambridge on a Sunday, and they chose today of all days to visit our old college. What are the chances?'

'Next to none,' Mum agreed lightly.

'Yes, well. I'm just glad we could help out. Sounds like they have quite a trip lined up. Cambridge today. Paris tomorrow. Then Milan. Or was it Madrid?'

'They're going to *Paris*?' It sounded like there was something stuck in Mum's throat. 'But what about—'

'I know the plan was for you to go with them, Amy,' Dad cut in. 'But your dad's right. They're going to be super busy with work. You'll be better off here. I know Thorpeness might look like a sleepy old place. Especially after London. But I promise you there's loads of fun to be had.' He winked. 'If you know where to look for it. Isn't that right, Holly?'

I nodded mutely, eyeing the girl's shiny patent leather shoes, wondering how she kept them so clean. I doubted she'd be interested in the games I played with my best friend Jane. Or any of the kids in the village. In fact, she didn't look like she belonged there at all.

17

'Especially in summer,' Dad continued, when it was clear I wasn't going to offer more. 'Third week in August, this place comes alive. There's the Marmalade Ball. We all get dressed up for that. Then the regatta on the Meare. You know, the boating lake. We passed it on our way here. That ends with the biggest fireworks display you'll ever see, and—'

'The ball's in two weeks, Adam,' Mum cut in. 'Surely Luke and Isabella will be—'

'And it's wonderful to have you stay with us. *Isn't* it, Olivia?' Dad said firmly. 'I haven't seen Luke, your daddy, for years,' he went on, turning back to Amy, and it seemed to me that the jollier he sounded, the more withdrawn Mum became. 'But he was always like a brother to me. Which makes *you* pretty much family, too. Yes?'

'I've always wanted a sister! Haven't I, Mummy?' I appealed to her with a small sense of triumph that faded as I took in her flushed cheeks and watery eyes.

'Me too,' Amy said huskily.

And then she smiled. You know the one. Long and slow, it starts with her eyes, indigo-blue and fringed with thick, dark lashes. They narrow and crinkle, while her mouth curls up, just slightly, almost as though she's trying to hide her smile – like it's only for you. It took me years to realise that's exactly what she wants you to think.

'Excellent!' Dad clapped his hands together. 'Holly's been rattling around this holiday, I'm afraid. Her mummy's setting up a floristry business. I've got work to finish. That's why I was in college today. Like I say, lucky timing, yes? Now I don't have to worry about Holly being lonely. Everyone's happy. You'll look after Amy, won't you, sweetheart?'

'Of course.' I tried to put on my best, most grown-up voice. 'Welcome to Sea View,' I said politely, as I always heard Mum say whenever she greeted visitors at the door.

'Oh, wait, I have something for you, Amy.' Dad looked excited again. 'I took the opportunity while you and your daddy went back to the hotel to pack. Hang on. I'll fetch it.'

'Is that yours?' As Dad disappeared into his study at the front of the house, I nodded at a smart black holdall with shiny buckles. It was almost as big as Amy.

She shook her head, her dark hair so fine, it rippled like black silk around her oval face. 'It's Mummy's. She has lots. She's a designer. Her label is *Isabella's*.'

I had no idea what that meant; the idea of a person wearing some kind of *label* seemed very odd to me. I looked at Amy's suitcase. *That* had a label on it. In case it got lost, I supposed. Amy's parents obviously travelled a great deal, which must explain why her mum had such a massive case. And a label. In case *she* got lost.

I was desperate to ask but didn't want to appear ignorant in front of this pretty, confident stranger with her glittering, watchful eyes and fancy luggage. So I simply nodded and smiled. I was still smiling when Dad returned with a glossy white oblong box.

'Here we are. I hope you like them, Amy. Red was always your mum's favourite colour. I hoped it might be yours, too. I should have asked her, of course. Only she and your dad wanted to catch an earlier flight. Now that you're staying here, I mean. She told me how much you love fashion too. Shoes especially. And your size. But I didn't think to check—'

'Open it! Open it!' I interrupted, stepping closer, eager to see what was inside that glossy, enticing box. *Sparkly red shoes*. I recognised them immediately, and all my excitement at having a pretend sister was washed away by a hot rush of hurt.

'Thank you, Mr Aitken,' Amy said politely.

But she didn't take them out of the box; she didn't stroke them, or fawn over the shoes I had coveted for months. I glared at my mum, baffled that she could have forgotten how I'd dragged her the long way home from school every day, just so I could gaze

19

at those very shoes in the shop on the high street. *How could she have bought them for another girl?*

'Oh, let's not be formal. Call me Adam,' Dad said. 'And you're welcome. I'm glad you like them,' he added, even though Amy hadn't said any such thing.

I felt sorry for him then: he was trying so hard and getting little in return. I felt guilty for thinking badly of my mum, too. The shoes had clearly been Dad's idea; Mum looked equally startled by the gift. In fact, she'd hardly said a word, and she was usually so chatty.

It was only after Mum was gone that I realised, for all her chattiness, how little she actually told me; how little I knew her, not just as my mum but as a *person*. She colour-washed my life with her quiet elegance and warm, bustling ways, but I never really stopped to look at *her*. Olivia Aitken née Howard.

'My favourite colour's red, too,' I said, although from that day on, I hated it.

'Holly, why don't you take Amy upstairs and show her your room?' Mum suggested at last. 'I'll call you when lunch is ready. You need your medicine, too, don't forget.'

'Are you ill?' Brazenly, Amy looked me up and down.

'I've got a hole in my heart,' I declared somewhat grandly, hoping it might make me sound interesting enough to impress this bored-looking girl.

'How did you get *that*?' she asked, finally showing a gratifying glint of interest.

'I was born with it. Daddy said I should have an operation, but Mummy—'

'Said she can't risk losing you,' Mum jumped in with a smile. 'I've got your pills ready, love,' she added. 'I'll give you a call in a bit, OK? I just want a word with your dad.'

'Yes. You girls will want to get to know each other,' he agreed. 'Room-mates. Just like Amy's daddy and I used to be at Cambridge. It'll be fun, hey?'

'She's going to share my *room*?' I stared at him in shock.

Dad hated me leaving my things around the house, and my cosy bedroom had become my private refuge: a place where I could be as messy as I liked. I loved it when Jane came for sleepovers, but that was only ever for a night or two. My eyes fixed on the oversized suitcase in the hall that clearly held enough clothes for a great many nights.

'Only for a few days,' Mum said, her eyes drifting to the suitcase too. 'Just until Luke and Isabella . . . just until her parents are back from Europe.' She smiled at Amy, then turned back to my dad, resting a gentle hand on his arm. 'Right, Adam?'

Chapter 4

Three weeks later, Amy was still sleeping on the spare bed next to mine, and it had become clear that for her, 'sharing' meant taking the best for herself. Her clothes filled my wardrobe, although on that particular late-August bank holiday, most were spread across my bed: Mum had suggested Amy and I pick out something to wear for a 'musical soiree' she was hosting.

Apparently, Amy played the piano *exquisitely*: 'just like her mother', Dad said, while Mum was always telling everyone what a 'fine ear' I had for the violin. In truth, I didn't, and I dreaded being shown up by Amy, who seemed to outshine me at most things.

I knew all eyes would be on her at the party, just as they had been at the Marmalade Ball the week before, and I'd deliberately chosen my best dress to wear. I'd thought the green velvet pinafore looked fancy and grown-up, until I saw Amy's long, silky red dress with its diamante neckline. As it turned out, however, that wasn't the worst part of the evening.

'I have a feeling this might be our last party this summer,' Mum sighed, as she swished into our first-floor drawing room and set a vase of peonies on the mantelpiece. Smoothing down her dress, for once a plain gold linen rather than her usual chintz,

22

she frowned as though realising she'd forgotten something. Her frown deepened as she studied herself in the mirror.

She always looked pretty, I thought, but that evening Mum seemed to glow. Her cheeks were flushed, and her long chestnut hair was loose and glossy. One hand toyed with an amber-jewelled butterfly brooch I'd never seen before. Pinned close to the sweet-heart neckline of her dress, it caught the light and sparkled enticingly.

'Oh, is it school next week?' I was still staring at the brooch, thinking how expensive it looked, how unlike anything I'd ever seen my mum wear – wishing *I* could wear it.

'Term starts on Monday, love. Or is it Tuesday?' Mum's breath came in jerky puffs as she plumped cushions on the cream chester-field sofa. 'I'll ask your teacher, shall I?' Her brown eyes twinkled. 'You'll be pleased to hear Miss Shaw is joining us this evening.'

'Oh *no!*' I dashed to the window to watch for the kind but gossipy woman who seemed obsessed by my family. Miss Shaw was always asking questions about us, all under the guise of our home, the former St Mary's Church, being of 'historic interest'.

'The summer's gone in a flash,' Mum continued wistfully. 'You were in hospital the first week, of course. Then Amy . . .' She frowned, before nodding at a tray of snacks. 'Pop those on the side tables, would you, love? People can help themselves. Saves me running up and downstairs. I don't know what's wrong with me today. I feel completely wrung out.'

'You can have one of my pills,' I offered, grimacing. I hated the tablets I had to swallow with my juice each morning. Beta blockers and anticoagulants; even they weren't always enough to stop the palpitations and breathlessness that could grip me out of the blue.

'Ah, sweetheart. That's kind of you. But I'm fine. Today was just a bit busy, that's all. What with our picnic at the beach this afternoon. The allotment this morning. I probably shouldn't have gone, but I just needed to see . . .' She broke off, frowning again. 'Anyway, we're all good. And you'll be my little helper this evening, Holly, won't you?'

'OK!' I skipped across the room, eyeing the dishes of nuts. 'Please may I have some?' Just in time, I remembered to ask. *Manners cost nothing*, was Dad's perpetual mantra.

'I *should* tell you to wait,' Mum teased. 'But go on. I know how hard it is to resist temptation.' Her forehead creased, and for a moment she looked sad, then she seemed to force a smile as she crossed the room to the baby grand piano. 'Where is Amy, anyway?'

'Don't know. And don't care,' I growled under my breath. That was one good thing about the new school term starting: surely Amy's parents would have to return from Paris in time for that, and I'd have my bedroom, my home – and my parents – all to myself again.

'I haven't seen her for hours. Guests will be arriving soon. She'll miss her star turn, if she doesn't hurry up. Your dad picked up some film this afternoon especially.'

'Oh, no! Is he *filming* us?' I'd always been camera shy, but Amy wasn't. Photos of the regatta a week ago had filled the local *Gazette*, but it was Amy's pretty face that had stared out from the front page.

'Just a few snaps. He's making an album for Amy's parents. A "memory book", he calls it. He's doing the words *and* pictures,' Mum added, with the hint of an eye-roll.

'Amy loves having her photo taken.' Suddenly I lost my appetite for the nuts.

'She certainly does,' Mum agreed, and I wondered if she was remembering the headlines, too. Dad had tried to quash village gossip by insisting it was just a case of 'high jinks', but Amy had relished her fame, cutting out all the newspaper photos of herself.

'I bet she'll be a model when she grows up,' I mumbled, picturing her pirate costume at the regatta, sapphire eyes glittering behind a black sequinned mask, and recalling how she'd adored the competitive parade of decorated floats afterwards.

The theme for our family's entry that year had been Peter Pan, in honour of the author who'd helped create the original design of the Meare: the seventy-acre lake dotted with Neverland-themed islands. After insisting on dressing up as a pirate, Amy had smirked when my mum showed me the flouncy Tinker Bell costume she'd spent days sewing. I knew Mum had sensed my disappointment, and, irrationally, I'd blamed Amy. I was secretly convinced that her actions that night were a deliberate effort to pay me back for being grumpy with her.

'A model?' Mum's gentle query broke into my fractious thoughts.

'Like in the catalogue. Modelling clothes and stuff. She's got loads,' I said enviously.

'Ah, yes. She's, um, very striking, too. At least, the papers seemed to think so. I can see her parading along a catwalk. Maybe not dressed as a pirate, though.' Mum winked.

'Or Tinker Bell.' I grinned, perking up at the rare sense of conspiracy between us.

'Right, now, let me see.' Almost immediately, Mum snapped back into busy hostess mode. 'I'll just nip down to the kitchen again for the hot snacks, and then—'

'Mrs Aitken! Olivia!' Amy's husky voice was a shriek, her usually pale, infamously pretty oval face blotchy red as she appeared in the doorway.

'Oh, there you are.' Mum turned to smile at her. 'I was starting to worry.'

'My shoes are gone!' Amy whined. 'The ones Mr Aitken – I mean Adam – gave me.'

'Oh, dear. Where on earth can they have got to?'

Mum looked all around the room, from the vaulted ceiling to the tall, arched stone windows, as though the missing shoes might suddenly plop down the chimney into the inglenook fireplace, or roll out from behind one of the low Queen Anne armchairs.

I stared at Amy's bare feet. Her skinny legs were smooth and white, while mine were brown from spending so much time at the beach. Amy hated it and rarely went there; she'd moaned all afternoon that she wanted to go shopping in Cambridge with my dad instead.

I had, too, but he rarely took me anywhere with him anymore. Or Mum. In fact, she hardly ever left the village at all. It puzzled me, but every time I asked her why, she just smiled and said she preferred home to anywhere else she'd ever been.

'Your shoes are still in the box,' I said carelessly. 'On my dressing table.' I didn't add that it seemed to have become *her* dressing table.

'No, they're not.' Amy's bottom lip quivered. 'They're gone. And I really, really wanted to wear them. They're the best present I've ever had!'

I scowled at her. 'I didn't think you liked them. You haven't even tried them on.'

'Is that why you took them, Holly?' a low voice said from the hall landing. 'Is that why you threw Amy's new shoes into the log shed?'

My legs trembled as Dad walked slowly towards me, one hand hooked over his brown cords, the other holding up a familiar pair of sparkly red shoes. 'In the . . .? *No!*' I gasped.

'Tell the truth now, Holly.'

'I didn't do it! Mummy?'

'Oh, love. Don't upset yourself. Please.' Mum moved quickly to my side, resting a hand on my shoulder. 'You don't want to bring on another attack.'

'But I didn't *do* anything!' I protested again. 'Honestly!'

'So who did, then, pickle?' Dad bent over, his face close to mine.

'I don't know!' I waited for Amy to confess, to do the right thing, as I always tried to, but seconds stretched silently into minutes. Avoiding my dad's eyes, I held my breath, picturing the Bible quotes he'd hung in his study – and over my bed.

Neither of my parents were religious; those needlepoints were simply a legacy of our home's former life. *Sea View*. People always puzzle over its name, and I can't blame them. Even though you could hear the gentle rush of waves from every room, it was only from my bedroom at the top of the old church tower that you could catch a glimpse of the water.

But Mum dreamed of a sea view, so that's what she called our house, gradually eliminating anything 'churchy' – except for the framed commandments. Dad refused to part with those, calling them 'laws to govern the moral chaos'. He loved them; they terrified me.

'I hope you're not lying, Holly.' His deep voice was calm; *too* calm.

'Maybe Amy was playing outside? Perhaps she slipped on some stones?'

'Sweetheart.' Dad shook his head as he straightened up. 'You heard Amy. The shoes were in their box. And Amy hasn't left the house. She's been in my study this last hour.'

'Oh, has she?' Mum's voice had a slight edge to it now. 'I wondered where she'd got to. Holly didn't know, either. Probably because she's been right here, helping me.'

'That's as may be, Olivia. But the shoes are still ruined, and we both know how much Holly wanted them,' Dad countered softly, before frowning at me. 'We don't blame other people for our mistakes, OK? We own up and take responsibility for them.'

'But I haven't done anything *wrong*!'

'I know you *think* you haven't, pickle. You like to have fun. I understand that. I enjoy our little games, too. But you know the rule, yes?'

'Which one might that be, Adam?' Mum queried lightly.

Dad raised his eyebrows at her. 'It's not fun if only one of you is laughing.'

'But it wasn't a game,' I protested again. 'I didn't do it. *She* did!' I saw Amy smirk, and I just knew. She must have thrown her own shoes away, to get me into trouble.

'Poor Amy.' Dad sighed, sweeping a hand back and forth across his hair. 'Not only are her shoes ruined, her best friend is telling fibs about her.'

'Jane's my best friend,' I muttered, gritting my teeth to hold back my tears, suddenly deciding I wouldn't give Amy the satisfaction of seeing how upset I was.

'Little Jane Price.' Dad's eyes narrowed. 'Does she tell fibs too?'

I shook my head, even as I remembered Jane telling my mum that she hadn't picked all the blackberries off the bush at the end of our garden. I knew she had, and I'd tried to reassure her that my mum wouldn't mind, but she'd said: 'Grown-ups *always* mind.'

'Right, well. Let's try this one last time,' Dad said with exaggerated patience. 'Are you or are you not going to own up?'

Feeling trapped, I finally gave in. 'OK. I did it.'

Dad nodded curtly. 'Good girl. Now, what do you have to say to poor Amy?'

'Sorry,' I mumbled.

Amy said nothing at all. She only smiled as I ran past her and out of the drawing room, before bounding up the spiral staircase, holding back my tears until I had crawled into the only place in the world that still felt like it was completely mine: under my bed.

Chapter 5

MONDAY – SIX DAYS BEFORE

'Jordan – *look*!' I was trying to whisper discreetly, so you wouldn't hear, but I practically had to shout to get your daddy's attention as he hummed while beating eggs for our breakfast.

That was one thing that hadn't changed over the last few weeks. Jordan might have started spending weekday nights on the living-room sofa and weekends on his boat, but he always made time to cook and prepare fresh food for us. Even on a Monday morning, when he was rushing to get to his early shift at the country club restaurant.

'Got my hands full here, babe. What's up?' he said, without turning around.

'Marley's posted something. In the worry box.' I carried it to the kitchen table and sat down, staring at the wad of yellow paper inside, recognising it as a page you must have torn from the journal I bought for your birthday. It struck me that I hadn't seen the diary since; you'd tidied everything away so well that I couldn't find *any* of your new books or toys.

Curiously, given his own messiness, Jordan seemed to approve of your newfound perfectionism. But I hated it. I didn't want you to sit quietly, saying 'please' and 'thank you' but little more. I *wanted* to see your flaws; I worried about what was making you hide them.

'Worry box?' Jordan finally stopped whisking and set the glass bowl aside on the worktop, wiping his hands on his jeans as he turned to frown at me.

'Like a post box. You know, for Marley to leave me notes.' I rolled my eyes. 'I *told* you, she hasn't been herself for weeks. I'm worried about her.'

'Ah. So is this *your* worry box, then, or hers?' he teased.

'Marley's, of course.' I glared at him. 'So she can share what's on her mind.'

'Sure.' Blond eyebrows arched. 'Well, go on, then, open it. You'd better be quick, though. Marley will be down in a minute. She's got school today, hasn't she?'

'Yes, she has.' I looked at him in surprise; he never usually remembered term dates.

'Poor kid. First days are the worst. No wonder she's dragging her heels.'

'Actually, she seems super keen to go back.' I glanced at your school bag, propped against the dresser, sighing as I thought of your insistence yesterday on staying home to pack it, rather than going out to play. Then I recalled you letting slip that Jordan had taken you to the beach in the morning – and that he'd called your sandy, tangled curls 'a nuisance' . . .

The thought reminded me of my own dad's impatience with *my* curls as a child, and suddenly I was gripped by an uncomfortable sense of déjà vu; it intensified as I watched Jordan rake a hand across his thick, tawny hair, the gesture weirdly mirroring my dad's.

'Earth to Holly?' he quipped loudly, making me jump.

'Sorry?' I glanced up, then stared closer at him as I noticed he'd had his hair cut. 'Ah, right,' I mumbled, figuring you must have misunderstood his irritation. He'd probably been complaining about his *own* curls, hence the haircut. I smiled. 'Sorry, I was miles away.'

'No kidding. But Marley will be down any second. Hopefully.' He checked his watch. 'I thought I'd drop her off before work.'

'Really?' Most days Jordan practically sprinted out of the door; recently, he'd barely paused to say goodbye. 'Won't that make you late?'

'Nah. I'll take her on the bike.'

'Oh. Are you sure?'

'Of course. We'll be there in a flash. The school's only ten minutes up the road.'

'No, I meant . . . on your motorbike?'

'Is that a problem?'

'Well, I . . .' I wanted to ask if he'd taken you out on it before, or on his boat; I wanted to press him about what had happened at the beach yesterday morning. But we'd had enough misunderstandings, lately, and I was already picking up a thread of tension from him.

'Well, you ...?' Green eyes widened questioningly as I continued to hesitate.

'Actually, you know what? I'll take her. Might as well, I'm dressed and ready.' I glanced down at the jeans and blue sweatshirt I'd pulled on hastily while BB cried for his morning feed. 'And I'd like a quick word with Mrs Hart, in any case.'

'Mrs . . .?'

'Marley's teacher. You remember. Tall, long brown hair. Liverpool accent. You met her at the school summer fair. She's married to Joe at the bank.'

'Right. Of course.' Jordan grabbed his keys out of a china bowl on the dresser, then turned back to look at me. 'It's no hassle for me to take her, you know? In fact, I'd like to.'

'It's fine. Honestly.'

'Sure? I know it's a pain getting on and off the bus with the buggy.'

31

'We'll manage. We do every other day.' Realising I sounded frosty, I added more gently: 'I need to get BB out, anyway. We could both do with a bit of fresh air.' I'd lain awake half the night worrying about you, and my head was muzzy.

'Right.' Jordan tucked the keys in his jeans pocket. 'Wait . . . did you just say *BB*?'

'Yes. Short for Benji Boy.' I leaned over to smile at him, fast asleep in his carry-cot tucked, as usual, under the kitchen table. 'Marley's decided she prefers that to Benjamin.'

'What? *Why*? Does she know another Benjamin? Some kid she doesn't like?'

'Not that I know of.' *Won't Daddy be cross?* I remembered you asking. 'At least she's finally showing an interest in her brother. And BB is kind of cute, don't you think?'

'Huh,' Jordan grunted.

'Well, I like it, and I'm happy to call him that. But I did wonder what made Marley suddenly come up with the idea,' I admitted. 'Which is exactly what *this* is about.' I flapped the lid of the worry box. 'To help me find out what's going on in her head.'

Sighing impatiently, Jordan dragged out a chair and sat down opposite me at the kitchen table, slanting me a sardonic look. 'You could always try asking her.'

'Do you honestly think I haven't?' I bristled. 'Maybe *you* could have a chat with her? Or perhaps you have already,' I added lightly. 'At the, uh, beach, or—'

'Marley and I talk all the time.' Jordan leaned back, folding his arms across his chest. *Daddy Is Our Hero*, it said on the khaki sweatshirt I'd given him the day we brought BB home from hospital.

It matched his eyes, and I felt a jolt of sadness as I remembered telling him so as he'd unwrapped it. 'Sure, sorry,' I pacified. 'I know you two are close. It's just, you haven't been around much lately, and . . .' Seeing his lips tighten, I added: 'Not that I'm blaming you. I realise work has been—'

'It's not just work, Holl. There's . . . other stuff.'

'Oh?' I watched a blush spread over his tanned, handsome face and felt one scorch my skin too. That was the first time he'd openly admitted we had a problem.

'Yeah. And you're right,' he said quietly. 'I know I haven't been here a lot. It's—'

'Life's got so busy, hasn't it?' I jumped in, suddenly wanting to bury my head in the sand, pretend everything was fine. 'We've barely had a minute to *think*, let alone talk, or spend any proper time together, or—'

'It's not just that.' Jordan leaned towards me, one hand resting casually on the table. 'You and me. Things have been . . . What with a new baby, and you worrying about Marley.'

'You mean you're *not* worried?' Yes, I was a coward. It was far easier to argue about your problems than to confront our own: to fill the gap that had opened up between us with anger rather than honesty. 'You think I'm blowing things out of proportion?'

'No,' Jordan said mildly, but I saw his hand ball into a fist. 'Actually, I agree with you. We've both had a lot on our plates. It's got between *us*. Stopped us talking, laughing. Doing *anything*. I wouldn't be surprised if it's had an impact on Marley, too.'

'Are you saying I don't do enough with her? Because I—'

'Calm down, Holl, you'll make yourself ill.' He frowned. '*Again*.'

'I'm fine.' I refused to let him blame all our problems on my health. The end of my pregnancy *had* been traumatic, but I thought I'd done OK since then, recovering well from the emergency C-section. I'd been a bit sore and tired, but that hadn't stopped me getting on, getting *out*. The point wasn't that I didn't take you anywhere, but that you didn't want to go.

'Good. I'm glad to hear it. But things are pretty chaotic right now.' Jordan glanced down towards BB. 'Maybe Marley can sense that. Perhaps she's feeling a bit left out.'

'She certainly doesn't seem too keen on being around her

brother,' I acknowledged. 'Babies are pretty all-consuming, though. I guess it's only natural if Marley feels jealous.'

'*Exactly*. Busy parents. Lack of attention. You of all people know how kids can be. You've spent enough hours in the classroom.'

'Yes. Although, in my experience, kids who want attention play up,' I said thoughtfully. 'They mess about. Cause trouble. Do anything to put themselves in the spotlight. They don't act like they're competing for a gold medal in good behaviour.'

'Unless there's something they want. I used to creep round my dad when I needed parts for my bike and stuff. Perhaps Marley's got her eye on a new toy.'

'She had plenty for her birthday. That was only eight weeks ago.'

'Maybe she didn't like what she got.'

'Oh.' I chewed my lip, remembering. 'But we made a wish list together.'

'Hmm. A list. There's your answer, then. Kids like surprises, don't they?'

'Not always.' *I hadn't*; not since Amy came to live with us. She'd turned up out of the blue one day and never went home, and I had never stopped dreading more surprises around every corner. Guiltily, I realised I'd simply assumed you would feel the same way.

'Well, whatever,' Jordan dismissed. 'You've got to stop *worrying* so much, babe. I realise you have a lot on your plate, and we might live in a sleepy seaside backwater, but—'

'You said you *liked* the peace and quiet,' I chipped in, detecting a complaint.

'I did. I *do*,' he corrected quickly. 'I just mean, these are crazy times. Worry becomes like a habit, for all of us. We're always waiting for the next tragic news story. Another horrible headline. Imagining the worst and tormenting ourselves that it's already happened.'

I paused, thinking of my anxiety about him secretly taking you to the beach – the bruises on your knees that could simply

34

have been caused by tripping as you played. Jordan was right, yet something still niggled at me. 'I know I probably worry too much, but I—'

'Then *stop*. It's not going to help our daughter if you put yourself back in hospital.'

'You think I don't know that?'

'Well, then. Seriously, Holl, you're driving yourself mad over nothing. Everything's *fine*. With Marley, anyway,' he mumbled, before adding more assertively: 'I guarantee it.'

He sounded so sure of himself, but rather than feeling comforted by his confidence, it grated on me. Somewhere beneath Jordan's calm, slightly patronising reassurances, I sensed a dig: that I was being neurotic, *driving myself mad* imagining problems that didn't exist.

'I get what you're saying. But I think you're wrong.' I stared at the worry box on the table between us, remembering your little hands struggling with pots of glitter and slippery piles of fiddly gems, your tongue poking out in concentration as you glued buttons and shiny shapes all over the shoe box. It was like you'd known it was important: something beyond a pretend pirate's treasure chest, or a game of post offices.

'I guess there's only one way to find out.' Jordan nodded at the folded-up piece of paper I realised I'd been putting off reading, secretly scared of what it might say.

'Yes,' I said, finally opening it, the first note you'd ever left me.

Chapter 6

'Hey!' I yelped a moment later, as the little piece of paper was snatched out of my hands, before I'd even had a chance to read it. 'Give that back, Jordan.'

'See? Panic over.' He shook his head with a wry smile. 'It's nothing. Just a drawing.'

'What?' I grabbed the paper back and stared at it, trying to make sense of what I was seeing: a surprisingly accurate pencil sketch of a cake with seven candles . . .

It was cleverly drawn, and, after all, it had been my suggestion that you might like to draw something. But I couldn't help feeling disappointed that there were no words. It hadn't been that long since your birthday; a picture of a cake seemed obvious. It didn't reveal *anything*, certainly not that you hadn't liked your presents, as Jordan was suggesting.

'It's the birthday cake I made for her,' he said proudly, clearly taking your sketch as a compliment. 'Nice to know I can do something right.'

'You did a great job,' I affirmed, deciding to ignore the hint of sarcasm. Tracing a finger over the fat bumblebee you'd drawn, just like the one Jordan had iced on your cake, I couldn't help smiling as I thought of how much you loved bees. And butterflies. *Mum would have loved showing you her garden*, I thought, suddenly wishing she was there.

I'd missed her so many times over the last eight years, but never more than in that moment. Her death had been so sudden, so shocking. I had only just begun to feel I was getting to know her when she was snatched away from me, our family home sold soon after.

'Anyway. Happy now?' Jordan stood up and crossed the kitchen to the counter, briskly covering the eggs he'd prepared for breakfast with cling film, before shrugging on his leather jacket and grabbing his khaki backpack from next to the dresser.

'Sorry?' I was still lost in thought about Mum.

'Marley's drawing. Surely that's put your mind at rest. Nothing remotely sinister about birthday cake. So, can we give the conspiracy theories a rest now, please?'

I threw him a sharp look. 'I don't know what you mean.'

'Oh, come on, admit it, Holl. You were expecting Marley to confess some terrible, deep, dark secret, weren't you? I mean, far be it for me to say *I told you so*, but this – this is nothing.' He stepped forward and snatched the note off me, flapping it carelessly.

'Is it?' I retorted hotly. 'Are you absolutely sure about that?'

'One hundred per cent.' He crumpled the paper in his hand. 'This proves nothing.'

'Proves? You make it sound like a criminal investigation. I'm looking for answers, Jordan, not evidence. Proof of *what*?' I held out my hand insistently for the note.

'You tell me.' Grudgingly, he handed over the balled-up paper.

'Well, excuse me for being concerned.' I pushed back my chair, too, and carried the worry box back to the dresser, tucking your note under the rose-painted teapot Jordan had bought me that summer as a surprise. A flash memory of him saying he thought it would remind me of my mum instantly made me regret the flare of conflict between us, and I turned to appeal to him. 'It's just, I've never seen Marley so subdued. This has to mean *something.*'

Jordan rolled his eyes. 'It's just a silly drawing. Hardly a cry for help.'

'Unless Marley doesn't know how to put her fears into words.' Once again, I felt a wave of frustration that I had no idea what, or who, you might be frightened of.

'Fears?' Jordan let his backpack drop to the floor. 'What fears?' he demanded, closing the gap between us in two long strides.

Automatically, I stepped back. 'I don't know,' I said hoarsely, even as my head filled with childhood memories of Sunday mornings in my dad's study. The unsettling images merged confusingly with pictures of Jordan taking you to the beach, and I hesitated, terrified to give shape or voice to the sickening fears clawing at me.

'Well, then.'

'But maybe Marley doesn't, either,' I protested urgently. 'Sometimes children aren't even sure themselves what they're frightened of. They just sense that—'

'Oh, please, spare me the child psychology lecture,' Jordan huffed. 'Look, I know you miss your old job, babe, but you're not in the classroom now.'

'*What?* What do you mean?' I bristled.

'I mean, you're Marley's mum, not her teacher. Sure, she's been a bit quiet. So what? You've got to stop grading her. Overanalysing. Looking for trouble where it doesn't exist.'

'Why the hell would I *want* Marley to have problems?'

'So you can help her? Rescue her from whatever minor catastrophes happen in a seven-year-old's world? A lost toy. Or a broken one.' Jordan sighed. 'OK, look, if you want me to spell it out, I think you're this anxious because you're not sure she still needs you.'

'Now who's psychoanalysing,' I snapped. Feeling hurt, I strode to the sink and clattered dishes into it. 'I don't need proof that my own children need me, Jordan,' I threw over my shoulder, before muttering: 'I'm just not sure my husband does anymore.'

'Ouch.' He winced, clearly having heard. 'I guess we're getting to the nub of it now.' Slowly, he crossed the kitchen to stand behind me, resting his hands on my waist.

'You said it first.' I fought the urge to lean back against his strong body, to wrap my arms around him and take the comfort he no longer seemed to want to offer. 'We've got problems. That's what you said.'

'You don't agree? You think everything between us is ... perfect,' he finished softly, and I knew we were both remembering that was how he used to describe our relationship. Eight years ago, before grief and marriage and two children came along to muddy the waters.

'I didn't say that.' I turned to face him, but I couldn't meet his eyes. Part of me still wanted to throw myself into his arms; the bigger part wanted to punch him for being so complacent. 'But our *problems*,' I said deliberately, 'have nothing to do with Marley.'

'Really? Are you absolutely sure you're not inventing worries about her as a distraction from what's happening between *us*?'

It was my turn to wince. He was half-right: it *was* easier to focus on you than our marriage. 'What *is* happening to us, Jordan?' It came out as more of a plea than I'd intended. 'You're either at work or on your boat. You don't seem at all bothered about what's going on with Marley.' *Or me*, I didn't add, deciding to tackle one problem at a time.

'Oh, for God's sake, how many times? *Nothing* is going on with her.'

I shook my head. 'She's changed. You must see that. Marley's always been so lively, carefree. *Chatty*. Now she barely says a word. She hardly leaves her room, either. She refused to go to the playground all half-term. She never even wants to go to the beach, or—'

'I took her there yesterday morning.'

Goose bumps feathered up my spine. 'Yes, she did tell me that. So, um, how was she?'

He shrugged. 'Quiet.'

'Exactly!'

'It was six in the morning, Holl. You were asleep. I didn't want to wake you. You've been looking so tired lately, I thought—'

'Gee, thanks.'

'Please don't get the hump. I just mean I thought it was better if Marley and I snuck out. I took her to the bakery. We wandered back along the beach. She seemed happy enough.'

'Which is precisely my point. She just goes along with whatever she's asked to do. It's like she's turned into a polite little robot, and I can't *bear* it.' I drifted back towards the kitchen table, slumping down on a chair. 'I know something's wrong. I *know* there is.'

Jordan came to sit next to me, laying a hand on my arm. 'Look, I'm sorry. I didn't mean to sound dismissive. I'm sure whatever is going on in her head feels very real for her.'

I shook him off. '*Feels* real. You don't think it is, though? And does that even matter? If Marley is worrying about something, that's real enough for me.'

'Or maybe she's not worrying at all. She can probably see you have your hands full.' Jordan huffed as, bang on cue, BB started crying. 'Perhaps she's just trying to be helpful. Staying out of the way, causing no fuss.'

'She doesn't have to do that.' I reached for BB, feeling guilty.

'No, she doesn't. So maybe try praising her, not setting her little tests, or whatever the heck that is.' He nodded at the worry box, a glittering, silent witness on the dresser.

'It's not a test. It's . . . I thought it might . . .'

I scooped up BB, jiggling him until he stopped crying and snuggled into me. But even as he settled, my mind churned in confusion. *Was I over-reacting?* Everything Jordan had said made perfect sense, even if I was too proud to admit it to him. He'd always had good instincts. He was a good *dad*. Things might have become strained between us, recently, but he clearly adored you.

Only my blood is in your veins – my emotional DNA. I was a

seven-year-old girl once, too, and I was starting to remember how tough it could be. Even on birthdays. The pressure to be thankful for what you're given, when you were hoping for something else. Not to spoil the day by demanding more attention than anyone wants to give. Especially when a new member of the family comes along. In your case, a baby. In mine . . . Amy.

Parents hold all the power, don't they? Ironically, Amy was the one who told me that. But she was right. Grown-ups are always making decisions without asking children first, and sometimes they forget how hard it is for kids to put up their hand and say they disagree.

I knew all this, but maybe I'd forgotten. I was beginning to remember, though. And to worry that someone had already taught you what it took me years growing up at Sea View to learn: that if you say nothing at all, no one can accuse you of lying.

Chapter 7

NOVEMBER 2001

The 'shoe theft', as Amy called it, remained a sore point for weeks. Neither my mum nor my dad ever mentioned it again, but I almost wished they had: to clear the atmosphere, the sense of blame, that seemed to hang over me from that day. Even as the years passed, if anything got lost, broken or damaged at Sea View, I still felt – or imagined – that once again everyone believed it was my fault.

Something had changed in our family. In *me*. I guess it wasn't all down to the shoes. Luke and Isabella Jackson had never come back, you see. They had another research trip, then another. And when the summer ended, Dad said it would be best if 'poor Amy' went to school with me. Just until her parents 'sorted themselves out'. He'd made all the arrangements, he said; he and Mum now had 'legal guardianship' of Amy.

I didn't understand what that meant, or how it was even possible that a girl who wasn't my sister now took the place of one. I'd always wanted a sibling, but the arrival of one fully formed, the same age as me, was a huge shock. Sharing my home, my bedroom, my toys . . . and my parents. I didn't get why Amy's didn't seem to want her anymore, and no one would tell me. Eventually, I stopped asking, and Amy didn't seem to care at all.

If I changed, she changed more. Not in front of my mum and dad, of course. As far as they were concerned, she remained *poor Amy*, and whenever they were around, she became *perfect Amy*. Only she wasn't. I knew it, but I soon realised it was pointless trying to convince anyone else. Take my tenth birthday . . .

'Such a cute little bunny. You're so *lucky*, Holly.' Amy sighed as she stroked the floppy ears of the cream-and-fawn rabbit that had been my special present. '*Isn't* she, Fluffball?'

'Is that her name?' Mum's soft voice was muffled as she entered the drawing room, her face flushed, chin tucked against her chest as she struggled to hold the local newspaper under one arm, while unhooking her ubiquitous flowery apron.

'No, it's Treacle,' I said, before Amy could reply. Reaching over, I lifted the fluffy bundle out of her arms; she'd been sitting on the sofa holding the baby rabbit for the last hour, and I wanted her back. 'Ouch!' I exclaimed as I felt Amy's thin fingers pinch my arm.

'Oh dear, did she catch you with her claws?' Mum asked, clearly oblivious to Amy's spiteful actions. Dropping her apron onto an armchair, she hurried towards me. 'Let me see?'

'No, it was . . .' I caught Amy's eye and swallowed what I was about to say, knowing that if I made a fuss, she would pay me back tenfold later. Besides, I didn't want to upset my mum. Not when she'd gone to so much trouble to make my birthday special, baking homemade waffles for my breakfast and buying a pretty little pot of treacle to go with them.

'It was what?' Mum prompted anxiously.

'Nothing.' I shook my head. 'I'm OK.' Ignoring Amy's smirk, I smiled.

'She's probably frightened,' Mum said gently. 'Animals do tend to lash out if they feel cornered. You remember Maria's old collie

43

up at the Cartwright farm? Poppy. Gorgeous dog. Friendly as anything until you got too close. Maybe give Treacle a bit of space, hmm?'

'Treacle doesn't suit her,' Amy insisted. 'She's the colour of biscuits. We should call her *Cookie*. Shouldn't we, Olivia?'

Mum cocked her head to one side, pondering. 'Hmm. You might have a point. She *is* more of a biscuit colour.' My heart sank until she added: 'What do *you* think, Holly?'

'She's Treacle,' I said firmly. 'Because treacle was my birthday treat, and so is she.'

'Ah, good thinking. Clever girl.' Mum gave me an affirming nod, before crossing the room to hand my dad the *Gazette*. 'Sorry, it's a bit soggy. The boys have taken to just lobbing it towards the door.' She sighed. 'I was sure I asked Karen to mention it to them. I stopped by the post office last week especially.'

'Don't worry, I'll have a word.' Dad leaned forward to set the damp newspaper to dry in front of the roaring fire that was also a birthday tradition. Settling back in his armchair, he added briskly: 'I need to pop into Leiston in the morning, in any case. Next chapter of my thesis is done. Professor Wilkins offered to take a look. I said I'd mail it to her.'

'That's a bit of a hassle, isn't it?' Mum perched on the arm of his leather wingback chair, giving him a puzzled look. 'Can't you just email it to her? Or better still, give it to her at work tomorrow?'

'Well, I would, but it's a big file, and you know how unreliable our internet is. And I'm off next week, Olivia, remember?'

'Oh, is it the end of term already? No, it can't be. Sorry, I'm mixing up my dates.' Mum frowned, pressing a hand to her forehead. 'I can't seem to shake off this headache.'

'You're overdoing things, love. As usual.' Dad patted Mum's knee. 'Term ends middle of December. Same as every year.' Smiling, he turned to nod at me and Amy. 'You girls have got all this to come. Homework. College deadlines.' He laughed at

44

Treacle, who was now burrowing into the sofa cushions. 'Maybe one of you will become a vet, hey?'

'I'm going to be a fashion designer,' Amy announced.

The words *like my mum* seemed to hang in the air, and I felt a flash of pity for her. Amy was infuriating, but there were good reasons for her spikiness, I supposed. 'I want to be an art teacher.' I smiled shyly at her, hoping we might be friends, at least for the day.

'You might change your minds once you meet the vet,' Dad said with another chuckle. 'Sally gets to hang out with a dozen Fluffballs all day, every day.'

'I wish I had one,' Amy sighed. 'Let me cuddle her, Holly? You're hogging her!'

'She's my rabbit,' I pointed out, regretting my brief attempt at friendliness.

'Oh, come on, Holly.' Dad frowned. 'Share and share alike. Give poor Amy a turn.'

Amy beamed as she scooped Treacle back onto her lap, and I felt her shoulder nudge against me. I got the message: she could wrap my dad around her finger any time she wanted.

'You can both have as many cuddles as you like when we take Treacle for her check-up,' Dad continued. 'Sally always has a packed surgery. Bunnies, cats and dogs. You name it. We'll go after school tomorrow, yes? You can stay with Sally while I go to the post office.'

'So, you're definitely not at work tomorrow,' Mum said slowly.

'I'm off the whole week. *Study* leave, Olivia. I did mention it.'

'Oh, yes, right. Sorry.' Mum chewed a thumbnail, looking thoughtful. 'Ah, for your *thesis*!' Her face lit up as though she'd suddenly remembered something vitally important.

'Of course.' Dad's dark brows furrowed, his eyes lingering on Mum's flushed face. 'It's about time I finished the damned thing. It's being published next summer.'

'Same time as Luke's book,' Mum mused softly.

'Quite.' Dad flicked her an irritable glance then. 'I realise my little paper's not quite in his league, but—'

'Your thesis is brilliant, Adam,' Mum soothed instantly. 'I'm so very proud of you.'

Dad shifted in his seat, looking uncomfortable, and I couldn't work out if he was embarrassed by the praise, or still irritated by the comparison to his old friend's greater success. 'It's an achievement in its way. Even without a fancy launch dinner in Paris.'

'Paris?' Amy crushed Treacle against her chest so hard, I was worried she was suffocating her. 'Do my parents live there now? Am I going to live with them?'

It was Mum's turn to throw my dad a cross look. 'They're just there for work, darling,' she told Amy quietly. 'Your mum has a fashion show coming up. Your dad . . . well, as Adam said, he's got his book coming out, and he . . . But it's not permanent. They—'

'Send their love,' Dad interjected, firmly back in control.

'You said that last week,' Amy snapped, for once forgetting to act polite.

'Because it's the truth.' Dad smiled as he sat back in his chair, crossing his legs.

'The truth. Yeah, right. No one in this house *ever* tells that!'

Amy glared around the room, her flash of anger echoing into an awkward pause that seemed to stretch endlessly. I stared incredulously at her, waiting for my mum to gently contradict her, or my dad to lecture her about rudeness, as he would have me.

Amy had a point, though. No one *did* ever explain what was going on with her parents; conversations about them were always cut short, any questions hushed or left to drift off into loaded silence.

'Right, who fancies a trip up to the allotment?' Mum spoke first, leaning forward to tickle Treacle. '*Someone* is having a special lunch today.' Her brown eyes twinkled at me. 'We need to pick some fresh veg. I bet *this* little one would love some carrots, too.'

Her deft change of subject was typical of my mum's easy,

46

placid diplomacy, but something about her struck me as different. In fact, she didn't seem herself at all, and I was consumed by a sudden sense of foreboding.

For all her gentleness, Mum had this incredible quiet strength. She got things *done*: gently, unobtrusively. Suddenly she seemed preoccupied, forgetful; a little frayed around the edges, as though she might unravel at any moment.

'I'll come with you,' I offered, eager to save her more work. Dad must be right: she was overdoing things. Mum was always busy cooking and baking, organising charity events or working up at the allotment.

'We might need our wellies,' she warned, glancing at the window. 'Fingers crossed those clouds blow the other way. It would be a shame if the display has to be cancelled later. Such perfect timing that Bonfire Night coincides with your birthday, Holly.' She smiled, beginning to look more like herself again. 'It's like the fireworks are especially for *you*.'

'I love fireworks. I love *Treacle*.' I stood up and gave Mum a hug, wanting to say I loved her too and was worried about her. But we never said things like that in our family.

'You might want to keep her inside tonight.' Mum hugged me back, then nodded at Treacle. 'If it rains, she won't be a happy bunny,' she added with one of her tinkling laughs.

'No need to worry about that,' Dad said mysteriously. 'That rabbit's going to be living in the lap of luxury. I finished building her hutch – or should I say palace – last night.'

'She has a *house*? Come on, Treacle. Let's go look!' I thrust my hands determinedly towards Amy, demanding she hand over my new pet.

'Oh, you can't take Cookie out into the rain,' she said with a small smile. 'I'll wait here with her. I don't want any *more* of my shoes to get ruined,' she added, and I knew she was reminding me of the ones I had supposedly spoiled three years ago – and that I still owed her.

Chapter 8

The rain held off, and the fireworks display went ahead. Even so, Amy refused to come outside and watch it. As she disappeared up the spiral staircase to our room, I heard her muttering about not having had fireworks on *her* birthday the month before, and Mum reminding her that we'd had a party and invited everyone from our class.

I hadn't wanted a party. I didn't want to wear a 'special dress' and talk to lots of people. I wanted to put on my new shop-bought jeans and play with Jane. She loved fireworks, too, and we'd wandered happily down Church Road towards the Meare, smiling at locals we had grown up with, staring curiously at visiting strangers.

It never ceased to amaze me how busy our quiet village became during festivals. It was only as an adult that I realised the tourists we'd whispered about were as curious about us as we were about them. As a child, it never dawned on me that, to the outside world, our tiny village was considered charmingly locked in a time warp, with its quaint traditions and quiet lanes lined with mock-Tudor homes bumping shoulders with vast modern beach houses.

Unlike Amy, I never fell out of love with Thorpeness. While I always had the feeling that she was biding her time, waiting to grow up and leave, I couldn't imagine living anywhere else. Butterflies of happy excitement danced in my stomach as Jane and I found a quiet spot on the green, as close to the Meare as we could get, and sat watching the spectacular display that lit up the sky and cast glittering reflections onto the misty lake below.

'I wish it could be my birthday every day,' I sighed, then gasped as a particularly loud rocket soared above the boathouse. I watched transfixed as it arched over the House in the Clouds – the whimsical holiday home converted out of a water tower – before spiralling towards the windmill. All the familiar landmarks of our little world. I felt strangely possessive of them and was almost glad Amy didn't cherish them as I did.

'Then you'd be at least a hundred and even more wrinkly than Miss Shaw,' Jane teased, laughing as I punched her arm in disgust; neither of us were fond of our nosy former teacher, who continued to take far too much interest our lives, despite no longer being responsible for us.

After the fireworks finished, we ran back to Sea View, eager to play astronauts in the space station Mum had created for us in the back garden. Tin foil turned a bench into a rocket, while spotlights trained onto the patio created a launch pad, with sand and pea shingle recreating the surface of the moon. Immediately, Jane mimed a languid moon walk.

'Wow, it feels like we're really in space,' she said, swaying across the garden as though battling a lack of gravity. 'Your mum's so clever.'

'I know,' I agreed proudly. For all my dad went on about Amy's mum being 'such an artistic talent', my mum would surely have given her a run for her money. The clothes she made may not have carried any designer label, but her imagination was glorious.

'There's a shooting star! A *real* one!' Jane almost tumbled over in excitement as she pointed upwards.

Traces of smoke from the village fireworks still drifted across the now dark sky, but the bright tail of a meteor was clearly visible. I craned my neck to follow the progress of the glittering arc. 'Quick! Make a wish, Jane!' I said, grabbing her arm.

'You first,' she invited shyly, hooking her arm through mine.

'I wish . . . I wish we'll be best friends for ever.'

'Me too. That's a double wish. That means it *has* to come true!'

We hugged each other, then took it in turns to cuddle Treacle. 'We need to make her a bed,' I said. 'So she can sleep on the rocket ship back to Earth.'

'We can use this,' Jane offered, slipping off her cardigan.

'Watch out for flying saucers!' I called out, as we loped like astronauts towards Treacle's palatial wooden hutch at the end of the garden.

'Here you go, Treacle. Time for sleepies.' Jane popped her into the hutch and spread her fluffy red cardigan across the soft hay.

'Girls! Who wants space juice and moon snacks?' Mum called out from the terrace.

'What?' Jane and I said in unison, grinning as we ran across the lawn, forgetting to moon walk as we raced to see what treats had been laid out for us.

Hot dogs and elderflower cordial, crisps and home-baked cookies. Mum had even lit a fire in the chiminea, setting out a bundle of skewers for us to toast fluffy marshmallows. But along with excitement, anxiety knotted in my stomach as I looked up at the shadowy mullioned windows above us.

I was convinced I could see Amy watching from our bedroom, and although she was the one who had refused to join us, I felt sad she was missing out. 'I should get Amy,' I said guiltily to Jane, when Mum disappeared to fetch my birthday cake. 'She'll want to watch me blow out my candles. Ooh, I get another wish!' I laughed, trying to ignore the thought that what I really wanted was for Amy to go home.

'You should wish for Amy to go back to her own house,' Jane said, uncannily echoing my thoughts. 'Why does she even live here?'

'Dad says it's our moral duty to help friends in need,' I parroted carefully. I'd heard him say it so many times, the phrase was ingrained in my mind.

'I'll never be Amy's friend.' Jane plunged a spindly skewer into a marshmallow like she was poking it into Amy's eye. 'She just pretends to be nice. She *begged* me to come to her birthday party. Then she stole my Bratz doll and poked her eyes out!'

'Oh, no. Not Chloe?' I knew how much Jane loved that doll.

'Yes! *And* she called me Mop Head. In front of everyone!'

'But you've got lovely hair.' It was one of the things I liked most about Jane – her chocolate-brown curly hair that was as wild as mine, not sleek and midnight-dark like Amy's.

'Amy doesn't think so.' Jane chewed the end of her tangled ponytail, looking cross. 'Everyone thinks she's so funny and pretty. But she's mean.'

'She misses her mum and dad,' I said, and deep down I knew that was the truth. For all Amy's spikiness and game playing, a big part of me genuinely felt sorry for her. I couldn't imagine what it must feel like to be without her family. And Amy could be fun. Sometimes.

'At least she *has* a mum and dad,' Jane said unsympathetically.

Her own had been killed in a car crash when she was a baby, and she'd grown up with her aunt and uncle. They were pleasant enough, but strict; her uncle Dave made my dad look positively laid-back.

'Sorry, Jane.' I gave her a hug, feeling bad that I had inadvertently reminded her of her loss. For all I hated sharing my parents with Amy, at least they were still around.

'I bet Amy's mum and dad didn't like her, either. I bet that's why they left her here.'

'No, I don't think so,' I said seriously. 'They're just very busy.' I wasn't sure why I was defending Amy, and neither was Jane. She looked at me like I'd gone mad.

'Why are you sticking up for her? She's always pushing people around! She shoved me off the boat at the regatta that time. Remember? I almost *drowned*,' she declared theatrically. 'Then she pretended to rescue me. But she didn't really. Craig pulled me out.'

I tried not to laugh at Jane's indignant expression. Even though it had been a shocking incident at the time, the Meare was only three feet deep. Like Jane, I'd always looked up to Craig, the twinkly-eyed boatman, but in truth she could easily have put her feet down, had she not been disorientated by the flamboyant floats crowding around her, the fireworks popping overhead. And yet . . . *How did she even come to fall into the lake?*

Amy had sworn blind it was an accident: that my friend had been messing around, and she'd only grabbed her arm to stop her falling overboard. If Jane hadn't panicked, she would never have become trapped between floats, Amy insisted. But the long skirt of her Tiger Lily costume had filled up with water as she'd struggled, dragging her under. My dad dismissed it all as 'high jinks', and, in Amy's defence, she did jump in after Jane. Craig had, too, although with typical modesty he allowed Amy to take all the credit.

While the *Gazette*, starved of news in our quiet village, undoubtedly exaggerated a 'local girl's brush with tragedy', I shuddered to think how differently the incident *could* have ended. Unwieldy and elaborately decorated, the floats easily obscured a child thrashing in the water. I had to admit it was thanks to Amy that the alarm had been raised.

'She didn't mean to,' I said loyally. 'It was an *accident*.'

'Was it? She pushed Claire off the swing last week. Then told the teacher I did it! Uncle Dave had to go into school to speak to her. He told me off all the way home. He said I'm a "naughty girl", and I'm not allowed any pocket money for a month!'

'Oh, no. Really?' Losing pocket money was the worst punishment I could imagine.

'Aunty Helen only let me come today cos it's your birthday.'

'That's not fair. You're not a naughty girl. You didn't *do* anything!' I knew exactly how it felt when Amy wriggled her way out of things – how badly the injustice rankled.

Deep down, I knew my parents didn't really favour Amy over

me – that they were only trying to make up for the family she had lost. In truth, I did the same, always making excuses for her and letting her get away with things. She intimidated me, but I also pitied her. Mostly, I couldn't figure her out and simply took the path of least resistance.

'It doesn't matter.' Jane shrugged philosophically. 'Did you like my present?'

'I love it.' I didn't add that I'd instinctively hidden the pretty shell-covered jewellery box under my bed, because I feared that if Amy saw it, she would break it. Or steal it. 'I haven't got anything to put in it yet, though.'

'Here, you can have this.' Jane's hazel eyes shone as she reached behind her head to unfasten a silver chain bearing a delicate heart pendant.

'Oh, no. That's yours. I can't take it. I've got nothing to give *you*.' I mentally scoured my bedroom for anything I could offer in return, but I had nothing of any real value. Everything in our home was either home-grown or handmade.

Looking back now, I realise how special that was – the effort Mum put into giving me things that were unique. At the time, I wanted to look like everyone else. My new jeans with butterfly patches, the same as Jane's, were my favourite thing to wear for months to come.

'You don't have to give me anything,' she said firmly, wrapping her skinny arms around my neck. 'We're best friends for ever, aren't we?'

'For ever and ever.' I gazed longingly at the necklace, trying to remember the framed commandments in Dad's study. I was sure there was something about not coveting things.

'So you have to wear this,' Jane insisted, fastening the necklace around my neck.

'OK.' I smiled, feeling happy and grateful. 'You can come and play with Treacle every day, if you like,' I offered eagerly. 'She's the most special thing I've got.'

'Really? Thanks, Holly. You're so kind. Can I have another cuddle with her now?'

Neither of us had any clue that it would be the last time *anyone* would cuddle Treacle. Somehow, the hutch door had come undone during the night, and a fox had snuck inside. It had only managed to steal one bite before the fireworks scared it off, but it was enough. By the time I skipped across the garden next morning, clutching the bundle of carrots my mum had picked at her allotment, Treacle was dead.

I hadn't wanted to let go of her; Mum had to prise her out of my arms. She said we needed to wrap her up and put her in something: 'a final resting place', she called it. I didn't hesitate. I flew up the spiral staircase and looked under Amy's bed, finding the glossy white box her sparkly red shoes had come in. After tipping out the pens and toys she'd filled it with, I retrieved a couple that were mine and left the rest scattered over the bedroom floor.

There was no ice cream that day, or school. Instead, I spent the morning sobbing, before solemnly carrying Treacle into the garden in Amy's shoe box. At the last moment, I couldn't bring myself to lower the pristine box into the claggy earth, so Mum and I wrapped Treacle in Jane's red cardigan instead, before burying her under the oak tree. Mum didn't say a single word, but she cried too as she pressed crocus bulbs into the soil to mark the spot.

Afterwards, I ran upstairs, cradling the now empty box, weeping into it until I had no tears left to cry. Then I wiped the box clean and hid it under *my* bed. Amy didn't once ask for it back, even though she must have known I had it. But I think she also knew that I'd realised what she had done. In a horrible way, I think she wanted me to know. That she'd deliberately opened the hutch door – and that no matter how many times I told my dad, he wouldn't believe me.

Chapter 9

TUESDAY – FIVE DAYS BEFORE

'Treacle? Or maple syrup? No, I know – honey. Yes?' The pancake almost slid onto the terracotta floor, because I was concentrating so hard on the purple shadows under your eyes that I wasn't paying attention to what I was doing: making a special breakfast to cheer you up. Or, rather, heating up the crepes Jordan had made before he left for work.

I'd heard the front door click shut before I had even opened my eyes, and when I crept downstairs with BB, I was greeted by the warm, sweet doughy smell of freshly cooked batter – and an empty kitchen.

'Yes, please. Honey,' you said politely, taking your usual seat at the end of the table, and tucking a napkin neatly into the collar of your blue school jumper. Your head was down.

'Good choice. It's organic. Made by happy bees,' I joked, hoping to make you smile. 'See the pretty label?' I reached up to the shelf above the Aga, then held out the jar to show you. 'I bought it from the village tea shop. We can go there after school, if you like? Or the library. Unless Mrs Hart gave you a new reading book yesterday?'

'She said to bring one in from home,' you said, so quietly I barely heard you.

'Sorry, darling?' I smiled encouragingly as I grabbed your favourite bumblebee plate and scooped a pancake onto it, covering it with honey before setting it down in front of you.

'A book.'

I eyed the stack on the dresser, trying to remember the last time we'd read a story together; the last time you had made one up for me. 'Ah. How about your new poetry one?'

'OK,' you agreed, without looking up.

I reached for the little hardback, then pulled out a chair and sat down next to you, flicking through the colourful pages, waiting for you to say more. Usually, you loved learning poems and little rhymes, reciting them to me as we walked and talked.

'I think I like this one best,' I said, when you remained silent. Holding up the beautiful, intricate illustration to show you, I read aloud: '*The friendly rabbit had no fear. Her legs were fast, her eyes were clear.*' I smiled. 'Have you got a favourite poem yet?'

You shrugged.

'Too many to choose from, hey?' I set the book down, watching you push the pancake around your plate with your knife and fork. 'What did Mrs Hart read at story time yesterday?'

Another shrug, this time accompanied by a frown.

'I expect you and Leah sat together, hey? I know she loves books and stories, too,' I prompted, still wondering if the two of you had squabbled about something.

Your chin sank even lower onto your chest, and I resolved to phone Leah's mum, Rachel, to ask if she was aware of any fallout out between the two of you.

'You know what that pancake needs?' I said, watching you slice your special breakfast into pieces without eating so much as a morsel. 'More honey!' I spooned on more of the golden, sticky liquid, remembering other times when you'd lavishly sprinkled sugar onto Jordan's crepes, giggling uncontrollably as the two of you had a lively-fought competition to eat them without licking your lips.

Smiling at the thought, I waited to see the same excitement at the unexpected treat of having your favourite breakfast on a school day, but all you did was shake your head before taking a tiny mouthful. I had the feeling you were forcing yourself, just to please me.

'Well, it looks so good, I think I'll have one myself.' I stood up and moved to the hob, serving myself a pancake I didn't want, before returning to the table. 'Mmm. Delicious.' I forced a mouthful, too. 'Lucky us having a chef in the house, hey? Imagine if Daddy was a policeman! Or a—' I broke off as your cutlery clattered onto the table, your hands flying upwards to cover your mouth as you leaped off your chair like you'd had an electric shock.

'Sorry, Mummy,' you said tearfully, then bolted out of the kitchen.

'It's OK, love. No harm done.' Jumping up too, I quickly cleaned everything up and stacked our plates on the worktop, before following you into the living room.

'I don't like policemen.' Your voice came from behind the sofa.

'Oh? Why's that, darling?' I thought of our local community officer, wondering if he'd had occasion to have words with you about something. I racked my brains to think what on earth that could possibly be. 'Sergeant Robins is nice, isn't he?'

There was a long pause. 'Does he have a . . .'

I kneeled down and reached behind the sofa, gently coaxing you out and pulling you onto my lap. 'Does he have a *what*?' But I never got to hear what you wanted to ask about Sergeant Robins, because in that moment Jordan bowled in through the back door.

'Anyone home? I forgot my locker key! Hey, little man,' I heard him say to BB, who was asleep in his carry-cot tucked, as usual, under the kitchen table. 'How's my honey bee today?' he asked cheerily, striding into the living room and planting a kiss on your cheek.

He didn't hang around long enough to see you surreptitiously wipe your face on your sleeve; he disappeared into the hall and up the stairs before I'd even said *good morning*. He didn't bother to say it to me, either, just as he hadn't wished me goodnight the day before.

Jordan had hurried off to work after our disagreement yesterday morning, only returning long after I was in bed. It was becoming a familiar routine: his empty side of the bed; his even emptier excuses that he 'didn't want to wake me' when he came home late.

'You wait here, sweetheart,' I said, settling you on the sofa. Your body was rigid, only your eyes moving, tracking the sound of your daddy's boots as they thumped up the wooden stairs. I hurried into the kitchen to fetch BB, and when I returned, you were still frozen to the spot, hunched on the sofa. 'I promise I won't be long, darling,' I reassured you softly. 'I just want a word with your dad.'

Chapter 10

'Did you find it?' Still picturing your pale, tense face, I caught up with Jordan in the bathroom, although why he was looking in there for his locker key baffled me.

Automatically, I glanced at the Victorian roll-top tub we'd salvaged from a local scrap merchant and carefully restored, installing a shower attachment on the white-tiled wall above it. A shower curtain covered with little blue anchors protected the blue-painted tongue-and-groove panelling that disguised the bumpy bathroom walls.

As in every room, the ceiling sloped and the wood floor was uneven, but together we'd made it a clean, inviting space. Jordan had grown up tinkering with bikes and boats, and he was confident tackling anything from plumbing to electrics, while I had indulged my love of colour to create a pretty if – at least according to Amy – predictable nautical theme.

'What? Oh, yeah. My key. It was in the back pocket of yesterday's jeans.'

'Good job you left them on the bathroom floor, then.' I nodded at the crumpled heap of faded blue denim, then smiled in a last-minute attempt to counteract the sarcasm.

'Ah. Sorry about that. I know you've got enough to do. Don't worry, I'll bung them in the machine on my way out.' Jordan bundled his jeans under his arm as I reached for them.

'Oh!' I jumped back as we almost bumped heads. 'Really, it's no problem,' I said truthfully. Although the house was messier than usual, I was proud of our home and liked looking after it. Routine domestic tasks actually helped switch off my brain, after I'd been grappling with mountains of paperwork. 'But OK. Thanks. I do need to put a wash on.'

'Great,' Jordan said absently, his attention already drifting. Leaning closer to the mirror over the sink, he ran a quick hand through his thick, freshly trimmed hair before stroking the square angles of his jaw, as though checking whether he needed to shave as well.

A strange feeling of awkwardness flooded through me – a prickly sense that I was intruding on his private space. I turned away, feeling a pang as I remembered the early days of our marriage, when Jordan would light scented candles and coax me into sharing a bubble bath, teasingly inviting me to do the 'stubble test'. Knowing how much I disliked beards, he would rub his cheek slowly against mine, asking if it was 'too rough, too soft, or just right'.

'Don't even think about it,' I teased softly, my heart aching at the memory.

'Sorry, what?' Jordan jumped, almost banging his head on the sloping ceiling.

'Growing a beard.' I grinned, waiting and hoping the same memory would surface for him, too. My eyes drifted to the tub: plastic toys now sat in place of candles, and luxury toiletries had been replaced by a range of baby-friendly products. I sighed.

'Oh. Right.' He followed my gaze, green eyes narrowing. 'Sorry, hon, gotta go.'

'Sure,' I said quickly, feeling myself blush.

'Catch you later, OK?'

He paused briefly as he brushed past me, and for a second I

thought he was going to lean in for a kiss. He didn't. After stroking BB's head, he hurried out of the bathroom, leaving me to stand watching him, heart thudding as I breathed in the lingering smell of his familiar citrus cologne, wishing I had simply kissed him first.

'Hang on a minute!' I called out impulsively, filled with a sudden urge for us all to spend the day together: for Jordan to phone in sick; for you to skip school. 'Jordan, wait!'

'Not now, Holl. I'm late already.'

'Please. We need to talk.' Suddenly desperate for him not to leave, I shifted BB to my other shoulder and reached out to stop Jordan going down the stairs.

'I thought we did enough of that yesterday.'

'Sorry, I didn't realise there was a word limit,' I said, feeling rejected.

'OK, fine.' He checked his watch, frowning. 'Two minutes, then I really have to go.'

'Oh, don't be late on my account.' I knew I was being unreasonable, but my pride was smarting, and I hated that Jordan always seemed to be hurrying out the door – and I wasn't always sure where he was going.

'Look, Marley's *fine*,' he said impatiently. 'We've been through this. You've just got to stop worrying. Why not ditch work today? Get yourself out. Blow out the cobwebs.'

'It wasn't Marley I wanted to talk about, actually,' I snipped, my yearning to be close to him vanishing in a puff of hurt. It was almost a relief when BB started to cry, giving me an excuse to push past Jordan and head for the changing table in our bedroom.

The back of my neck prickled again as he followed and stood watching me. When I glanced up, his gaze shifted quickly to the stripped-pine floor littered with baby toys, then to the bed covered in clothes, most of them BB's. The house looked like a bomb site, I thought ruefully; and our marriage was lost somewhere in the wreckage.

'So what *did* you want to talk about?' Jordan asked irritably.

61

'Doesn't matter,' I muttered, unpopping BB's sleepsuit.

'Sweetheart, I'm late.' Jordan sighed with exaggerated patience, leaning a shoulder against the doorframe. 'If you have something to say, please, just spit it out.'

It wasn't that easy, and I used the distraction of changing BB and dressing him in a fresh sleepsuit to give myself time to think, deciding it was the wrong time to try to unpick what was going awry between us. Jordan didn't seem that bothered, anyway.

'Maybe you're right. Maybe I just need to get out more.' *With you*, I thought sadly. A night out was probably all we needed. Or, better still, I decided, my eyes lingering on the bed where Jordan rarely slept these days, a night *in*. Just the two of us.

Only neither option was that easy to arrange. I wasn't comfortable asking my dad to babysit, and Amy seemed to be out every evening. At least, her phone went to voicemail whenever I called her. Lately, she'd stopped calling me back.

'Yeah. You do. You're on your own way too much, Holly. Just like your mum was.'

I jumped, taken aback by the unexpected comparison, hating that Jordan might feel our once passionate marriage was sliding into the same sort of affectionate but semi-platonic relationship my parents had. About to make a joke about it, I looked up at him with a smile, but his expression was blank, his eyes glazed with a faraway look.

'You're right,' I whispered, wishing I knew what he was really thinking. 'Maybe you and I could—'

'Why don't you invite Amy round?'

'Sorry?' Her name, plucked out of nowhere, made my pulse leap. 'Why?'

'She's your best friend, isn't she?'

No, you are, I thought. 'Perhaps you should remind her of that. I haven't heard from her in weeks. Anyway, it's too short notice. She'll be busy. The start of term's always crazy.'

I realised how much I missed it and wished again that Jordan wasn't rushing off – that we could talk things over, figure out if there was a way I might combine my floristry work with part-time teaching. Home tutoring, perhaps. Surely the life insurance company couldn't deem that an 'unacceptable health risk', as they had my ASD?

I was suddenly desperate to know what Jordan thought of the idea. He'd seemed so pleased when I took over my mum's business, saying the money would be 'a lifeline'. But while it had surprised me how much I'd enjoyed the flower-arranging courses I'd taken, in truth it had never been my passion, but Mum's – and I knew that was the real reason I'd taken over her company: to cling on to what felt like the last piece I had left of her.

'Tomorrow night, then,' Jordan countered, oblivious to my turbulent thoughts, my yearning to share them with him. 'I can cook. Give us an excuse to open a bottle of bubbly.'

'Champagne?' I couldn't imagine what he thought we had to celebrate.

'Sure. Why not? Strikes me we've both forgotten how to have fun.' He glanced at the bed before heading for the bedroom door. 'At least with each other,' I was sure I heard him mutter as he strode off down the stairs.

Chapter 11

By the time I returned to the living room with a freshly changed BB, you were gone. I found you perched on an old milking stool at the kitchen sink, washing our breakfast plates. Glancing at the nautical-style brass clock on the wall, I wondered if Jordan would make his shift on time, then realised *we* were going to be late too, if we didn't hurry up.

Your school was only a fifteen-minute bus ride away, and we could skip our usual meander along the beach beforehand; you hadn't wanted to go there yesterday, anyway. Only by the time I'd settled BB in his buggy and hurried you both to the bus stop on the Thorpe Road, we would still be cutting it fine to beat the morning bell.

I was planning to leave the washing up until later, to save time, but you seemed to have taken care of it – of *everything*. 'Wow, what a busy little bee you've been!' *Honey bee*, echoed in my head, my mind's eye picturing your rigid body and frozen expression as you'd secretly wiped away your daddy's kiss.

'I tidied up, Mummy.'

'So I see.' Obligingly, I turned around to admire the neat stack of place mats on the table, the mugs washed and set to drain on the rack next to the gleaming butler's sink. 'Thank you, darling. You're a gem.' I switched BB to my other arm and pulled you against me, wishing you would hug me back, but you remained stiff and aloof.

'And I put my books away. Daddy didn't even have to ask me.'

'Huh. I can't believe he's *ever* asked you.' Jordan had always been unashamedly messy – except in the kitchen, where he was a stickler for neatness. As you looked down, I frowned at your flushed, anxious face. '*Has* he?'

You shrugged and carried on carefully soaping your plate.

Gently taking it from you, I set it down and caught hold of your hands. 'I realise the house is a bit messy at the moment, darling.' I glanced guiltily at the dresser, half-buried under paperwork I kept meaning to sort out. While I was still teaching, I'd only kept the floristry business ticking over; now it was my full-time job, and after taking time out to recover from BB's birth, I was behind with it – with everything. 'Is that bothering you?'

Another shrug.

'Hmm, well, it bothers me,' I said, guessing you didn't want to say. 'I'll find somewhere else to put all this.' I pulled a face as I waved at the piles of paper on the dresser. 'Boring old accounts. Maybe I'll dig a great big hole and bury them.'

'At the 'lotment?' Your head jerked up, green eyes widening.

'Well, no.' I smiled. 'Sorry, I was just joking, love. Much as I'd *love* to bury those ugly binders under a big fat pile of earth at the allotment, I didn't actually mean—'

'Leah said there's other st . . . st . . . stuff buried there,' you stuttered.

'There certainly is. Hopefully, next year's spring crop. Daffodils, snowdrops, crocus. All the delicate seedlings are in Maria's greenhouse, but some bulbs have to be planted in . . .' I broke off as you looked down again. 'That *is* what you meant, isn't it?'

I could see your shoulders hunch, your arms hugging yourself in what was becoming a familiar gesture. 'What, then, sweetheart? What kind of stuff?' I pressed, picturing the half-acre site Mum had rented at the back of Maria and Bill Cartwright's farm.

The plot was sheltered by tall trees that the hardworking couple had planted especially around its perimeter, to shield budding plants from the biting winds that could whip across the flat Suffolk landscape. It was an isolated, purely functional nursery, not somewhere I took clients – not somewhere I ever encouraged you to play. You loved our occasional treasure hunts, but not at the farm. With agricultural machinery around, it wasn't safe.

'A doll. Leah found it,' you said, so quietly I had to stoop to hear. '*Buried.*'

'Buried?' I frowned, jiggling BB as I tried to think. 'Ah, it was probably left over from the Easter Egg Hunt.' I thought back to the last one, which, under doctor's orders to rest during my pregnancy, I hadn't been able to take part in. Jordan being Jordan, rather than simply hiding chocolates around the village, he'd tucked away little toys, too.

That day had also been the annual Good Friday Beach and Village Clean, and I remembered pointing out that for every bit of plastic people cleared, Jordan was replacing them with ten more. 'Spoilsport,' he'd teased, saying I'd 'forgotten how to have fun'. Thinking of his parting words to me just now, I wondered if it was true.

'And bones,' you whispered, your eyes widening even further.

'Sorry? *What* did you say?'

'They were buried next to the doll. A big pile of bones. Leah said so.'

'Oh, I very much doubt that.' I prayed it hadn't been the remains of a dog; I knew the Cartwrights had always buried their old family pets on the farm.

'Leah *said* so,' you insisted. 'She said that's where they bury *naughty girls.*'

'*No*, sweetheart,' I said, more firmly. 'Who told her that?' I was positive it wouldn't have been Maria. She had two children herself, albeit grown-up men now, both working as labourers on the farm. They had children too, and I knew they would be as sensitive as Maria to the impressionable nature of young minds.

You shrugged, eyes flicking around the kitchen, avoiding mine.

'Well, it's not true.' I tried not to show how angry I felt, but inwardly I was seething. I'd always liked Leah; I liked her mum Rachel, too. But I really needed to have that chat with her. First Leah called you Mop Head, now this. Making up stories to frighten you wasn't on.

'Look, I promise you there's nothing buried up at the allotment but bulbs and a few old vegetables.' I plopped a kiss on BB's head. 'The three of us can wander up there after school, if you like, and I'll show you. I need a chat with Maria anyway.' I realised it had been days since I'd checked in with her about the orders she was caretaking for me.

You shook your head so hard, you almost fell off the stool. I caught you just in time, almost dropping BB as you clung on tightly to my sweatshirt.

'Or we can play here,' I soothed, hugging your trembling body before gazing around the cramped, cluttered kitchen. 'Babies certainly need a lot of stuff, don't they?' I sighed.

You nodded mutely, your eyebrows puckering as you glared at BB.

'I'll have a sort-out, darling. I promise. It was super helpful of you to tidy up this morning, but that's my job, OK? Besides, a bit of mess never killed anyone.'

'Really?'

Your fingertips dug into my arms now, and I wondered again if Jordan had been dropping hints. Maybe that explained your worried face as he'd charged through the house . . .

Perhaps it was also the *real* reason he'd taken you to the beach early on Sunday morning: to have a quiet word with you about keeping things tidy, to avoid tiring me out. After all, Jordan was the one who'd brought up my health yesterday, I recalled, also remembering your insistence on pushing the buggy. *To spare me the effort?*

'Yes, really,' I said firmly. 'This is our *home*, not a museum.' I remembered all too well my own dad telling me off for being messy. 'I tell you what. I'll do a proper tidy-up this week, while you're at school. It'll take no time at all. I'll hardly even be out of breath!'

You stared up at me, and I could tell by your wide, shadowed eyes that I'd touched a raw nerve. I hadn't seen that frightened look since the final days of my pregnancy, when the ever-present threat of pulmonary hypertension had begun to loom dangerously large. Jordan had called an ambulance, chasing behind it in our car – and you were with him.

The sirens, the flashing blue lights, the oxygen masks. I knew it must all have been terrifying, and that you probably still remembered every tense, bewildering moment. Maybe you were scared it might happen again. I knew how it felt to worry about my own mum's health; I kicked myself for not realising sooner that you might have been doing the same.

'I'm absolutely fine, love. And to prove it, I'm going to ask Aunty Amy round for dinner tomorrow. You'd like that, wouldn't you? And try not to worry about what Leah said. She's just telling silly stories.' I gave you another hug, pleased when you wrapped your arms around me this time. 'Come on, then. Let's get a wriggle on, or we'll be late for school.'

I hummed with deliberate cheerfulness as I settled BB in his buggy, before pulling on my boots and jacket, but my mind was working on overdrive. I was concerned and more than a little cross about the things Leah had told you, but, that aside, I was convinced I'd hit on what had been making you so quiet lately: worry about me overdoing things and falling ill again.

I spent the whole of our little bus ride trying to think what I could do to reassure you. I already hid my medication and made excuses whenever I had hospital check-ups; I tried not to ever let you see how, sometimes, just getting through the day was a physical effort. Clearly, my little act wasn't fooling you. But maybe dinner with Amy would do the trick. She was always lively company, even if she hadn't seemed so keen on mine, lately.

In fact, I hadn't heard from her in weeks, so it was a surprise when, seconds after I texted inviting her to 'pop over about 7.30 tomorrow night', her reply flashed up:

Great. Something to tell you xx

After dropping you at school, I pondered that message all the way home, jumping in confusion when Martin, the bus driver, called out my stop. 'You're away with the fairies today, love,' he said, as I manoeuvred BB's buggy off the bus. 'That little guy keeping you up all night? My Lily was in a right daze after Eddie was born. Hormones, Dr Henry said.'

I must have said something in response, but I don't remember what. I was still preoccupied by Amy's text and barely noticed my surroundings as I made my way home. I blinked in surprise when I arrived at our cottage; an even bigger surprise awaited me inside.

After letting myself in and carrying BB through to the kitchen, settling him in his carry-cot, I found another note in the worry box. 'At least you're communicating with me. Sort of,' I mumbled, unfolding the scrap of paper. This time, there were words rather than a drawing, although, frustratingly, your second message was as puzzling as your first:

I wish I could fly away

'Huh. Just like Amy,' I mused, and at first it truly did seem like pure coincidence. You'd sat at our kitchen table with her dozens of times, watching her draw and cut out patterns, listening to her talk about when she could finally quit teaching and become a fashion designer. She always said the same thing: 'I wish I could fly away.' Our chat about her coming round for dinner must have planted the thought of her in your mind, that was all.

But the longer I stared at your note, the more I worried that there was something else you were trying to tell me – that maybe your note was a secret nod to your anxiety about seeing Amy: my oldest friend, who, for all her vivacious charm, has always had a dark side that only seemed to intensify the older she got.

Chapter 12

MAY 2007

'I just don't see the point of learning all this crap. I won't need GCSE Chemistry for fashion college. And what use is the freakin' periodic table to anyone, anyway?' Amy kicked higher on the swing, thrusting her pale, skinny legs into the air until her feet brushed the feathery tips of the big oak tree that dominated our back garden. The ropes looped around its ancient branches creaked ominously.

'You're going too fast. Slow down!' I yelled from the safe distance of the bench under the pergola. Covered with roses, it was Mum's favourite shady nook to sit and watch us play when we were little. But we weren't little anymore, and I was worried the homemade swing would break. 'Amy, seriously, that branch looks like it's about to snap!'

'Don't be a spoilsport, Holly! I'm *flying*! I wish I could fly away,' she sang, urging the swing higher until her skirt flew up around her thighs.

I glanced around, relieved the garden wasn't overlooked. Even if Amy didn't value her modesty, it had become my habit to worry about it. I hadn't forgotten having to drag her out of the school

71

Easter Disco, after watching her flirt tipsily with two older boys. With her leather mini skirt, crop top and bad attitude, Amy had been any father's worst nightmare.

Only she hadn't seen her father for ten years; he obviously didn't care *what* she got up to. It was *my* dad who worried about her, gave her pep talks and imposed curfews. And even though Amy was now a permanent part of our family rather than a guest, Dad still seemed to hold me responsible for her wellbeing. If she messed up, I usually paid the price.

I'd given up protesting that it was Amy, not me, who left cigarette butts behind the shed. Nor did I snitch on her for sneaking out of our room most nights. When she crept back in hours later, I didn't ask her where she'd been, or why she hid crying under the covers. I never said a word at breakfast, either. We all simply pretended everything was fine.

I knew it wasn't, but I also knew that if I said anything, it would provoke an explosion from Amy that would leave us all trembling in its wake, especially my increasingly frail mum. I was never quite sure if she and my dad were genuinely oblivious of Amy's wily ways, or if, like me, they simply chose to turn a blind eye in order to keep the peace.

Despite everything, though, I still cared – still worried about Amy. 'Slow *down*, Ames!' I called out anxiously again that afternoon. 'You'll break it!'

'Are you calling me fat?' She swivelled precariously on the swing to glare at me.

'Of course not! We need to get back to work, anyway.' We'd only come out for a break from revision because Amy was bored. 'If you lose any more weight, you'll disappear.'

'It's your mum's summer solstice party soon. I've got my outfit all planned out. Just need to starve off a few pounds first. Do you really think I look chubby?'

I sighed as she executed a dramatic dismount and came to sit next to me. '*No*, Amy. It's just that the swing is meant for little kids, not teenagers. Dad made it as a replacement present for Treacle, remember?' I tried not to sound bitter, but I hadn't forgotten that while it had been my rabbit that died, Amy had claimed full share in the consolation gift.

'Oh yeah. Poor Cookie. I mean Treacle.' She gave me one of her shoulder bumps.

'Don't act so innocent,' I huffed. 'I know *exactly* what you did.'

'What? I did nothing.' She grinned. 'At least, not to your rabbit. Shame I can't say the same about your friend Jane. No, enough said. Ask me no secrets, I'll tell you no lies.'

'What do you mean?' I turned to stare at her pretty face. She was sixteen by then, but looked, and acted, a lot older. 'Don't be a drama queen, Amy. Jane fell into the Meare, that's all. Maybe you pushed her. Maybe she fell. Either way, it's no big deal. We were seven.'

'Sure.' She winked. 'Anyway, I meant after that. Before secondary school.'

'What?' I frowned. 'Jane moved to London with her family. So what?' I shrugged carelessly, even though I hadn't forgotten my hurt surprise that I'd never heard from my best friend again. We'd been so close, and then it was as though she'd vanished into thin air.

'Oh, Holly. You still believe that? I guess you were an oversensitive kid. No one wanted to tell you the truth. About *anything*. We knew you couldn't take it. You still can't.'

'Oversensitive?' I glared at her. 'And take *what*?' I said through gritted teeth. Mostly, I felt sorry for Amy. Occasionally, I liked her. Sometimes, like in that moment, I hated her. Who the hell was she to say my own parents were scared to tell me things?

I'd grown up feeling our home was full of secrets. Conversations that stopped when I walked into the room; evasiveness when I asked questions. I had thought it was all to do with Amy's parents; now she was hinting there was something I didn't know about Jane?

'Jane didn't move away, Holly. She died.'

'She . . . *what*?'

Amy took hold of my hands, lowering her voice. 'She fell off the swing at school. And no one told you, because they knew you'd be devastated. Because you liked her better than me.' Her eyes narrowed. 'Which is why I pushed her in the first place.'

'No. Stop!' I put my hands over my ears, trying to block out what she was saying.

'I tried the lake first,' Amy continued, yanking my hands away. 'But that didn't work. Too many people around at the regatta. So I had to come up with something more subtle.'

'What are you *talking* about?' I stared at her, horrified at what she was saying. Amy had always made up stories to gain attention, but this was her worst one yet.

'It took me a couple of years, but it was worth the wait. Jane was history.' Amy's blue eyes glittered triumphantly. 'Finally, I had you all to myself.'

'What the fuck?' I didn't usually swear – Dad didn't approve – but I was furious. 'What is *wrong* with you? You're always lying. Twisting the truth. Now you're telling me you're a *murderer*?' I could feel my hands trembling as I wrenched them away from Amy.

'See? I told you.' She folded her arms, looking smug. 'Everything has to be perfect for *little Holly*. Everyone always has to walk on eggshells around you, in case your stupid heart packs in.' She rolled her eyes unsympathetically. 'Well, news flash, life isn't perfect. But you just shut your mind to anything you don't like. You live in your own twinkly little bubble thinking everyone's lovely. That your mum's an angel and your dad's a fucking hero.'

'That's not true! I *don't* think that!' I loved my parents, but I wasn't blind to their faults. Mum was preoccupied with her allotment and seemed increasingly absent-minded; Dad was too strict, and I only really relaxed during his many trips to London 'for research'.

74

I wondered if that was where he'd got the idea to tell me Jane had moved there, then mentally berated myself for letting Amy's nonsense get into my head. 'And Jane *did* move to London,' I insisted.

'Didn't.'

'Did.'

'Oh, Holly, Holly.' Amy shook her head. 'You can't see what's going on right under your nose. Jane never went anywhere other than a cold, dark grave. Over there.' She nodded in the direction of St Andrew's Church, just outside the village. 'Go look for yourself, if you don't believe me.'

'So why did no one *tell* me?' I was humouring her, I told myself. I wouldn't fall for her lies, her crocodile tears. I wouldn't give her the chance to poke fun at me and yell, *Got you!* as she usually did after stringing me along with one of her tall tales.

'Because no one can tell you *anything*,' she said quietly.

'What? *Why*?' I forced her to look me in the eye. 'Such as?'

'Such as . . .' Amy stared back at me, her pupils widening until the blue of her irises almost disappeared. Then she laughed. 'Got you!'

'I hate you, Amy Jackson.'

I pulled away from her and ran into the house, jamming my fingers in my ears to block out the sound of her mocking laughter – and the voice in my head whispering that Amy might have lied about Jane, but there was obviously another confession burning in her mind. And she was right: I was too scared to ask what it was.

Chapter 13

'Can I ask you something, Dad?'

The niggle about Jane wouldn't go away. I had wanted to speak to Mum, but she was nowhere to be found. Amy had disappeared, too. I was glad; I didn't want her teasing me for asking my dad about her stupid lies. I didn't want another lecture about maligning *poor Amy*, either, and my 'stupid heart' pounded as I knocked on his study door.

'What is it, sweetheart? Be quick.' He didn't look up from the papers he was rifling through on his desk. 'I'm trying to find something. A . . . a poem.'

'A poem?' I looked doubtfully at the pile of official-looking papers in front of him.

'Your mum has got this, um, verse stuck in her head. She wanted me to find it. Just to check if she'd remembered it correctly. I printed it out earlier. Now I can't find it *anywhere*.'

'Have you checked Amy's desk?' I said dryly.

'Sorry?' Dad glanced distractedly at me over his shoulder. 'Of course not. I don't go into her room. That's her private space. And yours,' he added, seemingly as an afterthought. Frowning, he pulled open his own desk drawers, rifling briskly. 'Where *is* the darned thing?'

Muttering to himself, he stared around the room. I followed his gaze, scanning the tall, neatly alphabetised bookcases and squat leather trunks where he kept his 'curiosities', as he called the odd assortment of antiques he collected.

Glancing at the sofa by the window, I felt a pulse throb in my neck as I pictured my younger self, recalling how I used to sit there for hours every Sunday morning, playing with the strange objects Dad showed me, laughing as he tickled me when I couldn't remember their names. Then Amy came along, and she was the one he invited into his study, not me.

'I've got loads of poetry books,' I offered awkwardly. 'I could give you—'

'*No.*' Dad slammed the door of a walnut cabinet. 'Sorry. Thank you, darling. But it's a particular, er, sonnet. I hoped it would soothe Olivia. She's been feeling a little tired today.'

'Tired?' I perched on the sofa, feeling a flash of panic as I remembered spotting Dr Henry's car outside our house when I came home earlier. 'Is Mum in bed?' That would explain why I hadn't been able to find her. It hadn't occurred to me to look upstairs at five in the afternoon: Mum was usually at the allotment at that time of day. 'She's not ill, is she?'

'Bit under the weather, that's all. Working too hard, I expect. Florists are in extra demand at this time of year. Business always booms – or should I say blooms – during spring.' Dad finally looked in my direction, giving me a wink. 'Easter services, weddings—'

'Funerals?' I blurted out, my thoughts still full of my friend Jane.

Dad's tanned face paled. 'Well, yes, I suppose so. But let's not get ahead of—'

'So Dr Henry didn't say anything's wrong?' I half stood up again, eager to see Mum for myself. 'I think I'll just go and check.'

'She's resting, sweetheart.' Dad's height blocked my path. 'Best not to disturb her.'

Immediately, I regretted announcing my intention. I should have expected the subtle veto of me having time alone with Mum; for some reason, Dad always found a reason to interrupt whenever I tried to have a quiet chat with her. 'OK.' I sank back onto the sofa in resignation, but I couldn't shake off my anxiety.

Dad gave up searching for his poem and came to sit next to me. 'Don't worry, love. Dr Henry's visit was purely social. A quick catch-up about hospital fundraising. Anyway, you wanted to ask me something?'

'Doesn't matter,' I mumbled, wishing I'd never said anything.

'No time like the present.' He crossed his legs, one arm resting lightly behind me on the back of the sofa. 'We haven't had one of our daddy–daughter chats in months, have we?'

Years, I thought. 'No.' I chewed my lip, feeling unaccountably nervous.

'You used to come in here all the time. I remember you sitting right there. Playing with your toys. Making up stories. I guess you're too old for all that now. Exams soon, hey?'

'I haven't got much time for anything now. Too much revision. In fact, I should—'

'No hurry, is there? I can see something's bothering you. Don't be shy. Spit it out.'

'OK.' Half-formed fears tangled in my mind. So many, I didn't know where to start.

'Well?'

'It's about Amy, actually,' I said, before I could change my mind. 'And Jane.'

'Jane who?'

'You know, my old best friend. She used to come here all the time. Until Amy . . .' My heart hammered, and I looked quickly away, my gaze falling on the silver-framed photo on Dad's desk of me and my 'almost-sister', as Amy called herself.

'Until Amy . . .?'

I took a deep breath. 'Until Amy moved in permanently. Jane

78

was always round here before then.' I deliberately hinted at a connection between the two events, hoping to flush out a revelation. 'We used to have loads of sleepovers. But none after Amy came to live here. Except on my tenth birthday. That was such a special night, and then . . . nothing. I never got to play with her again.'

'Ah. I see.' Dad nodded, sitting forward. 'I remember that time. Your mum was setting up her floristry business. I was trying to finish my thesis. And Amy . . . Well, it was tough for her, wasn't it? Adjusting to a new family. Even though it was for the best. What with her parents travelling so much, and Olivia and I being able to offer her a more stable—'

'I get it, Dad. I'm not complaining that I didn't have enough play dates. I'm just asking if you remember my friend. Where she went. What happened to her. Jane Price.'

It was only in that moment that I managed to recall her surname. I'd been desperately trying to think of it as I wandered up to the church a couple of hours before. Not to look for any gravestone, I'd told myself. I still didn't believe what Amy had said. No, I just needed to stretch my legs after being stuck inside revising all day, that was all.

But as I'd crossed the golf course, trying to kid myself I wasn't heading straight for St Andrew's on the other side, I felt increasingly agitated: that I couldn't remember my friend's surname; that I was even allowing head space to the idea of Amy having killed her.

It was crazy. Surely there would have been a special assembly or church service if a pupil had died? Yet I remembered nothing. Jane was definitely there on our last day of primary school, but she never appeared at secondary school. For a while, I'd pestered my parents to know why, and then, with the fickleness of an eleven-year-old, I'd simply resigned myself to playing with someone else.

'Sorry, pickle.' Dad pulled a rueful smile. 'I don't recall any Jane. I guess I'm used to seeing you with Amy. Thick as thieves, you two always were. Two clever, pretty girls together. Everything's turned out for the best, yes?'

'Sure.' It was pointless telling him that he only saw what he wanted to see. 'Don't be a tell-tale, Holly,' I remembered him saying, so anxious to make sure his best friend's daughter felt part of our family that he was blind to how often she tried to push me out of it.

'Something else worrying you?'

It had become so rare for my dad to ask about my feelings that, caught off guard, I blurted out: 'Yes. I'm scared something really bad happened to Jane.'

'Such as?'

'I don't know. Kidnap? *Murder?*' The word sounded darkly incongruous in the light, tranquil surroundings of our elegant family home, and as I saw Dad's thin lips tighten, I knew I'd made a mistake.

'Holly Aitken, I'm surprised at you. How can you joke about such a horror when that poor little girl is still all over the news?'

'What girl?' My mind went blank. I felt crestfallen at his disapproval, but at the same time bewildered that another girl might have come to a grisly end. 'Who? What's happened?'

'Madeleine something or other. And nobody knows. She was stolen from right under her parents' noses. Not two weeks ago. You really mustn't joke about these things. Making up stories is all very well when you're a little girl. But you're a young woman now. I thought you'd left off playing make-believe years ago.'

'I have. I mean, I'm not making things up.' The injustice stung, and I almost wanted to laugh at the irony of *me* being accused of making up stories, not Amy. 'Right under your nose', I remembered her saying, struck by the coincidence of her using the same phrase, baffled at the idea that terrible things could happen without anyone noticing. 'I wasn't joking, Dad, honestly. I was just thinking about my friend. I'm worried that—'

'Worried that *what*?' He was clearly getting impatient now. His blue eyes flicked repeatedly to the door, and I could tell he'd had enough of our 'little chat'.

The thought made me angry. It was *me* he'd spent time with before Amy came to live with us. Not anymore, though. Now it was Amy he took everywhere. They'd even stayed overnight in London a few times. I never had. No doubt because Dad thought I couldn't cope with the big, bad world – because I was 'over-sensitive', as Amy said.

She'd also said everyone walked on eggshells around me; that no one felt I could handle the truth. Now was my chance to prove otherwise. If something bad *had* happened, I wanted to know about it. 'I want to know if Amy hurt Jane,' I said as firmly as I dared.

'Holly.' Any hint of a smile disappeared. 'It's a good job poor Amy's not here. Imagine how she'd feel if she heard you accusing her of . . . goodness knows what.'

'But she said—'

'Enough! Sorry, love. I didn't mean to shout.' A nerve twitched under his eye. 'It's just . . . there are enough tragedies in the world without inventing fictional ones, OK?'

'Sorry.' Long-ingrained habit kicked in, compelling me to accept the blame rather than reveal Amy's outrageous claim, which had obviously been nothing more than yet another cruel joke at my expense.

'Look, I don't want to come down too hard on you. Your health, your heart . . .' Dad pulled me against him, and the stubble on his jaw was rough and familiar against my forehead. I could feel the heat of his armpit against my shoulder. I pulled sharply away.

'I'm *fine*, Dad,' I said irritably. I wasn't an invalid, and I hated being treated like one.

'I just don't want you upsetting yourself. You've grown up so fast. You're so clever and hardworking. But what you've just said about poor Amy.' He shook his head. 'That's cruel. *Irrational*. I'm surprised at you. Amy's a good girl. She wouldn't hurt a fly.'

Chapter 14

I felt ridiculously nervous about dinner that evening and changed three times before settling on my old standby of black jeans and shirt. I didn't want to give Amy any cause to tease me about becoming 'mumsy', as she had the last time I'd seen her. I frowned at my reflection in the dressing-table mirror, shocked to realise that had been two months ago, on your birthday.

'You don't look bad for almost thirty,' I reassured myself, pulling my hair out of its ponytail and tousling it in a vague attempt at a sexy-casual look. 'I can be fun when I want to be,' I muttered, still smarting from Jordan's dig yesterday morning.

Hunting through the box where I kept my earrings, I realised it was the one Jane had given me. 'Where did you go, Jane?' My fingers shook as they found the silver heart she'd also given me, twenty years ago. I'd forgotten I still had it, but, to be honest, even if I *had* remembered, I wouldn't have given it a second thought. Now it reminded me of questions I'd thought were buried in the past. Such as: *Was Amy really as bad as she liked to make out?*

I thought of her text, wondering if she'd done something to scare you and wanted to confess. As I fastened Jane's necklace around my neck, I felt haunted once more by my old friend's sudden, inexplicable disappearance. I'd failed to solve that mystery, but I wouldn't rest until I'd got to the bottom of yours.

'Sorry I'm late. Couldn't get a taxi.' Amy wafted perfume as she stepped into the porch. Awkwardly, she was also wearing black jeans and shirt, although hers bore a designer label.

'You're fine. We're running a bit behind, too.' I didn't bore her with the details. Amy lived alone, rarely cooked and employed a cleaner. It seemed extravagant to me, given her compact, modern flat next to the Aldeburgh Yacht Club. But then she'd never been domestic.

'You seem different,' she commented, looking me up and down as she followed me into the living room. 'Have you had your hair cut?'

'No. But Jordan has. Amazingly.' I mimed shock, acknowledging his usual scruffiness. 'He must have a secret admir—'

'You look like you've dropped a couple of pounds, though. I guess it's the breastfeeding. Wendy's been raving all week about it being a "miracle diet". You remember Wendy? The head's PA. She's just back from mat leave, and boy don't we all know about it.'

'Ah, yes.' I felt a pang as I realised how I'd lost touch with friends from my old job.

'She's turned into some bloody earth mother. It's all *baby this, baby that*. But I can't deny she's skinny as hell. She puts it all down to breastfeeding the little parasite.'

'Amy!' I shook my head but couldn't help chuckling at her disgusted expression.

'What? So I don't like babies. Or kids. Shoot me.' She raised her eyebrows.

'Bit of a disadvantage for a teacher,' I pointed out.

'I teach them. I don't have to love them. Apart from yours, of course. Where are they, anyway? Hiding from their wicked godmother?' She batted her eyelashes. 'Evil Aunty Amy.'

'Upstairs. Jordan's putting them to bed. He'll be down in a minute. But please don't joke, Amy. You might not mean to, but you'll scare Marley,' I cautioned.

'Rubbish. She's a smart kid. Way cleverer than all the others in her class. I had to babysit them on Monday.' She sighed, slumping wearily onto the sofa.

'You did?' I wondered why you hadn't mentioned it. Perching on the armchair opposite, I watched Amy closely. 'Did Marley seem OK to you?'

Amy shrugged. 'She was in cahoots with Rachel's daughter most of the time.'

'Rachel Smith? Yes, Leah is Marley's best friend. Supposedly.' I wrinkled my nose.

'Oh? Problems? They certainly seemed as thick as thieves in class.'

'Right. That's good. I think.' Maybe the name-calling had been a joke, but you'd taken it seriously, along with stories about 'naughty girls' being buried at the allotment. Although, thinking about it, that sounded more like Amy's style, I pondered, recalling her dramatic story about my friend Jane, wondering if she'd told *your* friend a similar one.

'You *think*?' Amy cocked her head, navy eyes widening questioningly.

'Something's worrying Marley. I wondered if she'd had a fallout with her friend. Did you, um, speak to Leah at all? Read her any stories, or anything?' I said carefully, not wanting to rub Amy up the wrong way by accusing her of spooking a child. I wanted the evening to be a success; I didn't want Jordan accusing me of being a 'spoilsport' again.

'Nothing I can recall. The pair of them were too busy ransacking the dressing-up box. Leah dresses just like her mum. *Badly.*' Amy rolled her eyes. 'There's no hope for Rach, of course. But I did my best to enlighten her poor daughter.'

'You are *so* in the wrong job,' I teased, shaking my head.

'Not for much longer, thankfully.'

'Sorry? Oh, hang on, I'll take those.' I groaned as Amy carelessly shoved at the blankets I'd folded so neatly on the sofa, letting them tumble onto the floor.

'Don't tell me Jordan's still sleeping on this thing?' One thin eyebrow quirked.

I hid my blush in the blankets. 'Night feeds are so disruptive, and what with Jordan working extra shifts . . .' I wondered how Amy knew where he slept; I hoped she didn't also know that he spent weekends on his boat. I knew she'd never believed our marriage would last; I didn't want her thinking she was right – even if I was worrying about it myself.

'Sure.' She gave me a look that was half pity, half curiosity. 'The joys of parenting.'

'Do you ever hear from *your* parents?' It was a clumsy attempt to divert attention from my marriage, and I regretted the question as soon as it was out of my mouth.

'Nope. Not since Olivia . . .' Amy tailed off, frowning. 'My dad sent flowers for her funeral, remember? I mean, for fuck's sake, who sends flowers to a florist? Even a dead one.'

'I know you were disappointed they didn't come to the church,' I said softly, all too familiar with Amy's habit of disguising her true feelings with black humour.

'Oh, I didn't expect it. They were settled in Paris by then. Happy. Successful. Free.' She shrugged. 'There wasn't exactly a lot to entice them home.'

'There was *you*,' I said, dumping the blankets in a corner. I knew how hurt Amy had been by her parents' absence – that it was the reason she put on such a tough, prickly front.

'Huh. Well, I guess I wasn't enough. I tried to find them once, you know? When I was at art college in—'

'Paris,' I finished for her, feeling bad that it had never occurred to me that was probably the real reason she'd chosen to apply for a college placement there.

'Yeah. I got the run-around even then. Charming, hey? I mean, I wasn't asking for anything. I was a grown woman. Independent.' Her lips pursed. 'Not like when I was younger. Frankly, I get why they wanted shot of me then. Which would you choose? Dragging an obnoxious kid around Europe, or being free to jet off at a moment's notice?'

'I'd choose my child. Every time. But I can't believe it was that simple. I mean, I know they travelled a lot. Dad always said it was better you stayed with us than had to move from city to city, school to school. But is that what your parents—'

'You know what? Let's not do this now, OK? The past is the past. As far as I'm concerned, Adam and Olivia were my mum and dad. And I've always been glad about that.'

'Sure.' I didn't add that I hadn't always felt the same. 'Wine?' I hurried into the kitchen, heading for the bottle of cava chilling in the fridge. I badly needed a drink myself.

Amy followed. 'Thanks. Or vodka, if you have it. Fewer calories.' She patted her flat stomach before sitting down at the kitchen table, admiring the gold and cream place settings. 'This looks nice.'

'Thanks. Marley helped me.'

'See? I told you. She's such a clever girl. And *something* smells awesome.'

'My equally clever husband's creation.' I set the wine down on the table, then glanced at my watch. 'He's taking his time.' I frowned, wondering what was going on upstairs – if there was some kind of problem; if he was talking to you, what he was saying . . .

'Holl, I'm dying of thirst here.' Amy grabbed the wine and poured herself a glass. 'Sorry, I should have brought a bottle. I forgot. You know how crazy the start of term is. Still, like I said, it's not for much longer. I'm handing in my notice. Finally, I get to fly away!'

Chapter 15

I almost dropped my glass as I sat down abruptly at the table. 'You're *what*?'

'Yep. Oh, I know I've been saying it every year since I started teaching. I mean it this time, though. Things have . . . changed. If I don't take the plunge now, I never will.'

'Never will what?' Jordan asked, strolling into the kitchen at last, a full nappy sack held out in front of him like an unexploded bomb.

'Follow my dream.' Amy pulled a wry face. 'I've only been chasing it for a decade.'

'Ha. Maybe that tells you something. Like, you're chasing the wrong dream. It's not too late to switch, you know? Reading bedtime stories and changing nappies was never meant to be at the end of *my* rainbow. Look at me now!' Jordan feigned a look of comic disgust as he flipped open the kitchen bin and dropped the bulging blue plastic sack inside it.

'Yes, look at you,' Amy said, and this time she didn't laugh. She gazed between us, swilling wine around her glass. 'You've certainly found your pot of gold. Both of you.'

'I like to think so,' I agreed, watching Jordan wash his hands before checking the food, feeling surprised and hurt by his comment that life hadn't turned out as he'd imagined.

'Marriage. Babies.' Amy screwed up her nose. 'I guess my parents did a great job putting me off that particular dream. Now *fashion*. That never gets dull.'

'Hey, Jackson, watch who you're calling dull,' Jordan teased, shutting the oven door and wafting away fragrant steam before joining us at the table. 'Although I reckon I might be heading that way,' he added, rolling his eyes as he sat down, hooking one leg over the other.

His hair was still wet from his shower, and his green T-shirt clung damply to his chest. I glanced down to see tanned bare feet, the anchor tattoo on his right ankle visible beneath the hem of his jeans. There was nothing dull about Jordan; he was the most vibrant, interesting person I'd ever met. I wondered if he would still say the same about me.

'Says the guy who's sailed halfway around the world!' Amy poked out her tongue.

'Which means there's still a good fifty per cent I *haven't* seen,' he countered with a chuckle. 'My passport has probably expired.'

'Well, mine hasn't.' Amy sighed. 'That's what I love about fashion. The chance to travel. The constant buzz of change. Always a new trend. Different cities. Different clients. I totally get why my mum loved it. No two days are ever the same.'

'You get a different class of children every year,' I pointed out.

'And after ten years, they blur into one. Lucky you, Holl, getting out when you did.'

'Not by choice. I'd still be teaching if it wasn't for that stupid insurance company.'

'They were right to be cautious, babe,' Jordan interjected. 'Your heart condition *is* unpredictable. That last time you fainted at school, the doctors said—'

'I know!' I cut in, hating the reminder. 'Anyway, working from home lets me focus on the kids, too. Having a family was always at the end of *my* rainbow,' I said pointedly.

'Well, this lady for one isn't going to inherit a pot of gold in a couple of months.' Amy raised her glass, toasting herself. 'I've got to get out there and earn one for myself.'

'Cheers to you, Ames.' Jordan poured himself some wine and clinked glasses with her. 'And your next adventure.' He winked. 'Wherever you go . . . whoever you go with.'

I didn't join in with the toast. 'We've had this conversation so many times, Amy. I've got no intention of touching that money. Selling Sea View was Dad's decision, not mine. And as for the proceeds, I don't get why they weren't split equally between us any more than you do. But the trust fund will pass on to Marley when I'm gone. I don't need it.'

'Wish I could say the same.' Amy rolled her eyes. 'Sorry, ignore me. I'm just miffed because no doubt all I'll get on my big three-oh is a crappy card from the kids in my class.'

'You love them really.' I forced a smile. I couldn't blame her for feeling bitter that while a small fortune was held in trust for me when I turned thirty, my mum hadn't left Amy a penny. I had no idea why. Like so many things in my family, it remained a mystery.

'Seriously, I don't. You're the maternal one. Just like Olivia. She may have brought me up, but I'm not like her. Never was. Which is probably why she left everything to you. Oh, don't look so guilty, Holl. Your dad did all right out of it too. Selling Sea View gave him a healthy pension pot.' She smirked. 'I'll just guilt-trip him into paying for the party instead.'

'Party?' Jordan's eyes lit up.

'Yeah. Why not? I've still got a few days to book something. Maybe we could even have a joint thing,' she added, turning to me. 'Your thirtieth's only a month after mine.'

I gave her a dubious glance, surprised she would want to share her big moment. She never had before. 'I wasn't really planning anything,' I muttered. 'Parties are expensive.'

'Yeah. Shame we can't hold one at Sea View. Imagine what your mum . . .'

I gave her a sharp look. It still hurt unbearably that our old family home was now a holiday rental. Every time I thought of other families staying there, cooking in Mum's kitchen, sleeping in her bedroom, it felt like they were walking over her grave.

'They do special rates for locals at the Dolphin,' Jordan offered quietly, watching me.

'Or maybe you could get us a discount at the country club?' Amy raised her eyebrows at him, and cynically I wondered if that was the real reason she'd accepted my invitation so fast – if she'd had a party in mind all along and had seized the chance to beg a favour.

'That's not a bad idea,' Jordan agreed, so quickly that I wondered if the idea hadn't been a surprise to him, either – if he and Amy had in fact already discussed it, and that was why he'd suggested we ask her round in the first place, to 'open a bottle of bubbly'.

'Fabulous!' Amy clapped her hands together.

'I'll do the catering,' Jordan added. 'I did Marley's when we had her party there. I'm sure your friends will be easier to please than a bunch of seven-year-olds. And less messy.'

Amy pulled a face. 'I wouldn't count on it. But that was one hell of a party.'

'Marley enjoyed it, too,' I chipped in ironically, remembering Amy's wild mood that afternoon, how much wine she'd drunk. 'Although, she's been weirdly quiet ever since. Actually, I wanted to ask you about that.' I'd already tried twice, and suddenly I realised that Amy had distracted me both times. 'I know Marley had fun on her birthday, but—'

'Fun. Yes, she certainly had plenty of that.' Amy rolled her eyes. 'Especially when she covered my favourite dress in strawberry milkshake. *Didn't* you, pickle?'

We all turned to look in the direction of the kitchen door. 'Oh, Marley, love.' I wondered how long you had been standing there, listening. You looked freezing, your little body rigid beneath your yellow nightie, your face white as you peeped through the tousled curtain of your hair. 'Can't you sleep? Come on, let me take you back upstairs.'

'I can take her,' Amy offered, half standing up from her chair.

I'd never seen you move so fast; you flew across the kitchen into my arms before I'd even had a chance to reply. Pulling you onto my lap, I held you close, trying to absorb your trembles. 'It's OK. I'll take you, darling. Say nighty night to Daddy. And Aunty Amy,' I made myself add, even though I was puzzled by your reluctance to go with her.

'Night,' you whispered against my neck.

'Sweet dreams, Marley.' Amy patted your back as I carried you out of the room.

Jordan stood up to kiss you. 'Sleep tight, honey bee. Don't let the bed bugs bite.'

You didn't respond; you didn't say a single word as I carried you upstairs and helped you back into bed. You didn't explain why you had come downstairs, or complain of bad dreams. You simply held on to me as I bent to kiss you, wrapping your arms around my neck.

'Everything's OK, darling. Was it a bit funny seeing Aunty Amy out of school?' I suddenly recalled my surprise when you'd claimed to be too tired to wait up for her to arrive, once again worrying that there was something about Amy that was bothering you.

'Don't go downstairs, Mummy,' you said breathlessly, ignoring my question.

'I'll be up soon, darling. I'll pop in and check on you when I come to bed.'

'Can you sleep with me? *Please?*'

'Oh, sweetheart.' I sat down on the edge of your bed. 'I don't think there's room for me in here.' I patted your blankets. 'I might squash Wally.'

'He's not here.'

'Not here? Where's he gone?' I looked around your room in disbelief.

You *never* slept without the little grey koala Jordan bought for you after BB was born, pretending the soft toy was a gift from your new brother. I remembered how your eyes shone as you'd unwrapped Wally, as you later christened him, unable to pronounce *koala* – how like Jordan's they were. How much I loved you both.

'He's lost.' You squeezed your eyes shut, shaking your head.

'Oh!' I peeped under your blanket. 'Nope, not there.' I hesitated, guessing you must have tucked him away with your other toys. Not wanting to dwell on your recent obsession with tidiness, I let it go. 'Let's find him in the morning. He must be fast asleep somewhere.'

Your eyes snapped open. 'Don't go! Stay with me, Mummy. Please?'

'One more cuddle.' I stroked your arms, then froze as I realised I was unconsciously checking for more bruises. 'Dreams aren't real, love,' I whispered. 'Your imagination gets bored while you sleep, that's all. It makes up stories to pass the time till you wake up.'

Your eyes widened. 'Daddy said dreams come true if you wish on a shooting star.'

'Did he now?' I bit back a harsher response, still peeved by his comment that having children hadn't been *his* dream. 'Let's find one, then.' I pointed to the fluorescent stars I'd painted on your ceiling, smiling as I waited for you to spot the one with a long, silvery tail.

'There it is!' Your arm sprang out, pointing.

Instantly, my head filled with pictures of Jane Price doing the same thing on my tenth birthday. 'Well done, darling,' I said huskily. 'Now you have to make a wish.'

You squeezed your eyes closed again, your little face screwing up in concentration.

'Have you thought of one? Tell me what you wish, Marley,' I whispered, fighting tears as I remembered Jane's wish all those years ago – and recalled the one in your note. I hadn't been able to stop thinking about it; I was desperate to know what was making you want to 'fly away'. Just like Amy – *or because of her?*

Almost making me jump out of my skin, you grabbed hold of my hand and squeezed it hard, saying: 'I wish . . . I wish Daddy didn't have a boat.'

Chapter 16

By the time I went back downstairs, Jordan and Amy had served up dinner and were brainstorming plans for her fashion business. I sat listening, but I was still thinking about your wish. *You missed Jordan too.* That had to be what it meant. You didn't like it that your daddy spent all his time on the boat any more than I did.

I was burning to talk to him about it, but Amy, having found the limelight, wasn't going to relinquish it. Funnily enough, it helped calm my nerves to sit and listen to her chat about how she couldn't wait to 'get the hell out of our boring old village'. It rekindled my sympathy for her: she'd known sadness, too, and had no doubt taken refuge in fantasy – in dreams of becoming a famous designer, like the mum she hadn't seen since she was seven.

The lies Amy had made up when we were kids were most likely fantasies, too, and although she claimed to dislike the pupils in her class, it was probably that she envied their happy childhoods. Sadly, I could all too easily believe that Amy had tried to spook Leah with stories about 'naughty girls' buried at the allotment. But she was your *godmother*; I was sure she would never know-ingly hurt or even try to scare you.

My certainty evaporated when I read your third note, but I didn't find that until the next morning, when BB woke me just before dawn. After feeding and settling him back in his cot, I grabbed the baby monitor and decided to clean the kitchen before the school run.

At first, I was baffled as to when you'd posted it. Then I realised you must have slipped it into the worry box when you'd come down during dinner. As soon as I opened it, I knew I was right, and that you'd overheard far more than any of us had realised last night.

I hate parties

'You and me both, darling,' I mumbled, folding up your note with a sigh.

After tucking it under the teapot with the other two, I abandoned the washing up and sat down at the kitchen table, my head buzzing with thoughts. I'd forgotten to pull on my dressing gown, but the warmth of the Aga permeated the thick stone walls of the cottage, which rarely felt cold, even on a drizzly October day just before dawn. Wind whistled down the chimney breast, and rain tapped on the sash window over the sink.

The tick of the brass wall clock seemed to keep time with my heartbeat, but otherwise the cottage was quiet, in semi-darkness. Only the streetlight in the narrow alley behind our terrace cast a glow into the kitchen. I looked up as the light flickered – then went out.

'Damn, not again.' Power cuts were common during windy weather, but they always spooked me. Deciding to double-check if the electricity had gone out in the house as well as outside, I felt my way blindly across the kitchen, working my fingertips along the worktop to the wall, before sliding my hands upwards to locate the light switch.

'Oh! Strange.' The overhead light came on immediately. So too did the floor lamp next to my rocking chair in the corner. Puzzled, I was about to go back upstairs to check on you and BB, when I heard the unmistakable sound of footsteps in the alley.

Hurrying to the window, I peered out, but all I could see

through the glass was the black mirror of the sky. *'Jordan,'* I whispered, rushing through to the living room where, as usual, he'd made a makeshift bed of the sofa. Judging from his snores, he must have drunk more last night than I'd noticed, and I didn't want to disturb you or BB by yelling.

'Fabulous,' I muttered, grabbing Jordan's coat from the hall and pulling it on over my pyjamas. Hurrying back to the kitchen, I opened the back door, at the last moment turning to grab a sharp-tipped beach umbrella from the stand. Better safe than sorry.

'Holly? Is that you?'

'Oh, Phil. Thank *God*!' I let out a sigh of relief as I recognised our neighbour.

'Is your power out too?' he asked, shuffling down our garden path towards me.

'Bloody hell, Jordan,' I mumbled to myself. *'You left the gate open.'* I smiled at Phil, not wanting to appear rude. 'Actually, no. I thought it was. I came out to check. But we're fine!' I called out, blinking as the bright beam of his torch blinded me. I looked away, but not before I'd registered that Phil was wearing a short towelling dressing gown that hung open.

His chest and legs were bare, shoulders hunched against the soft mizzle. A fierce wind whipped off the sea, charging in gusty swirls across the coastal path to batter our huddled terrace. I shivered, wishing I hadn't come outside.

'The streetlight's out, too,' Phil said needlessly: the alley behind our cottages was pitch-black. 'Oh, sorry.' He swung his torch to the ground as I shielded my eyes.

'I noticed that – the streetlight. But our power's fine,' I repeated, also needlessly: the kitchen window behind me was brightly lit. 'Is, um, is yours definitely out?'

I felt a thrum of awkwardness as Phil finally came to stand in front of me. I hardly ever saw him, and all I knew about our immediate neighbour was that he lived alone and worked from home; having no electricity would be a big problem.

'Yeah. It went off just now. I was making myself a coffee, and then – pfftt – lights out.' He chuckled. 'Almost scalded myself on the damned kettle.'

'Oh, no. Do you, uh . . . do you want to pop into our house? Jordan is good with electrics.' I deliberately mentioned that I wasn't alone, then felt stupid as Phil grinned.

'No, it's fine. If you guys aren't having problems, it must be a fuse. I just thought I should check in with you, to see if it was a more general problem. Thanks, anyway.'

He turned and strode back along the footpath towards the alley. After a moment's hesitation, I followed, deciding to check on Jordan's motorbike. The bright red vintage Triumph was his pride and joy, only his new yacht coming higher in the pecking order – just above me, as I sometimes teased him.

The bike was fine, and I could see lights on in the other cottages along the terrace. Phil was right: if only his house was affected, it was probably a popped fuse. But as I turned to go back inside, I heard the crunch of broken glass beneath my slippers. Looking up, I could just about make out that the streetlight bulb had been smashed.

'Oh, God.' I looked all around, feeling a rush of alarm. The alley was empty, and I turned to stare nervously at Phil. Had he been lying about coming to check on us? Was the power cut simply a ruse, and the broken light meant to intimidate me?

'You OK?' His voice sounded deeper, somehow more threatening, in the darkness.

'Totally,' I lied. I guessed Phil was in his forties, but he clearly kept himself in shape; his muscular physique was obvious through his open robe. I edged backwards, holding the beach umbrella in front of me. If he took one step further . . .

'Good. I was worried about you – and the little ones. I know your husband works shifts. I thought I should pop round to check you were all OK, in case you were home alone. Hey, I hope I didn't scare you?' he added, as though the idea had just occurred to him.

'Well, maybe a bit.' My heart was still pounding, but his gentler tone and concerned expression reassured me a little. Phil was just being neighbourly; I was freaking out over nothing. 'It was very kind of you,' I said politely.

'No probs.' He winked. 'Although, if I might ask you a quick favour in return?'

'Sorry?'

'Would you mind holding this for me?'

'What?' I lifted the umbrella, fully prepared to spike him with it.

'The torch, Holly. If you could hold it while I check the fuse box?'

'Oh. Right.' I let out an awkward laugh. 'Yes, sure. Of course.'

'Actually, I think I've got something of yours,' he said over his shoulder as he pushed through his back gate. 'I've been meaning to return it to you. We can kill two birds with one stone, as it were.' Without waiting for me to reply, he set off down his garden path.

Hesitating again, I looked back towards our cottage, then gave myself a mental shake. Phil was a bit creepy, but pleasant enough. I was letting the darkness, and the eerie sound of the wind, get to me. Coming to a decision, I nipped back to wedge the umbrella in our back door to stop it blowing shut, then dashed after Phil and followed him into his kitchen.

As my eyes began to adjust to the dark, I realised the layout was different from ours, and it occurred to me that I'd never been inside his cottage; I suddenly wondered if *you* had.

'Did you find one of Marley's toys?' I called out, annoyed to hear my voice tremble.

'You tell me. Here you go.'

I jumped as I felt his sudden grip on my arm, pressing something soft into my hands. Automatically, I lifted it to my face, immediately recognising its smell. It was Wally.

Our kitchen was still brightly lit when I returned, having left Phil with his own lights working perfectly again. It had turned out to be a tripped fuse in his cottage, after all, and, declining his offer to share a pot of fresh coffee with him as a thank-you, I hurried home.

I was desperate to get out of there. The brief but strange encounter had rattled me, and I couldn't stop trembling. I was worried you might have been in Phil's cottage, alone; I wanted to mull over how your favourite toy had gone astray – and how he had come to find it. I also wanted to think some more about your third note: *I hate parties* . . .

Jordan had booked the morning off and was still fast asleep, and thankfully neither you nor BB had been disturbed when I left the house. I knew you wouldn't be getting up for school for a couple of hours: more than enough time for me to ponder whether it was Amy's birthday celebrations you were dreading, or your own party that you hadn't enjoyed – and why. Enough time to remember the worst party of *my* life. At Sea View, eight years ago.

Chapter 17

If I'd known it was to be my mum's last party, I would have tried harder to get into the spirit of it. But I've always hated parties, too. The annual Marmalade Ball, beloved by everyone else, was something I dreaded. The excitement, gossip and speculation that rippled through the village leading up to it only added to my nerves.

I especially hated fancy dress. It wasn't that I didn't enjoy make-believe; I loved it, and Thorpeness had been the perfect playground for my childhood imagination, from exploring the secret islands, coves and creeks of the Meare, to rambling through the woods and misty marshes. Living at Sea View fuelled my sense of adventure, too. One day I was a pirate scaling our spiral staircase to keep look-out; the next I was a princess locked in the tower.

I was always happy to play dress-up, and Mum's homemade costumes were amazing. I loved that she made so much effort; I've borrowed many of her ideas in the classroom over the years. What I found so excruciating, so *exhausting*, was Amy's need to always be the centre of attention. Over the years, I got used to it – then, gradually, more and more tired of it. The day I brought Jordan home to meet my parents for the first time was the final straw.

'Mum. Dad. This is Jordan. Jordan Mayhew. My, um, boyfriend.' I still felt self-conscious saying the word, and I cursed the tell-tale blush I could feel heating my cheeks.

The weather didn't help. It was a blisteringly hot day, oppressively humid after weeks of thunder storms. My neck felt sticky, my palms clammy as I gripped Jordan's hand and we stood in the hall, watching my parents watching us.

'I promise I'm not a closet arsonist,' Jordan joked to break the awkward silence, holding aloft the cardboard and tissue paper torch I'd spent my lunchtime making in the school staffroom. 'Alas I can't claim to be a Greek god, either.' He laughed, glancing down at the toga costume that showed off his strong, tanned legs.

'Ah. The Olympic flame. *Thank you.* Lovely of you to get into the spirit of the party.' Mum, also wearing a toga, stepped forward to embrace Jordan, her petite frame emphasised by his height. 'Better not light that till later, though. You might set off the fireworks.'

'There's enough gunpowder out back to get us all arrested.' Dad's usual brown cords and checked shirt suggested that he *wasn't* getting into the spirit of things. 'Come and see for yourself.' He led the way briskly through the kitchen into the blessedly cool dining room.

Jordan and I followed, exchanging relieved glances now the parental introduction was over. I *had* wanted to talk to Mum alone, but I still rarely got her to myself. Either Amy was hovering, or Dad would call her away. My hopes of a private chat rose as he suddenly turned back to the kitchen. I looked around for Amy, but for once there was no sign of her.

'Wow, this is awesome,' Jordan complimented as we stepped out of the dining room onto the terrace. 'You've done an incredible job, Mrs Aitken.'

'Olivia,' Mum corrected gently, looking pleased. 'And thank you. I did my best.'

I smiled at her typical modesty; I knew she would have spent days organising every detail. The compact but lush garden had been transformed by the Olympic theme, with Greek statues peeping out from neat borders and international flag bunting lining the fences. Parasol-covered tables and chairs around the lawn turned it into a dance floor, while music played from discreetly placed speakers, and orange flames burned in a fire pit on the terrace.

'Kind of puts your homemade torch in the shade,' I said, laughing at Jordan's stunned expression. 'How many people have you invited, Mum?' We were the first to arrive, but parties at Sea View were rarely small, and this one looked set to be more lavish than most.

'Oh, not many. Maria and her husband, Bill. You know, the Cartwrights. Dr Henry. Miss Shaw, of course.' She smiled. 'A few people from the village. The usual suspects.' She laughed, acknowledging her favourite catch-all phrase.

'Of course.' I laughed too, pleased to see her looking so happy and relaxed.

'What with one thing and another, there's quite a lot we've neglected to celebrate lately,' she said wistfully. 'Your degree. First teaching job. Moving into your flat.'

'Bedsit,' I corrected, laughing again. 'But thanks, Mum.' I gave her a hug, frowning in concern as I felt how thin she had become; I knew the reference to 'one thing and another' was her way of glossing over her illness. As usual. 'How are you, anyway?'

'Exceptionally well, darling. Although the heat's getting to me a little,' she admitted.

'I know. What a change from all the rain. It's been stifling this weekend.' I lifted my ponytail to cool my neck, then flapped my own toga, a last-minute effort after Amy had phoned to nag me that it was a costume party and 'not to bother showing up without one'.

'Ah, so you must be the mysterious boyfriend.'

Speak of the devil, I thought as Amy half walked, half danced towards us, deliberately drawing all eyes to her Union Jack mini dress. With her wide mouth slicked with red gloss, and her long hair silkily loose, she looked dressed for a nightclub rather than a family party.

'Mysterious? I'm not sure this outfit leaves much to the imagination,' Jordan joked.

Or hers, either, I thought, discreetly looking Amy up and down, while she assessed Jordan's appearance a little more slowly and obviously.

'You're certainly made of flesh and blood,' she said suggestively. 'I was beginning to think Holly must have made you up. Either that or you'd hightailed it back to Australia. That is where you're from, isn't it?'

Jordan shook the hand she held out to him. 'Sydney.'

'Oh, I'm Amy,' she quipped, not letting go of his hand.

'Yeah, I meant—'

'I know what you meant, silly.' She pouted. 'We're not all country bumpkins in Suffolk, you know. I went to art college in Paris.'

'For a six-week exchange,' I couldn't resist pointing out.

We'd both done our teacher training at a local college, Amy because it was the only course that would accept her low A-level grades, while I had turned down a university place in London so I could stay closer to Mum. Her health didn't seem to have got worse, but she certainly wasn't any better.

'Sydney, eh?' Dad reappeared with a bottle of champagne, popping the cork as he walked. 'Beautiful city. What brought you to Suffolk?'

'Lucky chance.' Jordan grinned. 'I've been travelling, the last couple of years. I originally came to London for the Olympics, but boats are my passion. I took a trip up the coast, stumbled across this village. And this gorgeous lady.' He hugged me against his side.

'Travelling, hey? Sounds exciting. So, where's next on the itinerary?'

'Dad!' I felt a rush of irritation that he was already discounting my new relationship.

'What? Young man like this. Twenty-five? Twenty-six? You've got your whole life ahead of you, Jordan. America. That's the place to visit. If you're looking for work, I can—'

'Dad, Jordan's moved in with me,' I cut in crossly. 'He's got a job at the country club. He's twenty-seven and a classically trained chef. We're going to be looking for a place of our own. Together,' I added firmly.

'Wow. My little girl's all grown up. You won't be needing your old dad anymore, eh?' He gave me a crooked smile, before adding quietly: 'I won't have anyone left soon.'

'Rubbish.' I smiled too, but my gaze was pulled across the lawn to where Mum was mingling happily with her guests. She loved talking to people, and she seemed as lively and animated as ever. But I wondered fearfully how much of it was an act, and I was glad she hadn't overheard my dad's uncharacteristically tactless comment.

'Just you look after her, young man,' he added, patting Jordan on the back as though to emphasise his greater age and experience, even though he didn't actually look that much older than him. Dad was in his mid-forties by then; he looked much younger.

'Oh, my drifter days are over, Mr Aitken.' Jordan took hold of my hand, pressing it against his chest. He addressed his comments to my dad, but his green eyes were fixed on mine. I could feel his heart thumping, and my own beat faster, too, as he said softly: 'I'm not going anywhere. Why would I? When you've seen as much of the world as I have, you know perfection when you find it.'

Chapter 18

'I just don't want you to get hurt, pickle.'

Dad handed me one of my mum's hand-knitted blankets as he sat down next to me on the bench – *Mum's* bench – under the pergola. The last of the fireworks fizzed against the night sky, drawing slightly muted *oohs* and *aahs* now. It was gone midnight. Most of the guests, bar a few stragglers, had left. The party was over, although someone had clearly forgotten to tell Amy. She was still dancing with Jordan in the middle of the lawn.

'I won't. Jordan's a good man,' I said, watching Amy drape herself all over him.

'I'm sure he is. But he's not a *family* man. I hope I'm wrong, but I don't think so. He said it himself. He's a drifter at heart. Can you really see him settling in our little village?'

'If he wants to be with me, yes. I'm going nowhere. At least, not until I'm sure Mum's properly well.' I decided to change the subject and ask the question I'd felt hanging over me all evening. 'She seems tired, Dad. Has the cancer come back?'

'Holly, it's a party. I don't think now's the time to—'

'Everyone's gone. And when *is* the time? Mum's got an inoperable brain tumour. We don't know how long she's got left. We have to come to terms with that.'

'I have, darling. And so has your mum. Six years ago.'

'Six . . . *what?*' I thought back to the day after I sat my final A-level exam, when my parents had first broken the news to me. They'd looked as devastated as I had felt, and I'd assumed they must have only just found out themselves. Now here was Dad saying they'd known two years before. 'When exactly did you find out?' I said hotly.

'We didn't want to worry you, love. It was benign at that stage. And, thankfully, so it remained for a long time. Dr Henry has managed things superbly. The medication prevented further growth. Your mum kept her beautiful hair.' Dad paused for a moment before clearing his throat and continuing quietly: 'Daily doses of morphine have—'

'*When*, Dad?' I cut in impatiently.

He sighed. 'The initial diagnosis was confirmed just before Amy came to live with us. At that stage, we were told there was nothing to worry about. So we didn't. Or tried not to.'

'Shit.' It took me a few moments to digest the revelation, my mind tracking back over the years, reinterpreting Mum's behaviour – our whole family life – in light of how such a dreadful diagnosis must have changed it, without my ever knowing.

'Double shit,' Dad agreed, giving me a wry smile.

There was no point having a go at him, insisting he should have told me sooner. I had long since got used to the feeling of secrecy at home, and I understood now why he'd always tried to stop me having time alone with Mum: in case she told me herself, I surmised.

'Does Amy know?' I said tightly, wondering if that sense of secrecy at Sea View had explained her tears in the night – if she, too, had been troubled by the undercurrents of tension over the years that I now realised must have arisen from Mum's secret illness.

'Actually, she guessed.'

'What?' I found that hard to believe. Amy was always so

wrapped up in her own feelings, she never noticed other people's. 'How? *When?*'

'When we discovered the tumour had progressed. Spread from Oliva's brain into her bones. Become malignant.' Dad swallowed hard. 'Just before you both took your GCSEs, I think it was. You were both about, oh, let me think, sixteen or—'

'Are you serious?' I reeled back in shock. I could accept that my parents hadn't wanted to upset me, but the fact that Amy had known Mum was seriously ill and never told me . . . That felt like a betrayal. Or yet another deliberate, spiteful game . . .

I remembered her strange, wild confession that she'd pushed my friend Jane off the swing. That had been around the same time. Maybe Amy had been toying with me, hinting at tragedy while withholding the truth: that my mum was the one staring death in the face.

I just prayed my parents hadn't been party to it – that there hadn't been a conspiracy between them all to protect me. Because I was 'oversensitive', as Amy had also taunted me that day. I knew they worried about my health, but I hated being wrapped up in cotton wool.

'Yes. Turns out Amy is extremely . . . intuitive,' Dad said, oblivious to my turmoil.

'I can think of other words,' I snapped. I didn't mean to be cross; it just hurt so badly that he considered Amy more attuned to my mum's health than I was.

I hoped Mum didn't feel the same. Whenever I asked how she was, she responded with a breezy 'fine, love'. Until a few weeks ago, she had even convinced me. Now there was no hiding the blinding headaches, the memory loss I'd assumed was her being endearingly scatter-minded, until the day she forgot my name. Not Amy's though. She never forgot hers.

'Don't bad-mouth poor Amy, love,' Dad said, resting a hand on my arm. 'Please.'

'I'm not. I don't have to. Her behaviour speaks for itself.' I gritted my teeth as I watched her gyrate to the music, pouting at Jordan, one hand pressed against his chest.

'Amy loves life,' Dad said, following my gaze. 'And why shouldn't she? She's had a tough time. She deserves to enjoy herself. Maybe you should take a leaf out of her book. I know your heart condition is a worry, love, but it doesn't have to stop you living—'

'It doesn't,' I protested heatedly. 'I don't let it stop me doing *anything*,' I added fiercely. 'And I wish everyone else would just stop bloody going on about it!'

'If I'd had my way, you'd have had an operation as a baby. But your mum—'

'No, don't blame her, Dad. Please. She only wanted to protect me.' I felt my temper about to boil over and fought to hold on to it. This was Mum's party; she'd gone to tremendous effort. I didn't want to spoil it for her with an argument.

'I know she did,' Dad pacified. 'Please don't get the hump, darling. I just want you to live life to the full. Like Amy does. We never know how much time we're granted, do we?'

'Sure.' I took long, slow breaths to calm myself down.

'And your mum was probably right. Surgery *would* have been a risk. As parents, we have to make tough choices. Your mum knows that better than anyone. Whatever it takes to help the ones you love, whatever we have to do, we do it. No matter what. Olivia understands that.' He reached for my hand, lacing his fingers deliberately through mine. 'And so do I.'

Chapter 19

'Dad seemed in an odd mood tonight. He didn't even get dressed up for the party,' I said to Mum when the house was finally quiet. The last of the guests had gone, Jordan was helping my dad clear up, and Amy was supervising. For once, I had Mum all to myself. She slept in her own room by that time. Pain kept her awake at night, and she didn't want to disturb Dad. Plus, her new bedroom overlooked the garden, which she said helped to soothe her.

I could believe it. As I stood by the open sash window, I felt the stresses of the evening drift away on warm summer air laden with the heady, almost soporific fragrance of flowers. I smiled at Mum. She looked tired but happy as she sat at her dressing table, slowly removing her make-up. She was in her mid-forties by then; she looked much older.

'You know your dad.' She gave me a vague smile in return. 'He's never been one for parties. It was lovely, though. Your *chap* seems lovely, too.' Mum stopped dabbing her face with cotton pads and turned to face me with solemn eyes. 'Are you happy, darling?'

'Very,' I said firmly, wanting to reassure her. 'Although Dad seems to think it won't last. He reckons Jordan isn't a family kind of guy. That he'll be off travelling again.'

'Your father's just worried about you, sweetheart.' Mum reached for a pot of moisturiser and started smoothing it over her pale, gaunt face; it broke my heart to see the sharp prominence of her cheekbones. 'He wants to be sure you'll be OK, when I'm . . .'

'Mum!' Panic fluttered in my chest. 'Dr Henry said you're doing really well.' I'd made a point of speaking to him, after my dad's tactless comment. The dour, middle-aged doctor had been reassuring; I wondered now if he'd been lying as well, to spare my feelings, as everyone seemed determined to do. I dry-swallowed. 'Is there something you're not—'

'I'm fine, love. Honestly.' As though to prove it, she started humming as she unhooked her dangly gold earrings and tossed them carelessly into a little china dish.

'Then what's Dad so worried about?'

'Jordan's a few years older than you, that's all.' Mum seemed to hesitate, then turned to look at me. 'To be honest, I think your dad also sees quite a bit of himself in him.'

'You mean because Dad was an outsider too, not from the village?' I teased gently.

'That as well.' She smiled obligingly. 'But I was thinking more about the travelling. Jordan's done an awful lot, hasn't he? So did your father, when he was younger.'

'He did? I didn't know that.' I'd always believed the reason my dad moaned constantly about the dreariness of the North Sea, the claustrophobic monotony of our quiet village, was that he longed to see other places but had never properly had the chance.

'Yes. He and Luke worked their way around America during their gap year. If college gossip is to be believed, they broke a lot of hearts along the way.' Mum's dark eyes lingered on mine for a moment. 'I expect he's worrying Jordan might do the same to you.'

'Luke as in *Jackson*? Dad went travelling with Amy's *dad*?' I wondered how many more surprises the day had in store for me. First discovering I'd been the last to know about Mum's illness; now the revelation that there was a whole chunk of history between my dad and Amy's that I knew nothing about.

Mum nodded. 'The two of them were quite a pair. Clever. Charming. Not to mention handsome. Half the college was in love with one or other of them.' Reaching up to remove her gold-leaf headdress, she released the pins from her hair and let it cascade down her back.

Like a river of silk, I thought, recalling my dad's familiar compliment, turning over the idea of him having had other relationships before he met my mum – having 'broken a lot of hearts'. With Luke. Amy's dad, whom I had never met.

It wasn't unreasonable, I tried to tell myself. I knew my parents had met at university, and I'd certainly had boyfriends at college before meeting Jordan. Nothing serious, though. No hearts had been broken, including mine. I suddenly wondered if my mum's had been.

'Did that bother you?' I asked carefully. 'I know you and Dad weren't married then. But were you a couple?' *Was he unfaithful to you?*

'Oh, I had plenty of boyfriends of my own,' Mum insisted. 'I could have had my pick.' She unpinned her butterfly brooch, then closed her slim fingers around it, squeezing it so tightly I worried it would pierce her skin. 'I chose your father, though.'

'And he chose you, right?' I said, picking up on a slight undertone. 'He went to America, sowed his last wild oats, or whatever, then came home and married you. Yes?'

'Of course. And Luke married Isabella,' she added huskily.

I leaned against the wall, trying to figure out what was bothering me. 'Did you know her? Amy's mum? I mean, I know Dad was room-mates with her dad, but—'

'Isabella was my best friend,' Mum said simply, and I could see tears in her eyes now. 'And my maid of honour.'

'She . . . really?' I stared at her in astonishment.

'Not that she thanked me for it. She was pregnant with Amy at the time, you see. She didn't want it to show in the wedding photos, I suppose.'

'I had no idea. About *any* of this.' I moved to sit next to Mum, gently removing the butterfly brooch from her clenched fist. Turning it over in my hands, I remembered the first and only other time I'd seen her wearing it, at the 'musical soiree' after Amy came to live with us. 'Did Amy know you were so close to her mum?' I asked curiously.

'Isabella made her own dress, of course.' Mum stared into the distance, and I couldn't tell whether she hadn't heard my question, or was ignoring it. 'I thought she might have offered to make mine, too. But alas no. She did buy my wedding veil, though. I've saved it for you, Holly. And for what it's worth, I hope Jordan is the one who gets to see you in it.'

'Thanks, Mum.' I gave her a long hug, pressing pause on my questions, even though my mind was bursting with them.

It was a shock to discover that Amy's parents and mine had been far closer than I knew. No wonder they'd felt confident letting their daughter stay with us. But that still didn't explain why they left her in the first place. Or why they'd never come back.

'He's right. You *are* perfect.' Mum almost seemed to cling to me.

'Oh, Amy's the perfect one,' I said, hating how self-pitying I sounded.

'No, *you* are, my darling.' Finally pulling away from me, Mum brushed away a tear. 'And you'll look even more so in that veil.' She smiled, then nodded towards the wardrobe in the corner. 'Hand me that, would you? There, on top.'

'This?' It felt like there was a rock in my stomach as I stood up and crossed the room, reaching up towards a familiar-looking white box.

'Yes. That's the one.'

It was heavier than it looked, and, taking off the lid, I half expected to find sparkly red shoes nestled inside. Instead, there was a soft cloud of almond-white silk. I stared down at it, my head spinning. 'Where did you get this?'

'I told you, Isabella bought it for me. In Paris, or somewhere, I don't—'

'No, I mean the box.'

'Ah. I don't remember, sweetheart. It's been up there gathering dust for years.'

'It was under my bed, Mum.'

'Was it? Oh, well, I must have found it when I cleared out your room. You know, when you moved into your flat. Bedsit, I mean,' she corrected herself with a teasing smile.

'That was six months ago.'

'Sorry, love. I do tend to get confused. It's the pills, you see.'

I sat down heavily on the bed and gave her a direct look, holding up the box. 'Mum, did you take Amy's shoes when we were kids? Did you put them in the log shed?'

'She was such a *devious* child.' Mum turned back to the mirror, picked up her brush and jerked it through her hair with vigorous strokes. 'Acting like butter wouldn't melt. But I saw. I saw *everything*. And I didn't like how she picked on you.'

'But you let me take the blame! All those years.'

'I never blamed *you* for anything, darling.'

'Dad did. Amy might have sucked up to him, but he let her get away with murder.' Out of nowhere, Jane Price's face flashed across my mind, and I felt my eyes fill up.

'Oh, please don't upset yourself, love. I can't . . . I can't bear it.'

Abruptly, Mum put down the brush and came to sit next to me on the bed. Her silky white toga clung to delicate bones; her hand was almost translucent, and icy cold as she took hold of mine. Close up, I realised that her beautiful long hair was a wig.

'Sorry, Mum. I'm so sorry. I didn't mean to upset you.' I hated seeing how illness had ravaged her body; I wished she hadn't hidden it from me. 'I just feel like there's something I'm *missing*. About you, Dad. My friend Jane. She vanished into thin air, didn't she? She was there one day, and gone the next. Then there's Amy. Always dropping these cryptic little hints. I

113

feel like there's so much stuff no one has told me about. What *else* don't I know?'

'It's been a long evening, darling. You're tired. Call me tomorrow, OK?' Mum planted a gentle kiss on my forehead. 'I'll explain everything then. I promise.'

But I was still upset the next morning. I didn't phone my mum, and I almost didn't pick up when I saw the number for Sea View flash up on my phone.

Then I thought of the frailness Mum had tried to hide beneath the layers of her Greek goddess costume. I thought about her wig, her relentless cheerfulness. I pictured her secretly, impulsively throwing Amy's shoes into the log shed, because this *devious child*, this stranger in our home, had picked on me.

Mum couldn't confess what she'd done, I realised, or else she would have had to explain the tumour that had most likely affected her personality and altered her behaviour, compelling her to do something so irrational, so completely out of character. And my mum hated to see me upset. All she ever wanted was for me to be safe, healthy, *happy* . . .

I thought of all this the morning after that dreadful party, and I was already babbling a tearful apology as I swallowed my hurt and finally answered the call. But it wasn't her. It was Amy. Phoning to tell me that Mum had died in the night.

Chapter 20

'Here. I brought you a coffee. It's freezing out here.' Jordan looked impossibly gorgeous even when he was hungover and half-asleep. Bundled up in a navy parka over last night's jeans and T-shirt, he joined me on the beach wall just before seven.

'Jordan, you can't leave the kids.' Ignoring the steaming mug he held out, I was about to stand up and stalk back to our cottage when he put out his free hand to stop me.

'They're fast asleep. And I've got the monitor.' He pulled the compact device out of his pocket. 'Just a few minutes, OK? There's, uh, something I've been wanting to tell you.'

'Oh. Sounds ominous.' I immediately thought about Amy's text and the revelation about her intended resignation. 'Seems to be a big news week round here,' I joked nervously.

Jordan didn't laugh but pushed the mug towards me again. This time, I took it, grateful for the warmth. Although I was wearing Ugg boots and a long, grey cardigan – hand-knitted by my mum – over my pyjamas, the wind scything off the North Sea was bitter.

I'd only stepped outside to clear my head after the rain had

115

stopped. I wasn't sure how long I'd been sitting on the wall between the coastal path and beach, but my fingers ached as the heat of the coffee worked its way into my bones.

'Jesus, my head's banging.' Jordan ran his hands through his hair as he sat down beside me. 'It was worth it, though, hey? Good to relax, for once. Catch up with Amy. Although, actually, I'd been hoping for more of a serious chat. I wanted her to tell you—'

'What time did she finally leave?' I cut in, my own head starting to pound with a sudden, horrible premonition of exactly what he wanted Amy to tell me.

'God knows. An hour or so after you called it a night. One? Maybe two.'

'She managed to get a taxi all right?' I glanced back to see Jordan's beloved motorbike parked in the alley behind our cottage; our ancient VW Beetle was in the garage for repairs, and for an awful moment I wondered if he'd given Amy a lift home on his bike.

'Yeah. And she sent a text to say she'd got home safely.' He groaned. 'Although, to be honest, I only saw it a minute ago. I must have crashed out on the sofa after she left.'

'Hmm, you were dead to the world – you missed all the drama. Phil next door had a tripped fuse. Allegedly.' I frowned, still not entirely convinced. 'I had to pop round to help him. Which reminds me, you forgot to lock the back gate, Jordan.'

'What? No. I can't have. I always double-check it. Are you sure?'

'I guess I could have forgotten,' I pacified, not wanting to provoke yet another argument. I didn't want to prove Jordan right about 'worry becoming a habit', either, so I decided not to mention that I'd spooked myself imagining an intruder. Or that I was still wondering how your koala had ended up at Phil's house . . .

My best guess was that you'd dropped it in the alley one day, and Phil had picked it up. I hoped so. I didn't like the thought of you going inside his house alone. But I was equally puzzled why you'd have thrown away the special toy your daddy had given you.

'So Phil was making a song and dance about a tripped fuse, was he?' Jordan pulled a face. 'Sounds about right. He's always struck me as one slice short of a loaf. I didn't hear a thing, though. Huh, too much cava. I'll say one thing for your sister, she can hold her drink.'

I almost choked, swallowing my coffee the wrong way. 'She's not my sister.'

'Sorry. My mistake,' Jordan appeased quickly. 'It's just that's what she called you last night. It stuck in my head, I suppose.'

'Amy likes to pretend. She dreams up the life she wants, then acts like it's real.'

'That's a bit harsh. She idolises you, you know?'

'What? Rubbish.' Despite everything, I was very fond of Amy, but I had no illusions about how self-centred she was, and it hurt to hear Jordan sticking up for her.

'She does, Holl. She didn't stop talking about you after you went to bed. And there's nothing wrong with dreams. She's serious about changing career. It's tough. I sympathise.'

'Why, because telling bedtime stories and changing nappies was never *your* dream?'

'That was a joke, and you know it. Since when did you lose your sense of humour?'

'Oh, I don't know, Jordan. Maybe about the same time you started sleeping on the sofa.' *And your boat*, I thought, remembering your odd wish as I'd kissed you goodnight.

'Right. Sure. I guess I deserved that.' He lapsed into silence, staring out towards the sea that was slowly turning from grey to orange as the sun inched its way above the horizon.

Over the years, we'd sat in exactly that spot so many times, but rarely alone. I got pregnant so fast after our wedding, we never even had a honeymoon, only weeks of mourning followed by months of crippling regret that my mum would never get to hold my baby.

Grief had consumed me, and while motherhood rescued

me – to an extent – maybe it hadn't left enough room for our marriage to grow. I never stopped loving Jordan, but we'd gone from infatuation to marriage to parenthood in such a short space of time. Maybe that was what he'd meant about nappy-changing not being his dream . . .

'BB is sleeping so much better,' I said, resting a tentative hand on his arm. 'I know it was tough at first. I get that's why you wanted to sleep downstairs. But it's not so bad now. I don't expect you to settle him when he wakes, you know? Not when you're working shifts.'

'I know. Thanks. But it's not that.' He turned to look at me, and I was surprised to see his eyes glinting with tears. 'I don't mind if the little chap gets me up all night long. After what happened when he was born . . . Jesus, it's a miracle he's even here.'

'Yes. It is.' He was right. It hadn't just been my life under threat; BB's breathing had been touch and go at first. 'But he's doing brilliantly. Marley not so much, but . . .'

'We need to think about *us*, for once, Holly,' Jordan said, taking hold of my arm. 'If we don't get that right, we're lost. We need to fix us first.'

'Fix us?' Our marriage was under strain; I hadn't realised he thought it was broken. I pictured Amy's face again, her glittering eyes and knowing smile, and my heart started to thump. 'Is that what you came out here to tell me?'

'Not entirely. Look, I . . .' Jordan hesitated, then took my mug, setting it down on the wall before grabbing my hand and drawing me across the slippery pebbles towards the sea.

'This is another thing we haven't done for a while,' I said, relishing the wide expanse of sea and sky. 'I miss it. I miss *you*,' I added, but I wasn't sure if he heard me.

The wind had picked up again, booming as it stirred the grey sea into white peaks, blowing my hair in all directions. Jordan reached out with both hands to catch and tame it, twisting it into a ponytail and pulling me gently towards him, holding me against his body.

118

'There are lots of things we don't do anymore,' he said huskily.

'I know. I was thinking the same. Maybe we could—'

'You should come out on the boat, Holl. I didn't buy it just for me, you know? God knows I'll be paying off the loan for the rest of my life.'

'Mm, whose fault is *that*?' I said wryly. Jordan had continued to insist that he hadn't taken out that loan with my inheritance in mind, but the possibility still rankled between us.

'Mine. All mine, I know.' Letting his hands drop, he bent to scoop up a handful of stones, then lobbed them into the sea. 'Even so, we should make more use of it. As a *family*.'

'You're right,' I acknowledged sadly, regretting my sharpness, wishing he would hold me again. 'It's just . . .' Excuses whirled around my head, and I turned to gaze along the beach, tracing the misty bay towards Aldeburgh, where Jordan moored his new yacht.

It was also where Amy lived, her apartment building so close to the marina that she could see it from her balcony. She always seemed to be hovering at my shoulder: waiting in the wings, on the periphery of my family. Seeing her last night had been confusing, I realised, stirring up unsettling fears about the past as well as worries about the present.

'Well?' Jordan pressed, watching me. 'Why *do* you never want to go on the boat?'

'Why are you so keen to get me out on it?' I parried. 'Planning to shove me overboard, are you?' I only half-joked. 'I guess that would solve everyone's problems.'

'Don't be daft, and stop avoiding my question. You do realise you change the subject every time I ask it? Don't you trust me with the kids, or something?'

'I . . . well, I . . .' His green eyes bored into me. 'I guess I'm waiting until they're a bit older, that's all. To be honest, I'm a bit nervous about them being on the water.'

'Seriously?' Jordan frowned. 'You've never said. Anyway,

Marley's been out on the Meare dozens of times. She could row herself around it blindfolded.'

'That's the lake. The sea's . . . different.' I bit my lip, feeling uncomfortable now.

I wasn't sure why I'd never told him about my fear of drowning – the nightmares that still haunted me. Lately, I'd been dreaming a lot about that night at the regatta, watching Jane flail about in the dark, swirling water of the Meare, her terrified face bobbing on the surface. I hadn't been able to reach her . . . then, three years later, I'd lost her for ever.

But my fear of the water went deeper even than painful associations with my mysteriously missing friend. The last time I'd ventured onto the North Sea had been to scatter my mum's ashes, and the bereavement counsellor I'd seen after Mum died suggested that might have planted an unconscious association in my mind between the sea and death . . .

'I wouldn't take any risks,' Jordan insisted.

'Sorry?' I looked at him blankly.

'If you come out on the boat, Holly. You could hold Benji – BB – the whole time. He'd love it. Marley certainly did. I took her out on *Liberty* a while back. She had a *whale* of a time.'

Chapter 21

'You did *what*?' Adrenaline coursed through me. '*When*?'

Jordan shrugged. 'A few weeks ago. Can't remember exactly. Maybe—'

'You mean, you snuck off with Marley . . . alone?'

'Snuck off?' He reeled back. 'Hardly. I think you had a health visitor appointment. No, hospital check-up. Whatever. Anyway, why is that a problem? I've been sailing my whole life. You won't find a safer pair of hands. And Marley's my daughter. I can take her out wherever and whenever I like. Can't I?' A hint of belligerence hardened his voice now.

'Of course. You should have told me, that's all.' I looked away, not wanting him to read the doubt in my eyes, as I recalled his secret early-morning trip to the beach with you and pictured your bruised knees. 'You shouldn't *keep* things from me, Jordan.'

'Ditto.'

'What? I tell you *everything*.'

'Do you? So how come I had to hear from your dad that you've skipped your last few Sunday visits with the kids? Where've you been going, Holly?'

'Nowhere special,' I snapped, cross that he was making me account for my movements, when he never explained his own.

'Which tells me precisely nothing.'

'Marley hasn't seemed keen to see Dad, that's all,' I said impatiently. 'I didn't want to force her. I didn't want to bother you with it, either. You were at work, and—'

'Exactly. I was at *work*. Trying to earn enough to pay for a wife and two kids.'

'Who you don't seem exactly eager to be around,' I pointed out. 'Unlike Amy,' I couldn't resist adding. 'Everyone always wants to hang out with her.'

'Amy?' Jordan let out a heavy sigh. 'Look, none of this is her fault, Holly.'

I felt a pang of jealousy that, once again, he was defending her, even if he was right: I *was* using her as target practice, both for insecurities about my marriage and my relationship with my dad. It was true that you'd seemed reluctant to visit him lately, but, in all honesty, I hadn't pressured you. I wasn't sure why. Maybe because it felt weird seeing Dad in a modern flat rather than at Sea View; or maybe I was worried that Amy would be there.

'Anyway, for the record, Mum and Dad had guardianship of Amy, but they never made it official. She's not even my *adopted* sister. Strictly speaking, she's not family at all.'

'Family is as family does, hey?' Jordan stooped to pick up more stones, skimming them one by one across the water. 'My old man said that the day my best mate took a punch for me in a bar brawl.'

'What?' I stared at him in shock. 'Was it serious? How old were you?'

'Twenty-three. And, yeah, it was. For my mate, anyway. I got out pretty much unscathed. Matt wasn't so lucky. He was in a coma for weeks.'

'Oh, my God.' A shiver ran through me, and I dug my hands into my pockets.

'Yeah. It was just one of those freak incidents. Wrong place,

122

wrong time. But it broke me, seeing him like that. That's why I left Australia. Or ran away, should I say. And didn't stop running till I met you.' Jordan's eyes blazed as he stared down at me. 'I've hated hospitals ever since. I freak out every time you have to go there. All those tests. Wires all over your body. BB's birth was a nightmare. That C-section scared the shit out of me.'

I groaned, frustrated that he'd kept such a life-changing secret from me, just as my parents had. 'You've never said. Why have you never *told* me any of this?'

'Because I've learned to deal with it. And if I'd mentioned it back then, it would have given *your* dad an excuse to stop us getting married. Adam's never liked me.'

'He couldn't have stopped me marrying you if he'd tried,' I said fiercely.

'Likewise.' Jordan took a step towards me, reaching out to sweep my hair off my face again. He leaned in closer, but I'd already turned away, stalking off back up the beach.

The moment passed; I immediately wished it back. Only it was too late. By the time Jordan caught up with me, I was almost back at the cottage, worrying about you and BB being left alone for so long.

'Keeping secrets, bottling things up. It never helps,' I whispered, as we let ourselves into the kitchen. 'Which is why we need *that*,' I added, my eyes drawn to the worry box.

Jordan huffed loudly. 'Really? *Do* we?'

'Yes, and keep your voice down. You'll wake the kids. Marley needs help, and—'

'Or maybe you do,' Jordan said quietly.

'What?' Shock fizzed through me, and I turned to stare at him. His arms were folded, his expression guarded. I tried to say more, but my throat dried, my heart pounding with a dizzying feeling that we were two strangers standing in our own kitchen.

Jordan took a step towards me, but I backed away. 'Look, please don't take this the wrong way,' he said, holding up his hands. 'It's just . . . you're all over the place, babe. It's making you ill, all this worrying about every little thing, imagining—'

'*Imagining?*' I was so angry, I forgot to whisper. I'd spent my entire childhood being told I was worrying about nothing; I couldn't believe the same thing was happening with Jordan. 'You're saying I'm just *imagining* Marley being so withdrawn. That her notes—'

'Hardly notes,' Jordan muttered. 'More like random scribbles.'

'*What?*' I couldn't believe what I was hearing.

'OK, if you really want the truth, I still think you're reading too much into them. This whole worry box thing is just a game to Marley. I told you, she's *fine.*'

I tutted, furious at his dismissal of your notes, and even more suspicious as to why he was so keen to repeatedly invalidate them. 'What makes you so sure, Jordan?'

'I'm her dad, aren't I? I just know.'

'Well, I'm her mum, and I don't. And I'm not prepared to take that risk.'

'What risk?' he scoffed, his fleeting softness on the beach well and truly gone now.

I fiddled with the silver heart around my neck, thinking about an eleven-year-old girl who disappeared without trace two decades ago. 'All I know is that I don't want to wake up one day, years from now, and find out that something truly awful happened to my daughter when she was little, and I never knew.'

'*Our* daughter,' Jordan corrected. 'And something awful like what, exactly?'

'Like . . .' My mind was a blur of images. Of Dad, Amy, Jane . . . the last time I saw my mum. 'Stuff that happens in childhood. It goes deep into the corners of our mind. Sometimes we don't even realise it's there, but it is. It shapes who we are, what we become.'

'Not always in a bad way, but whatever.' Jordan shook his head, sighing as he checked his watch. 'Marley will be down soon, so tell me, has she posted anything else?'

'This morning, actually.' I crossed the kitchen and picked up the teapot. 'Or maybe last night. Sometime after I took her up to bed, anyway.' I hesitated before handing him your latest note, still cross and hurt that he thought *I* was the one who needed rescuing, not you . . . still wary that he might be the one you needed saving from.

Jordan screwed up his face as he scanned the note. 'So, she doesn't like parties? Her birthday one was pretty full on. Perhaps Marley found it all a bit overwhelming.'

'Or maybe she overheard us planning *Amy's* party.'

'Why the heck would *that* bother her?'

'I don't know, but last night . . . Marley looked at Amy like she'd seen a ghost.'

'She was half-asleep.'

'She was terrified. When I carried her upstairs, she was shaking like a leaf.'

'Well, if Marley doesn't want to go to Amy's party, she doesn't have to. I'll just stay home with her.'

My fingers tensed around the teapot. 'You don't have to do that. I can stay with her.'

'No way. It's your thirtieth, too,' Jordan pointed out reasonably. He was calm; *too* calm. 'You have to be there. Marley and I can have a daddy–daughter night. It'll be fun.'

'A daddy–daughter . . .' The phrase reminded me once again of my own dad, and I felt the back of my neck prickle. 'Well, let's see, shall we?' I prevaricated. 'Maybe there won't even be a party. I'm not that fussed, and Amy changes her mind every other minute.'

'Fine,' Jordan said tightly, heading for the kitchen door. 'I thought it would be a nice thing, but whatever.'

'Jordan—'

'It's fine. I'll take a shower then head over to Amy's. She mentioned that her bath's leaking. I offered to fix it for her. I've got the morning off and nothing better to do.'

'Fine,' I echoed frostily, swallowing hurt that he'd choose to spend his spare time with Amy, not me. I detected a hint of retaliation, too, but steeled myself not to rise to it.

'Think about what I said, though, hey?' Jordan said seriously, pausing in the doorway. 'Maybe book a check-up with the doctor. Or, uh, your old counsellor.'

I forced myself to set the teapot carefully on the kitchen table, before I was tempted to hurl it at him. 'I'm not suffering from delusions, Jordan, if that's what you're implying.'

He shrugged. 'Maybe. Or maybe a touch of overactive imagination.'

'Over . . .' I felt my head spin and grabbed at a chair. If Jordan was now questioning my state of mind, would his next move be to cast doubt on whether I remained a fit mother? I gritted my teeth, livid that I was being made to doubt myself, just as I had been as a child whenever I'd asked my dad what was really going on at Sea View – with Mum, Amy . . . 'Are you suggesting I'm *irrational*?' I felt sick as I remembered Dad saying the same thing.

'I'm *suggesting* you're going to worry yourself into an early grave.' Jordan held my gaze for a second, then turned away. 'Anyway, I'd best get on. That bath won't fix itself.'

'Sure. *No worries*,' I said deliberately, even though my head was actually spinning with worry: about you, Jordan, and the thought of him in Amy's flat. I wondered if she'd given him a key. Or if he already had one . . .

Chapter 22

'How was school, sweetheart?' It was an effort to keep my tone jolly. I'd had a terrible day.

I couldn't stop going over and over my row with Jordan. That, along with paranoia about him and Amy, had distracted me from asking what he'd come out to the beach to tell me in the first place, and it was preying on my mind. Then I noticed Phil staring up at your bedroom window as he left his house, and my anxiety about him returned in full force . . .

To busy my mind with other things, and remembering my promise to you, I'd put off tackling the accounts and talking to Maria about floristry orders, and had tidied the cottage instead. But BB had been unusually fractious, crying for hours; a few times, I'd simply sat on the sofa cuddling him, and joined in.

'School was OK.' You scuffed your black leather shoes, staring down at them.

'Just OK?' I bent down to give you a hug. 'Oh, my God. Marley, what's happened? Who *did* that do you?' I traced my fingertips over a vivid scratch along your cheekbone.

You shrugged, hugging your book bag.

'Did you get into a fight?' I found a clean tissue and gently dabbed your face. I was sure I could see nail marks where the skin was broken. 'This looks nasty, darling.'

'We were just playing, Mummy.' You pulled away. 'It was just a . . . a game.'

'A game? What sort of game?' *I don't like games*, I remembered you saying. 'Who were you playing with? Was it *Leah*?' I straightened up, looking around for Mrs Hart.

I'd planned to have a follow-up chat with your teacher in any case, after my conversation with her before school on Monday. She'd been at pains to reassure me then that you'd seemed happy in class, if a little quiet, which had actually made me worry more. Why would you be relaxed at school, but tense at home – and who was it you were scared of?

Despite being furious with Jordan, I couldn't bear to think that it was him, and I was sickened by the idea that it could be Phil. When I'd asked you about him, your blank looks had left me none the wiser. Looking at the gouge on your cheek, I was convinced Mrs Hart must have missed a squabble between you and Leah. I was determined to press her on it.

'Can we go, Mummy?' You tugged on my arm, your face flushing so deeply now, the scratch almost disappeared, blending in with the heated skin around it.

'In a sec, love. I want a quick chat with Mrs Hart.' I glanced around again.

'No, Mummy. *Now*.' Your eyes widened, bottom lip quivering.

I was worried and upset, but I hated seeing you distressed. 'OK, all right,' I acquiesced, deciding to call your teacher later. 'Let's get you home.'

'Is Daddy there?'

Your quietly spoken question brought a smile, reassuring me that, whoever was scaring you, at least it wasn't Jordan. 'Not yet, sweetheart.'

'Where is he?'

'At work. *I think*,' I added under my breath, recalling bitterly that he'd spent his morning off at Amy's, fixing her bath. *Supposedly*. I hadn't heard from either of them all day.

'Will he be home before bed?'

'Sorry?' I frowned, puzzled now by your persistence. 'I don't know, love. Daddy . . .' A loud beep distracted me, and I reached into my coat pocket, checking to see if it had come from my phone – hoping Jordan might have sent a text, even an apology for earlier.

'Is that him?' you demanded, chewing the toggle on the hood of your duffel coat.

'No. Silly me. It wasn't even my phone.' I swallowed disappointment as I watched another mum take out her phone, laughing at a text as she shepherded a group of giggling children towards the ice-cream van parked, as ever, outside the school gate.

I stared at the boisterous group, wondering if one of them was called Benjamin, remembering your dislike of the name. Perhaps it wasn't just *Leah* picking on you. Yet you'd seemed so keen, almost desperate to go to school, and your withdrawal had lasted all through the half-term break. My thoughts spiralled: was the root of your fear at school, or at home?

'Mum, you said we can go.' You yanked impatiently on my arm.

'So I did. Come on, then. Uh, fancy an ice cream first?' If there *was* a Benjamin in that giggling group, I was determined to find him and put a stop to any spiteful games.

'*No*, Mummy. I want to *go*. I want to . . . to go to . . . to the park,' you stuttered. 'I want to go on the swings.'

'Really?' I said dubiously. 'It'll be getting dark soon.'

'Please?' you begged, pulling me away from your chattering classmates.

'OK, sure.' Perhaps now wasn't the best time, after all. I could hardly confront a seven-year-old boy in the street. If there was a problem at school, I would talk to your teacher properly about it, later. 'Only for a little . . .' But you'd already sprinted off.

I followed as fast as I could, bumping BB's buggy out of the playground and along the pavement, still wondering who had scratched you. The goose bumps breaking out all over me had nothing to do with the chill breeze, and everything to do with the thought of someone intimidating you into pretending that whatever they'd done to you, it was 'just a game'.

The park playground was empty when we arrived a few minutes later, and for once I was glad. Checking BB was still soundly asleep, I tucked his buggy next to our usual bench and reached for my phone, deciding I couldn't wait to call Mrs Hart, after all. *Someone had hurt you.* I wanted to know who, why, and exactly what the school was going to do about it.

'Oh, Marley. Slow down!' I called out, watching you urge the swing higher.

'I'm flying, Mummy!'

'You certainly are.' It was the happiest I'd seen you in weeks, I realised sadly. *I wish I could fly away*, I recalled you writing in your note, and my heart squeezed.

'I can almost touch the moon!' You reached out a starfish hand, fingers stretching.

'Watch out for flying saucers!' I bit my lip as memories of Jane stirred once more. I couldn't seem to get my old friend out of my head; I found myself constantly thinking of her; *dreaming* about her. The mystery of her physical disappearance, and your emotional one, had become unconsciously, disturbingly, entwined in my head, I realised.

'Catch me, Mummy!'

'Careful, darling!' I tucked my phone into my pocket and ran to stand in front of you, just as you propelled yourself into the air. 'Got you!' I crushed you against my chest, the pair of us almost tumbling over onto the soft grass. 'Now *that's* what I call a crash landing.'

'Are you OK, Mummy?' Your eyes were huge in your bright-pink face.

'Absolutely.' I gave you a hug, remembering my earlier conviction that you'd been worrying about my health. 'Come on, let's go get BB and head home.'

'Do we *have* to? I like it when it's just us,' you said quietly, dragging your feet.

'You do? Why's that, then? I mean, I love hanging out with you as well,' I continued when you didn't reply. 'I especially enjoy our new post box. You like that too, don't you?'

You nodded, but I could feel you closing off once more, your thoughts folding inwards, leaving only a shadow of them on your face, like clouds passing over the sun.

'I love your notes,' I encouraged. 'Thank you for leaving them for me. Grown-ups send each other such boring texts.' Feeling my phone buzz in my pocket, I pulled it out, a rush of adrenaline coursing through me as I saw a new message.

It was from Amy, thanking me for dinner last night. She didn't mention Jordan fixing her bath, and I wondered why; I wondered if she'd been there, and, if so, what the two of them had talked about. Me? My 'overactive imagination'? *Amy's party?*

The thought reminded me of your last note. 'You know, you don't *have* to go to Aunty Amy's party. Not if you don't want to.'

'She'll be cross,' you said, climbing onto the gate as we reached the park exit.

'Whatever makes you think that?' I frowned, remembering Amy's terse comment last night about spilled milkshake at your birthday party. '*Has* she ever told you off? At school, or . . . anywhere else?' I stopped myself asking if Amy had come out on the boat with you and Jordan. Whatever questions I had for my husband, I refused to make you a go-between.

You shrugged, then leaped off the gate. 'Can we go home now?'

'Well . . .' I looked along the street, feeling prickles of apprehension as I pictured our cottage, its wonky walls once echoing with laughter and joy, now shrouded in tense silence and dark suspicions. 'How about a trip to the tea room?' Suddenly, I too felt reluctant to return home.

You shrugged your shoulders again, which I took as agreement. 'Mind BB,' I cautioned, as you climbed onto the buggy board, and I couldn't have been more astonished when you bent forward to kiss him.

'Don't worry, Mummy. I'll protect BB. I won't let him get hurt. I promise.'

Chapter 23

Later that evening, once we'd had dinner and both got changed into our pyjamas, I curled up on our saggy blue velvet sofa, watching you play with BB, and pondered that promise. You'd barely shown any interest in your baby brother since he was born, yet there you were, hovering over his carry-cot, holding up different toys to make him smile.

Maybe the last few weeks had been a period of adjustment, I reflected, and now, finally, you were getting used to being a big sister and we'd see a return of your previous playfulness. I hoped so. 'Ah, he's chewing your finger,' I said, feeling my heart melt.

'Is he hungry?'

'Probably.' I laughed. 'But I won't feed him until bedtime. Another half-hour, OK?'

'Can I have my doughnut now?'

'Of course, sweetheart.' You'd seemed eager to choose a treat at the tea room, then all of a sudden had demanded to go home. No one else had been in the café, apart from Sergeant Robins collecting a takeaway coffee, but nothing I'd said could persuade you to stay. 'As long as you're happy to share,' I teased, heading into the kitchen.

I chuckled as I reached for the cake tin on the dresser, feeling more relaxed than I had for ages. We'd had a nice evening, and after I'd bathed your cheek with soothing calamine lotion, even that hadn't looked so bad. Maybe it had been an innocent accident, after all.

After setting the doughnut on a plate, I glared at the worry box. I'd had such high hopes of it helping me discover what was bothering you; all it had achieved was stirring up my own worries – and conflict with Jordan.

I sighed, lifting the lid, expecting to find the box empty. It wasn't. 'Oh, Marley. Have you written me a proper letter this time?'

My heart beat faster as I carried a white envelope into the living room, encouraging you to sit next to me as I opened it. Breathlessly, I scanned the note – your fourth – before reading the words softly aloud:

Secrets make me sad

'Oh, love. Me too.' I stroked your cheek, tracing the faint, lingering scratch. My heart felt like it was beating out of my chest. 'Is there a . . . a particular secret? Do you want to tell me?'

You shook your head. 'It's not my secret.'

'Ah.' I paused. 'Can you say whose secret it is?'

You chewed your hair. 'It's Leah's. She said not to tell. I *never* tell, Mummy.'

'I know, darling.' I tried not to sound cross, but I wondered how many more stories your so-called best friend was going to make up. 'Maybe, though . . . maybe I can help her?'

You hunkered against my side. 'She's . . . Leah's getting a new daddy.'

'Sorry?' That wasn't what I'd expected you to say at all. '*Who?*' For a crazy moment, I thought of Jordan and the 'news' he hadn't got around to telling me at the beach.

'It's Mrs Hart's husband,' you whispered, as though frightened of being overheard. 'He's going to live in Leah's house and be her daddy.'

'Really? Is that *true*?' I banked at a different branch than the one Joe Hart worked at, and I'd only met him a few times. But he'd seemed nice. *Ordinary*. Not the kind to be having a secret affair with the parent of one of his wife's pupils.

You nodded emphatically, your head bobbing up and down.

'Oh, dear.' I wondered if that explained why Mrs Hart hadn't come out to the playground after school – if she feared gossip and speculation. I was concerned about Leah, too, but what bothered me more was why her secret bothered *you*. 'It's very sad, but these things do happen sometimes. Is Leah OK?'

You shrugged.

'Well, like I say, it's very sad. For all of them.'

I thought of Amy's scathing reference to Rachel Smith's fashion sense, recalling that I'd seen her looking more dressed-up lately. Leah had also been going home with a childminder. It all seemed to tally with big changes, so perhaps it *was* true. Leah's recent behaviour definitely indicated something was wrong. Like you, she didn't seem to be her usual self – although if her daddy was leaving . . .

'Oh!' A penny dropped. 'Are you worried that *your* daddy might go away? Is that why you keep asking where he is?'

'No,' you said, but you tucked up your knees, resting your chin on them.

I cast my mind back over the last twenty-four hours, the conversation you'd most likely overheard with Amy last night, the row I'd had with Jordan this morning. You had also shunned Wally after I'd washed and returned him to your bed.

'Sweetheart.' I tried again. 'Did you hear Mummy and Daddy talking this morning?'

You shrugged but didn't look up.

'You know, all parents quarrel sometimes. It doesn't mean they don't love each other. It's very sad what's happened, and I'm sure Leah is upset.' No doubt that explained why she'd been making up stories – perhaps even lashing out at you, as Amy lashed out at me, growing up. 'But that won't happen to you. To *us*. OK?' Mentally, I crossed my fingers.

'OK,' you said, your voice muffled against your knees.

'Daddy loves us, so much. I know he spends a lot of time on his boat.' I paused, hoping you might volunteer more about your wish the night before. 'He just misses being out on the sea,' I continued quietly when you didn't. 'Exploring.' *Feeling free?* I wondered, reflecting on the name he had given his new yacht: *Liberty*. 'But he's going nowhere. Neither am I. We're a *family*. Forever-together-whatever,' I whispered, kissing the top of your head.

Still thinking about Jordan as I took you upstairs and settled you in bed, I remembered that before our bedtime promise belonged to you and me, it had been mine and Jordan's. Only it was years since he'd said it: eight, to be precise. On our wedding day, when Amy tried everything she possibly could to convince me not to marry him.

Chapter 24

'You don't have to go through with this, you know?' Amy stood in front of the full-length mirror on the back of my mum's bedroom door, finessing her already flawless make-up. 'People break off engagements all the time. Brides get cold feet. Guys get jilted at the altar. Shit happens. Better a shitty day than regretting it for the rest of your life.'

'Well, if I don't marry him, I'm going to look a bit daft in this get-up.' I fussed anxiously with folds of ivory silk that already felt a little strange, like I was playing dress-up for the Marmalade Ball. 'Anyway, it's too late to return it now. I've cut the labels off.'

'You should have let *me* make your dress.' Amy came to stand behind me, resting her hands on my shoulders, her eyes meeting mine in the dressing-table mirror. 'Then it wouldn't have mattered what you did with it. It would make a fab evening gown. You could cut it—'

'Amy, you're not listening.' Nerves made me snappy. 'I *want* to marry Jordan.'

'Are you sure about that?' She reached across me to pick up

her red clutch bag, pulling out a packet of cigarettes and lighting one. 'Or do you just want to be married?'

'What the heck?' I swivelled round on the stool, glaring at her.

'OK, fine, spoilsport. I'll open a window.' Her long, crimson taffeta dress rustled as she sauntered across the room and flung open the sash window overlooking the back garden.

'I didn't mean that.' I shook my head as she made a show of blowing smoke out of the window. 'Although Mum would have a fit if she could see you smoking in her bedroom.' I felt sick as I realised it was the first time I'd mentioned my mum for weeks; I still found it almost impossible to talk about her. Especially to Amy.

I'd been so cross with her after that final party at Sea View, for how outrageously she'd flirted with Jordan. Amy always tried to take everything from me, but there was no way I was going to let her steal the love of my life. Worse than that, though, the last conversation I'd had with my mum had been about Amy, and it hadn't been a good one.

After our cross words about the shoes, I'd been desperate to leave. Only while I'd gone, Amy had stayed. She was still living at Sea View then, and it was her, not me, at Mum's side when she drew her last breath. I'd never forgiven myself for that; I was struggling to forgive Amy.

'You'd probably get the blame anyway, hey?' she acknowledged.

'The blame?' Lost in thought, I had no idea what Amy was talking about. 'For what?'

She blew smoke towards me. 'The illicit fags, of course. Remember your dad ranting at you about the butts behind the shed? You were so sweet not telling on me. You never told, did you, Holly?' She paused, then added softly: 'About anything.'

For a moment, we both lapsed into memories. Mine were still all of my mum. She would have loved to organise my wedding, I reflected, but she didn't even live to know I was getting married. It was the week after her funeral when Jordan had unexpectedly proposed, taking me out on his old motorboat so I could scatter Mum's ashes at sea.

We'd spent the whole day on the water, saying very little until, as the light began to fade, he asked me to be his wife. It wasn't a 'sympathy proposal', he insisted repeatedly. It was simply that my mum's sudden, premature death had brought home the need to seize happiness with both hands. And, for him, happiness meant being with me. 'Forever-together-whatever,' as he went on to promise me three months later, in the vows we wrote ourselves.

That moment was still two hours away, and if Amy had got her way, it wouldn't have taken place at all. 'What have you got against Jordan, anyway?' I said, turning back to the mirror to touch up my own make-up. I was wearing far less than Amy, even though I was the bride, and while her hair had been professionally styled, I had pulled mine into a simple ponytail. I wanted to get married, but without Mum there, I wasn't in the mood for a party.

She shrugged, then lit up another cigarette. 'You've only known him a few months.'

'How long does it take to know you love someone?'

'Love. I'd forgotten about that. It isn't a cure for grief, though. You know that, right?'

'I'm not marrying Jordan to get over losing Mum, Amy. Nothing can replace her.'

'Sure. It sucks. I know, and my mum's not even dead. Just missing in action.' She stubbed out her cigarette on the window-sill, then lobbed it towards the oak tree. 'God, do you remember the hours we hung out on that swing? Bitching about everyone at school.'

'*You* did, you mean. You were a nightmare teenager,' I told her, but with a more sympathetic smile now. Amy was Amy. Spiky, restless and straight-talking. But in fairness, she had good reason to be. After all, she'd been through a lot, too.

'But you stuck by me.' Her eyes darkened to navy as she turned to look at me.

'I was stuck *with* you, more like. We shared a room for ten years, didn't we? In a tower, no less.' I grinned. 'Some prisoners get less for murder.'

'Ha bloody ha.'

'But I'm glad you're going to be my bridesmaid.' Despite everything, I meant it. I'd grown up with Amy; she knew me better than anyone, even Jordan.

'Family tradition.' She winked. 'My mum was your mum's maid of honour, too.'

'Oh. You knew that?' I looked at her in surprise. 'Who told you? My mum?'

'Well, it definitely wasn't mine. I haven't heard from her in years. Or my dad.'

'Really? I guess I kind of assumed you were secretly in touch with them.'

'Nope. No contact at all. I don't think they even paid maintenance for me.'

'Well, that wouldn't have bothered Mum and Dad. Money might have been tight when we were kids, but they never—'

'What are you talking about?' Amy's eyebrows flew up. 'Your mum was *loaded.*'

'Sorry?' I stopped fiddling with the catch on my bracelet and stared at her.

'Here, let me,' Amy offered, deftly fastening it. 'God, you really do know nothing, Holl. This house was *Olivia's*, inherited from her parents. Huh, along with a hefty bank balance. The Howard family owned a hotel chain along the East Coast. Didn't you know?'

'No. I didn't.' I stared at her, wondering if she was making it all up – half hoping she was. I thought of my quiet, unassuming mum, finding it hard to reconcile her make-do-and-mend philosophy with the image of a woman who had unknown wealth at her disposal.

Why had she never mentioned it? Or my dad? Why had they

always lived so modestly – and, more importantly, refused the option of private medical care for her cancer?

Mum always insisted that if our local hospital was 'good enough for my daughter', it was good enough for her. She never complained. Or explained. Or told me *anything*, I thought, struggling to breathe as my chest tightened with grief, and anger, and questions it seemed would never be answered now.

Chapter 25

'Honestly, you're hopeless.' Amy rifled through Mum's jewellery box, picking up bracelets, rings and necklaces as though examining them for value and authenticity. 'You need to wake up and smell the coffee, hon. For all your talk about love, your dad married for money. He might head up a law department now, but he was a penniless student when they met.'

Feeling cross that, yet again, Amy had been privy to secrets that I wasn't, I snapped at her. 'You're wrong. Dad *loved* Mum. And she chose him because she loved him too. For richer, for poorer.' I thought back to my last conversation with her, Mum's surprising admission that she could have 'had her pick'. At the time, I'd puzzled over what that meant; I thought I had all the time in the world to ask her. I was wrong.

'Well, your dad will definitely be richer now,' Amy said archly.

'He'd rather still have his wife,' I said hoarsely. 'And I don't care *how* much money Mum had. I've never known anyone less materialistic. She grew her own veg, for God's sake. *And* made all my clothes.' I stared at my wedding dress, feeling tearful as I imagined Mum fussing with it, but also confused. I'd always thought she was being frugal out of necessity, not . . . *guilt*? Misplaced shame about wealth she'd inherited not earned?

'You're right,' Amy conceded sheepishly, putting down the jewellery box.

I grabbed it, not liking how she was picking over my mum's things. 'I'm also pretty sure she gave away more money than she spent. Mum always put others before herself.'

Glancing down at the tangle of beads and necklaces, I frowned when I couldn't spot the amber butterfly brooch Mum had worn on her last evening. I'd had the feeling then that it was special to her; significant, even. Suddenly I wanted to know why; I wanted to know who gave it to her, where it had gone – if she had given it away, or if someone had taken it.

'Gave away money?' Amy's husky voice rose in surprise. 'What do you mean?'

'I *mean*, every single person who came to her funeral had a story to tell about Mum. How she'd helped them in some way.'

'Ah, the endless bake sales.' Amy huffed; she hated anything domestic.

'And the rest. Volunteering at the hospice. Donating produce from her allotment. Mum kept nothing for herself. She gave to *everyone*.'

'True. Greedy bloodsuckers. There won't be a penny left for us in the will.'

'I've no idea. And you know what? I don't care. The last thing I ever wanted from Mum was money.' All I'd wanted was love. And honesty. But suddenly I was overcome by a feeling that I'd been brought up by a stranger – one I'd adored but hadn't known at all.

'I'm not sure your dad feels the same,' Amy said cynically. 'I heard him on the phone earlier, banging on to his solicitor about some probate hitch. He was using his best Head of Law voice.' She rolled her eyes. 'Has he changed his mind about today, by the way?'

'Sorry?'

'Walking you up the aisle. Handing over his only child to a man he can't stand.'

143

'Amy. Don't. Please.'

'What? I'm only speaking the truth. That's what almost-sisters are for, isn't it? That and making regretful announcements to the guests if you *do* change your mind. Last chance?'

I didn't bother to answer her. I stood up and swished across the room, reaching up for the box on top of Mum's wardrobe. Then I sat down on her bed, lifted the lid and stared down at the almond-white wedding veil.

I hope Jordan is the one who gets to see you in it, I remembered Mum saying, and as I stroked the soft material, I felt paralysed by regrets. That I hadn't had the chance to say goodbye to her. That I hadn't ever told her properly how much I loved her – that she'd never told me. And, most of all, that she hadn't seized the moment on the night of the party to tell me whatever it was she'd promised to explain on the phone the next morning . . .

I regretted, too, that I hadn't booked a different church for the wedding. I had organised the whole thing in a daze of grief. I'd thought getting married at St Andrew's, where my parents had said their vows all those year ago, might bring me some comfort. Now I realised that with every step up the aisle, I'd be remembering Mum's coffin at the end of it.

Struggling to get my breath, I stood up and lurched towards the window, leaning out. But on summer days like that, the air was thick and heavy. Not even the faint breeze drifting off the sea could blow away the sudden claustrophobia that choked me. All at once I felt oppressed by regrets . . . and secrets. Trapped by my own inability to unlock both.

Amy came to stand at my side, so close I could smell her perfume and the sweet-sharp smell of her honey-lemon shampoo beneath the cigarette smoke that still hung about her.

'Look, I know you said it's too late,' she said, taking hold of my hand. 'But it isn't really. It's never too late to change your mind. To wise up to reality – and be brave enough to do something about it. To stop lying to yourself and speak up.'

'What on earth do you mean?' I pushed her away. 'What are you *talking* about?'

For a moment, she seemed to hesitate. Then she stepped away from me, wandering back to the dressing table to sit gazing at her reflection in the mirror. But her indigo eyes looked too bright, too fixed, as though she wasn't looking at herself at all.

'I guess there's divorce,' she said at last. 'Actually, you don't even have to go that far. You could simply walk away. Women do it all the time. Not just from their husbands, either.'

'Ah.' It finally dawned on me that she must be thinking of her own parents. No doubt that explained her wariness about the commitment I was about to make. 'You know, what your parents did, Amy. They must have had their reasons. I don't believe they didn't love—'

'Although we never truly escape our past, do we? It gets stuck in *here*.' She balled her hands into fists and punched her stomach. Then again. Over and over, harder and harder.

'Amy! Oh, my God, don't. Stop that!' I ran to her side in shock. She was really starting to worry me now. Her flushed face and sparking eyes made her look almost wild.

'I suppose there's always death,' she said bitterly. 'After all, they write it into the damned vows, don't they? *Till death do us part.*'

Automatically, I turned to look at Mum's bedside table, remembering the bottles of pills that once covered it, the low, muffled moans of pain I used to hear in the night. I hated that Amy was the one who had been with her when she spoke her last words. For the last three months, I'd felt too traumatised by guilt and grief to ask what they were. Now I had to know.

'That night,' I said quietly. 'It must have been . . . terrible.' The memory of it was clearly still affecting Amy. I felt for her, but I had so many questions. Even more after Amy's revelation about Mum's wealthy background. But one above all others burned in my mind. 'You stayed with her after the party. You were alone with her. In this room. Did she . . .' I cleared my throat and tried again. 'Did she mention me?'

Amy shook her head. 'Not that I'm surprised. They say there's nothing like death to crystallise what matters most in life.'

'What?' I glared at her, racked with grief, loneliness and angry, futile desperation. 'I was her *daughter*.' *Not you*, I thought but couldn't bring myself to say. For all her spite towards me, I would never knowingly hurt Amy. 'Are you saying she didn't love—'

'Oh, Olivia adored the bones of you, Holly. You must know *that*, at least.' She reached for another cigarette and lit up. 'No, it was me she hated the sight of.'

Chapter 26

'Oh, bless you, Holly, you look like a fairy-tale princess.'

'That's so kind of you to say, Miss Shaw,' I replied politely, disguising a sigh. Of all the guests mingling outside the church, my gossipy old teacher had to be the first to greet me. 'You look lovely too,' I added, trying not to wince at her pink chiffon dress, remembering her love of garish colour: 'to brighten up the school day'.

'Kind, piffle,' she dismissed, enveloping me in a vanilla-fragranced hug. 'I speak as I find. You're positively glowing, my dear. Although you need to fix that veil before you walk up the aisle. Brides need an air of mystery, don't they?' she tittered.

'You're right. I'll just . . .'

I offered an apologetic smile and attempted to brush past her, at the same time reaching up to grasp the wispy voile that twisted and curled on a sudden breeze. Although the gusty wind was playing havoc with my hair, I was glad of it: the weather was altogether too hot, too sticky. I felt almost faint from the humidity – and nerves.

'Here, let me help you with that, duck.' Miss Shaw bustled at my side, briskly capturing the elusive cloud of almond-white silk. 'Exquisite,' she sighed admiringly.

'Thank you. It was Mum's.' My chest felt tight, and I turned away on the pretext of looking for my dad and Amy. I knew they'd arrived before me, but there was no sign of them. I hadn't even seen Dad's BMW parked on the lane. While he'd driven himself and Amy, I had opted for a taxi, wanting time alone to digest everything Amy had said to me.

I still felt raw, shocked and deeply confused. Walking to church might have cleared my head, but while St Andrew's was only a short stroll from the rented flat Jordan and I shared at the time, I was wearing a full-length wedding dress and satin high heels.

Miss Shaw took out a pink lace hanky and dabbed at her eyes. 'Your mum might not be here in body, but she's with you in spirit, dear.'

'I hope so.' I bit the inside of my lip, dreading how many times I was going to have the same conversation, regretting my choice of our local church for the second time that day. It was going to be hard enough not bursting into tears each time I thought about Mum; if every guest pointed out her absence, I wasn't sure I could bear it.

'We're all here for you, Holly. You're one of us. We've got your back,' Miss Shaw added with unusual, slightly incongruous fierceness.

'Thank you. Today is definitely going to feel a bit strange,' I admitted. 'It's nice to see so many friendly faces.' I nodded towards the pretty, flint-stone medieval church, where guests were beginning to saunter into the gabled porch. 'Thank you for coming, Miss Shaw. I'm glad you could make it at such short notice.'

'Oh, I wouldn't have missed it for the world. I was a little surprised, as you say.' Her blue eyes turned misty. 'What with it being so soon after your . . . Olivia's funeral.'

I drew in a long breath, then released it, trying to let go of the pain. 'When we're lucky enough to catch a glimpse of happiness, we have to seize it with both hands.' I smiled. 'That's what Jordan says.' Suddenly, I wished I hadn't said no when he'd suggested we arrive together, just as we'd defied tradition by spending the night before our wedding together at the flat, eating fish and chips before wandering down to the beach at midnight.

Jordan hadn't let go of my hand as I stood staring out across the North Sea, letting myself be lulled by its rhythm, imagining I could hear the whisper of Mum's voice. Her heart, body and soul were in that sea; simply being next to it always gave me a feeling of peace. Strangely, last night it hadn't. I'd felt restless and unsettled, and I wasn't sure why.

'I know Olivia thought Jordan was perfect for you,' Miss Shaw said kindly. 'She told me so that evening. At her party.' She sighed, eyes misting over. 'Oh, what a night that was.'

Her last, I thought, digging my nails into my palms. 'Mum was in her element at parties. She was a born hostess.' *Heiress*, I heard in the back of my head.

'She would have burst with pride if she could see you now, dear. Little Holly Aitken. Soon to be Mrs Mayhew. The belle of the ball at last.'

'I suppose you're thinking of Amy,' I said, for once not taking offence at Miss Shaw's directness. Everyone in the village knew about Amy's penchant for theatricality; she'd made enough dramatic entrances at the annual Marmalade Ball.

'Although, in that dress, there's no danger of her fading into the background.' Miss Shaw turned to stare as Amy swept towards the church, one arm linked through my dad's, her long silky hair trailing behind her on the breeze like a dark veil.

'Finally,' I muttered, wryly acknowledging that if Amy couldn't be the first to arrive, she had to be the last. I knew Jordan was already inside; I'd spotted his battered orange Beetle as I arrived. He'd also texted me just as I was finishing getting dressed with Amy at Sea View, saying he was so worried about being late, he was planning to be an hour early.

'Still, Amy will be company for your dad, at least, now you're flying the nest. She might even carry on the tradition of Olivia's parties. At least until there's a new owner.'

'New owner?' I frowned, still watching Amy – watching my dad pause, hand on her waist, stooping to untangle the floaty, scarlet taffeta hem that had got caught in a stiletto heel.

'Don't worry, dear. I'll be discreet. I know your dad asked Mr Jones to keep it hush hush. I only know because I popped into the estate agency last week. Old spinster like me, I'll soon need to swap my little cottage for a comfy modern flat. There are some nice—'

'But what does that have to do with Sea View?' I turned to stare at her, completely baffled. Then I recalled Amy muttering about heated conversations she claimed to have overheard between Dad and a solicitor. 'Did Mr Jones *tell* you he'd been instructed to sell it?'

'I proofread the particulars myself. Mr Jones knows I'm a fiend for punctuation.' Her prim look took me right back to her classroom. 'I'll admit I was surprised. But perhaps a fresh start is best for you all. I'll say no more, though.' She tapped the side of her nose. 'Mum's the word.'

'Dad,' I whispered urgently as we loitered in the blessedly cool vestibule, waiting for the first note of the organ that would give us our cue to start walking up the aisle. The musty smell of spare hymn books piled on a bench mingled with the slight earthiness of the ancient stone walls. I took a calming breath, inhaling the sweet scent of white peonies from my bouquet. Immediately, I was reminded of my mum. *'Dad!'* I called out huskily.

'Sorry, darling.' He hurried back to my side, looking flustered. 'Didn't mean to neglect you. I was just sizing up the audience.' He jerked his head towards the congregation. 'Are they *all* invited to the reception?'

'No. Don't panic. Most are courtesy guests. People who knew Mum. Just a few of our closest friends are coming back to Sea View.'

'Ah. The usual suspects, as your mum would say.'

'Exactly.' I looked at him in concern. The day would be tough for him, too, and not only because Mum wasn't there. In truth, Amy had been right about the tension between my dad and Jordan. I knew Jordan was sociable enough to ride it out, but Dad was a traditional man with strong values; if he didn't like someone, he found it hard not to show it.

'Where did your mum *find* all these people?' he said, shaking his head. 'I can count on one hand the number of close friends I've got.'

'You don't need loads. Just good ones.' I wished I'd dare ask him if Luke Jackson was still one of them, and if so why he never saw him . . . why Luke had never returned to see his *daughter*. I thought of the hearts Mum said he and Dad had broken, and Amy's odd statement that my mum had hated the sight of her. So many secrets and hidden agendas . . .

Were all marriages like that? I wondered, glancing towards the oak door separating us from the nave. It stood ajar, seeming to mirror my sudden indecision. 'It's never too late to change your mind,' Amy had said. I loved Jordan; I wanted to be with him. But was our marriage all just too much, too soon? Miss Shaw had probably only said what everyone else sitting in the church was thinking . . .

'Your mum had both.' Dad's heavy sigh cut across my thoughts. 'Good friends and many of them. She saw the best in everyone. I was always far less patient. This place—' his arm made a wide sweep encompassing the church and beyond '—I was always looking for a way out. Olivia never wanted to be anywhere else. She was born here. She died here.'

'So why are you selling her house?' I blurted out, unable to bite back the question any longer. 'Sea View was her home, Dad. She loved every brick of it. Besides, it's all I have left of her,' I said, choking up.

'I need the money, love.'

'*What?*' I shook my head, thinking about Mum's secret wealth. Surely my dad would have inherited most, if not all of it? 'But Amy said—'

'Amy doesn't know everything, whatever she thinks,' he said crossly. 'Sorry, I didn't mean to be sharp. This is your special moment.' Dad smiled, but as he rested his hands on my shoulders and stared down at me, his eyes were sad. 'You look beautiful, pickle. Your mum would have been so, so proud of you.' He coughed gruffly. 'As am I.'

Chapter 27

'I'm so proud of you, Mrs Mayhew. I know today was tough for you. Without your mum being there, I mean. But you were sublime. I'm the luckiest man alive. Hey, we *did* it!'

Jordan spun me around on the lawn that served as an impromptu dance floor, even without the fairy lights, parasols and bunting I knew Mum would have brought out to dress our garden for a lavish wedding reception. Without her there, I hadn't wanted one and had only invited a handful of people back to Sea View for drinks and nibbles. It was Amy who had switched on the music, turning it into a party.

'Jordan!' I leaned into him, resting my blushing face against the softly padded shoulder of his hired silver-grey wedding suit. 'Everyone's watching.'

'Good.' He spun me round again. 'You deserve to be the centre of attention.'

'For once,' I mumbled, spotting Miss Shaw offering around a tray of drinks to guests and remembering her slightly pointed comment outside the church.

'Sorry?' Jordan paused mid-spin, changing direction so fast, I felt dizzy.

'Nothing. Don't stop, I'm having fun!' I didn't want to make churlish remarks about Amy. She'd actually been the perfect bridesmaid, although I couldn't deny I'd felt a pang as she stood next to me in the church. Closing my eyes for a second, I'd taken a moment to remember another best friend who, had things been different, would have been at my side.

I'd made one last, futile effort to find Jane Price before the wedding, but every enquiry had led to a dead end. Perhaps it was for the best, I decided, after Jordan and I had exchanged rings and I turned to see Amy's eyes shining with emotion. She'd never liked my old friend, and I knew she would have hated to play second fiddle to her. To *anyone*.

Amy always had to be number one, which made it all the more astonishing that she politely stood aside to let one of my teacher friends catch my bouquet. In truth, I'd been planning to keep the peonies and air dry them. Maria had made my bouquet as a gift, copying it from a photo she'd found of Mum and Dad's wedding. But Amy's chant to 'Throw it! Throw it!' as we left the church had rippled through the guests, until I'd felt compelled to comply with tradition and toss the bouquet into the air.

'Fun's all very well,' Jordan said, stepping back and extracting a handkerchief from his pocket, 'but maybe now's a good time to pause for cake. And champagne. Preferably chilled. Jeez, it's hot.' He wiped his forehead. 'We should have got hitched at the beach.'

'That would have been perfect.' I smiled at him, wishing I'd thought of it. But the last three months had been such a blur. I had given scarcely any thought to wedding planning beyond printing off homemade invitations; I'd bought the first wedding dress I tried on.

'No, *you're* perfect,' Jordan said softly. 'And I should know. I've been to the four corners of the world, and there's nowhere else I'd rather be than right here.'

'Mum used to say that.' I leaned against his chest again, needing his strength.

'I'm so sorry she's gone, babe.' He wrapped his arms around

me, holding me tightly, half holding me up. 'But I'll *never* leave you. Forever-together-whatever, remember?'

'You two love birds need to get a room.' Amy swayed slowly towards us, three flutes of champagne cradled precariously in her hands. Jordan and I jumped apart, reaching for our drinks before Amy spilled them. 'Not *my* room, though,' she added cheekily.

'Ours, don't you mean?' I pointed out, raising my eyebrows. 'It was mine first.'

'Squatters' rights.' Amy grinned. 'I've taken full possession now. At least until my flat sale completes. The bank's getting arsy about the deposit.'

I studied her face, remembering Dad's comment about needing money, wondering if there was a connection between him putting Sea View up for sale and Amy buying her first flat. Jordan and I were also house-hunting, but we both had savings. Besides, I wanted our home to be exclusively ours; I didn't want to owe anyone, not even my dad. Not even if he had a secret inheritance from my mum that, for some reason, he seemed determined to keep private.

'It won't belong to either of us soon.' I took a huge gulp of champagne, coughing as bubbles went up my nose. 'It'll be someone else's bedroom.'

'Sorry?'

Jordan and Amy spoke in unison, but only one of them seemed genuinely surprised. Turning away to grab another glass of champagne from Miss Shaw, who, as ever, seemed to be loitering, Amy seemed to deliberately hide her face.

I turned away too, gazing up at the cream-rendered façade of our Grade II listed townhouse. Closing my eyes, I could hear the rush of the sea and feel summer heat scorching the back of my neck. I imagined my mum calling me in from the garden, wiping her hands on her apron as she offered homemade lemonade and vanilla sponge hot out of the oven.

Blinking away tears, I stared up at the window of my old

bedroom. The curtains were closed, almost as though the house, too, was in mourning. I had the feeling I was looking at the familiar face of a much-loved old friend, one I would soon lose, just as I had Mum.

'Dad's selling Sea View,' I said flatly, watching Amy for any sign that she knew.

'What? *Why?*' Jordan gazed around incredulously, as if he too was trying to imagine new owners sipping cocktails on Mum's terrace and enjoying her pretty garden.

I shrugged. 'You tell me.' I deliberately directed my words at Amy.

'That's a shocker,' she said, although she didn't seem that shocked. 'Don't let it spoil the party mood, though, Holl. This is your special moment,' she added, weirdly echoing my dad's words at the church. 'Sod everyone else, just enjoy it.'

'I've had a whole day of moments,' I said with a sigh. '*Most* of them amazing.'

'There's probably been some kind of mix-up,' Amy said. 'I'll go have a word with Adam. See what I can find out. Be good while I'm gone, you two. You've already set tongues wagging. At least it's not me they're talking about, for once, but you,' she added ironically.

I stared at her with a sinking feeling in the pit of my stomach. Amy had been on her best behaviour all day; now, it seemed, she couldn't keep up the act any longer. I gritted my teeth as I watched her eyes widen innocently, convinced she was finally going to cause a scene, make herself the centre of attention, as she always did. 'What do you mean?'

'Oh, surely you realise, Holly? You two married so fast, you've got the whole village convinced you're expecting the patter of teeny tiny feet.'

'The whole village? Or just you, Amy?' Miss Shaw chipped in unexpectedly, hovering briefly at my side as she drifted past with her tray of champagne.

But Amy was already gone, sashaying across the lawn to the French doors that stood open to the terrace. She paused for a moment to glance back at me with dark, glittering eyes, before disappearing inside the house in a flash of scarlet.

Jordan came to stand at my side, looping an arm around my waist as he frowned at Amy. I smiled up at him, before turning to see Miss Shaw still watching her, too. Immediately, I realised that it wasn't me but our old teacher Amy had been glaring at.

I stared curiously at Miss Shaw's round, flushed face and watery, pale-blue eyes, wondering what I was missing. But after a harried glance in my direction, she bustled away. 'Gold-digger,' I was sure I heard her mutter under her breath.

Chapter 28

FRIDAY – TWO DAYS BEFORE

'How'd you like to help me pick some flowers, darling? I've had an extra special order. For a *wedding* bouquet.' I smiled as you hopped onto the buggy board, holding on tightly as we set off through the school gates and down the road towards the bus stop. 'We could stop by the chip shop afterwards, too, if you like?'

I thought the idea might cheer you up; you'd looked so glum as we crossed the playground after school that I'd started to worry there had been another bullying incident. Surreptitiously, I scrutinised you for any more scratches.

'But you don't like flowers,' you muttered, without turning around.

'What? Well, that's not strictly true. I *do* like them. It's my job to know all about them, isn't it?' I still found it hard to get used to the idea myself: that I was a florist now, not a teacher. I needed to speak more positively to you about my business, I decided.

'We never have any at home.'

'OK, that's true. I just . . . They make me think of Grandma Olivia, sweetheart, that's all. She loved her garden. *And* her allotment. She started the business, you see, and I took it over. But having flowers around our home . . . it reminds me that my mum isn't here.'

'Is she in heaven?' You turned around to look back at me with wide, curious eyes.

'Heaven?' I pictured ashes floating on the sea, the rise and fall of waves carrying my mum away from me for ever. 'Yes, darling. She's in heaven.'

We both lapsed into thought as the bus arrived and we clambered on board, wheeling BB's buggy down the aisle to find a space at the widest point. Settling you by the window, I tucked the buggy securely against my seat, checking BB was still asleep.

'Does Mummy seem a bit sad sometimes?' I asked you quietly, guiltily wondering if your recent mood had simply been absorbed from me.

You shrugged, panting against the window to steam it up, before drawing a squiggly face with your fingertip; my heart sank as you gave it a big frown.

'I don't mean to, darling.' I leaned across to draw a round smiley face. 'I have everything I've ever wanted. You, your baby brother.' I drew a heart, then another face. 'Granddaddy. Um, Daddy.' I pressed my finger to the glass again, about to draw a third face, but you reached up and wiped the window with the sleeve of your duffel coat.

'Who's getting married?' you demanded.

'Oh. It's Karen's daughter. You know, Karen at the post office?'

You didn't reply but turned back to stare out of the window, leaning your forehead against the glass, watching quietly as houses and shops gave way to trees and open countryside. We passed the road leading to the church, and it dawned on me that you might have wondered if it was Leah's mum who was getting married: to your teacher's husband.

I'd spoken to Mrs Hart when I collected you – from your classroom this time, rather than the playground, where I suspected she felt uncomfortable surrounded by curious parents. She had indeed seemed edgy and distracted, tidying desks while I asked if there had been any fights between you and Leah, or if you'd mentioned our neighbour Phil. The answer was no on both counts, and she had no recollection of how your cheek came to be scratched.

As we'd left the school, I'd racked my brains to figure out why you continued to be so subdued, when nothing tangible seemed to have happened. I'd pondered again your story about a doll buried at the allotment, deciding it might help to put that worry to rest, at least.

'What colour flowers do you think Karen's daughter might like?' I said with deliberate cheeriness, as the bus trundled along the narrow, straight coastal road towards Thorpeness.

'Don't know.'

'Well, it's an October wedding, so . . . What does autumn make you think of?'

'Dead leaves.'

'Right. OK, yes, that's true.' I screwed up my nose, struggling to think how I could possibly put a cheerful spin on that. 'Maybe orange too? Like Halloween?'

You jumped. 'I don't like Halloween. Ghosts scare me.'

'They're not real, darling.' I kicked myself for introducing the thought.

'Is Grandma Olivia a ghost now? Will she come back and haunt us?'

'No, sweetheart. I told you, she's sleeping peacefully in heaven.'

'Aunty Amy said if you die in pain, your ghost *never* sleeps. She said it wanders around at night. Maybe Grandma's ghost will go back to her 'lotment.'

Your eyes were enormous with fear, and I gritted my teeth, feeling furious. I just *knew* Amy was behind the stories Leah had told you. She'd obviously done more than 'babysit' your class the other day; she had filled your heads with tall tales. Maybe she'd thrown in one about my mum for good measure, I thought crossly, vowing to have words with Amy later.

160

'Honestly, love, there's nothing there.' I forced myself to speak calmly. 'I promise. Look, here's our stop.' I quickly buttoned up your coat. 'Don't forget your book bag!'

Sensing your hesitation, I held on tightly to your hand as I manoeuvred the buggy off the bus, steering clear of the muddiest parts of the lane as we set off in the direction of the allotment. It was only a ten-minute walk to the Cartwrights' farm, but the closer we got, the more I could feel you tense up. Your hand gripped the buggy handle; as we approached the five-bar gate that marked the farm entrance, you let go of it and stopped walking completely.

'Come on, darling. There's Maria. Look, over there, waving to us!'

I waved back, feeling almost tearful at the sight of the greying hair and serene, rosy-cheeked face of my mum's oldest friend. Maria seemed to live in her green anorak and wellies, just as my mum had her flowery apron. I wasn't sure exactly when or how they'd met, but Maria had lived all her life in Thorpeness, too. If there was such a thing as a *second mother*, she was the closest thing to it for me.

'I *told* you, Mummy. There are *bones* in there.' You dug the heels of your school shoes in with all your strength, the sludgy mud of the road spattering your white socks.

'They don't keep animals on this farm, love, but maybe . . . you know, it's possible there might be one or two buried here. A sheep, perhaps. Or a rabbit.' I thought of Treacle, buried under the oak tree at Sea View, suddenly wishing she'd been cremated, too – that I had scattered her ashes at sea, where she could drift peacefully with my mum, rather than her grave being stomped over by the stream of tourists who rented our old family home.

'Naughty girls,' you hissed. 'That's what Leah said. She found a *doll*.'

'Did she say where, love?' I decided the best thing was to humour you and let you discover the truth with your own eyes.

'Behind the barn. She went to play there. A man shouted at her. He *scared* her.'

I frowned. That didn't sound like Bill. He barely spoke and was a gentle, mild-mannered man. 'OK, then. Let's just say hi to Maria first, then we can all go and look together, yes?'

You didn't say yes, but you didn't say no. You held on to my hand as though for dear life as I pushed BB's buggy towards where Maria stood waiting for us in front of the squat, cobbled farmhouse with its grey thatched roof and white walls criss-crossed with black mock-Tudor beams. The closer we got, the tighter your grip became, until you were squeezing my fingers so hard, I thought they might snap.

Chapter 29

'I know what *that* is,' Maria said twenty minutes later. 'My youngest granddaughter has one just like it. Ethan got it off eBay. Ask him, when we go back in.'

'No, it's OK, thanks. I know you're right.' I didn't need to check with Maria's eldest son; I recognised the Bratz doll perfectly well myself.

'It might even be hers,' Maria said, hooking it up and brushing away dark, claggy earth. 'Ethan often brings Lauren up here on his days off. She probably dropped it.' She examined it more closely, shining her torch closer to the doll's pale, mud-streaked face.

The light was fading now, and I was glad you'd stayed inside the farmhouse. In fact, you had refused even to set foot outside. I'd had to leave you and BB with Ethan, who thankfully was used to children, having two of his own. You played with them sometimes, and I knew you would be safe with their daddy, even if you didn't look too happy about it.

As Maria had hunted for a torch, I'd given you a reassuring hug, smiling as I watched Ethan set up a game of Snap at the kitchen table. You clung on to me, silently begging me not to go. 'Everything's fine, love,' I reassured you. 'I'll be back in three shakes of a lamb's tail!'

As I took the dirty, bedraggled doll Maria held out to me, I was glad you weren't there to see it. The sight of its torn dress, matted black hair and dead, broken eyes in their hollow sockets would have terrified you. Just as it did me . . .

'I'm sure you're right,' I said, deciding not to tell Maria that I knew she was wrong. The doll had a scribbled-out 'J' on her left hand. I'd have recognised it anywhere. It was Chloe. My friend Jane's favourite toy. The one Amy had taken from her twenty years ago.

'Not sure anyone's going to want to play with it now, though,' Maria said. 'Looks like the foxes have got to it.'

'Yes.' I glanced around, scanning the dark landscape between the corrugated hay barn and the allotment, the softly lit greenhouses in between. 'It's a fox's paradise round here,' I agreed, knowing you would also consider it the perfect playground for ghosts. What on earth had Amy been *thinking*, scaring you and Leah with spooky stories like that?

Instantly, I thought of the tale she'd spun about Jane all those years ago. I recalled her pointing towards St Andrew's Church, eyes glinting as she told me my friend was buried in a 'cold, dark grave . . . over there'. I'd assumed she meant the church, but from the garden at Sea View where we'd been sitting that day, the Cartwright farm was in the same direction.

Suddenly, I felt my heart rate slow down, and then speed up, faster and faster. Had Amy been pointing *here*? Could she have been telling the truth about hurting Jane? But how would that even have been possible? She'd been just eleven years old herself when Jane had either vanished or moved to London. It was high time I found out which, I decided.

'Stop it, already,' I said harshly, forgetting for a second that I wasn't alone.

'Sorry, love?' Maria shone the torch towards me, blinding me.

Immediately, I thought of Phil doing the same the other night – then I pictured Wally, mysteriously lost inside Phil's house. I

164

guessed our neighbour would have been in his late twenties when Jane had disappeared. Just a few years younger than my dad had been, I realised. *He* hadn't even remembered my school friend. But what about Phil?

'You've lived in Thorpeness all your life, Maria, haven't you?' I said slowly, as we began making our way back across the muddy, uneven field, picking our way with only lights from the farmhouse and Maria's torch to guide us. It was almost dark now.

'Aye. I have that. This farm's been in our family for generations. I'll never leave it. Ethan and Jake will have to carry me out of here in a box one day,' she said, with a typical lack of sentimentality. 'Are you thinking of your mum, love?' she added more gently.

'Actually, no. I was just wondering if you happen to know my next-door neighbour. Phil. I don't know his surname. He works from home, doing something or other.'

'Digital marketing. Yes, good-looking chap. Friendly but kind of quiet. Likes a pie and pint in the Dolphin on a Sunday. Plays golf once a month with his uncle from Ipswich.'

'Wow.' I looked at Maria in surprise. I knew the village grapevine was active; I had no idea everyone's daily habits were common knowledge. 'Has he lived here a long time?'

'Fifteen years or so. He took over the lease on his cottage from his uncle.'

'Oh. Really?' I frowned, curious about how she knew so much about the neighbour I had barely spoken to in all the years we'd lived next door to each other. 'How do you—'

'Bill and I own that whole terrace,' Maria said matter-of-factly. 'Or *owned*, should I say. We've gradually been selling off all the cottages. Yours was one of the first, being the nicest. We sold that to another young couple before you. But we still own Phil's. I'm his landlady, you might say. Why? Is he giving you any trouble? Playing loud music, or—'

'No. No trouble. I bumped into him, that's all, and was curious.

165

I should have asked you before.' I wished I had, then I wouldn't have spent so many hours worrying about him.

My fleeting paranoia about Phil having a connection with Jane's disappearance was crumbling by the second: he hadn't even lived in the area at the time she vanished. It was a huge relief, and I reminded myself that even if you *had* been next door, Phil was harmless and had no doubt simply found your koala on the beach by chance, as he'd told me himself.

'You can ask me anything, love.' Maria gave my arm a quick squeeze.

'Thanks. It's tough not being able to ask Mum. She knew all the local gossip.'

'Oh, she did that.' Maria chuckled. 'Far more than she ever let on. She was a good listener, Olivia.' She let out a long sigh. 'But not one for talking about her own problems.'

'I know.' I bit my lip, remembering. 'Dad's never taken much interest in the village.'

'Well, he's not from round here, is he?' Maria said abruptly. 'He's not one of *us*.'

'No.' I smiled at her slightly indignant dismissal of my dad. Even though he'd lived in the village for more than thirty years, he was clearly still not considered a local.

'We don't hold it against him,' Maria joked. 'So, we're all good?' She turned to me with a concerned frown as we arrived at the back door that led straight into her kitchen.

'Yes. Sorry, yes. I was just letting myself get freaked out by this . . .' I shook the doll, hating the way the black eyes rattled in its head. It was macabre, but hardly incriminating evidence of any crime – especially one I wasn't sure had even been committed in the first place.

There could be any number of reasons Jane's doll had come to be buried at the allotment. Amy could have thrown it away and it was scavenged by foxes. It could have ended up in a box of jumble, then bought and discarded by another child. All kinds of random objects turned up on farm land, just as they did at the beach.

'Farms are pretty spooky places in the dark,' Maria agreed, glancing around the yard. 'And we dig up all sorts,' she added, confirming what I was already telling myself.

'Bones?' I said, remembering your worry about 'naughty girls' ending up here.

Maria shrugged, concentrating on cleaning her wellies on a metal boot-scraper. 'We've always buried our dogs here. I remember your mum . . .' She straightened up, her rosy cheeks even redder in the glow of the outside light. 'Sorry, maybe now's not the best time.'

'No, please, go on.' I was greedy for any scrap of information.

'Well . . .' Maria's head tilted. 'This is going back a fair few years, mind. It was sweltering hot. August, I think. I remember the heat particularly because I was about to take a jug of my homemade lemonade out to your mum. She was on the allotment, as per usual. But all of a sudden, she comes haring into the kitchen, like the very devil was at her heels.'

'Oh?' I found it hard to picture my calm, graceful mum in such a state. There had only ever been one day I could recall seeing her genuinely ruffled. I took a punt. 'It wasn't by any chance a bank holiday, was it?'

'You know, I think it was. Yes, because I remember Bill's surprise when your mum turned up that day. I remember him saying she should be at the beach with you all.'

'Mum took us there that afternoon. For a picnic. Well, Amy and me. Dad hates the beach, as you know. He went shopping instead, I think. To buy film,' I suddenly recalled.

'That's what your mum said when she got here. She just had to check on something, she said. I remember it distinctly because she came flying back into the house not ten minutes later. All pale and trembling, she was, like she'd seen a ghost or something.'

'She was flustered all day. We had one of Mum's musical

soirees that evening. Actually, it was more of a party to welcome Amy.'

'Ah, yes. I remember now.' Maria frowned. 'I don't remember the party, though.'

'You and Bill couldn't make it, as I recall.' I also recalled Mum explaining her jitteriness that evening, telling everyone that a labourer cultivating land by the allotment had unearthed the remains of Maria's old dog. 'Mum being so agitated that day . . . it was because of Poppy, wasn't it?'

'Best dog ever.' Maria's mellow voice turned gruff. 'Yes, her poor old bones had been turned over by the tractor blades, your mum said. Shook her up something rotten. She loved that daft old collie.'

I thought of how tenderly Mum had encouraged me to find the perfect 'final resting place' for Treacle. 'Knowing Mum, I expect she asked you to bury Poppy somewhere else. Her bones, at least.' I shuddered. 'Did you?'

'Actually, no. Weirdly, we never found any. Not for want of looking, either. Which reminds me. That's why Bill and I couldn't make the party. We spent the day searching our entire plot. Found nothing. No bones, nothing at all. Whatever Olivia saw that put her in such a tizzy, I can safely say it wasn't a dead dog.'

Chapter 30

You ran straight upstairs when we got home an hour later. After taking off my muddy boots and hanging up my coat, I was tempted to do the same: to check if Jordan had returned to collect fresh clothes before heading over to his boat as usual. I forced myself not to. I was still hurt by his insinuations about my state of mind; if he wanted us to sleep apart, fine.

In fact, I was glad of the chance to spend some quiet time with BB. I gave him a warm, gentle bath then settled down in the rocking chair to feed and comfort him to sleep. He was so precious, and I had come so close to losing him when he was born. Jordan had been right about that, at least: it was a miracle we even had our little boy.

Tracing his velvety blond brows, I wiped away a tear that plopped onto his sleep-flushed face. I'd meant what I said on the bus: you, BB and Jordan were all I'd ever wanted. 'Mummy needs to do better, hey?' I whispered, gingerly transferring BB into his carry-cot.

Moving to the fridge, I peered inside for something I could whip up for dinner, straightening up in surprise when I spotted a pasta bake only Jordan could have left there. 'Daddy's been home, then,' I told BB. He wriggled, but the sleepy snuffles continued.

Tiptoeing past him, I headed for the stairs. 'Oh!' Peeping into my bedroom, I was taken aback that the pile of laundry I'd left on Jordan's chest of drawers was still there. Did that mean he was coming home tonight?

I was still mad at him, but I couldn't deny I felt lighter in spirit as I popped into your room to check on you, surprised to find you already undressed and in bed. 'Sweet dreams, darling. I love you,' I said softly, bending to kiss your forehead before tiptoeing out again.

I had wanted to have a chat with you about the doll, to reassure you there was nothing to be frightened of, but I wasn't surprised you were exhausted. We'd stayed far longer than I'd intended at the farm, with Ethan playing a particularly energetic last game of Snap with you, while Maria and I discussed Karen's daughter's bouquet and caught up with other orders.

Checking the time on my phone, I debated whether to text or call Jordan, finally deciding to wait and see whether or not he would contact *me*. I didn't want to ask if he was coming home; I needed him to make that decision himself. I *should* call Amy, I reflected, but I knew I wouldn't get a straight answer from her: not about the stories she'd obviously been telling you and Leah, nor about what happened to Jane and her doll twenty years ago.

Stepping back into my bedroom to put Jordan's clothes away, I realised there was another reason I didn't want to speak to her: I dreaded hearing Jordan in the background . . .

There. I'd admitted it to myself: I was worried they were having an affair.

The thought had been bubbling away for some time, I acknowledged, but, preoccupied by worry about you, I had ignored it. Only I couldn't keep packing it away like yesterday's jeans, I thought, shoving Jordan's into his bottom drawer and ramming it closed.

Hurrying downstairs to check BB was still asleep, I peered out of the kitchen window to see if I could spot the red Triumph. Our car still wasn't back from the garage, and I knew Jordan had ridden to work on his motorbike. There was no sign of it, but I positioned myself at the table where I would be able to see him when – *if* – he turned into the alleyway.

Broken nights, combined with the adrenaline rush of finding Jane's doll, finally caught up with me, and my head started to nod, my mind filling with turbulent images of my mum running into Maria's farmhouse on that hot summer's day twenty years ago. I pictured her standing over a pile of bones, shocked and weeping.

But something felt wrong. My mum *never* showed her feelings, and it struck me as odd that the remains of a dog, even a much-loved one, would have traumatised her. Her childhood had been a rural one, and I could recall countless family walks when we'd stumble across dead hedgehogs and squirrels in the woods, some bearing brutal signs of having fallen prey to foxes. Mum was never fazed; she simply nudged them into the undergrowth.

'What did you *see*, Mum?' I whispered, glancing towards the dresser, at the photo Dad had taken that August bank holiday: the same day Amy's shoes had gone missing; the day my mum secretly threw them into the log shed . . .

Amy, fresh from her predictably brilliant piano recital, was beaming triumphantly in the photo, while I was fake-smiling. Mum stood between us. Her head was tilted slightly towards Amy, but her hand was firmly on my shoulder. I smiled at that, standing up and crossing the kitchen to study the photo more closely.

'That brooch,' I murmured, staring at the jewelled butterfly on Mum's dress. 'Where is it? Who gave it to you? What *else* don't I know about you?'

Feeling frustrated once more by secrets locked in the past, I glared at the worry box, wishing I could open it up to find a letter from my mum inside. Impatiently, I lifted the lid – and discovered your fifth note.

'Oh, Marley.' I held my breath as I opened the small scrap of folded paper, frowning as I stared down at the words scrawled in blue crayon:

Aunty Amy is getting a baby

Chapter 31

'Now *that* is just plain silly,' I muttered, hurriedly tucking the note under the teapot with the other four. But I wasn't cross; I was relieved. I knew there wasn't a chance in hell that Amy wanted a child, and the fact that you'd written such a thing convinced me it was simply another sign of your jealousy towards BB leaking out.

Whatever was causing your anxious behaviour, I had to stop 'chasing shadows' and worrying that there was some 'deep, dark secret', as Jordan had scathingly teased me. I sighed, once again regretting the conflict between us, realising that my doubts about him were probably, in part, transference from my own childhood experiences: past unresolved anxieties about my dad that, in my emotional turmoil, I'd projected on to my husband.

When the landline rang in the living room, I leaped up in anticipation. 'Jordan,' I whispered hopefully, as I hurried to answer the strident call before it woke you or BB. My heart was in my mouth as I lifted the phone. 'Hello?'

'Holly, love, it's just Maria.'

'Oh. Maria. Hi.' I swallowed my disappointment.

'I hope I haven't woken the little ones?' she said, clearly picking up my tone.

'No, you're fine. Marley's out for the count. Ethan wore her out good and proper with that last game of Snap.' I smiled, settling down on the sofa and tucking my legs beneath me.

'Ha. He's relentless. Bill refuses to play *anything* with him. He didn't, um, upset Marley, I hope? Ethan can come on a bit too strong. He gets a bit loud and, um, boisterous.'

'No, of course not,' I said quickly, wondering what she meant, instantly thinking of you saying that Leah had complained of a man shouting at her. Could that have been Ethan? 'Don't worry. I think Marley just burned herself out. She's been a bit anxious, lately. Not her usual chatty self.'

'Ah, bless her. It must be tough adjusting to a new baby brother.'

'You're right. That's *exactly* what I think it is,' I said, pleased to have my suspicions validated by someone I trusted.

'Things will settle down, love. Ethan was a pain in the backside when his baby brother came along. Always prodding and pinching him. I used to worry my socks off that he'd proper hurt him. Not that Marley would do anything like that. She's a good girl.'

'Yes, she is,' I agreed, but I felt a niggle of panic as I cast my mind back to yesterday evening, remembering you playing with your baby brother. 'I won't let BB get hurt,' you'd said so emphatically. But I'd caught you staring intensely at him a few times, your foot nudging his carry-cot under the table – when you thought I wasn't looking? I knew you were worried about my health; perhaps, secretly, you blamed BB for making it worse.

'Marley wouldn't hurt a fly,' Maria continued, as though reading my mind.

'Or a bumblebee,' I said, forcing a laugh.

'Still bug crazy, is she?' Maria laughed too. 'Or perhaps it's just the honey she loves. I've got plenty of jars in the pantry. She's welcome to come and help herself. Why don't you both pop over for tea tomorrow? You could do with a bit of pampering.'

It dawned on me that I was being subtly checked up on. 'I'm fine, Maria. Honestly.'

'Are you sure?'

'Totally. Why, don't I look fine?' I stood up and crossed the living room to study my reflection in the mirror over the mantelpiece.

My hair was messy, tangled from the wind as I'd tramped across the fields with Maria, and my jeans and jumper had definitely seen better days. But I didn't *look* like a woman on the verge of a nervous breakdown. *Did I?* Jordan had all but suggested it; now here was Maria seeming to imply the same thing.

'You look as pretty as ever, love,' Maria reassured me. 'Only you did seem a tad on edge earlier. Is it work? I know we agreed I'll just handle orders for the time being, but I can take some paperwork off your hands too, if you like? I helped your mum out plenty of times.'

'I know you did. And I'm very grateful for the offer, Maria. It's really kind of you.' So kind, in fact, that it brought tears to my eyes.

'I just wish I could do more. I'm so fond of you, Holly. Oh, don't get me wrong, I like Sarah and Elaine well enough,' she said quickly, referring to her daughters-in-law. 'But Olivia was like a sister to me. Which makes *you* my honorary daughter.'

'I like that,' I said, dashing away a tear. 'Thank you.' It was so quiet in the cottage, and chatting to Maria made me realise how alone I felt – how I missed the closeness I once had with Jordan. I didn't even have the chatter of the classroom anymore, or the camaraderie of the staffroom, to cheer me up. I needed a good friend, but Amy clearly wasn't it.

'No problem. I like it too,' Maria said softly. 'If there's anything I can ever do . . .'

'Actually, there *might* be something you can help me with.' I curled up on the sofa again. 'Some information about a missing person, around twenty years ago. A schoolgirl. Her name was Jane Price.'

Half an hour later, I put the phone down feeling calmer than I had for days, possibly weeks. You were clearly just jealous of your baby brother, and if my mum had been around, she would no doubt have put her finger on it immediately – as Maria had.

Mum's oldest friend was also able to trawl her memory of village history to confirm that Jane had indeed died in a tragic accident, aged eleven. Maria couldn't recall the exact details, but she was certain no foul play had been involved.

Jane's aunt and uncle had moved away to London soon after, she said, because they'd just had a baby and didn't want social services involved. Apparently, they'd already felt under intense scrutiny when Jane's parents died, after which they were investigated to determine their suitability as adoptive parents.

That must have been where I got the idea that Jane had moved to London, I reflected, feeling sad as I tiptoed upstairs to settle BB in his cot. The second he was asleep, I ran myself a hot bath, deliberately lighting candles and tipping in all the luxury bath oil I could find. Then I sat in the tub, thinking it all through, and had a good cry: for the lost friend I'd never had a proper chance to mourn, and for the mum I had never stopped missing.

I told myself I didn't care if Jordan was with Amy at that very moment, maybe even enjoying a bubble bath of his own. In the tub he'd fixed for Amy. My supposed best friend. 'Gold-digger', I recalled Miss Shaw muttering.

But who did she have her sights set on – my dad, or my husband? One thing was certain, it wasn't you, and it wasn't BB. Your note about Amy 'getting a baby' had to be a misunderstanding. I knew full well that was the last thing my 'almost-sister' wanted. She'd made that crystal clear at your own christening, seven years ago.

Chapter 32

'I know life moves a little more slowly in Thorpeness,' I remember Jordan saying as he brought out yet more trays of food. 'But we've come a long way since post-war rationing. People don't have to eat like they don't know where their next meal is coming from,' he pretended to grumble, all the time grinning as we watched a queue form at the table where he'd just laid out extra pasta dishes, assorted curries and a selection of delicate pastries.

'You should take it as a compliment. Everyone loves your food,' I pointed out, as a group of six or seven people drifted past us, their plates piled high.

'I might need to get that in writing.' Jordan grimaced, surveying the rapidly dwindling buffet. 'My boss paid for all this grub. He said to call it his christening present. The rate this lot are packing it away, he might live to regret not going for the gift vouchers I suggested.'

'Wow.' I knew the manager of the country club was generous; he regularly sponsored village events, many held in that elegant first-floor space, with its vaulted ceilings and breath-taking sea views. But hosting our christening reception was above and beyond my expectations. 'He must really rate you.'

Jordan winked. 'I'm the best.'

'You certainly are. Best *chef*, best *husband*, best *daddy*.' I beamed at him, loving the sound of each word; loving the pride on Jordan's handsome face. I still got butterflies calling him my husband. It had been less than a year since our wedding, and already we had a baby daughter. After the pain and sadness of losing Mum, I felt fit to burst with joy.

'It's easy when you have the perfect wife,' he said, stooping to kiss my cheek. 'And *this* gorgeous bundle is the cherry on the proverbial,' he added, scooping you out of my arms.

'Isn't she just,' I agreed, smiling even more broadly.

'What a clever woman you are, Mrs Mayhew.' Jordan's face was transfixed with wonder as he rocked you in his arms. 'Not only did you marry me, you made us a miracle.'

'It took two of us,' I said, suddenly feeling shy as Jordan's green eyes burned into mine with such intense intimacy that everyone else in the room faded into the background.

A familiar husky voice punctuated the moment. 'What *is* it with you two and public displays of affection?'

'Ah, here comes the perfect *godmother*,' Jordan teased, turning to Amy with a grin.

He held you out expectantly, clearly waiting for Amy to seize the chance for a cuddle. All day, from the moment we had arrived at the church, to the second we pulled up outside the country club for the reception, people had been begging for 'just a little hold'.

'Er, thanks, but no thanks.' Amy held up her glass of champagne, rearing back as though Jordan had offered her a live grenade. 'No offence. I just don't do babies.'

'Oh, come on, Ames,' Jordan urged. 'Look at those little cheeks. Those big eyes. Marley is adorable. You don't have to change her nappy, or anything. Just give her a kiss!'

'Don't force her if she doesn't want to,' I said, the look on Amy's face making me nervous. Her summer-gold skin had turned pale, and as I watched her eyes glaze over, I was worried she might actually faint. I grabbed hold of her arm. 'Are you OK?'

'Am *I* OK?' Quickly pulling herself together, she flicked back her hair and cocked her head to one side. 'It should be me asking *you* that.'

'Sorry?'

'She's right, babe.' Jordan's smile dropped. 'I'm such an idiot. You've been on your feet all day. You should take a break. It's only a week since you got out of hospital. Have you taken your beta blockers today? The doctors said you need to be extra—'

'OK, OK! I know when I'm not wanted,' I teased.

'As if.' He rolled his eyes. 'You're irresistible, woman. I can't get enough of you.'

I blushed and looked down, feeling self-conscious. But as I looked up again, I was puzzled to see Jordan wink at Amy.

Telling myself I was being paranoid, I smiled brightly, but I was conscious of a sinking feeling of insecurity as I took in Amy's typically flawless appearance. While I'd chosen a loosely flowing navy pinafore to disguise my post-baby curves, her high heels and tight-fitting black shift dress showed off toned, tanned arms and legs, and her long black hair had a glossy sheen I doubted my hormone-infused curls would ever achieve again.

'I guess I am feeling a bit tired,' I admitted. 'I thought pregnancy was exhausting. It's got nothing on breastfeeding every two hours.'

'Ugh.' Amy shuddered. 'The very idea of it.'

'It's lovely, actually,' I said, smiling as she looked at me like I'd gone mad. 'I adore our quiet moments in the night, don't I, darling?' I whispered, stroking your golden wisps of hair. 'I could do with a bit more sleep, though,' I admitted, trying to smother a yawn.

'You must be knackered. You certainly look it,' Amy said bluntly.

'Cheers.' I rolled my eyes.

'Oh, I say it with the utmost sympathy. Childbirth is brutal. I'm not sure which is worse – getting a fat belly, or having to push the damn thing out.'

She sucked in her midriff, stroking it almost unconsciously, and all of a sudden I pictured Amy on my wedding day, punching her flat stomach over and over, as though she hated it . . . or was punishing herself, her body? I tried to imagine what could have fuelled such self-loathing; she had the perfect figure. But Amy's behaviour was so often a mystery.

I sighed. 'Maybe you'll feel differently, one day.'

'You mean, when I meet the man of my dreams and find myself overcome by an *irresistible* urge to breed with him?' She laughed, but it sounded hollow.

'Well, I . . .' I bit my lip, wondering if I'd imagined her sideways glance at Jordan.

'Did you hear that, Miss Shaw?' Suddenly, Amy turned to grin at our old teacher, who as ever seemed to be hovering nearby. 'What do you think? Is being desperately in love enough to convince a sane woman to subject herself to unbearable pain?'

Miss Shaw tittered, plucking at the ruffled neckline of her canary-yellow dress. 'Never married, dear. Never had a husband. Or children.'

'Never been in love?' Amy pressed, suddenly swivelling around in the other direction, staring across the room to where I could see my dad chatting with the vicar.

'Ignore her, Miss Shaw.' I gave Amy a warning glance, then glanced curiously at my dad again, wondering if Amy knew something I didn't.

Miss Shaw had become almost a permanent fixture at every family gathering over the years. I had assumed it was because my mum had been fond of her; now I wondered if the affection was all on her side – for my dad?

'You're never too old for romance,' Amy teased as Miss Shaw's blush deepened.

'Or too *young*, it seems,' she bit back with unusual sharpness, before bustling away.

Staring at Amy's furious expression, I wondered again what I was missing. 'I think I'll take Marley and go for that sit-down,' I said quietly. 'Why don't you join me, Amy?'

'Thanks, but I was hoping for a top-up.' She hoisted her glass in Jordan's direction.

'Take all the time you need, babe.' He passed you to me as gently as if he were handing over a piece of fragile bone china, obligingly taking Amy's glass from her and gesturing towards the buffet. 'We're all done here anyway, bar cutting the cake.'

'Oh, yes! I'd almost forgotten.' I glanced towards the spectacular creation Jordan had been working on for days, feeling excitement overlay my concern for Amy.

The christening cake stood on its own table, a gleaming white, five-tiered tower ringed with red rosebuds, at my request: a personal, private reminder of my mum.

'First one I've made in ages.' Jordan beamed. 'I reckon I've found a new hobby.'

'Luckily, you'll have plenty of opportunity to indulge it.' I smiled, thrilled at the thought of cutting the cake – and all the birthday cakes to follow. 'Once a year, in fact.'

'Or maybe twice. If I get *really* lucky.' Jordan leaned forward to kiss me again.

'Oh, man.' Amy rolled her eyes as she snatched back her glass and headed for the bar.

Chapter 33

It was two more hours before guests started leaving. My back was aching, my voice was hoarse and my feet were killing me by the time I had a chance to find a comfortable sofa by the window and steal a quiet moment to myself. Holding you asleep in my arms, I gazed out at the most glorious orange sunset, with hazy streaks of purple just beginning to smudge the horizon. The sea seemed almost alive, dancing in a spectacular display of light and shadows.

'You would have loved your granddaughter, Mum,' I said softly, closing my eyes for a second and trying to imagine her sitting there with me. *I miss you*, I added in my head.

Three months before, each of us had marked the first anniversary of Mum's death separately, in our own different ways. Heavily pregnant, I hadn't felt confident going out on Jordan's boat, as he'd suggested. Much as I had longed to feel as close as possible to my mum, I was struggling with nausea – and fear.

My first child.

While the doctors fussed endlessly about the strain on my heart, my only concern was for your safety. The possibility that I might slip and fall overboard felt all too real. Hormones intensified every nightmarish scenario conjured up by my imagination;

181

all I'd felt able to do was spend the evening quietly at our cottage looking through photo albums.

It had turned out to be a bad idea. Revisiting snapshots of my childhood – Amy posing at the Marmalade Ball, Jane pulling faces in the background, with my parents looking on with benign smiles – I'd been sucked into a tunnel of grief. Only the thought of you being born pulled me out the other side. I'd tried to call Amy, but her phone was switched off. So was my dad's. The following day, neither could account for where they'd been.

'Congratulations again, dear.' A gentle voice broke into my thoughts.

'Oh, sorry, Miss Shaw! I was miles away.'

'It's been an emotional day.' She smiled kindly.

'Very.' I smiled back, telling myself to enjoy the present rather than dwell in the past.

'Such a lovely gesture to give this little one your mum's name,' she continued, as though guessing my thoughts. 'Marley Olivia Mayhew. I wonder if she'll be like her.'

I smiled. 'I guess time will tell. Perhaps she'll take more after my . . . dad.' I coughed to cover up my slight hesitation. Amy's hints about Miss Shaw being in love with Dad were ridiculous. She was years older than him. 'Or me and Jordan, of course.'

'Well, you're certainly a mixture of both *your* parents. Family resemblance is funny like that, isn't it? People always used to tell me I looked exactly like my father. I could never see it myself. Sometimes we only see the truth in photos, don't we?'

'Of course,' I said politely, wondering if Amy had any of her parents, realising I'd never seen one. I wondered, too, if my dad had ever sent Luke and Isabella the infamous 'memory book' he had so carefully compiled of their daughter. I'd never seen that, either.

After saying goodbye to Miss Shaw, I couldn't help watching as she stopped to speak to my dad on her way out. He embraced her awkwardly, while Amy point-blank ignored her. 'Oh, Amy. You are your own worst enemy,' I sighed.

I pondered again the acerbic exchange between her and Miss Shaw, considering the possibility that Amy had been projecting her own frustration over a thwarted romance. 'Jordan!' I called out, deciding to ask if he'd ever heard Amy mention one.

'You OK, babe?' Jordan hurried to my side, green eyes glinting with concern.

'Absolutely.'

'Marley?'

'She's perfect.' I grinned, holding you out for him to see.

'Then it must be more cake you're wanting,' he teased. 'Awesome, wasn't it?'

'Even if you do say so yourself.' I laughed. 'But no. I'm not hungry. I'm . . .' *Suspicious. Jealous?* 'Curious. Has Amy ever mentioned any guys to you?' I asked casually.

Jordan rolled his eyes. 'Loads. You know how she loves to flirt.'

'I mean any one in particular. Like, someone she may have loved – and lost?'

'As if. To fall in love, there's this little thing you've got to have. It's called a *heart*.' Jordan thumped a fist dramatically against his chest. 'Cut Amy Jackson open, and I'm pretty sure all you'll find is a big, fat Swarovski crystal in its place.'

'Huh. You mean, you think she's a *gold-digger*?' I frowned, recalling another of Miss Shaw's pointed comments that had obviously been directed at Amy.

'I wouldn't go that far. But if Amy ever marries, I'm pretty sure she won't pick a poor, struggling chef with only a beaten-up VW and a clapped-out Triumph to his name.'

I just about managed to stop myself from saying: *Like you, you mean?* 'Amy likes the good things in life, it's true. And I'm sure she'll figure out a way of getting them.'

Jordan huffed, sitting down next to me on the sofa. 'Anyway, what's brought all this on?'

'Oh, just thinking. Wondering what makes Amy so cynical. About love. Babies.'

'She spends all day around kids. I bet there are loads of teachers who can't stand the thought of going home to their own. Anyway, all Amy cares about is Amy. Self-centred people don't make great parents,' he added tersely, and I saw him glance at my dad.

'Maybe he'll do better as a grandfather. He's retired now. He'll have a lot more time to spend on his family.'

'And money,' Amy said behind me, making me jump.

'Oh, my God!' I jumped, feeling heat flood into my cheeks as I wondered how much she'd overheard. 'Don't creep up on us like that!'

'Why, got a guilty conscience, have you?' Amy smirked. 'Budge up,' she instructed Jordan, perching on the sofa next to him, casually splaying a hand on his thigh.

'No. I haven't. Have *you*?' I asked boldly.

'Me?' Amy batted her eyelashes, then said: '*Keep a clear conscience before God, so that when people throw mud at you, none of it will stick.*' She glanced at my dad, but addressed her words clearly, almost defiantly at me: 'You remember that, don't you, Holl? You must do. Your darling dad hung it over your bed.'

Chapter 34

FEBRUARY 2015

'Did I over-season it?' Jordan put down his knife and fork, leaned his elbows on the kitchen table and nodded at the lasagne I was pushing around my plate.

'What? Oh, no. It's delicious.' I forced a mouthful, giving him a thumbs-up. The food genuinely was mouth-wateringly tasty; I was just exhausted and had very little appetite.

'So how come I've already finished seconds while you've barely nibbled a corner?'

'Sorry.' I pushed the plate away, giving up on the pretence of eating the romantic early Valentine's Day dinner he'd made especially, in the knowledge that he would be working flat-out the following day, one of the busiest nights of the year at the restaurant.

I glanced at the candles he'd lit, the pile of washing that, for once, had been taken care of by the time I'd returned home from work and collected you from the childminder. I had been back at my teaching job for six months by then; you were happily settled with Maggie round the corner, already best pals with her own eighteen-month-old toddler.

'Don't apologise,' Jordan said, clearing our plates. 'I'm not cross. Just concerned.'

'I'm fine. But I am sorry.' I sighed. 'You went to a lot of trouble.'

And not only with the food. While I was still dressed in my black work trousers and grey jumper, Jordan was wearing fresh jeans and a white shirt, the sleeves rolled back to show off tanned forearms. His usually messy hair was combed, and he'd also shaved; I could smell his favourite cologne. He must have come home early especially, to get everything ready as a surprise.

'I tried my best.' He turned away, stacking the dishes in the sink, shoulders hunched.

Feeling bad, I leaped to reassure him. 'You've been brilliant, Jordan. I know how hard you're working, too. Taking on extra shifts at the restaurant.'

'We need the money.' Crossing his arms as he turned to face me, he leaned back against the worktop. 'I wish I earned more. I wish you didn't have to work at all, but—'

'I love my job,' I said quickly. 'I don't do it just for the money.'

'I know, babe. But you know how much I worry about your health.'

'I'm fine,' I insisted, deliberately not mentioning the palpitations I'd been having, not wanting him to worry. He was working increasingly long hours; in fact, that Friday-night dinner together was a rarity. Usually, Jordan was at work, or at the Yacht Club. With no spare cash to pay someone to fix up his old boat, he'd been doing it himself.

'Are you sure?' He came to sit next to me at the table again. 'You will say if it all gets too much, won't you? I know you're carrying all the domestic stuff. Housework, Marley's childcare arrangements. Maybe she'd be happier, too, if you were at home full-time.'

'Marley's super happy with Maggie. In fact,' I said slowly, 'I've been thinking . . .'

'Always a dangerous thing,' Jordan quipped lightly.

'I know money's tight. I know we agreed to wait before trying for a second child . . .'

'Not because of money. You know I'd love us to have more kids. I thought we'd get cracking straightaway, too.' He winked cheekily, making me blush. 'But the doctors were right. You need to give your body a proper chance to recover first. Luck was on our side when we had Marley. The birth went well. We might not get so lucky next time.'

'I know. I just . . .' I sighed. 'Marley is growing up so fast. I really want her to have a little brother or sister. I don't want her to feel . . . alone.'

'Like you did,' Jordan said intuitively. 'Huh, with Amy around, it's hard to imagine you ever got a moment's peace. I bet she was a proper wild child. She hasn't changed much.'

'You don't know the half of it.' I shook my head. 'Anyway, she didn't come to live with us till I was seven. If we wait that long, it would be a huge age gap for Marley.'

'Although, looking at it another way, things will be financially easier for us by then.'

'Sorry?'

'I should make head chef in a couple of years. Then there's your inheritance.'

'My . . . Jordan, I've been meaning to say. Mum's money. I don't want it. I've arranged with the solicitor to put it in trust for Marley, when she's older.'

'Seriously?' Jordan frowned, digging his fists into his jeans pockets.

'I'm sorry.' I could feel the subtle shift in atmosphere, and I was cross with myself for causing it. 'I should have said. I just hate talking about money, and—'

'It's fine. You do whatever makes you feel comfortable. I'm just surprised, that's all.'

He smiled, but I could tell he didn't really understand. I barely grasped my own reasoning. All I knew was that I didn't want anything to do with a secret fortune that, for reasons known only to my mum, she hadn't seen fit to tell me about herself.

'We're doing OK, aren't we?' I said, suddenly feeling insecure. 'We're covering the mortgage. We've got no debts.'

'None,' Jordan said quickly. 'And you're right. We're getting by. It's just . . .' He gazed around the kitchen. 'You and Marley deserve better than this.'

I looked around too, at the cluttered dresser, saucepans hanging from an improvised ceiling rack. 'I know it's small, but it's *ours*. Bought with our money. And there's nowhere else I'd rather be,' I said, finally understanding why Mum used to say that.

It didn't matter that Driftwood Cottage was cramped and scruffy, and that we would struggle to find room for a second child, even if Jordan did agree to try for one any time soon. It was our *home*, and as long as we were all together, that was all that mattered to me.

'I love it too, babe,' Jordan said, less convincingly. 'We could do with some new furniture, though. We had to scrounge most of it from your dad's house before he sold it.'

'Mum's house,' I said deliberately. 'Sea View was hers.'

'Does that matter?' Jordan countered, sitting down opposite me again. 'Husbands and wives share everything, don't they?' He topped up our wine, then raised his glass in a pretend toast. 'For richer, for poorer. What's mine is yours, and all that.'

I smiled. 'For the record, I will *never* want your rusty old motorbike. It's a death trap. But seriously . . .' I picked up my wine and took a gulp of Dutch courage. 'I'm sorry if you thought you were marrying an heiress.'

Jordan sat back, hooking his arms behind his head. 'Er, I hate to break it to you, but I'm not the one sniffing round the family fortune.'

'You mean Amy? You really think she has her eye on my dad's money?'

I thought back to the day, soon after our wedding, when Dad

had finally revealed the terms of Mum's will. In hindsight, the angry phone calls with a solicitor Amy claimed to have overheard made complete sense: my dad had clearly been as surprised as we all were that the bulk of her estate had been left not to him, but to me.

To Dad's credit, not a single churlish word about it had ever passed his lips. Amy was far more vocal, and to be honest, I *was* surprised she'd been left nothing. I knew Amy took it as further evidence that Mum 'hated the sight of her', as she'd claimed on my wedding day, but I still had no idea why she thought that. I'd never seen Mum be anything other than kind to Amy, nor had I shared her confession that she'd thrown away Amy's shoes in a fit of maternal pique when we were children.

'You have to feel for Amy, though,' Jordan said, swirling red wine around his glass. 'If she *did* fancy herself as mistress of Sea View, it must have been a blow when your dad sold it. Any plans she had to become a lady of leisure were scuppered.'

'I can't believe she's *quite* that calculating. She still spends a lot of time with Dad. More than I do,' I added guiltily.

'You take Marley to see him every Sunday, don't you? I haven't seen my old man since I left Australia three years ago. Or my mum. Another reason I wish I had a bit more cash. Can't you just picture Marley cuddling a koala?'

I laughed. 'Can *you* picture a twenty-four-hour flight with a lively toddler who never stops chattering?' I leaned across the table, taking hold of Jordan's hand. 'But I know you miss home.'

'*This* is home now.' He squeezed my hand, lacing his fingers through mine. 'Wherever you and Marley are. Sod Amy Jackson. If she really believes money will buy her happiness, good luck to her.'

Chapter 35

'Really, this is all a lot of fuss about nothing,' I protested as Amy urged me into the taxi waiting outside the school gates the following Monday morning.

'I'll be the judge of that,' she said, climbing in next to me and taking out her phone.

'Who are you calling? Not Jordan?' I groaned. It had been just three days since our Valentine's dinner, when I'd promised him I was fine. If Jordan got wind that I wasn't, I knew he'd insist I left my job, and I couldn't give up my salary now: I'd already looked into the cost of flights to Australia and planned to surprise him by saving up for a trip.

'He needs to know, Holl. You passed out in the staffroom. And not just because the deputy head wears too much aftershave.'

'Ha. But I love how you tried to blame him anyway. The look on his face!' Amy had only been teaching at the same primary school as me for a couple of months; she already had half the teachers terrified of her. The other half, I suspected, were in love with her.

'He's so vain, he makes *me* look like a slob.' Unconsciously, she smoothed the fitted jacket of her black trouser suit. 'But it was smart of him to call a cab. An ambulance would have to come all the way from Ipswich. You'd have been dead by then.'

'Cheers for that happy thought,' I said, although I knew she was trying to keep my spirits up. I could see the fear in her eyes. I was scared too, not of going to hospital, but of not coming out again – of you losing your mum, just as I had mine.

'Dammit, why doesn't he pick up?' Amy tutted in exasperation, pressing redial. 'I'll phone his boss. What's the number of the country club?'

'Really, Amy. I don't want to bother him. I'm fine. Jordan doesn't need to know.'

'Keeping things from your husband? Tut tut. Hardly a recipe for a happy marriage.'

'We *are* happy,' I insisted, surprising myself by the note of desperation I could hear in my own voice. 'I love Jordan. And he loves me,' I added, only making it sound worse.

'You don't need to justify yourself to me, hon. Or yourself,' Amy said astutely. 'I know I had my doubts about Jordan in the beginning, but, to be honest, that was more about how fast you rushed him up the aisle.' She grinned.

'Amy!'

'OK, you weren't desperate, just desperately in love. Anyway, I thought it was all a bit shotgun. And you weren't even pregnant.'

She turned to stare out of the taxi window, and I had the feeling she was hiding her face from me. 'Is everything OK, Amy? You can talk to me, you know?' I added, remembering her once saying no one could tell me anything.

'Thanks. Actually, I . . .' She seemed to battle with herself, then the shutters came down over her indigo eyes. Leaning forward, she addressed the driver impatiently. 'Go straight to A&E, OK? No taking the long route to bump up the fare,' she added rudely.

I sighed wearily, recognising that I'd been brushed off. Again. 'Well, whatever. I'm glad Jordan finally has your stamp of approval. Whatever he's done to earn it.'

'Oh, I always liked him. He's gorgeous. What's *not* to like?' Amy turned to me with a wink. 'I just didn't think he'd stick around, is all. Men usually don't, you know?'

'Like your dad, you mean.'

'And the rest.'

'Oh?' I stared at her, wondering again if Amy had been involved in a relationship that ended badly, hoping this might be the moment she finally opened up about it.

'Ask me no secrets, I'll tell you no lies,' she teased.

I gave her a knowing look. 'I'm wise to your ways, Amy Jackson. You might get a kick out of being mysterious, but you're a primary school teacher in a seaside town, not the star of a Netflix boxset.'

'Worst luck.'

'There are plenty of people who'd think that's more than OK. Life doesn't have to be one big drama. You don't always have to act like there's some big mystery, when there isn't.'

'You're right. No skeletons in *my* closet. I do know a secret, though.'

And then she smiled. You know the one. It starts with her eyes; they narrow and crinkle, while her mouth curls up, just slightly, almost as though she's trying to hide her smile – like it's only for you.

'Go on, then,' I said breathlessly. 'I'll bite. What is it?'

'Jordan's buying a new boat. Actually, he's already bought it. A yacht.'

'What? But we can't afford . . .'

'That's what banks are for, honey. He's taken out a big fat loan. Still, you'll be able to pay it off with interest when you get your inheritance, hey?'

'We've *talked* about that, Amy. I don't *want* Mum's money.' I'd lost patience with her constantly bringing it up, and the coincidence of Jordan having just mentioned it, too – while mocking Amy's obsession with money – niggled at me.

'You don't want your inheritance?' The coy smile dropped, and Amy's expression hardened. 'That *is* a shame, because I'm pretty sure your husband is already spending it.'

Chapter 36

SATURDAY – THE DAY BEFORE

'Whatever happened to weekend lie-ins?' I mumbled, dragging a second load of washing out of the machine, groaning as I realised I'd forgotten to separate it: BB's sleepsuits had mutated from cream to dingy grey. 'What we need is a shopping trip.' I turned to smile at him in his carry-cot. 'Shall we see if Marley fancies that?'

The prospect of a day out with you made happiness unfurl inside me. Although tired from feeding BB in the night, I'd woken up feeling much more positive: my phone chat with Maria the evening before had left me with lingering questions about my mum, but it had put my mind to rest about what might be going on with *you*.

Amy's story about Jane was clearly nonsense she'd made up, probably after overhearing village gossip. Her tale of naughty girls buried at the allotment was equally ridiculous, but I understood why it had scared you. Now I was in full possession of the facts, I felt confident I could reassure you. I'd also walked past Phil's cottage the night before without giving it so much as a second glance.

All my worries were mere cobwebs in my mind; I simply needed to get out and blow them away, just as I hoped the worry box was helping you to clear *your* mind. Glancing at it, my gaze slid to the calendar hanging by the dresser, and I realised it was Jordan's day off: maybe a spot of retail therapy was what we *all* needed.

'Jordan?' I called softly, wandering into the living room. Even though he hadn't slept in our bed the night before, he had at least come home after his shift. I took that as a good sign. 'Are you awake?' I whispered again when he didn't stir.

As ever when I stopped to look at Jordan, I marvelled at how lucky I was to have met him. It had been a purely chance encounter in the Dolphin pub, where he'd popped in to ask about local boat clubs. Out for drinks with teacher friends, my ear had already been caught by the Australian accent. But the tall, tanned, golden-haired man was so good-looking, it didn't cross my mind that he was making a beeline for me. Gorgeous men with ocean-green eyes never looked at *me*, and I'd offered directions without a jot of self-consciousness.

When he'd asked my name, I assumed he was being polite; when he'd pressed me for my number, I thought it was in case he had trouble finding the marina. I was astonished when he called the next day to ask me out. And again the day after, and the day after that . . .

Jordan was the love of my life, and it broke my heart that he might no longer feel the same about me – and that it was my fault. All the time I'd been conjuring up mysteries about Jane, and imagining bad things happening to you, my marriage had been slipping through my fingers. I'd tried to address the situation; I needed to try harder, I decided.

'Aaargh,' Jordan groaned, almost rolling off the sofa as he started to wake up.

'What time did *you* get in last night,' I teased, then bit my lip as I realised how like a nagging wife I sounded.

'Not late. Around two.' He sat up, yawning widely. 'What time is it?' He checked his watch then threw back the blanket. 'Damn. I need to shower. Got to head over to the boat.'

'Oh. Really?' Disappointment flooded through me. 'I was hoping we might spend the day together. Go shopping. Grab some lunch. You know,' I tailed off awkwardly.

'Sorry, babe. I've got an outboard motor to fix. I would have made a start yesterday, but I was bushed. Big party of tourists in last night.' He yawned again, stretching so hard, yesterday's T-shirt rode up around his midriff, showing off his taut, tanned stomach.

'Sure.' I looked away, hating that I felt so awkward looking at my own husband's bare skin, mentally counting the weeks since we'd shared a bed together. 'Will you be home for dinner?' Even to my own ears, I was sounding increasingly like an old-fashioned housewife. I cringed as Jordan flashed me a comic sideways glance.

'No need to set out my pipe and slippers,' he said, waggling his eyebrows.

'That's not what I meant,' I snipped, feeling embarrassed. 'I just thought you might like to have dinner with your *family*. You've hardly seen Marley this week.' Determined to stop acting so suspicious, I bit back the question: *Have you?*

Jordan frowned. 'I didn't want to crowd her. I thought about what you said about Marley feeling anxious. I reckoned she needed a bit of space.'

'Right, because that's what we do when someone's having a tough time, isn't it?' Disappointment made me crabby. 'We leave them to struggle by themselves.'

'Is that Marley you're talking about, or yourself?' he said, one eyebrow quirking.

'Oh, *you* figure it out,' I snapped, spinning around and stomping back to the kitchen.

By the time Jordan had come downstairs after his shower, I'd conquered a week's housework in under an hour. Anger had spurred me on, and as I'd cleaned and tidied the cottage, I reminded myself that I wasn't a nagging housewife: I was a loving wife and mother trying to do the best for my family, whereas Jordan seemed concerned only with pleasing himself.

'Catch ya later, little man,' he said, wandering into the kitchen and bending to pick up BB, kissing him gently before settling him back in the carry-cot. 'Look after Mummy for me.' Unhooking his backpack off the peg by the back door, he leaned over to plant a quick kiss on my cheek. 'I'll text you when I'm done, OK? Have a good day. Treat yourself, yeah?'

'Sure,' I muttered. 'I might even go wild and clean the bathroom.'

Cross that he was leaving, I turned away and continued scrubbing the sink. I felt Jordan hesitate, but when I glanced at him out of the corner of my eye, he was looking past me to the kitchen dresser. I wondered if he was about to look inside the worry box. I hadn't checked it yet that morning, nor had I shown Jordan the note you'd left in it yesterday.

I didn't want to talk to him about Amy, or whether she did or didn't want a baby. I didn't want to hear him joke about her – or, worse, defend her again. I didn't want to think about the possibility that she was joining him at the Yacht Club, fifty metres from her flat . . .

'You haven't tidied away my log book, have you?' Jordan said with a slight huff of impatience as he stepped across to the dresser, yanking open a drawer and rifling through it.

'No. I haven't.'

'Damn. I must have left it in the car. We should get it back this weekend, by the way. Maybe we could take it out for a spin along the coast tomorrow afternoon. We could visit Bawdsey Cliff. Let Marley go fossil hunting.'

'Maybe,' I agreed shortly, not ready to accept any sort of olive branch. 'It can be a bit dangerous there, though. The cliffs are unstable. There are warnings to stay away.'

'I'd catch you if you fell,' Jordan quipped absently. 'But

whatever. I'll be off, then.' He frowned as he glanced around the kitchen one more time, then pulled on his leather jacket and headed for the back door, reaching for his phone in his jeans pocket. 'Are you there yet?' I heard him say as the door closed behind him.

'Wait!' I called after him, catching sight of a familiar leather-bound notebook under a pile of paperwork on the dresser. But the roar of his motorbike confirmed he'd already left.

Wiping my hands on my jeans, I picked up the log book, tracing the gold embossing on the cover with one finger. '*Liberty*,' I read aloud, pondering again the significance of the name Jordan had chosen, this time unable to stop myself wondering who he'd been calling . . . who he was meeting.

Chapter 37

The house felt curiously quiet and empty after Jordan had left, and I sat down at the kitchen table, flicking through his log book, my eyes skimming lists of details about repairs and upgrades. Jordan loved all that stuff; I should try to take more interest in it, I decided. Maybe he was right, and I should brave my fears and go out on the boat with him.

Teasing out a sheet tucked between the end pages, I opened it to discover a coastal map, with a series of co-ordinates scribbled on one corner in Jordan's scruffy handwriting. 'Hmm, looks like someone's planning a trip.' I traced a finger over a long line from Thorpeness to Brighton. 'A big one,' I mused anxiously. 'Oh, you idiot, Holly. This was his journey *to* Suffolk! June twenty-twelve.'

Immediately, I regretted having been so sharp with Jordan. The map was like a snapshot of our journey towards each other, and I was touched that he'd kept this little memento of our meeting. Reaching for my phone, I decided to call and tell him so – and apologise for being snippy. 'Jordan?' I smiled as the call connected. 'It's me. I—'

'*The person you have called is unavailable right now. Please leave a—*'

I didn't hear the rest of the message; a piercing scream from upstairs drowned it out.

'Mummy? MUMMY!'

'Marley?' Disconnecting the call, I threw my phone and the log book onto the kitchen table, then sprinted through the house. 'What is it? What's happened?' I bowled breathlessly into your bedroom, my eyes scanning the small room for signs of a catastrophe.

'She pushed me!'

'What? Who did?' I looked around frantically again, then began to calm down as I saw you rub your eyes and yawn sleepily. 'It was just a dream, love,' I soothed, sitting down next to you and pulling you onto my lap.

'She hates me.' Pressing against me, you sobbed until your voice was hoarse.

'Oh, sweetheart, who does? Do you mean Leah?' I held you tightly, absorbing your trembles. 'Was she the one who scratched you?'

You huddled closer against my side, gripping my hand with both of yours.

'You know, Leah's going through a really tough time right now. But she's still your friend, Marley. Did you have a bad dream about her?'

You shook your head, clinging on to me even tighter.

'Or . . . Aunty Amy?' I suggested tentatively, and as you buried your face into my jumper, I knew I'd guessed right. 'Oh, Marley. I know she told you and Leah some silly stories. But I explained about the doll, didn't I? It was very old. Someone lost it a long time ago. A little girl just like you. But she wasn't a *naughty* girl. She was called Jane, and she was Mummy's best friend,' I said huskily.

You looked up at that, eyes wide in your pink face. 'Did she die?'

'I'm afraid she did. But no one hurt her. It was an accident. And Jane wasn't buried at the allotment. She's in heaven now.'

'With Grandma?'

'I reckon so, don't you?'

'If *you* die, Mummy, will you go to heaven too?' Your eyes filled with tears, and I felt mine fill up too as you added croakily: 'Will Grandma Olivia look after you?'

'Oh, sweetheart.' The thought of seeing my mum again hurt so much; the thought of leaving you hurt more. 'I'm going nowhere. You can't get rid of me that easily.'

'Get rid of you?' Your body went rigid.

'I don't literally mean . . .' I frowned, puzzled by your reaction. 'It's just an expression, Marley. Like, when you don't want or need something anymore, and it's just sitting there, in the way. Or if it's broken and no longer works.'

You thought for a moment. 'Like Grandma?'

'What? No, darling. My mum was poorly, but she—'

'Or my old bike?' you added, eyes widening. 'Daddy said he has to get rid of it.'

'Yes, that's more like it. It's getting old and rusty, isn't it? You need a new one.'

'I like the old one. Can't I keep both?'

'I'm not sure we have room. I know it's sad when we have to say goodbye to things. But sometimes it's for the best. New stuff can be fun too, can't it?' I looked around your bedroom, noticing that some of the toys I'd bought for your birthday had finally found their way out of the cupboard and onto your shelf. 'Change can be tricky, hey?' I said softly.

You nodded. 'I don't want a new mummy.'

'Oh, silly bean. Like I said, you're stuck with me. So no more worrying about things that aren't going to happen, OK?' *Me too*, I lectured myself. 'In fact, I have a secret plan.'

'A secret?' Your head jolted up.

'A good one,' I added, sighing at how jumpy you were. 'We'll start by getting you up and dressed. Then breakfast. Waffles?' I grinned. 'After that we'll pop BB in his buggy. Then . . . wait for it,' I teased, doing my best to build anticipation. 'We're going shopping!'

'Just us?'

'Absolutely. You can look round that nice art shop. BB needs a few things, too. You can help me choose. *And* we can treat ourselves to pizza. Is that a good secret plan, or what?'

You sagged against me. 'I hate secrets.'

'Quite right, too.' I kissed the top of your head. 'So, let's have no more of them.'

Yes, I was deaf as well as blind. I couldn't see what was staring me in the face; I couldn't hear the terror you were trying to communicate to me. And when we went downstairs, after I'd helped you get dressed in your favourite jeans and bumblebee jumper, I was still none the wiser, even after I saw you staring wide-eyed at the worry box. I actually laughed as I crossed the kitchen to open it; I smiled when I found your sixth note inside.

'What's this, darling? A drawing of a butterfly?' I beamed, happy that you'd drawn something so pretty. 'We should frame it. Ooh, that gives me an idea. How about you do a drawing for Aunty Amy's birthday? We could frame *that*. What do you reckon?'

You shrugged, chewing the end of your ponytail.

'I tell you what, how about you pop back upstairs and get out your new pen set? I'll finish sorting the washing and get BB dressed. Then we'll make those waffles, yes?'

Obediently, you turned and crossed the kitchen. I watched your shoulders hunch, baffled that you still seemed so anxious. 'What do you think she'd most like a picture of?' I asked, to encourage you.

You wrapped your arms tightly around yourself; your voice, when it came, sounded like it was being torn from your throat. 'Daddy's yacht.'

201

Chapter 38

'Oh! I wasn't expecting . . . I didn't think you were . . .'

I'd never seen Amy lost for words. Not once since she was seven years old. But as she stood stuttering on the doorstep five minutes later, our front door key in her hand, my vacillating doubts finally crystallised, and I knew without any shadow of doubt that something was going on between her and Jordan – and that, somehow, you had discovered it.

I glanced up the stairs to where you were busy drawing a picture for *Aunty Amy's birthday*. Serve her right if it was a big, ugly, frowny face, I thought angrily.

'You didn't think I was home,' I said, finishing Amy's pathetic excuse for her. I cradled BB with one arm, holding the door firmly ajar with my other hand.

'I thought you were going shopping. I, um, I bumped into Jordan at the gas station. He was filling up his bike. I was . . .'

'You were . . .?' I prompted. I didn't rescue her this time; I wanted to see her squirm.

'I was on my way back to the village. I stopped off to pick up some chocolates. I've been driving. Pretty much all night, actually.'

'Driving. All night.' I rolled my eyes at Amy's typical

over-dramatics. 'Running away from something? A guilty conscience, perhaps?'

'Yes. You're right. I *am* guilty. As hell. I'm sorry I was going to use your spare keys. Here, take them.' She handed over the fob I had given her when we first moved in to the cottage. 'You might as well take these, too,' she added, shoving a brown paper bag at me. 'I, uh, I'll leave you to it. You've obviously got your hands full.' She nodded at BB.

Aunty Amy is getting a baby. That was what you'd written in your last note. Well, she might not 'do babies', but maybe my son came as part of a package deal, I thought bitterly: Jordan and his baby boy. You were older, more complicated; you might hold them back while they sailed off into the sunset. On my husband's boat. *Liberty*.

I stared at Amy's beautiful face, my head filling with all the resentment I had bottled up over the years. *She stole my parents.* She came into our family and took it over. Now she was trying to steal my husband, break up *my* family. Or maybe Jordan wanted to go, I thought sadly. Well, if so, the pair of them could just leave – hold hands as they chased their own rainbow, pursued their own dream. But I would never let them take my babies . . .

About to slam the door shut, I glanced down at the package in my hand and realised what Amy had handed to me. 'Oh. Chocolates.' I frowned, looking closer at her flushed face and smudged make-up. She had obviously been crying, and her black jeans were creased, her red sweatshirt crumpled beneath her leather jacket. 'So you weren't . . .'

'Lying,' she finished for me. 'Correct. Although I get why you might have doubted that. I know I haven't always . . . I realise I'm sometimes a little . . . creative with the truth.'

'Huh,' I scoffed, glancing upstairs again, wondering if you were listening to this, if it would help you to hear Amy admit that she was a liar and a fantasist.

'Stories are easier to live with, that's all,' she said quietly. 'Give me a lie any day. Just make it a good one. I'll happily take that over reality, thank you very much.'

I took that as a confession, but I stopped myself grilling her about why she'd thought it was OK to scare a classroom of seven-year-olds. I had other, more pressing questions, such as: *What the hell was going on between her and my husband?*

'You can't mean that,' I said warily, suspecting I was being played, as usual. Only this time we were adults; Amy could hardly run off yelling, *Got you!* But the stakes were even higher now: childhood humiliation was nothing compared to the survival of my marriage, the security of my children.

'Oh, but I do. Why tell someone the truth if it's going to destroy their entire world?'

I gave her a sharp look, even more convinced that she was working up to another strategic confession. About Jordan. Only, Amy being Amy, she had to twist things to make out that she was a hero – that she'd been doing me a favour by keeping quiet. 'Well, whatever,' I said tartly. 'I think it's time we had a little honesty between us, don't you?'

'Huh. Honesty. Never a strong point in our family, hey? Adam and Olivia constantly danced around it. Can you blame me if I grew up thinking it was OK to do the same?'

'Depends on why you're being dishonest. It's not a sin to tell a few little white lies. Parents want to protect their children.' Although the air of secrecy at Sea View had always driven me crazy, instinctively I protected my mum and dad.

'I wouldn't know about that. But it's nice to see you've inherited your dad's moral consciousness. You'll be hanging Bible quotes on your walls next.'

'If you've come here just to insult me . . .' I started to close the door.

'No. I haven't. Sorry,' Amy apologised swiftly. 'It's just . . . the whole parent thing. It's a sore point with me, I guess.' She sighed, rubbing a hand over her face, seemingly uncaring that she had wiped away the rest of her make-up.

Instantly, I felt contrite. 'Your mum and dad . . . Luke and Isabella . . .'

'Oh, I wasn't talking about *them*. I meant, I don't know what it is to be a mother.' Her expression turned surprisingly wistful as she looked at BB.

I held him closer, my heart pounding as I pictured Amy taking my baby – and Jordan letting her. 'I didn't think you liked children. You made that crystal clear over dinner the other night,' I said, hating the vulnerability I could hear in my own voice.

'Yeah. Sorry about that. I was on one that evening. I'd just handed in my notice, you see. That's why I was late. Got stuck having a massive showdown with the head.'

'But you said . . .' I distinctly remembered her saying she was *planning* to resign.

'I didn't want to spoil the evening, OK? I hadn't seen you in ages. I couldn't just turn up and dump that news on you. I was trying to be *cheerful*.' She shrugged. 'Whatever. My head was a mess. It has been for weeks. I realise I haven't been quite . . . myself.'

'I had noticed,' I admitted, recalling how Amy had been avoiding me lately – and that her elusiveness had coincided with Jordan spending more time on his boat. No doubt that explained why he hadn't picked up his phone earlier: because he was with Amy . . .

'To tell you the truth, I've crashed and burned. That's why I've ended up on your doorstep.' She shrugged. 'Nowhere else to go.'

I shook my head. 'That's not true. You have loads of friends, and I'm sure my dad—'

'*No*,' she said sharply, startling BB. 'Sorry. I didn't mean to scare you, little man.' She reached out to stroke his head. 'Evil Aunty Amy. I always fuck everything up. I've got so good at acting tough, everyone believes it, don't they? Even me,' she mumbled.

'We all make mistakes,' I conceded. 'Acknowledging them is a start.'

'Maybe. Look, I'm sorry,' she apologised yet again, shoving her hands into her jacket pockets. 'This really isn't your problem. I shouldn't have come here. I'll leave you to—'

'Wait! Please.' Awkwardly, I tucked the chocolates under my arm, then reached out to grab Amy's hand, my head spinning with anger mixed with curiosity – and scepticism.

Was she playing me for a fool again? Did she think I could be pacified by a box of chocolates while she waltzed off with my husband? Or was her distress real? I couldn't tell. I simply had no idea if her remorse was genuine, or yet another attention-seeking act.

'Jordan mentioned you've been worrying about Marley,' she said, pulling away. 'You're a good mum, Holly. You should concentrate on your family. Forget about me.'

'Family is as family does, hey?' I said, stealing Jordan's line with a sigh as I decided to give both him and Amy the benefit of the doubt. *For now.* 'Look, at least come in and have a coffee, OK? You look like you could use it,' I added, feeling the tiniest flicker of satisfaction that, this time, *perfect Amy* was the one who looked like hell.

Chapter 39

'So, what's been going on?' I said ten minutes later, after settling BB in his carry-cot and making a pot of coffee. I didn't bother offering Amy any breakfast; she never ate it.

'Do you mind?' She peeled the cellophane wrapping off the chocolates I had left on the kitchen table, lifting the lid of the box and taking two at random. 'Sorry, I'm starving.'

I stared at her in astonishment. 'I can make you some—'

'These are fine.' She shoved them into her mouth. 'Sugar fix. Exactly what I need.'

I pulled out a chair and sat down opposite her, raising my eyebrows. 'OK, who are you and what have you done with my friend?'

'Friend.' Amy wrinkled her nose. 'Yeah, I haven't exactly been one of those.'

'We all have bad patches. But like I said, it helps if we understand the reason for them,' I prompted leadingly.

'I've had a shitty few weeks,' she admitted vaguely, pinching the bridge of her nose.

'It'll be over soon, though, yes?' I deliberately assumed she was talking about work, to flush out whether she meant something more personal. 'How long is your notice period?'

'Actually, I've already left. I came to an arrangement with the head.'

'What? You haven't been fired, have you?' Immediately I thought about Leah's mum, wondering if Rachel had made a complaint about the spooky stories Amy had been telling. Then I pictured the nasty scratch on your cheek. It was beginning to heal, but you still hadn't told me who inflicted it. Could it have been *Amy*, and the head teacher had found out?

'No, I wasn't fired. I resigned.' She rolled her eyes. 'Although the head didn't exactly try to make me stay.'

'What about your flat?' Remembering her heated reaction when I'd suggested she could have turned to my dad, I didn't dare ask if she expected him to cover her mortgage. But I could imagine Miss Shaw's knowing looks when she found out that Amy had left her job, as she inevitably would.

'I'm renting it out. To another teacher, actually. It's in pristine condition. Has all the mod cons. Great location, too. Not far from the beach. Close to the school.'

And the Yacht Club, I couldn't help thinking, picturing Jordan's boat moored close to Amy's apartment – and the map I'd found hidden in his log book . . . 'So, um, are you going away?' *Is my husband going with you?*

'Paris. I leave tomorrow night.'

'Tomorrow? Wow.' She didn't need to spell out her connection to that city, and for a moment my heart ached for her. I poured coffee for us both, almost spilling it as I watched Amy reach for another chocolate; things must be really bad if she was comfort eating.

'There's just something I wanted to tell . . .' She bit her lip, then drew in a deep breath. 'To *give* you,' she corrected herself. 'Before I go. In case I, um, don't come back.'

I surveyed the remaining chocolates, pulling a wry smile. 'You've eaten most of them. What were they, anyway? Early birthday present? Guilt offering?' I suggested lightly.

Amy blushed as she reached into her jacket pocket. 'I didn't mean the chocolates.'

'Fuck.' Shock surged through me as I stared at the jewelled butterfly brooch she placed carefully on the table between us. 'Where did you . . . when . . . how long have you had this?' I glanced towards the dresser, suddenly realising that the drawing in your last note was an uncannily accurate copy of the brooch in front of me. 'Have you shown it to *Marley*?'

'What?' She frowned. 'No. Of course not.'

'But she must have seen it. She drew a picture of it. Look.' I stood up, about to retrieve your note to show Amy, but she grabbed my hand to stop me.

'Please, Holl. Just give me a minute.' She sighed. 'This is really hard for me.'

'Hard for *you*?' I glared at her, my mind filling with words I wanted to fling at her. *Gold-digger. Husband thief. Cuckoo.* Yes, that was what she was: a cuckoo who made herself at home in other people's nests, then took everything for herself.

'You're right. I'm a horrible person.' She sat back, her eyes filling with tears. 'I saw this brooch on your mum's bedside table that night. After her party. And I took it.'

'You mean, her last *ever* party. On the night she died,' I said fiercely.

'I'm so sorry, Holl. I did think about telling you. So many times. I was even going to tell you at dinner the other night. I sent you a text, but then I couldn't bring myself to—'

'What stopped you?' My sharp tone woke BB, and I wondered if you were listening at the door, just as I used to as a child. I stood up, crossing the kitchen to check, then picked up BB. 'It's OK,' I soothed, pacing the floor, trying to calm myself as much as him.

'Nothing *stopped* me. Well, maybe guilt that I stole it. I'm giving it back now, though, aren't I?' Amy said with a touch of her usual defiance. 'I thought you should have it. I just didn't think there was any rush. I guess I never thought it would be that big a deal.'

'Not a big . . .?' I stared at her incredulously, struggling to believe that even she could be so insensitive.

She frowned, clearly puzzled by my anger. 'They're not real diamonds, you know?'

'How *dare* you?' I had to put BB back in his carry-cot, I was shaking so much. 'I don't give a toss if that brooch is made of tin and glass. Its value to me has absolutely nothing to do with what it's made of. It belonged to—'

'Your mum. Olivia. Yes, I know,' Amy said in a low voice. Then her head dipped, her shoulders hunching. 'But it was my dad . . . it was Luke Jackson who gave it to her.'

Chapter 40

'Your dad.' I stared at Amy, but all I could see was my mum's flushed cheeks as she checked her appearance in our living-room mirror the first time I saw her wear that brooch. I remembered her restless, distracted behaviour that I later attributed to her secretly declining health; I remembered her clutching the brooch in her hand the very last time I saw her . . .

Mum told me then that she'd married Dad even though she could have 'had her pick'. As I looked down at the brooch, it hit me like a tonne of bricks that her choice must have been between just two men: my dad . . . and Amy's.

'He was in love with your mum,' she said quietly.

'How do you *know* that? Did my mum *tell* you?' Sorrow bubbled up inside me as I was forced to accept that Amy had been privy to yet another secret that had been kept from me – this one so intimate, so significant, that it hurt more than any other.

That night – the last of my mum's life – she'd given her blessing to my relationship with Jordan. She gave me her own wedding veil, too; she asked if I was happy. I opened my heart to her about having found the love of my life, and yet, as ever, she'd kept her own feelings from me. They were a closed book I had never been invited to read.

'No, your mum didn't tell me, Holly. I was the last person she wanted to talk to about *anything*. I was the black sheep, wasn't I? The fly in the ointment. The thorn in her precious roses, if you like,' Amy said sarcastically, her mouth twisting.

'Amy, no. Don't start all that *Olivia hated the sight of me* crap again. Please.'

'Oh, I know you think your parents were saints. Believe it or not, I've never wanted to be the one to burst that bubble.' Amy leaned across the table to press my hand. Her skin felt ice cold; her usually vivid, indigo eyes were dull and shadowed. 'I guess that's why I've kept this to myself. You idolised your mum. What kind of bitch would I be to mess with that?'

'You mean, you lied to me for my own good.' I yanked my hand away, huffing. Same old Amy. Hurting someone then making out she was helping them.

'I didn't lie. I just didn't *tell* you. You don't have to be someone's parent to feel protective of them, you know?'

'Right,' I gritted out, cross that, as usual, she was turning my words back on me.

'I'm actually surprised you never guessed. I *half* did. All that prickly tension between your mum and dad any time someone mentioned the great Luke Jackson.'

I cast my mind back to the day Amy arrived at Sea View – Mum so flustered; Dad trying ridiculously hard to be jolly. 'I know how hard it is to resist temptation,' my mum once said to me. Was that what she'd been referring to? An affair she was trying to end? I recalled, too, Maria's story about something upsetting Mum at the farm that late-August bank holiday. Could she have been meeting Luke in secret?

'I thought Dad looked up to his old friend,' I said faintly. 'Or envied him.'

'Covering up,' Amy said emphatically. 'Over-egging his admiration to pretend he was cool with another guy fancying his wife. Isn't that what married couples do?'

I gave her a hard stare. 'All marriages have rough patches. Good ones can survive a bit of jealousy. Or flirtation,' I added, wanting her to know I hadn't given up on Jordan.

Amy returned my stare with an equally direct look. 'What about love? What if one of you is actually in love with someone else?'

Heat flooded through me; I couldn't believe how brazen she was. I felt like she was *toying* with me, using this trumped-up story about my parents to make insinuations about *my* marriage, to justify her breaking it up. 'Are you saying my mum was in love with your dad?'

'More fool her if she was. The man's a selfish jerk. Same as every guy I've ever met.'

'I know how much it hurt that your dad abandoned you,' I said, more gently. 'Your mum did too, though,' I pointed out. 'Luke never came back, but neither did Isabella.'

'I know.' Amy covered her face with both hands. 'But she . . . my mum . . .'

'How do you know what your dad felt, anyway?' I jumped in, staring at her curiously, wondering how all this had come to light.

'I'm not making things up this time, Holl.' Amy gave me a wry, watery smile. 'Here. Look at this.' She reached into her pocket and took out a creased, folded piece of paper. 'Dumb idiot only went and wrote it down. I mean, what's the first rule of having an affair?'

I raised my eyebrows. 'I don't know, Amy. You tell me.'

'No texts. No phone calls. No love letters.'

'Is that what this . . .' I stared at the blue, crumpled paper in Amy's hand.

'Yep. It's all in that letter. Your mum kept it in her diary. And I read it.'

My legs felt shaky as I returned downstairs a few minutes later, after checking you were OK playing in your bedroom. You hadn't made a start on drawing any pictures, and I was dying to ask you if and when you'd seen my mum's brooch. But my head was buzzing with thoughts of her secret diary . . . and an equally secret love letter from Amy's dad.

I left you organising your teddies and walked slowly back to the kitchen, delaying the moment when I would have to open and read the letter. Suddenly, I understood what Amy had meant by her curiously barbed comment that living with a lie was easier than confronting the truth. If I found out that my mum once had an affair – with anyone, let alone her husband's best friend – it would change everything I had ever believed about my parents . . .

'Here. I made us fresh coffee,' Amy said as I sat down at the kitchen table in a daze.

'Thanks. Was BB OK? Maybe I should give him a quick feed and—'

'Holly, quit stalling. Read it. Aloud,' Amy urged, handing me the letter.

'My dear, sweet Olivia. Words are never enough, so I hope this gift will say what I cannot express. A butterfly, as exquisite as you are, and equally elusive. If I must let you fly free, my darling butterfly, please allow me the small comfort of knowing this trinket may at least, on occasion, rest close to your heart – as I wish I could for all the days to come.

'I have no desire to hurt Isabella. My feelings for her, my sense of duty to my daughter, are bound up with the same respect and honour I know you have for Adam, my best and oldest friend. If only—'

'If only *what*?' I said despairingly. 'And there's no date.' I turned the torn scrap of paper over and over, frustrated that I couldn't read what else Luke Jackson had written to my mum – that I had no idea whether he had professed his love to her before or after

214

she'd married my dad. 'When did he write it? When did this . . . this *thing* between them even happen?'

Amy shrugged. 'Olivia took her diary off me. Actually, she threw it across the room. God knows what happened to it after that. I sat with her for an hour or so more. She was barely conscious for most of it, to be honest. Seeing me with that letter . . . she got pretty agitated, I'm afraid. I guess it wore her out. She didn't want me there at all, but you—'

'Had gone home,' I whispered, feeling guilt slice through me as I pictured my mum distressed and in pain, both physical and emotional. 'You didn't *ask* her about the letter, then? She didn't explain it?' I remembered Mum's promise to 'tell me everything' the next day. And then she died. 'I wish you'd told me, Amy.'

'Seriously?' Her eyebrows arched. 'And leave you with that picture in your head?'

'What picture?'

'The one you're imagining right now,' she said astutely. 'Your mum tormented. At the mercy of a woman she couldn't stand. The daughter of the man who loved then left her.'

215

Chapter 41

Amy's words seemed to hang in the air, resonating back through time, shattering the images I had carried in my heart: of my parents, quietly devoted to each other; of my mum's last moments, peaceful and pain-free, as my dad had repeatedly assured me. But he hadn't been there, either; Amy was the only one who knew the truth of what had gone on that night.

We both sat in silence for a few minutes. 'Maybe it was all in your dad's head,' I said at last. 'His letter is pretty flowery. Like he was in love with love. Or in the grip of a one-sided, unrequited infatuation. Maybe nothing happened between them at all, and my mum—'

'She kept the brooch, didn't she?' Amy's lips pursed. 'And the letter.'

I shook my head. 'Mum kept *everything*.' I thought of the basket under her desk, stuffed with scraps of material saved in case they 'came in handy'. 'Unless you read something in her diary that showed—'

'Sorry,' Amy said quickly. 'She grabbed it before I'd read much. Olivia didn't refer to this letter at all that night. She didn't say *anything* else. It was like she'd just . . . given up.'

Briefly, I closed my eyes, feeling unbearable sadness wash

through me. 'Dr Henry said he thought Mum had a stroke that evening. Is that what it looked like to you? You said she was barely conscious. Was she . . .' I tailed off, my chest feeling tight.

'Alive when I left her?' Amy hugged herself, for a second reminding me of you. 'I wish I could tell you. But it was all a bit surreal. I wasn't thinking straight. I—'

'Right, but you had the wherewithal to keep hold of *that*.' In anguish, I cut her off, nodding at the letter. *I should have been the one with her*, I thought for the thousandth time. Or my dad. I frowned as a thought occurred to me. 'I expect Dad took the diary.'

'Maybe. Odd he's never told you about it, though. Unless he destroyed it. To protect Olivia's reputation, as it were. He should have burned the letter, too. Although, I guess it's possible he didn't know about it. I didn't even realise I still had it until the next day.'

'Which you didn't tell me, either,' I reminded her.

'I'm sorry,' she said again. 'It's just that I had nothing of my dad, you know? He never sent *me* anything. The brooch, this letter . . . they felt like a connection to him. I guess I felt I had a right to take them. To keep these little pieces of him just for me.'

'Right. I suppose I can understand that,' I admitted slowly, picking up the letter again. 'I still can't believe it, though. My mum – and your dad.'

'You know, Holly . . .' Amy leaned forward, staring intently at me. 'Our parents were all at uni together. They were young. Away from home. You know what college is like. If the four of them knocked around a bit before getting married, is it that surprising?'

'Hmm.' I remembered Mum talking about Luke Jackson and my dad breaking hearts. Maybe hers had been one of them, after all, but then she married my dad and moved on. 'I guess this could all have happened way before they got married. It doesn't necessarily mean anyone was actually *unfaithful*.'

'No, it doesn't.' Amy frowned. 'Although that's not quite what I was getting at.'

'What, then?'

'Just . . .' She hesitated, frowning. 'Oh, it doesn't matter. It's all in the past, anyway. We've both got more important things to worry about. You've got the brooch back. Whatever happened between our parents is history. We should just forget about it.'

I stared incredulously at her; there was no way I could do that. 'If only we had more idea about the *timing*.' I glanced at the letter again, desperate to find a hidden clue.

Amy sighed. 'Well, if it helps, I found that tucked into February in your mum's diary. I can't remember the year, though. And it could have been put there at random, anyway.'

'Or the brooch might have been a Valentine's Day gift,' I mused, tracing the lavish curls of Luke Jackson's handwriting, looping across the thick, luxurious blue paper.

'Lucky Olivia,' Amy huffed.

'I know your dad never sent you anything,' I said, understanding her bitterness. 'But he clearly thought about you. "My daughter", he wrote. At least he *mentioned* you.'

'His duty towards me, you mean.'

'Perhaps he was writing about the *idea* of you. Like how I called BB "baby number two" for a while. Young babies do tend to feel like an extension of yourself.'

'I'll take your word for it,' Amy said flatly.

'Which again suggests your dad wrote this years ago.' I sat up straighter, convinced I was right. 'Maybe after Isabella fell pregnant with you. February. Hmm, the timing fits.'

'You mean, he did the noble thing. Gave up the love of his life and married my mum.' Amy huffed. 'No wonder he got shot of me as soon as he had the chance. I fucked his life up good and proper. Then I fucked up your parents' lives, too.'

'*No*, Amy.' It was my turn to grab her hand. 'Adults make their own decisions.' I swallowed hard, suddenly wondering if Jordan was out on his boat trying to make one at that very moment. 'Children can't be blamed for what their parents do. Or don't do,' I added meaningfully, thinking of the long years without any word from either Amy's dad *or* mum.

Amy took the letter from me, stroking its torn edge. 'Looks like *someone* wanted to destroy it. Huh. Maybe your dad found it after all. And ripped it up in a fit of jealous rage.'

'What, the man who wrote a thesis on conveyancing law?' I rolled my eyes. 'If you cut him open, you'll find a calculator inside.' Instantly, I recalled Jordan joking that Amy had a Swarovski crystal in place of her heart, and I couldn't help wondering if she'd found out about my mum's fortune before, or after, she spent that final evening alone with her . . .

Horrified at the direction of my thoughts, I told myself not to be so stupid. I was fully aware how much Amy resented my inheritance, but while she might have once joked about killing Jane, I knew that was pure fantasy. Amy was ambitious, materialistic – and deceitful. I refused to believe she was a murderer.

'Yes, Adam's a stuffed shirt.' Amy's eyebrows arched. 'But you can't judge a book by its cover. Your dad's not a saint any more than your mum was,' she said cryptically.

'What do you mean? Dad stood by my mum, didn't he? If she *did* have an affair, I mean. He might come across as a bit stern. And pompous.' I thought of your reluctance to see him lately, guessing that was the reason. 'But he's a good man.'

'Sure. He married poor, lovelorn Olivia. With her beautiful house. Her secret fortune.'

'That's enough, Amy,' I said irritably, wishing she'd never shown me that damned letter. 'My parents loved each other. I know they did.'

'Although, we never know for sure what's going on in people's minds, do we?' Amy met and held my gaze for long moments, before adding quietly: 'And the truth has a weird way of coming out when you least expect it.'

'Maybe. Sometimes you have to give it a nudge, though.' I glanced at the worry box.

Amy turned to look at it, too. 'Has Marley posted anything interesting?'

'She's left a few notes. A picture of that brooch. A drawing of her birthday cake.'

'Her *birthday* cake?' Amy's pale cheeks flushed as red as her jumper.

'Yes. I've no idea why, though, so don't ask me.'

'Children are so intuitive, aren't they?' She stood up and paced to the window, staring out at the broad sweep of pale sky. It was a bright, crisp, clear sunny day, in contrast to the suddenly tense atmosphere in the kitchen. 'I think I always knew my parents lied to me. Yours too,' she added, turning to face me. 'Like you said, kids can't be held responsible for grown-ups' choices. That doesn't mean we have to accept them.'

'What do you mean?' My mind was working frantically, as ever trying to keep up with the twists and turns of Amy's.

She'd arrived at the cottage in distress, seeming almost like a different person. But as her mouth curled in a smile, I had a glimpse of the old Amy. The one who deliberately left Treacle's hutch open; who pushed Jane Price into the Meare; who made up stories to frighten you. And as she returned to sit next to me at the kitchen table, she frightened *me*.

'You know, between you and me,' she said softly, 'I don't think Marley enjoyed her birthday party at all. I know *I* didn't,' she admitted bluntly. 'But parents hold all the power, don't they?' She leaned even closer, whispering: 'Only, sometimes, we have to take it back.'

Chapter 42

Your birthday fell on the day of the regatta this year, and I remember being glad that the carnival atmosphere in the village would do some of the work for us. I was feeling so exhausted – and guilty. BB's birth only a week before had been traumatic; the days since had passed in a blur. I wanted your seventh birthday to be fabulous. I was just in too much pain, my head fuzzy with medication, to think or do anything much.

Jordan was incredible. Worried about money being tight, he'd barely taken any time off work, yet he still found time to go out and buy all the presents from the wish list you and I put together. He also organised your party at the country club, making sure the upstairs room was decorated exactly as I wanted for you, with streamers and balloons, paper butterflies and bumblebees hanging from the rafters to create the atmosphere of a magical garden.

Somehow, he'd even managed to find time to decorate a float for the annual post-regatta competition, working on it before, after and even in between shifts. Yet despite all this time and effort, he barely quibbled when I expressed concern about you taking part in it.

'I just have a weird feeling about it,' I said, watching Jordan slice fruit for your birthday breakfast. 'I can't put my finger on why.' I continued pushing the rocking chair to and fro, even though BB was fast asleep in my arms. The motion soothed me; I was excited about your birthday, but I couldn't shake the feeling that something bad was going to happen.

'That'll be hormones. They're still raging, babe,' Jordan said, without turning around.

'Maybe. But the lake ... taking Marley out on the water ...' I stopped myself mentioning my fear of drowning; I knew it would sound like postnatal neurosis. Perhaps it was. I'd been plagued by nightmares, my sleep-deprived mind distorting my recurring dreams of Jane into images of you tumbling into the Meare, being dragged under the boats.

'It's fine. I get it.' Finally satisfied that he had everything ready before you woke up and came downstairs, Jordan wiped his hands and came to sit at the kitchen table, turning his chair to face me. 'We'll skip the regatta completely, if you like? I'll row Marley around the islands instead. She can enjoy the fun without getting caught up in the action. OK?'

'OK,' I agreed gratefully. 'Good idea. Thanks, Jordan.'

'No worries. Her party later is the main event, in any case. The regatta is just a bonus. Although it's pretty cool there will be fireworks afterwards.' He grinned.

'Like they're especially for her,' I said, smiling too as I remembered Mum saying the same thing to me on my birthday each year.

'Did you hear that, Marley?' Jordan said, as you bounced into the kitchen. 'Fireworks, just for you. My gorgeous birthday girl.' He stood up, throwing his arms wide, and as you ran into them he caught you up into a spin. 'How's my honey bee this morning?'

'It's my birthday!' you sang happily. *Happy birthday to me! Happy birthday to me!'*

'Happy birthday, darling.' I stood up from the rocking chair, shifting BB to my other arm so I could give you a hug. My muscles

222

protested at every movement, pain clamping deep inside, but I hung on to my smile. 'Now, let me think, how old are you? Six? No, eight?'

'Seven! I'm seven, Mummy! One, two, three, four, five, six, SEVEN!' you yelled, jumping up and down as Jordan set you back on the floor.

'Wow. You're a big girl now.' I stroked your sleep-messy hair, winding a curl around my finger. 'I'm so proud of you, sweetheart.' I bent to give you another kiss to hide sudden tearfulness. Jordan had been right, I thought: my hormones were all over the place.

'And look – the sun's come out especially!' He crossed the kitchen to point triumphantly at the bright-blue, cloudless sky. 'Perhaps we should go for a walk before—'

'Presents *first*, Daddy!' you interrupted, hands on hips, eyes glittering.

'Presents?' Jordan pretended to look puzzled. 'What presents?'

'*Those*, Daddy!' Your arm shot out towards the table, laden with colourful packages.

'Oh, wow. Are those all for *you*?'

'Yes! Yes, yes, yes!' you squealed, your face turning pink as you skipped happily around the table. After three circuits, you finally stopped dancing and started examining your presents, giving each a little shake. 'I think I might know what this is,' you declared wisely, picking up one of the biggest ones. 'It's a *jigsaw*!'

'Hmm, you might be right, smarty pants.' Jordan took the box from you and rattled it. 'Or maybe it's a few pebbles from the beach,' he teased. 'Yeah, that must be it.' He shook the box again. 'Just a big old box of sand and stones.'

'*No*, Daddy,' you corrected patiently. 'It's a jigsaw. Or Lego?' Your soft eyebrows puckered in a frown as you pondered the options.

'Go on, then, sweetheart. Open it and find out,' I encouraged, chuckling.

You looked so like your daddy when you were excited,

I thought. In fact, it was hard to tell which of you was *more* excited. Usually so laid-back, Jordan seemed to be buzzing, which surprised me after the tiny amount of sleep we'd both had.

The night before your birthday was the last time Jordan and I slept in the same bed. Although, in truth, we'd barely slept at all. I constantly checked the rise and fall of BB's little chest, to reassure myself he was all right. Jordan had tossed and turned all night. 'Anyone would think it was *your* birthday tomorrow,' I'd teased him at one point.

'Sorry, hon,' he'd replied, wrapping me in his strong arms and pulling me close. 'I guess I'm a tad keyed up. Tomorrow's a big day. I don't want anything to go wrong.'

'You mean with the party?'

'What? Oh. Yeah. I want everything to be perfect. I want Marley to have a day she'll never forget. Me too. Our little girl is turning seven. I want to remember it for ever.'

I pressed my cheek against his warm skin, loving how much he cared about making you happy. 'You make it sound like you're going off to war. Or it's the last birthday Marley will ever have. She's not going to vanish at midnight, you know? She's not Cinderella.'

'No. But she's my little princess,' he said hoarsely. 'I want her to know that.'

I must have finally nodded off after that, because when I woke up, the bed was empty. Checking my watch, I realised it was still early – a little after five. Hoping for a bit more rest, I snuggled down under the duvet, only for BB to wake up crying for a feed.

'OK, Benji Boy. You win. Mummy's getting up,' I said, yawning as I pulled on my dressing gown. Not wanting to disturb you so early, I crept downstairs and sat nursing BB on the rocking chair in the kitchen, watching Jordan busy himself making batter for waffles. He barely spoke as he whisked, humming under his breath, only looking up when you came downstairs an hour later and bounced into the kitchen . . .

I replayed all this in my mind as I watched you shake your presents, reminding myself to tell Jordan later how much I appreciated all the effort he had gone to.

My little family.

I was so lucky to have you all, and I wished I could hold on to that moment for ever. I smiled at Jordan, remembering his quiet words before dawn, guessing he felt the same.

'See, I told you! It's a jigsaw!' you announced ecstatically, tearing it open.

'Who's that from, love?' I asked, surreptitiously wiping away a rogue tear.

'Aunty Amy,' you said confidently, even though I hadn't seen you look at the label, and I knew a jigsaw hadn't been on my list. 'It's a bunny picture, see?' You held up the box. 'She told me she had one when she was little. I thought Treacle was *your* rabbit, Mummy?'

'She was. Let me see?' My hands shook as I took the box from you to have a closer look. 'But she didn't look like this,' I added, ridiculously relieved to see the rabbit in the picture on the box was black and white, not biscuit-coloured like Treacle.

I gave myself a mental shake, cross at the odd thoughts I kept having. First nightmares about Jane, now remembering Amy as a girl. I was being silly imagining that the rabbit jigsaw was a bad omen – or some kind of secret, toxic message. I took a breath, trying to refill my lungs with happiness.

'Cute bunny,' Jordan said, giving me a curious look as he jumped into the pause. 'No getting any ideas, though. A jigsaw is all very well, but we don't need the real thing, OK? Which is obviously what your mummy is thinking,' he said, to explain my silence.

I smiled gratefully at him. 'Yes, you got me. I was waiting for you to ask if we can get one, love.' I gave you a hug. 'I know you'd love a pet, Marley. Maybe when your baby brother's a bit older, OK? It was, um, kind of Amy, though. I thought she was getting you—'

'Red shoes! *Look*, Mummy!' Your face lit up as you opened the next package, and you danced around the kitchen in excitement, squealing and twirling.

They came in a jute bag rather than a white box, and they were patent leather rather than sparkly. But the Mary Jane shoes were definitely red – and Amy was definitely making some kind of point. I just had no idea what.

Chapter 43

'Two presents.' I forced myself to smile. 'How kind of her. You mustn't forget to say thank you to Aunty Amy later. She'll be at your party. Or you could—'

'I'll write her a note,' you cut in gleefully. 'With my new pen set! I love writing. I'll write thank-you notes for *everyone*.'

'Ah, that's a nice idea. Though I reckon it'll take you all day. Look at this lot!' I nodded at the table. 'And that might be the postman with more,' I added as the doorbell rang.

Handing BB to Jordan, I hurried through the house to the hall, glad of the chance to ponder what Amy was up to. Were her gifts nostalgic gestures, or something more spiteful? I knew I was feeling overemotional, and I didn't want to spoil the morning by jumping to the wrong conclusion, but Amy's presents had seriously rattled me.

'I see balloons, Mummy! I LOVE balloons!' you declared excitedly.

'Oh, sweetheart, you made me jump.' I hadn't realised you had followed me until I felt your hand tugging on my arm. 'But you're right,' I added, smiling as I opened the door to see an enormous bouquet of silver balloons, tethered with blue ribbons. 'Stevie, hi,' I said recognising one of the teenagers who helped Karen in the post office. 'What's all this?'

'Special delivery,' he said awkwardly, thrusting the balloons at me. 'Karen said sorry they're late,' he added gruffly, before sloping off, headphones already back in place.

'They're not late. They're perfectly punctual,' you lisped sweetly, arms outstretched.

'Actually, I think Stevie's right,' I said, reading the message on the card.

'But today's my birthday,' you insisted logically.

'Yes, but this is addressed to Master Benjamin Mayhew. See? But you just wait till you see how many balloons are at your party,' I added, picking up on your disappointment. Closing the front door, I turned to you with a smile. But you had already gone. 'Darn it.'

I had made a point of finally putting away all the 'New Baby' cards, and Jordan and I had gently explained that your party was to be a double celebration. At the time, you'd seemed excited; I wondered if that excitement was beginning to give way to jealousy.

'Oh, who's that now?' I sighed as the doorbell rang again. Eager to return to the kitchen to check you were OK, I pulled the door open impatiently.

'Have you got a minute?'

'Amy! Is something up?' I forgot all about her strange presents, more concerned that there had been a last-minute hitch with the party arrangements. 'I thought we weren't seeing you till later this afternoon. At the—'

'It won't take long. I just need a quick chat.'

Her eyes were covered by large, tortoiseshell-framed sunglasses, but she seemed jittery, flicking her hair and pulling at her short red sundress, as though self-conscious about how much of her tanned legs it revealed.

'Is there a problem at the country club?' I tightened the belt of my dressing gown, ready to rush out in my slippers and sort it out.

'At the . . .? Oh, yes. I mean, no. There's no problem. Shit.

Sorry.' Amy screwed up her nose. 'Of course, it's Marley's birthday. Never mind. I'll catch you later.'

'Amy?' I said quickly as she turned away. 'Are you OK? You're welcome to join us. Marley's opening her presents. She, um, loves the jigsaw. And the shoes. Why don't you—'

'No, it's fine. It'll keep.'

'Are you sure?' I said dubiously, struck by her jittery mood and the fact that she'd obviously forgotten it was your birthday. But she'd already hurried off, high heels clicking on the garden path. I watched her for a few moments, waiting to see if she would change her mind. She didn't. She climbed into her car and drove off, tyres spinning on the gravel lane.

'What was all *that* about?' Jordan asked, wandering into the hall with BB tucked against his shoulder.

'You tell me.'

'Probably nothing. Amy wouldn't be Amy if there wasn't some kind of drama.'

'Exactly.' I tried to smile, but I was gripped by a feeling that there had been more to her unexpected visit than that. If it was simply attention she was looking for, she could have waited until we were all gathered at your party – or even at the regatta beforehand. After all, Amy was no stranger to making a spectacle of herself at a village event.

A shiver ran through me as I recalled my dreams from the night before. I told myself there was no way Amy would pull any kind of stunt like that on your birthday. Even so, I was glad Jordan had offered to give the regatta itself a miss, and take you out alone afterwards.

It was the perfect plan: I knew you'd be safe with him, and you loved exploring the quirky islands and Neverland figures that turned the Meare into a living storybook. Only, as ever, Amy had a plan of her own.

The next time I saw her that day, I was standing on the wharf in front of the boathouse, holding BB. The lake was filled with a parade of colourful floats, and fireworks were beginning to pop and fizz overhead. I smiled as I watched you tilt your head back to gaze up at them, one hand resting trustingly on Jordan's arm.

He frowned, concentrating on steering the boat, setting a steady course away from the bustling regatta crowds. And Amy was sitting right next to him.

Chapter 44

'They'll be fine, love. Don't you worry.' Miss Shaw came to stand at my side, wrapping a bright-pink pashmina around her shoulders. 'Turned a bit chilly, hasn't it?'

'I suppose it's the mist.' Even though it was late afternoon, smoke from the fireworks mingled with a light fog to cool the summer air and make visibility poor.

'I hope Marley's got a jacket on. Wouldn't want her to catch cold before her party.'

'She's wearing her new birthday jumper.' I smiled, remembering your squeal of joy as you'd opened the soft yellow sweater with a bumblebee motif on the front. 'And red shoes,' I added, biting my lip. I could just about make out Amy edging her way along the seat towards you in the boat. I hugged BB closer, wishing we were all safely back at the cottage.

'Ah, that's nice. There she is. Marley, helloo, there!' Miss Shaw called out.

'I don't suppose . . . would you be OK holding Benji for a bit? Just while I wander over there to get a closer look?' I nodded in the direction of the boat, scudding away from us.

'Of course, dear. I don't blame you for wanting to keep an eye on her.' Miss Shaw gave me a knowing look, making it obvious that she wasn't talking about you.

'I just want to make sure Marley has fun,' I said deliberately. I knew my old teacher had mixed feelings about Amy, but I wanted to blot any doubts out of my mind. It had taken a lot for me to help you climb on board the boat, then stand watching Jordan push it out into the water. If it had been up to me, you would have watched the fireworks from dry land.

'Your chap will make sure of that.' Miss Shaw tutted approvingly. 'Now *there's* a man who knows how to have fun.'

I turned to look at her, wondering what she was hinting at, but she smiled, then laughed as Jordan pointed at the sky. 'He's still a big kid at heart,' I admitted. 'He loves fireworks. And parties. Anything loud, basically. He's been more excited about today than Marley. I love his enthusiasm,' I added, wondering if I told him that often enough.

'You two are chalk and cheese,' Miss Shaw said gently, pale-blue eyes glinting with reflected light from the boathouse. 'But opposites attract. Isn't that what they say?'

'It was certainly true of my parents.' I stared across the water at Amy, acknowledging that, deep down, I'd often wondered if she had more in common with Jordan than I did. They were both highly sociable and loved travelling. 'She hates the beach, though,' I muttered.

'Well, she wasn't born in the village, was she?' Miss Shaw said tartly, resting a hand on my arm. 'The sea is in your blood, Holly.'

'Yes. I reckon Amy has Prosecco running through her veins.' I no longer bothered to pretend we weren't talking about her. 'She's a city girl at heart. Always loved London more than here. Like my dad, I guess. Mum adored the village, as you know. Dad, not so much.'

'Such a shame Adam's feeling poorly,' Miss Shaw sympathised. 'I know he was never a big fan of the regatta, but he'll be upset to miss his granddaughter's party.'

'Dad finds these things hard without Mum.' I pulled a wry face. It was true he'd been battling a cold, but I knew my dad associated parties with my mum, as did I. Guessing the truth behind his absence, I hadn't pressed him when he'd sent his excuses.

'Olivia was the glue that held you all together, wasn't she, dear?'

'She certainly kept us all in check.' I bit my lip as I heard Amy laugh, and watched the dark swathe of her hair ripple around her shoulders. She seemed in a much better mood than earlier, I noticed, wondering what had changed. 'But so gently, none of us realised it.'

'She was a special lady.' Miss Shaw sniffed. 'Anyway, off you go. I'll take good care of this little one.' She lifted BB out of my arms, shooing me off with a watery smile.

'I won't be long,' I promised, kissing BB and hurrying as fast as I could along the wharf, picking my way between the crowds of people who were still milling around, chatting and laughing as they admired the colourful floats and enjoyed the spectacle of the fireworks.

I tried not to jump every time a rocket went off, but the further out into the lake your little boat went, the more anxious I became. 'Jordan! Over here! Don't go too far!' I called out. I wasn't sure whether he could hear me over the crackle of fireworks, though, so I waved frantically, hoping to signal for him not to disappear entirely from view.

I was too late. As the boat turned to navigate the narrow channel around an island, it vanished into the mist. I stood staring after you, my heart thudding and a feeling of panic clawing at my throat. 'Please come back,' I whispered, wishing I had never let you go.

Chapter 45

'I wish you'd stayed where I could see you,' I said to Jordan two hours later, as he put the finishing touches to your party buffet, setting out sandwiches, fairy cakes and jelly pots.

'Sorry, babe. The water was choppier than I thought. There must have been twice as many floats as last year. People really pushed the boat out.' He waggled his eyebrows.

'Oh, very funny.' I punched his arm but smiled at the same time. I was still a bit cross, but more relieved to have you both back in one piece.

'Marley was fine, Holl. I'm sorry I worried you, though. You looked as white as a sheet when we came in to dock. I thought something must have happened to Benjamin.'

'He was fine, too.' I kissed his soft head. 'It was me who was starting to panic. You were gone ages.' I didn't mention the dreadful accidents I'd been imagining the whole time. Nor did I confess how jealous I'd felt seeing Amy cosied up between you and Jordan. After all, it was my own stupid fault for not going with you.

'Only forty-five minutes. It would have been less, but we had to make an emergency stop on one of the islands. Marley was worried the crocodile might have got loose.' Jordan winked. 'She insisted on checking the swans were OK.'

I smiled. 'That sounds like Marley. Her heart is as big as her imagination.'

'She's caring and sensitive. Just like her mummy.' Jordan pulled me against him for a kiss, despite an audience of upwards of sixty guests. 'I'm so proud of you both. You too, mister.' He bent to kiss BB, cradled against my shoulder. 'You do look tired, though, hon. Why don't you take a break? Maria and Miss Shaw seem to have the party games in hand.'

'Don't they just.' I laughed, then felt my eyes well up as I watched two of my mum's oldest friends joining in with Musical Statues. 'It's a shame Dad couldn't make it,' I said, remembering my earlier chat with Miss Shaw. 'He's missed out on all the fun today.'

'I think your dad has a different idea of fun,' Jordan said dryly.

'I know.' I sighed. 'He used to take Marley to The Emporium all the time, for a browse through the bric-a-brac. He never does now. Every Sunday it's the same. *Chess.* Even Scrabble would be better. Marley loves word games, but chess . . .' I shook my head.

'I don't blame her. She's seven, and a bundle of energy. Look at the girl's *moves!*'

'She's adorable. Amy will have competition on the dance floor later.' I glanced around, suddenly realising I hadn't seen her since we arrived. 'Where is she, anyway?'

'Enjoying a private party of one.' Jordan nodded towards the sofas at the far corner of the room. 'That's not strawberry milk-shake she's drinking, by the way.'

'Something's definitely up with her today,' I said, recalling Amy's brief, strange visit to the cottage that morning. I looked at Jordan, battening down my jealousy of them being out on the lake together. 'Did she say anything to you on the boat?'

'Oh, just, ah, stuff. You know. The usual chat, I guess.'

'Ah. About your yacht,' I teased. 'And Amy's plans to become a fashion designer.'

Jordan threw his hands up in mock surrender. 'You know me too well.'

'I know Amy, too. At least, I thought I did.' I watched in concern as she helped herself to another drink from what I could now clearly see was a carton of wine.

'She's an enigma, it has to be said. Mind you, is it any wonder?' Jordan added, turning serious for a moment. 'Growing up at Sea View. The house of secrets.'

'Is that how you thought of it?' I stared at him in surprise. 'You never said.'

He shrugged. 'I didn't want to offend you. But there was always an undercurrent, wasn't there? Like a rip tide. I had the feeling I might get pulled under by it at any moment.'

'Slight exaggeration, but OK. I'll admit it did feel a bit like that growing up there.'

'Although, to be fair, it was probably different before your mum passed away. Sorry, sweetheart, I shouldn't have brought this up. I don't want to upset—'

'Although, honestly, the atmosphere at home wasn't much better before,' I said thoughtfully, watching Amy sitting alone, quietly getting drunk. I remembered her crying in the night as a teenager . . . the heavy silences at the breakfast table the next morning. 'Lots of things would have been different if Mum hadn't got sick,' I said sadly.

'Which is exactly why you need to look after *your* health. I know how much you miss your job, but it was the right thing to give it up and stay home.'

'Er, excuse me, but I'm working just as hard as you.' I threw him a teasing glare. 'Running a floristry business is full on. No wonder Mum was always so busy. Thank God for Maria helping me out.'

'She's a good sport.' Jordan laughed, watching her dance energetically.

'She certainly is,' I agreed. 'She actually hates parties. Mum was the one who . . . Anyway, enough talk about the past.' I smiled, pulling myself together. 'It's cake time, yes?'

*

'Make a wish, darling!'

Ten minutes later, I held my phone in one hand, and my camera in the other, clumsily attempting to film and photograph you at the same time. BB was strapped to my chest in a baby sling; you were poised awkwardly on a stool next to your birthday cake, your legs swinging backwards and forwards. You looked like you wanted to run away.

'Here, give me that. You're tying yourself up in knots. You film, I'll take snaps.' Jordan laughed as he held out a hand for the camera. But Amy beat him to it.

'I'll do it,' she said, and there was a hint of a slur in her voice.

'Oh, Amy. There you are. Where have you been hiding?' I asked pointedly.

'It's OK. I can handle it,' Jordan said lightly, taking the camera out of Amy's hands. 'Go stand with Marley. You too, Holl. My three favourite girls all together.' He grinned.

'Nuh-uh.' Amy made another grab for the camera. 'You need to be in the photos, Jordan. *Daddy and daughter*,' she said, her words slurring even more obviously.

'How much have you had to drink?' I whispered, frowning as I discreetly tried to pull her to one side before people started noticing.

'It's a party, isn't it?'

'A children's one, Amy,' I hissed. 'Most of these kids go to your school. Half of them are in your class. Not to mention that Marley is your god—'

'Hey! Slow down, pickle.' Amy reached out as you leaped off your stool and ran past us. 'Shit,' she exclaimed as the carton of milkshake in your hand spurted onto her red dress.

'Sorry, Aunty Amy,' you said quickly, looking up at her with wide eyes.

'It's OK, love.' I grabbed a bunch of napkins from the buffet table and gave them to Amy, before crouching down to reassure you. 'It'll wash out. It's nothing that can't be fixed.'

'Accidents happen,' Amy agreed tightly. 'People make mistakes. Your mum's right, Marley,' she added, scrubbing at her dress with the napkins. 'Some can even be fixed.'

'Come on, honey bee,' Jordan said quietly. 'Let's get you cleaned up. Don't want you all covered in strawberry milkshake in the photos, do we? I'll take you to the bathroom.'

It was only as Jordan intervened that I realised your new bumblebee jumper had been splattered as well. I hadn't noticed, too distracted by the look of inexplicable fear on your face, which seemed out of all proportion to a bit of spilled milkshake.

'No!' You grabbed hold of my hand, huddling against my side.

'It's OK, sweetheart. We don't have to take photos at all, if you don't want? Let's just light the candles, shall we? Then you can make a wish.'

You shook your head, looking down.

Hearing a few giggles among your school friends, I bit my lip, realising the party mood was slipping into something more akin to teasing. 'I tell you what,' I said, leaning close to your ear. 'Why don't you sit on my lap? We can cut the cake together.'

Your hand squeezed mine even tighter, but you didn't reply.

'Or maybe you'd like *Leah* to help you?' I suggested, running out of ideas.

For a moment, it seemed I'd hit on the perfect solution. Your head jerked up, your eyes seeking out your best friend amidst the chattering group sitting cross-legged on the floor in front of us. I looked at her too, biting my lip as I saw Leah whispering to the girl next to her. A second later, you pulled your hand out of mine, and bolted towards the exit.

'Sorry, folks. We'll do cake later,' Jordan announced jauntily, following quickly after you. As he reached the door, he turned and raised the camera above his head, adding jokily: 'I don't think the birthday girl is quite ready for her close-up.'

Chapter 46

TODAY – SUNDAY, 7.00 A.M.

Everything always came back to Amy, I thought, as I lay in bed this morning, cuddling BB, wondering if you were awake.

After dropping her bombshell at our kitchen table yesterday morning – about my mum's brooch, her missing diary and the letter from Luke Jackson – Amy had left as suddenly as she'd arrived. I'd even had the feeling she wanted to leave without saying goodbye: I was changing BB's nappy when I'd heard the front door open.

'Wait!' I called out, my fingers fumbling with sleepsuit poppers.

'I'll call you, Holly,' came the husky voice. 'I've got to finish packing.'

'No, please, hang on a sec.' Tucking BB into his carry-cot, I dashed into the hall.

'It's better this way,' Amy said, and I was sure I saw her wipe away a tear, before forcing a smile as I hurried towards her. 'For now, anyway.'

'What's better?' I frowned at her. 'What are you talking about?'

'You'll find out.' Resting her hands on my shoulders, she hesitated, then pulled me into a hug. 'I'm sorry,' she whispered, so quietly, I thought for a second I had misheard her.

'Do you have to go?' Suddenly, I realised how much I was going to miss her.

I was angry with Amy; at times, I hated her. But I also loved her. I couldn't imagine her not being in my life. If she went to Paris, I had a sinking feeling she really wouldn't come back, as she'd hinted. Especially if Jordan was planning to join her there . . .

'Yeah, I do,' she said hoarsely. 'I need to sort my head out. I need to sort my *life* out.'

I watched her hand drift into her pocket, and heard the rustle of paper. Amy may have left me Mum's brooch, but she'd kept the letter from her dad. It was rightfully hers, I supposed, although I had wanted to show it to *my* dad, to ask him about it.

'What happened between our parents doesn't have to affect us, does it?' I said softly. 'Like you said, it's history.'

Amy zipped up her leather jacket, then wrapped her arms around herself, giving me a rueful smile. 'Sure. Except we never truly escape our past, do we?'

'You said that to me once before, remember? On my wedding day,' I reminded her, at the same time recalling her strange mood that morning, eight years ago. Then, I'd been unsettled by her seeming efforts to stop me marrying Jordan; I wondered if she'd been carrying feelings for him all that time – if *he* had secretly felt he'd married the wrong person – and things had now come to a head between them.

'Yeah, I remember,' she acknowledged. 'And I meant it. Perhaps for slightly different reasons. But I still believe it's true. The past lives inside us. Like a cancer. Dormant. Possibly benign. Definitely incurable. We can't get rid of it, even if we want to.'

I guessed she was alluding to my mum, but I refused to be distracted. 'Life hasn't been *so* bad for you, has it? And what do you mean, *slightly different reasons*?'

'I mean, I've spent my whole life wanting to run away. From something. Some*one*. Now . . . well, I realise it's probably myself I'm running away from.'

'I don't get it. Sorry, Amy. I didn't know what you were talking about eight years ago, and I still don't. Please, just tell me. What's going on?' I could feel my heart pounding as I waited for her to confess that she was in love with my husband, and always had been.

She stood watching me for a few moments, then suddenly pulled me into another, longer hug. 'I'll call you tomorrow and explain everything. I promise.'

'No, you won't.' I pushed her away, remembering my mum making the same promise. She'd died before she could keep it, and a shiver ran through me as Amy gave me a sad smile and turned away. 'Don't go,' I called after her. 'Stay. Let's talk some more. *Amy!*'

But she was already stalking down the garden path. She didn't look back.

I was fractious and unsettled all day after that, and I couldn't sleep last night. I wanted to call Jordan, but I was still convinced there was something going on between him and Amy. That had to explain her odd behaviour, her vague but loaded explanations. Maybe they weren't planning to run away together, but perhaps they'd had an affair, which had now ended, and Amy felt unable to stick around any longer.

I sat up, reaching for Mum's brooch on the bedside cabinet, and as I turned it over in my hands, I remembered the picture you'd drawn of it. I wondered if you'd overheard Amy and Jordan fighting on your birthday, when the three of you were out on the boat.

It seemed too much of a coincidence that Amy had chosen to show the brooch to me now, and the letter, both of which she'd kept secret for eight years. I felt sure she was using them to hint at an affair, or at the very least an infatuation, that she was too scared to confess.

'She always wants whatever I have,' I muttered sadly as I

climbed wearily out of bed. 'But maybe this time she had the decency not to take it.' I wanted to believe Jordan had been the one to tell Amy to back off, to leave him alone, but I couldn't be certain. If he was so determined to be with us, why had he left me to sleep alone since your birthday?

'Marley, are you awake?' After checking BB was still fast asleep, I crept into your bedroom, smoothing back your hair until you opened your eyes.

'Is it school?'

'No, love. It's Sunday.' I sat down next to you, taking hold of your hand. 'I thought we might go out for the day. Just you, me and BB.' I needed to get out of the cottage – perhaps even the village. I wanted to be anywhere else but in our home if and when Jordan returned to tell me he was planning to leave us to be with my best friend.

'OK.' You yawned sleepily.

'Or maybe Granddaddy could join us, yes? We could go on a little adventure.'

You sat bolt upright, staring at me with wide eyes. 'An adventure?'

'Sure. Maybe a trip up the coast. Nothing dangerous. I'm no James Bond.'

'James Bond,' you repeated solemnly. 'That's Daddy's real name, isn't it?'

I laughed at that. 'Er, no. Your daddy's name is Jordan. Jordan Mayhew. Without the double-oh-seven.' I chuckled again. 'He might like to *think* of himself as—'

'But Aunty Amy called him that, Mummy. When we were on the boat. Daddy jumped onto the island. There was a gap. I thought he was going to fall in, but he didn't. He caught hold of a rope on the tree and swung himself. Aunty Amy called him James Bond.'

'Ah, I see. And what else did Aunty Amy say, love?' I said, my heart pounding.

242

'She said Daddy was on a *mission*. He said she'd blown his cover. He was cross.'

'Oh, I doubt that, sweetheart,' I reassured you, but my stomach clenched as I pictured the scene, the flirtation it suggested. '*Blown his cover* is like when a spy has a secret identity,' I explained. 'So no one knows who they are. Or, um, what they're planning to do.'

You gripped my hand, looking terrified. 'A *spy*? Daddy is a spy?'

'No, love.' I frowned, wondering why the thought bothered you so much. 'James Bond is a made-up character. He's in Daddy's favourite movies, actually. That's probably why Aunty Amy made the joke. He's an action hero, you see? Although he has guns, and—'

Your eyes widened. 'Daddy has a gun *too*?'

'No, love. I meant James Bond. In the movies.' I sighed at how literally you were taking everything. I tried again. 'Daddy isn't a spy, Marley. He's—'

'No one has to spy on me, Mummy. I never, never tell. Honest!'

'Of course you don't, darling,' I soothed, although I wished you would. I still had no idea who you were scared of – who you were refusing to tell tales about.

'But I don't want anyone to get hurt,' you said tearfully, tugging on my arm.

'No one is getting hurt.' Silently, I prayed I was right. Jordan didn't have to point a gun to my head to hurt me. If he'd fallen out of love with me, I would be broken.

'You don't know that! I don't want you to die, Mummy. I don't want Aunty Amy to take BB away.' Tears started running down your face.

'What? Oh, sweetheart. Is this what's been worrying you?' I reached out to pull you onto my lap for a proper cuddle, but as I did so, I spotted a piece of folded-up paper tucked underneath your bedside lamp. 'What's this, love?'

'I was going to post it.' You knotted your hands together, looking guilty now, as though you'd forgotten to hand in your homework.

I lifted the yellow paper. 'Well, I can just open it now. Shall I?'

You hesitated for a moment, then nodded. Carefully, without disturbing the grip you seemed desperate to keep on my arm, I unfolded the note – your seventh.

It had been torn almost in half, and I wondered if you hadn't forgotten to post it at all but had changed your mind and tried to rip it up. As I scanned the words written in red crayon, I understood your reluctance to share your final, darkest worry:

daddy wants to kill you

Chapter 47

I tucked the note into my dressing-gown pocket and pulled you onto my lap, kissing your hot forehead. I could feel your heart beating faster, but mine was racing. I wasn't frightened that my life was in danger, but I was terrified that it was about to change for ever.

Despite your confusion about the teasing exchange you'd over-heard between Jordan and Amy, everything made perfect sense to me now. At the very least, my husband and so-called best friend had obviously been flirting; worst-case scenario, they were chatting about plans for the future. Whatever, you had clearly perceived a far more sinister nuance; after all, you were a bright girl: you listened hard, and you loved words.

While I was glad to have finally got to the root of your worry, my heart sank as I reflected on what was surely the truth behind your misunderstanding: Jordan didn't want to kill me; *he wanted to leave me*. 'Sweetheart,' I said softly, 'try to remember *exactly* what Daddy and Aunty Amy said.'

'Daddy said no one gets what they want by being nice,' you parroted carefully.

245

'Hmm. I expect he was talking about work.' I recalled Jordan talking recently about how he got promoted to head chef. He'd used that line then; maybe he'd offered Amy the same advice – about quitting teaching to pursue a career in fashion? *Or about breaking up our marriage so they could be together?*

You shook your head. 'Aunty Amy said sometimes you have to bite the bullet.' Your eyes widened with fear. 'She said that's what Granddaddy always told her.'

'It's just a silly saying, darling.' I went to cuddle you again, but this time you pulled away. I sighed. 'The bullet isn't real, Marley.' I shook my head. 'There *is* no bullet.'

'But Daddy said it would *kill* you!' You flung your arms round my neck, burying your face against my shoulder.

'It won't,' I said confidently, but my mind was working furiously, trying to make sense of it all – to fill in the gaps between the jumbled snippets of what was beginning to sound like a serious conversation disguised as a jokey exchange. 'I know it's confusing, love. We use lots of funny expressions, don't we?'

I paused for a moment, reflecting on how many I used, all the time. Jordan, too. Partly to amuse you. I pictured you giggling when he complained that he was 'busy as a bee', grinning when I teased him for being 'cool as a cucumber'. I recalled Jordan's favourite rallying call when we set off anywhere: 'Anchors aweigh!' You loved silly rhymes and funny phrases; they had always made you laugh. But not this time, and I wondered why.

'*Bite the bullet* is definitely one of the strangest, isn't it?' I said brightly. 'But no one is spying on you. Or trying to hurt me.' *Not physically, at least,* I reflected bitterly. 'Daddy and Aunty Amy were talking about . . . something else.'

'Is it my fault, Mummy?' You looked tearfully at me. 'I'm so noisy. And messy. My curls are a nuisance. They get tangled. And you have to tidy up after me all the time.'

'Not lately, darling,' I said, trying to coax a smile. 'You've been *super* tidy.'

'Granddaddy doesn't think so. He said Grandma was always busy, too. He said it made her so tired she had to go to sleep and never wake up!'

'Well, that isn't quite what—'

'And Daddy told Aunty Amy that *you* get tired all the time. He said you're just like your mummy. He said something had to be done about it!'

'And what did Aunty Amy say to that?' I squeezed your hand gently, trying to reassure you, even as my own heart felt like it was breaking into a million pieces.

You thought for a moment. 'She said some people don't deserve to be parents.'

'Oh.' I gritted my teeth, fighting tears. 'Did, um, did Daddy agree with her?'

'I don't know. But Granddaddy does. Aunty Amy said so.' You rubbed your eyes again, yawning widely, and immediately I regretted asking you so many questions.

I could see you were exhausted. And confused. 'It's OK,' I said soothingly. 'I promise you, none of this is your fault. You mustn't worry. About *any* of it.'

'That's what Daddy told Aunty Amy. He told her not to worry, it will be all over soon. Then he won't have to sleep on his boat anymore. She said they should sail away on it. But Daddy said Sergeant Robins would catch them in his speed boat.'

'Ah, well. Sergeant Robins is a very nice man. I'm sure he—'

'And Aunty Amy said that would be the end of you!'

I thought of Jordan's eagerness for me to join him on his boat, for a fleeting moment imagining him pushing me overboard, before taking you, BB and the inheritance he and Amy seemed to covet, and running away with her. 'I'm going *nowhere*, darling,' I said firmly.

'I'm sorry, Mummy,' you said again, hunching into a ball and curling against my side. 'I'll try harder to be good. I love you. I don't want you to die because of me!'

You began to cry in earnest now, great big gulping sobs racking your body. 'Oh, Marley. I love you too.' I held you, letting you cry out all the pent-up tension of the last eight weeks. 'But Daddy and Aunty Amy . . . what you overheard . . . it was just silly grown-up chat. OK? Sleep now. Everything is absolutely fine.' Once again, I pictured Jordan's handsome face as I offered you the same reassurance he'd tried to give me: 'I guarantee it.'

After giving you one last cuddle, I tucked you back into bed, pleased when you fell almost immediately into a deep, exhausted sleep. You needed to rest; I needed to think.

I stood up to go and get dressed, pausing at the door to look down at you, my own eyes filling with tears too. It was a huge relief to know that no one had hurt or threatened *you*, but my heart squeezed with anguish that your fear hadn't been for yourself, but all for me . . .

No wonder you'd been so compliant lately, behaving perfectly so as not to make your busy daddy grumpy – to risk provoking him, as you'd obviously feared, into punishing me before escaping on his boat. I thought of your wish that he didn't have one at all, and berated myself for not joining all the dots sooner. 'Why didn't I *realise*?' I groaned, wandering into my bedroom and listlessly pulling on navy jeans and a soft grey jumper.

For a moment, I stayed doubled over in pain as I bent to pick up BB from his cot; carrying him downstairs felt like I was holding a tonne weight. Making my way breathlessly into the kitchen, I gave BB a quick feed before settling him in his carry-cot, then quickly gathered together all your notes from under the teapot on the dresser. Easing myself down onto the rocking chair, I reread them all.

'My poor, kind, clever girl. You were trying to tell me. I just didn't understand.'

Looking again at your notes, and thinking through the jumbled snippets of overheard conversation you'd been able to remember,

I was finally able to piece together the little trail of clues you had left for me, too scared to speak your worst fear aloud.

I could see now where you'd been trying to direct me: from the drawing of your birthday cake, to your wish to fly away, your dislike of secrets and the hint about not liking parties – your own being the stage on which all your worries first came so terrifyingly to life.

I felt dreadful that you'd been carrying such paralysing fear all these weeks; it broke my heart as I remembered you saying: 'I never tell.' But while you had obviously misunderstood the intent of the conversation between Amy and Jordan, there were troubling, even threatening undercurrents that I was still struggling to decipher.

A brisk hammering on the front door interrupted my turbulent thoughts. Tucking your notes into my jeans pocket, I levered myself slowly off the rocking chair, doing my best to ignore the familiar, increasingly insistent fluttery palpitations in my chest, and hurried as fast as my shaky legs would carry me to open it.

Chapter 48

'Oh, Dad!' Guilt rushed through me at the sight of him standing on our doorstep. I immediately realised he must have got so tired of waiting for me to visit him that he'd decided to come to us instead. The look on his face confirmed how he felt about that.

'Yes, I'm still your father,' he responded gruffly.

'Sorry. I realise I've skipped, um, a couple of visits.'

'Seven, to be precise.' He raised his eyebrows. 'Jordan said you've been busy?'

'Yes.' Despite everything, at least Jordan had been kind enough to cover for me. 'I was thinking of coming to see you today, though,' I said, trying hard to be conciliatory.

'Really?' He looked sceptical.

'Really. It would be good to chat. I've, um, I've had some stuff on my mind, lately.'

'So I gathered. You haven't been to the flat. Or called. I didn't want to just turn up like this, but I'm worried about my daughter. If that's allowed?'

'Of course.'

'Good. Well, are you going to invite me in?' He didn't wait for

250

a response but pushed past me and strode into the tiny hallway, hesitating for a moment at the bottom of the stairs before heading into the living room.

'The kids are asleep,' I said, guessing that's what he was wondering.

'Ah. That's a shame.'

'At least it gives us a chance to chat in peace.' I smiled, taking in his familiar cords and green sweater, immediately reminded of Sundays at Sea View and feeling a pang that our visits could no longer take place there. 'You know, you're welcome here any time, Dad.'

'That's nice to hear. I was starting to think I'd done something to upset you.' He ignored my gesture for him to take a seat and started pacing up and down the living room, muttering to himself.

'I know. I'm sorry,' I apologised again. 'But please, sit down. You're making me anxious.' I laughed nervously as I watched him continue pacing and mumbling.

'Was that Benjamin?' He stopped pacing and stared at the doorway. 'I heard a cry.'

'Ah, he's probably waking up. If you wait here, I'll go fetch him. Back in a tick.'

'I wasn't thinking of staying, actually,' Dad said when I returned with BB a couple of minutes later. 'I just wanted to see you. I meant what I said, Holly. I'm worried about you. I spoke to Maria the other day. She's worried about you, too.'

'Oh. I see.' The penny dropped. 'Yes, I was up at her farm the other day. Like I said, I've, um, had a few things on my mind. But I had a good chat with Maria. She offered to take some paperwork off my hands. So, you see, there's no need for you to worry about—'

'You're overdoing things,' Dad cut in with his usual directness.

'No, it's not that,' I said, sinking down onto the sofa and laying BB on the play mat in front of me. I waited for Dad to perch on the armchair, then I drew in a deep, steadying breath. I had seen how bottling up your worries had affected you; it was time to share my own, before the pains in my chest got any worse. 'I've just been a bit worried, that's all.'

'About?' He leaned forward, elbows resting on his knees. 'What's going on, pickle?'

'I'm not entirely sure.' I wrinkled my nose, hesitating. As much as I was worrying about my own marriage, I also had questions about his. I wanted to ask him about Luke Jackson's letter, and whether he knew about Mum having an affair. But the thought of Jordan loving someone else was so painful, I was loath to inflict the same hurt on my own dad.

'Come on, love. If there's something on your mind, just spit it out.'

'OK.' I took another breath. 'It's about Jordan. And Amy.'

Dad's eyebrows arched. 'Really? I thought you'd be over all that jealous nonsense by now. You two aren't kids squabbling over pet rabbits anymore.'

'Sorry?' I stared at him, and all of a sudden that was exactly how I felt: as though I was still a child wondering why everyone favoured Amy over me.

'Go on, then,' he said with exaggerated patience. 'What's she done now?'

'Nothing. It doesn't matter,' I mumbled, feeling small.

'Well, it mattered enough for you to stop me seeing my grand-children, so—'

'This isn't about you, Dad,' I said crossly. 'It's about me. And Jordan. In fact, I need to call him.' I picked BB up off the play mat and stood up. 'Let's talk later, OK?'

Dad stood up too. 'Fine. My mistake. I'm sorry, love.' He ran a hand back and forth across his short hair. 'I realise I haven't been the father you wanted.'

'No, don't you do that. Don't turn this around and make it *my* fault.' I'd had enough of Amy pulling that stunt. 'I'm not blaming *you*, Dad. I just think it's best we don't talk about Amy. Because we're not going to agree, are we?'

'Agree?' He frowned. 'About what?'

'About . . .' I hesitated, then took a deep breath, deciding to go for it. 'About how she always gets what she wants, and no one . . . I mean, neither you nor Mum ever seemed bothered about how she pushed me out. Why, Dad? I get that you wanted to make her welcome. But what about *me*?' I knew I sounded childish, but I couldn't help myself.

'Your mother and I did our best.' He looked sad rather than angry as I'd expected.

'I know, but Amy . . .' I tailed off as a feeling of hopelessness stole through me. Dad had never been able to see through Amy; she waltzed through life, dazzling everyone; now she'd bewitched my husband, too.

'Amy *what*?' Dad prompted, his jaw tightening again.

'I just wish you'd never brought her into our home,' I admitted painfully.

'Well, I'm sorry about that,' he said quietly, sitting down again. 'I guess nothing turned out quite the way I'd hoped.'

'What *did* you hope, Dad?'

'That you and Amy would become best friends, of course. That your mother and I would now be enjoying our retirement together. Me with my books. Olivia with her garden, her allotment. Spending weekends playing with our grandchildren.'

'If only she was still here,' I said softly, pointlessly. 'I miss her so much.'

'As do I. Every second of every minute of every day.' Dad twisted his hands together, and I could tell he was battling hard not to break down in front of me. 'Don't let the grass grow under your feet, Holly. Don't make the same mistakes I did.'

'Mistakes?' I stared curiously at him, noticing for the first time that he looked thinner than usual. I held my breath. 'What do you mean? You're not ill, are you?'

'Never fitter. Which only adds to the guilt, of course. If anyone deserved to live, it was your mum. After what she gave up for

253

me . . .' He cleared his throat. 'She wanted more children, you see. When you were born, she was the happiest I'd ever seen her.'

I swallowed hard. 'I always wanted a brother or sister. I used to ask Mum why we couldn't get another baby. She'd just smile and say: "Ask your father." For some reason, I never did.' I bit my lip, thinking how little I'd dared ask anyone, growing up.

'Yes, well.' Dad coughed as though embarrassed to talk about babies, even though he'd brought the subject up. 'We weren't blessed a second time. Sometimes we talked about adoption. Then I bumped into Luke. He and Isabella were going through a rough time, so—'

'They were?' I looked at him in surprise. 'I thought they were just busy with work?'

'That too. But marriage is tough, isn't it? Loving one person your whole life. Especially when you're not sure they love you back,' he added quietly.

I sighed, thinking of Luke Jackson's letter. 'I know about Mum's brooch, Dad. I know Amy's dad gave it to her. You did know that, right?'

He gave a curt nod, his lips pursing tightly.

'It must have been hard for you,' I probed. 'Mum having feelings for another man.'

His body seemed to jolt in shock. 'Sorry?'

'No, *I'm* sorry. I shouldn't have been so blunt.'

'It's fine. We should have talked about this before. Only the timing never quite felt right. First the whole infertility thing, then Amy coming into our lives. Your mum's illness.'

'I'm sorry, Dad,' I apologised again. 'I didn't mean to upset you.'

'It's not you, Holly. It's . . . It was just so hard watching your mum suffer. In the end, we both simply wanted it to be over. The pain, I mean.'

'Did you forgive her?' I whispered. 'Before she died?'

'Forgive her?' Dad looked puzzled. 'Oh, you mean because of Luke.' He huffed. 'That man could charm the birds out of the trees.'

254

I thought of his letter and nodded. 'Mum always said he had a way with words.'

'Yes, well. In the end, actions speak louder, don't they?'

'You stood by Mum, you mean?' I suddenly remembered him saying: *Whatever it takes to help the ones you love, whatever we have to do, we do it.*

He must have loved my mum very much to have forgiven an affair with his best friend, I thought – and then to take in that man's daughter. Perhaps that self-sacrifice even explained why he had become such an uptight, moralistic man . . .

'I did what I needed to do,' he said huskily, pulling me back to the present. 'Duty. Family loyalty. As you get older, family is all that matters, you see? Protecting your own.'

'I know, Dad.' I saw tears in his eyes and felt strangely awkward. I had never seen him cry; I wasn't entirely sure why he was upset now.

'Your old dad messed up, Holly, and you might not blame me, but it is my fault. I want to make it all right. Start again. Be a better man. A better father. *Grand*father.' He stood up, reaching for BB. 'Here, let me take him. You need to sleep.'

'Really, it's OK,' I said, holding BB away from him. Something about Dad's suddenly intense manner was making me anxious. 'Please, let *go*.' Panic began to take hold as his hands curled around your baby brother's soft, pudgy arms.

'You need to let me *help* you,' he insisted.

'No! Stop! Please!' I watched BB's face turning pink, and the scream gathering force in my chest was about to burst out of me when you appeared in the doorway – and Amy was standing right behind you.

Chapter 49

'What the fuck?'

I wasn't sure who spoke the words first, Amy or me, but I moved faster, switching BB to my other shoulder and hurrying to grab your hand and pull you against me.

Even though you'd got yourself dressed in your jeans and bumblebee jumper, you were shivering uncontrollably. I rubbed your shoulder, trying to comfort you. By then I had figured out that Amy wasn't a physical threat, but it was obvious she still intimidated you.

'How did you get in?' I asked, staring at her. 'I thought you were in Paris?'

'The door was open. And my train's not till this evening.'

'You're going to *Paris*?' Dad took a step towards Amy, his arms half-outstretched, typically switching his concern from me to her in an instant.

'Yes,' she said, uncharacteristically brief, her eyes fixed on me.

'Why?' Dad persisted, refusing to be rebuffed.

They'd always been so close; I was surprised Dad appeared to know nothing about Amy's trip – perhaps wasn't even aware that

256

she'd left her job. I was about to ask if that was the case, when Amy turned on him.

'You know why,' she said, and her eyes were darker and colder than a winter night.

'To find your dad?' I conjectured hesitantly, unsure whether I was trying to rescue Amy, or challenge her – force her to admit that she was planning to meet my husband there.

'Actually, Holly . . .' Amy stepped further into the living room, hands clasped in front of her, almost in supplication. 'That's not why I'm going.'

A dozen sarcastic responses flitted across my mind; I swallowed them all, tasting bitterness mixed with the acrid tang of defeat. *Amy had won.* She'd spent her life trying to steal everything that meant the most to me, and now she was about to claim her trophy.

'No. I didn't really think so,' I said sadly, feeling physically weak and unable to fight her any longer. I couldn't outsmart her; I had never been able to outshine her.

Perfect Amy. I glanced at her designer black jeans, the silky red shirt beneath her leather jacket, the wedge boots completing her polished look. I pulled self-consciously at my loose, seen-better-days grey jumper, feeling the pinch of my jeans waistband, mentally comparing the tautness of Amy's gym-honed figure with my post-baby one.

Jordan had always called *me* perfect; he'd promised me we would be forever together, whatever. My feelings hadn't changed one iota: I loved Jordan even more now than when he'd first burst into my life like a blaze of sunshine. But something must have changed for him, and while I'd blamed work, money worries, the demands of being parents, it seemed somehow inevitable that the true catalyst was Amy Jackson.

She rested a hand on my arm. 'I'm still going. But there's something I want to say before I leave. That I should have said yesterday. The other night. Weeks ago.'

'No apologies. Please.' I hadn't meant to beg, but my heart was thumping so hard, I knew it couldn't take a big emotional scene. 'If you have something to say, just say it. Then go,' I added firmly, holding BB closer and tightening my grip on your shoulder.

Amy may have returned to clear her conscience, and if absolution was what she wanted, she could have it. I wouldn't force Jordan to stay with me if he wanted to leave, and I refused to waste any more energy hating Amy. But she wasn't taking my children with her.

'I wasn't going to apologise.' She frowned, looking puzzled. 'I wanted to tell you—'

'Not now, Amy,' my dad said curtly. 'This isn't the time, or the place. This is Holly's home, and we were talking about *her*.'

I gave him a tart look, suspecting he was being ironic, but his expression was grave. 'Well, actually, I think we were done, Dad,' I said quietly. 'You were about to leave too, yes? Maybe you could give Amy a lift to the station,' I added, wanting them both out of there.

'I'm not going anywhere until I've said what I came to say.' Amy's voice was low and urgent as she pushed past me to sit defiantly on the sofa. 'This affects Holly as well.'

It was my turn to look confused. 'Too right it does. If Jordan is—'

'Jordan?' Amy sat back, eyes widening. 'What on earth has *he* got to do with it?'

'But you . . . he . . .' My legs started to feel even weaker, and I lurched towards the sofa, cradling BB as I sat down next to Amy. You curled into my other side, as far away from her as possible, and my dad stood by helplessly, clenching his fists as he looked between us.

'If you do this, Amy, I will never, ever forgive you,' he said darkly.

Amy gave him a sharp look, then turned to me, taking hold of my hand. 'I'm sorry I left you hanging yesterday. I was going to call you. Honestly, I was. Then I woke up this morning and I realised . . . I've never treated you fairly, Holly.' She pulled a wry face. 'I've always been jealous of you, I suppose.'

'Jealous? Of *me*?' I stared at her in shock.

'Of course,' she said simply. 'You had your parents. Your lovely home, Sea View. You knew exactly who you were and where you belonged. Then you met Jordan and had these two beauties.' She smiled sadly. 'You became a mum, whereas I . . .'

'I said *no*, Amy.'

Dad didn't shout; then again, he'd never had to. His displeasure alone was enough to make anyone feel guilty, and as he stood up straighter, he suddenly looked more like the father I remembered from twenty years ago. And with that memory came many more: Amy crying in her bed at night; my dad's endless jollity; my mum's anxious chatter . . .

'Why?' Amy demanded, and her eyes filled with tears. 'This has hung over me for too long, Adam. I want it off my chest. I won't be silenced any longer!'

I stared between her and Dad, suddenly registering that we weren't talking about Jordan, or any secret affair. At least not between them, I thought, feeling a chill run through me. 'Tell me,' I said, trying to ignore the voice in my head taunting me that I knew exactly what Amy was so desperate to confess – that, deep down, I'd always known.

'No one is trying to silence you, love.' Dad folded his arms, a proud man who refused to admit his crimes, even when they were about to be exposed for all to see.

'Oh, really?' Amy's cheeks flushed bright red. 'Olivia didn't even mention it on her death bed. I mean, she must have known, right?'

Dad sank down onto the armchair, looking as though Amy had punched him in the gut. 'No,' he whispered, running a hand over his face. 'I never . . . we never talked about it.'

'You expect me to believe that?' Amy's eyes flashed indigo. 'She never liked me.'

'She cared for you. Very much. She looked after you like you

259

were her own child.' Dad glanced at me then, and I saw the hint of appeal in his blue eyes.

I knew he was reminding me of Mum's sadness at not being able to have more children; I got that he was silently begging for me to take his side, to tell Amy how it was – that my parents had been good to both of us, and we should forgive their failings, because they were born out of love.

Only a terrible fear was taking hold of me. I couldn't ignore it, but I couldn't speak it aloud – not until Amy said it first. I'd jumped to enough conclusions over the last few days, and it had caused me nothing but heartache. I needed to hear Amy spell it out in her own words. Frustratingly, she lapsed into uncharacteristic silence.

Chapter 50

'I don't know which is worse,' Amy said at last. 'That Olivia could have been so ignorant of the truth, or that you *kept* it from her. To protect yourself,' she added scathingly.

'OK, it's possible she guessed,' Dad admitted in a low, strangled voice.

'But she died without ever admitting it,' Amy said bluntly. 'Funny that. Convenient, some might say.'

'Now hang on a minute.' Dad leaned forward. 'What precisely are you implying?'

Dad had never sounded more like the law lecturer he'd been for thirty years. But beneath his uptight manner, I detected genuine shock . . . *and fear?* I remembered Amy's snide comments about Mum's fortune, her sarcasm about my dad's generosity in standing by her after she had an affair with his best friend.

I still wasn't sure if that was true or not, but I did know that my mum had died suddenly and unexpectedly – taking all her secrets to the grave. *My dad's secrets, too?*

'I'll allow you to draw your own inference,' Amy said smartly, but there was no humour in her eyes.

'I loved Olivia. I would have given my life to save her. Don't you dare suggest—'

'Look, this isn't about you, Adam,' Amy cut in brusquely. 'I didn't even know you were going to be here. Why are you, anyway? What's going on?' She looked curiously between Dad and me, her eyes widening as she began to pick up that there had been an atmosphere in the room even before she had arrived.

'Dad came over to check we're OK,' I explained quietly, rocking BB and turning to give you a reassuring smile, even as my mind was working at a hundred miles an hour, trying to process everything Amy was saying. I would have suggested you go back upstairs to play, but I knew it was pointless: you were clinging on to my arm as though afraid I might vanish.

'Right,' Amy drawled sceptically. 'Adam Aitken. The perfect father.'

'I'm worried about Holly,' Dad insisted indignantly. 'She has a serious heart defect, in case you'd forgotten.'

Amy rolled her eyes. 'And your concerned visit, of course, had nothing to do with checking whether or not she and I had spoken.'

'Absolutely, categorically not. I hadn't heard from Holly in a while. I know she's had her hands full with the baby. I've left her in peace. But I was getting worried, and—'

'Yes, she has a new baby.' Amy flicked back her hair and sat forward. 'That's the *real* reason you haven't seen much of her, isn't it? So don't even think of trying to blame—'

'No, actually, it *is* my fault,' I said calmly. Whatever crimes my dad had committed, and a terrifying list was growing in my mind, negligence wasn't one of them. 'I haven't visited Dad for a while.' *Because you'd refused every time I suggested it.*

In fact, you hadn't seemed too happy to see him this morning, either, I reflected, turning to look at you, feeling my stomach flip when you buried your face against my shoulder. I wondered if it wasn't just Amy you were scared of, but my dad, too. Dark thoughts flitted at the back of my mind; I brushed them away.

'You don't have to pretend just to make him look good, Holly,' Amy said bluntly.

'I'm not,' I protested too fast. 'Like Dad said, I've had my hands full. We haven't been out and about that much. I've had some stuff on my mind for a few weeks.' *Eight, to be precise*, I thought: ever since your birthday party, which I still needed to ask Amy about . . .

'Haven't we all?' she said dryly, and I felt a renewed flicker of suspicion that whatever she wanted to reveal about my dad wasn't her only secret. Before I could ask her, she continued: 'That was one heck of a day, hey, pickle?' She gave you a lopsided smile, ridiculously attempting to lighten the mood. You only burrowed closer into my side.

'Marley has been feeling very anxious,' I said, hugging you. 'Things were said before her party that she didn't quite understand. They've stayed with her, and—'

'Shit.' Amy looked stricken. A hand flew to her mouth. 'That's *my* fault, isn't it?'

'Oh, surely not,' Dad said sardonically. 'Don't tell me *perfect Amy* put a foot wrong.'

I frowned, not only at the uncharacteristic nastiness of his tone, but also because I hadn't realised he knew my nickname for Amy. I was about to apologise to her for it, when she leaped off the sofa and strode across the room to stand in front of him.

'Perfect. No, I was never that, was I? I was an inconvenience. A cuckoo in the nest. A wild child who never did the right thing.'

'Amy . . .' I blushed to think that I'd thought all those things about her, and more, but I hated seeing her distress – and I didn't fully understand it.

'And what was my biggest crime?' she continued, jabbing a finger in the air. 'Falling for an older man's lies, that's what. Telling me I was beautiful. That I deserved to be loved. That he could make me happy, take care of me for ever.' She dragged in a deep breath. 'Then I got pregnant and all those promises turned to dust.'

'Oh, my God,' I whispered, pressing a hand against my chest as I felt my heart stutter.

'And when all I had left was my baby,' Amy continued, leaning over my dad like he was the child and she was the angry parent, 'you took that from me, too. You made me get rid of it. You made a *murderer* of me!'

My head started to spin as my heart seemed to slow right down, while at the same time my brain speeded up. As though watching a film on fast forward, I pictured a teenage Amy in our bedroom at Sea View, creeping back into her bed each night; I recalled her strange, angry confession that she'd killed Jane.

Then I rolled all these memories up into one big, horrible ball, and I thought I might faint from the horror of it. 'You had a termination before your GCSEs,' I said, feeling tears sting my eyes as I remembered Amy sprinting through the garden, yelling, '*Got you!*'

She'd wanted to tell me then, I realised. All these years I'd believed Amy had coped with her grief over my mum's death by projecting it into fantastical imaginings about a murdered child. My friend, Jane. Only it *was* a child who had died: her own baby . . . And as I remembered her pummelling her stomach on my wedding day, and recalled her sarcasm about my dad as we got ready at Sea View, the most horrific fear began to seep through me.

'Were you the father?' I stared at my dad, but suddenly he felt like a stranger to me.

'If you can ask me that, you're no daughter of mine,' he said, his face flushing dark red. 'And you don't deserve to be the mother of my grandchildren!' He jerked out of the armchair and strode towards me, arms outstretched, his face a grim mask.

'No! *No!*' My legs felt like lead as I hauled myself off the sofa, pulling you after me. I registered the shock on Amy's face as I brushed past her, but I didn't stop. I barrelled into the hall, clutching BB against my chest, looking left and right, uncertain which way to turn.

I made the wrong call. I should have run out of the front door, and kept on running, but instinctively I sought the sanctuary of our home, where I had always felt so happy, so *safe*. I hurried into the kitchen, but as I heard footsteps behind me, I realised my mistake. *Too late.* Stress and exertion had ramped up the strain on my weak heart; my lungs felt like they were imploding.

'Holly, wait!' Dad called out, launching himself at me, yanking BB from my arms.

'No! Please!' I gasped, reaching for BB, feeling anguish rip through me at the sight of his pink, crumpled face crushed against my dad's shoulder. 'Marley!' I cried out, my heart breaking as I saw you open your mouth in a silent scream.

Dad pushed, and I pulled, and I just had time to register the look of shock on his face before my legs gave way and I felt my head crack against the hard kitchen floor. Desperately, I fought the dark wave of unconsciousness I could feel steadily rising, but it pulled me under, exactly like the rip tide Jordan had guessed was lurking in our family.

The last thing I saw was the bumblebee on the back of your jumper, disappearing out of the kitchen; the last thing I heard was my dad whispering as he opened the front door: 'Now, you're going to be a good girl for Granddaddy, yes? I know you will be. You always are. Quite right, too. Because we know what happens to naughty girls, don't we?'

Chapter 51

'You must rest, Holly. Dr Henry said your heart rhythm has stabilised, but you may still need surgery. And you've got a corker of a bump on your head. Please. Stay in bed.'

The nurse's face is a blur. I know her name badge says Celia, because she's looked after me every time I've been in hospital since I was a little girl. I know she has blonde hair and green eyes, and that she's wearing a white uniform, with her hair up in a bun and a pink hairclip on one side that her daughter gave her. I know all this, but I can't see her: my eyes refuse to focus; my legs don't seem to work.

'Marley. I have to . . . get Marley,' I rasp, and my chest feels like I'm breathing fire.

'Your dad said he'll bring her to see you later, OK? Once you've had a bit more rest. I called Adam just now to update him on your progress. I haven't been able to get hold of Jordan, mind you. But your dad said he'll let him know as soon as.'

'NO! Please . . .' I try again to lift my legs and swing them to the floor, but suddenly the room seems to spin. I sink back against the pillows, feeling disorientated . . . defeated.

266

'Ah, here comes trouble,' Celia chirps briskly. 'Been pacing the waiting room these last three hours, she has.' She chuckles, and then I hear a whispered exchange.

'Who is it?' I say anxiously, staring blindly towards a dark shape I sense nearby.

'Fucking hell.' A familiar husky voice moves closer. 'Holly, you look . . .'

'I'll leave you two to have a natter,' Celia says brightly. 'No getting any more ideas about discharging yourself, though. Did you hear that, Amy? I'm putting you in charge. I'll be back shortly with more painkillers. Holly's to stay put till then. Understood?'

'Amy?' I hear the door close behind Celia and, for a moment, I panic that Amy has left too, and I'm alone. I reach out a hand, squeezing tightly the second Amy grabs hold of it. 'Thank God you're here. And yes, I imagine I look like shit. Good thing I can't see myself.'

'You look beautiful,' she says firmly. 'You always do. You just don't believe it.'

'I thought I was the one who banged my head. But thank you.' I smile, but in the next second I feel tears well up.

I hurt all over, and I feel lost and confused. It's only because I've been in this room on the cardiac ward so many times before that I have a mental image of where I am, and what has been happening to me: the white walls and ugly machinery; the thread-bare blue armchair by the window, with its dreary view of the car park; the army of doctors bearing defibrillators and syringes; the injections and scans, monitors and clipboards.

At least you were spared the drama. You were long gone before flashing blue lights lit up our street; you didn't have to watch, this time, as I was hauled onto a stretcher, lying flat on my back, staring at the worry box on the dresser while a paramedic performed emergency CPR in our kitchen. When I finally regained consciousness, my thoughts were still so locked in the past that I almost expected to see BB curled in a plastic crib at my side.

Worry returns in a pulsing, heady rush. Celia reassured me I'm stable, and while physically that may be true, emotionally, I'm a wreck. For all I have trawled my memory to understand what has been going on for you, I still have the feeling there is something – a stubborn canker deep in my brain – that I'm missing.

'Thanks for what?' Amy says, dragging my thoughts back to her as she rubs my hand. 'For telling the truth? You *do* look—'

'For not leaving,' I cut in, and my tears finally spill over. I'm so frightened, yet relieved at the same time. Amy is here; she will help me. Strange as it feels to trust her, I suddenly realise I do.

'As if. I'm always here for you, Holly. I may not show it, but I am.'

'You're not running away to Paris with my husband, then?' I try to laugh, but it hurts like hell. I let my head sink into the pillow, squeezing my eyes shut. 'I got that wrong, hey?'

'Big time.' Her voice is raw. 'Not that I blame you. It was a total car crash back at your house. But, you know what? In a funny kind of way, it helped.'

'Helped *who*?' I frown, recalling the trauma of the last few hours.

'Me.'

'Oh.' That surprises me. Amy has spent her whole life wanting to get away from our village. Now, as escape lay within her grasp, it has stalled at the eleventh hour. '*How*?'

'By helping me understand.' Her voice is unusually calm. Locked in darkness as I am, I tune in to each inflection. 'I've had my head buried in my own stuff, these last few weeks. I haven't had a clue what's been going on around me. I get it now, though.'

'Get what?'

'Your suspicion about me and Jordan. And Marley—'

'She overheard everything, Amy.' The heart-to-heart I had with you in your bedroom flashes vividly across my mind, along with your final, shocking note. 'She heard you and Jordan talking. On her birthday. The day of the regatta, when you were out on the lake.'

'Right. That makes even more sense,' Amy says in a flat voice.

'That's why she's been so anxious, you see? She got the wrong end of the stick. Misunderstood what was going on between the two of you. So did I,' I admit with a sigh.

'You thought I was scheming to run off with Jordan.'

'Yes.' I bite my lip in embarrassment. 'Which was bad enough. But Marley—'

'Is obviously terrified of me.' Amy sighs too. 'And probably hates me as much as you do. I'm sorry. It's all my fault. Jordan and I . . . we were just goofing around. I was in a really bad place. He was trying to help me – and keep Marley entertained at the same time.'

'She's seven,' I point out. 'She doesn't get irony. She's been terrified.'

'I honestly had no idea, Holl. It was just stupid banter. Because it was easier to joke around than be real. I guess neither of us realised how it was coming across to Marley. I wouldn't hurt her for the world. Or you. God, I'm such an idiot. I gave Marley the rabbit jigsaw and red shoes thinking it would remind you of us. Being girls. Best friends. But I guess they weren't good memories, were they? I'm so sorry,' she apologises again. 'For being a screw-up. And a flirt. You know I adore Jordan.' She pauses. 'But I love you more.'

Chapter 52

Amy squeezes my hand, and I let her. For a minute, neither of us speak.

'It's not all your fault,' I acknowledge at last, after silently replaying the conversation you told me about this morning, only this time hearing the words from Amy's perspective. 'I'd never have doubted you if Jordan and I . . . Well, I guess we've got a lot of talking to do.'

'He worships you, you know?' Amy's voice cracks. 'And I think he knows he's got some ground to make up. He's been fixing up his boat to take you guys on a trip. Get away for a while. He asked me to keep it a surprise. But you know what? I'm done with secrets.'

'A trip? With *us*?' Immediately, I picture the map in Jordan's log book and want to run to him and say how sorry I am for doubting him, too – for my fleeting, terrible suspicions about him bullying you as well as fancying Amy, and planning to hurt or leave me.

Deep down, I know he loves me; stress and worry poisoned that certainty, and fear turned it into a monster. But monsters

270

live in shadows; truth, honesty and openness can and will banish them. I brace myself to stand up, but pain shoots through my chest, spine, all the way down to my legs. At least they're not numb anymore, I console myself, gritting my teeth.

'Hey, no acrobatics. Remember Celia's orders. It'll be my head she has on a stick if you disobey them. For some reason, she has me pegged as a troublemaker.' Amy chuckles.

'I can't think why,' I say, but my smile won't come. 'I need Jordan,' I whisper.

'He must be out on the boat. Probably giving it a trial run.'

'Can you call him for me?'

'Already tried. Like, a zillion times. He's not picking up.'

'My dad . . .' I try again to sit up. 'I have to get Marley. And BB.'

'I know. But not yet, OK?' Amy rests a hand on my shoulder. 'Much as it pains me to admit it, old battle-axe Celia is right. You're not out of the woods yet, Holly. You almost didn't make it this time.' She lets out a ragged sigh. 'What would I do without you?'

'I'm not going anywhere.' I smack the bed in frustration; it feels like my prison, and I hate the feeling of powerlessness. 'Not even bloody Paris.'

'Huh, don't make me laugh. This is serious.' I hear the rustle of tissues followed by the sound of Amy blowing her nose. The bed dips as she sits down. 'Can you really not see?'

'It's just temporary. I hope. It always happens. My body kind of goes into shutdown. They've pumped me full of God knows what. It takes a while for everything to reboot, that's all.' I blink, and Amy's face finally starts to shift into focus. 'You've put lipstick on.'

'War paint.'

'Who are you fighting?'

There's a long pause, then Amy says quietly: 'Myself, I guess.'

I take a moment to digest her admission, memory gradually returning of the terrible scene at the cottage. I have no idea who called the ambulance, or whether my dad stuck around till it arrived. Celia said that Amy had been pacing up and down the

271

waiting room for hours, which means that you and BB are with my dad. At his flat? *Or somewhere else?*

'I'm worried about the kids, Amy,' I say, starting to panic. 'Dad won't hurt them, will he?' I have a flashback to Amy's anguished confession about the pregnancy she was forced to terminate. 'Did Dad . . . did he touch . . . has he ever hurt *you*?' As soon as the words leave my mouth, I realise how long they have lain trapped in my subconscious.

'No, never. Unless killing with kindness is really a thing.' She sighs. 'He smothered me, I guess. Trying to make up for me being lost luggage that washed up on your doorstep.'

'Pretty substantial luggage, as I recall,' I say dryly, picturing a seven-year-old Amy standing in the hall at Sea View, looking confident but, yes, also lost at the same time. She hasn't changed much, I reflect: always putting on a brave face; convincing everyone but herself that she's tough enough to cope with anything. 'He certainly doted on you.'

'I don't think it was all for my benefit. He was in love with my mum, you see? Oh, he loved Olivia too. But he really married her because she was pregnant with you.'

'What? No!' I sit bolt upright. 'That's not true. It was *your* mum who was pregnant when my parents got married. Mum told me so. Isabella was her maid of honour. She didn't want to be in the wedding photos, Mum said, because she was expecting *you*.'

'She may well have been,' Amy agrees. 'But so was your mum, Holly. Think about it. The timing. Your birthday is just a month after mine.'

'So?' I have a flashback to my dad saying it was hard loving someone when you weren't sure they loved you back. I'd assumed he was thinking of Luke Jackson's unrequited love for my mum, but maybe he was talking about himself: that Mum was unhappy because he loved Isabella. 'What about the butterfly brooch, though? And the letter from your dad?'

'Oh, Luke loved Olivia, for sure. But you were right about

272

your mum. She only ever had eyes for one man. Your dad. She was never unfaithful. Not in deed or thought.'

'But Dad let me think . . .' I close my eyes, trying to remember. 'He definitely gave me the impression that Mum was in love with his best friend. And that he *forgave* her.'

'Not true. Yes, Olivia was fond of Luke. But she only kept that brooch because she knew she'd broken his heart. Wearing it was her way of reminding herself never to take love for granted. At least, that's what she wrote in her diary.'

'Her diary. Right,' I say crossly. 'I thought you said you didn't read it?'

'Yeah. Sorry. I lied,' she says unashamedly. 'Not to hurt you. To save your feelings.'

'Oh, really.' I tut in exasperation, wondering whether to believe anything Amy says.

'OK, I got scared, Holl. I wanted to tell you more yesterday. I *tried* to, honestly. But, you know, you've always had your parents on a pedestal. I could see I was shattering your illusions, and I hated that. I didn't want you to feel as messed up as I've been. It's been an absolute nightmare trying to get my head around all this.'

'For eight *years*?' I can't hide my frustration.

'Actually, more like eight weeks.'

'What? Oh, my God. Marley's birthday. You're saying that all this . . . You only found it out that *day*? But you said you'd had the brooch since Mum died? And the letter.'

'That's true. Things, um, came to a head before the regatta, though.'

I thought of her strange mood and erratic behaviour when she turned up at the cottage on the morning of your birthday. Suddenly, it was beginning to make sense. 'You mean, before you went out on the boat with Jordan . . . and Marley.'

'Yeah. Look, I realise it's no excuse for my behaviour that day. Or for giving you a wide berth since. I've been avoiding you, and I'm sure you wondered why. In my defence, finding all this out . . . it was like a bomb going off in my head. Jordan said it would be the same for you. He said I just had to bite the bullet and tell you. But he was as scared as I was. He thought the truth would kill you. And he was half-right. Look at you.'

'Wait, what?' I grit my teeth, fighting nausea. 'Are you saying Jordan *knows*? He's known about my parents all this time – and he never told me?'

Chapter 53

TODAY – SUNDAY, 1.37 P.M.

Amy pauses for so long that if my eyesight hadn't more or less recovered, I would have imagined she'd left the room. For a moment, I almost wish my vision hadn't returned – that I didn't have to look at the guilt mixed with defiance on her beautiful face.

'We need to fix us first': that's what Jordan said to me. Now Amy has revealed that he's been privy to her secrets all along, and that both of them kept them from me, I'm no longer sure that's possible. My husband and my best friend may not have had an affair, but I feel like, somewhere along the line, their loyalties have switched from me to each other.

'Please don't blame Jordan,' Amy says urgently. 'It was deeply unfair of me to put him in that position. I realise that now. He wanted to tell you, he really did.'

'Is that why he's been sleeping on the boat?'

'I don't . . .' Her eyes widen innocently, then she sighs. 'Yeah, I guess. He's a terrible liar. Which is actually a good thing, don't you think?' Tentatively, she rests a hand on my arm. 'Give him a second chance, Holl. He deserves it.'

'Oh, suddenly you're a marriage counsellor, are you?' I say crossly.

'OK, I deserved that. You're right. I'm the last person to give relationship advice. I've got that in common with Miss Shaw, at least. Huh. She may dress like a clown, but we're both spinsters. Both so frightened of being hurt that we don't take the risk.'

The comparison is so ludicrous, I can't help smiling. 'Amy, I have to tell you, there is nothing remotely similar between you and Miss Shaw.'

'Well, thank you for that.' She wrinkles her nose. 'Although, in a way, she's braver than I am. She's in love with your dad. Has been for years. You knew that, right?'

'I know you've hinted at it.' I roll my eyes. 'Does *she* know about any of this?'

'I think she guessed about my termination. She's dropped enough snide hints. But I doubt she knew about your parents. They were so secretive, they'd have made great spies.'

My heart jumps at the word. 'Did you say that to Jordan, by any chance?' I recall more of the conversation you overheard on the boat, yet another piece falling into place.

'Yeah. He agreed with me. He even joked that Olivia's parties were some kind of elaborate cover. I told him I suspected your mum was burying state secrets in her allotment.'

'Better that than naughty girls,' I say, feeling goose bumps chase up my back.

'Ha. You sound just like me.' Amy smiles ruefully. 'Fabricating stories. Inventing mysteries where they don't exist. I like a bit of drama as much as the next person,' she admits. 'But, sadly, there's nothing at that allotment but a bunch of old turnips and potatoes.'

'Marley doesn't think so.' I give her a sharp look, remembering who planted the idea in your head about hidden bones in the first place. 'You know, I'm still cross that you made up all that nonsense about naughty girls being buried there.'

'Nuh-uh, sorry. I can't claim ownership of that one. I told the kids some guff about unhappy ghosts. Restless spirits walking the earth. I never mentioned *naughty girls*.'

'Are you sure?' I frown, trying to think who else could have told you. 'What about Mum's brooch, then? Marley drew an almost exact copy.'

'Ah, I guess that *is* down to me. I've had it in my pocket for weeks. I showed it to Jordan when we were out on the boat. Marley must have seen it.'

'And probably thought you stole it,' I say, groaning. 'I've shown her photos of her grandma wearing it. She knows how precious it was. To Mum. To me.'

'Which no doubt made her hate me more. Evil Aunty Amy. I told you, I fuck everything up.' She pauses, then adds softly, 'But I don't mean to.'

'We've all made mistakes,' I acknowledge a little tightly. 'It's what we do about them that counts.' My heart leaps as I remember Amy making a similar, drunken comment at your birthday party. I realise now what she was talking about. 'By mistake, I don't mean your baby.' I reach out, resting a hand on her arm. 'I'm so sorry that you lost . . .'

'I didn't *lose* it. I killed it,' she says harshly. '*It.*' Her voice cracks. 'Yes, not even *he*, or *she*. I have no idea if my child was a boy or a girl. It was too early to tell.'

'And my dad definitely wasn't the father?' I ask breathlessly.

'Fuck, no.' She pulls a grimace. 'Sorry. Adam was actually very kind. He took care of *everything*. The private hospital. The paperwork. There was shitloads.'

I think back to my dad's agitation the day I confronted him in his study about Jane, his defensiveness of Amy after I queried her wild tale about murdering my friend. He claimed he was looking for a poem, but his desk was piled high with official-looking papers. 'I can believe it,' I said quietly. 'Termination.' I wince at the word. 'It's a big thing.'

'The biggest. *Huge.* And I was just so *angry*. I guess I've never completely let go of that. What I found out on Marley's birthday . . . it brought it all back. How much I wanted that baby.

Adam telling me it would destroy Olivia. She couldn't have more kids, you know?'

'Yes. Dad told me that much, at least,' I say bitterly.

'Apparently, they discussed IVF. Until I came along, anyway. Then they dropped the idea. Olivia agreed to raise me instead. She'd had her cancer diagnosis by then. So, you see, your dad didn't have the heart to tell her that the cocky sixteen-year-old she'd taken under her wing got pregnant the first time. But he couldn't let me have a child, either. Not after—'

'The sacrifice my mum had made raising his best friend's daughter,' I finish for her, remembering Dad's comment about what Mum had given up for him. 'What a mess.' I sigh. 'But I'm glad he looked after you. I was worried that he—'

'Your dad isn't a monster, Holly. He's human. Fallible, in other words. He likes to think he lives life by the book. Doing the right thing. It's the lawyer in him, I guess. But he's made plenty of mistakes too.'

'I know. And I'd never have believed Dad capable of hurting *anyone*, until . . .' My voice dries up as I picture him dragging you and BB out of the cottage.

Maybe he genuinely *had* wanted to give me a break and simply became frustrated when I resisted, his hurt turning to anger when I asked whether he had abused Amy. I realise now that I got that wrong, but *he* was wrong to have kept such a big secret from me all these years. Growing up, I always made excuses for Amy, letting her off the hook for so much. If I'd known what she was going through, the pregnancy she'd either wanted or was persuaded to end, it would have changed so much. Now I'm left wondering what else I don't know.

'Until what?' Amy prompts impatiently.

'I heard Dad ask Marley if she knows what happens to *naughty girls*.' Goose bumps prickle across my skin. 'Marley still believes there are bones buried at the allotment. I took her to Maria's farm to put her mind at rest. But, Amy, I found Jane's doll there.'

'Jane from primary school? You found her Bratz doll? Wow. I took that off her, oh, it must be twenty years ago. Ugly thing. I chucked it in the jumble box where it belonged.'

'Ah, right.' I'd guessed as much, but it was a relief to hear Amy confirm it.

'I'm sorry if it scared Marley. And the ghost stories. The little sods in her class were running rings round me. I only meant to give them a bit of a fright to shut them up.'

'So it was pure coincidence, you think? Dad talking about naughty girls?'

'I reckon so. Why? What are you thinking?'

'Just . . . You're right that Dad has always tried to live by some kind of moral code. If we did something wrong, if we broke something, or didn't tidy our room, we got punished. Or I did,' I mutter, remembering how Amy always seemed to wriggle out of trouble.

'Yes, I remember,' she says, frowning. 'And? So what?'

'I'm not sure. All I know is that Jane died, and no one ever mentioned her again.' I pause, thinking. 'Maria said there was some kind of accident. And you told me once that Jane fell off a swing. Was that true?'

'I told you I *pushed* her, you mean.' Amy sighs. 'You know, I had to lie to everyone about the termination. Making stuff up sort of became a bad habit. Fantasy is a hell of a lot easier to deal with than the truth.'

'I get that. But what *was* the truth? How did you even know what happened to Jane?'

'Oh, that's simple. I overheard your dad talking about it. It all sounded very intriguing. I guess I hijacked the story and embellished it with a few details of my own.'

'You heard my dad talking about *Jane*? Who with?'

'A lawyer, I think. It was hard to tell through the door.' Her mouth twists wryly. 'He was on the phone in his study. I *did* gather that he was planning to represent Jane's aunt and uncle. They wanted to sue the Local Education Authority over the accident. It took place on school property, you see. Why? You didn't think that Adam . . .'

'I don't know. I don't know *what* I think anymore.'

'Oh, Holly. Look, your dad's done a lot of things I don't agree with. He's kept a lot of secrets, and I'm still mad as hell at him for that. But he was a good husband to Olivia, and he never hurt Jane. Or me, for that matter.'

'Are you absolutely sure?' I give her one last chance. 'Your baby's father—'

'Was just some guy I met in the pub.' She lets out a low, bitter laugh tinged with a hint of self-consciousness. 'Your neighbour, actually.'

'*What?* You mean *Phil?*' I stare at her in shock.

'Yeah. He was kind to me. Funny. Huh, I look at him now and wonder what the hell I was thinking. But to a sixteen-year-old . . . He had a cool job. A fast car. He was good-looking, too, in a preppy kind of way. What can I say? He flattered me.'

I picture Phil standing outside in the rain, his dressing gown falling open to reveal a muscular chest. 'Yeah. I can believe it. What an arse, though. You were *sixteen*.'

'Don't worry, you're not living next door to a paedo. Just a rather sad, immature guy. In his defence, I told him I was eighteen. I *didn't* tell him I was still at school. He soon got bored of me, anyway. Probably when I started to get fat.'

'Hardly. Oh. Shit. You mean, when you were *pregnant*.' I picture Amy in the garden at Sea View, forcing herself higher on the swing, worrying about being 'chubby'.

'Phil never had a clue, if that's what you're thinking. He still doesn't. *Loser*,' she hisses. 'I see him around sometimes. I always make a point of smiling. No way do I want him thinking his existence matters a jot to me. He looks right through me, though. I'm just glad I never told him about the baby. I never told *anyone*.' She pauses. 'Nor did you, come to that.'

'Sorry?'

'Oh, don't worry, I'm not blaming you. I'm just saying I know you turned a blind eye to me creeping out of our room every night when we were kids.'

'I wish I hadn't now.' I sigh. 'Maybe then I'd have found all this out a lot sooner. You say you've always looked out for me. Well, it was the same for me, too. I didn't want to get you into trouble. I just watched, listened and kept my mouth shut.'

'You protected me, I know that. I was a bitch, but you never dobbed me in it. I want us to always be that close, Holl. When I get back from Paris . . .' She coughs then starts again. 'Once I've sorted myself out, I'd like *us* to start again. Be the friends your dad wanted us to be. We need to stick together, you and me. After all, that's what sisters do, isn't it?'

'Almost-sisters,' I say, smiling as I think of the term she has always used. I haven't always liked it. Amy told me she grew up feeling jealous of everything I had, but in truth I've always been jealous of her, I acknowledge.

'Actually, no,' Amy corrects softly. 'That's what I came back to tell you.' She shifts closer on the bed. 'You're not my almost-sister. You're my *half*-sister.'

'I'm . . . what?' I feel as though the world has just spun on its axis, and it has nothing to do with the medication still fizzing through my veins.

'Holly, the brooch, the letter . . . what I've been trying tell you, in my usual cack-handed way, is that Adam is my dad, too.' Reaching into her jacket pocket, she takes out a piece of paper and hands it to me. 'Don't worry, you don't have to take my word for it this time. I realise I'm not the most reliable witness. But I know someone who is. Here, read this.'

I stare at her in shock. 'No. I . . . I can't.'

'Please. You have to,' Amy insists, pressing the folded paper into my hand. 'It's a letter. From Luke Jackson. It explains everything.'

'No, I mean I *can't*, Amy.' I push the letter away, blinking rapidly. 'My eyes . . .'

'Oh. Right. Sorry.' She lets out a long, ragged sigh. 'OK. Then I'll read it for you.'

Chapter 54

'*My dearest Amy,*

'*I wish I had the courage to speak to you in person, but by now you'll have realised I'm not the father you deserve. I apologise unreservedly for my absence from your life – the pain I know it will have caused you. My only excuse is that I've been battling my own pain, my own losses. I don't have the right to ask this of you, but, if only for curiosity's sake rather than mine, please let me share my side of the story with you.*

'*I was just eighteen and a cocky, ambitious law student when I first met Olivia Howard. And she was the sweetest, kindest, most modest woman I'd ever met. Like me, she came from a rich family, but she taught me that it wasn't important how much wealth we had been born into; all that mattered was what we did with our own lives to earn that privilege.*

'*I knew Olivia was in love with my best friend. She never led me on; she let me down gently. Still, her decision to marry Adam Aitken was a pain I bear to this day. To my shame, I would have continued to pursue her, had it not been for*

Isabella, your mother and the woman who was to become my wife. I know it hurt Isabella deeply that I refused to give up hope that, one day, Olivia would get tired of Adam and turn to me. Olivia was Isabella's best friend, you see, and while your mother was funny and generous, she was also fiery. She did everything possible to make me jealous, flirting with everyone – with Adam.

'If this sounds as though I judge her harshly, please know I loved your mother very much. She was strong, beautiful and immensely talented. I was simply obsessed with Olivia, and I struggled to let go of that. But when Isabella told me she was pregnant, I didn't hesitate. I wrote to Olivia to say goodbye, allowing myself only the consolation of sending her a small trinket as a memento of my affection. But I was happy to do my duty. In time, that grew into the genuine joy of being a husband and father – to you, my dearest Amy.

'I adored you from the second I held you, and for the first seven years of your life, we were a happy family. Isabella loved London, and her fashion business thrived. So too did my law career, and when Isabella decided to expand into Europe, I was thrilled that it coincided with publication of my first book. It seemed the world was our oyster, and we couldn't wait to show it to you.

'Alas, the stress of planning our European tour was immense. I'm not ashamed to admit that Isabella and I fought, but I do regret that I pushed her too far. In the heat of a row, I told her she was being selfish, putting her career before being a mother. She responded by sneering at me for caring about a child who wasn't even my daughter, taunting me that while I'd been "dithering over Olivia" at university, she'd had a one-night stand. With my best friend.

'I know Isabella was right to be angry with me, but I was devastated. With the benefit of hindsight, I've learned to accept that no one set out to hurt anyone. We were young and free, and college life had revolved around parties and alcohol. Isabella only slept with Adam once, but it was enough. I've often wondered, if she'd told Adam at the time, how different things might have been. I think he was in love with her, you see. But Isabella didn't return his feelings. She merely used him to make me jealous, and she used being pregnant to force me to stop "dithering" and make a commitment.

'When Olivia fell pregnant too, our fates were sealed. Adam married her, I married Isabella, and our lives moved on. No one was any the wiser, until that day in Paris when Isabella threw the truth at me. My best, closest friendship died for me that day. So too did my marriage. To put it mildly, I struggled – and I made the worst decision of my life. I phoned Adam and told him that if he loved Isabella so much, he was welcome to raise their bastard child.

'Forgive me, Amy. My only defence is that I wasn't in my right mind. Not a day has passed when I haven't regretted the choice I made. Even though you were not my daughter, I loved you. It tore my heart into pieces when I arranged to meet Adam at our old college to hand you over. But I was consumed by anger – towards him, and towards Isabella.

'She didn't know that the "visit" with Adam and Olivia was to be permanent; I let her think you were going to Sea View merely to meet their daughter. Your mother had no idea that I'd packed a suitcase for you, and when I returned to the hotel without you, she wept until the doctor insisted on her being sedated. I'm ashamed to admit that I then bullied her into leaving – returning to Paris.

'I visited Suffolk only one more time, after that. It was a bank holiday, I believe. Three weeks or so after I'd left you with Adam and Olivia. I was desperate to see you, but when it came to it, my courage failed me. I did see Olivia, but only from a distance; I didn't dare approach or speak to her. I'm not a bad man. I made a terrible mistake, but I didn't want to rock the boat for any of you. I knew that I alone should pay the price for what I had done, and the consequences of my actions. I returned to Paris alone, a broken man.

'I'm sorry, Amy. Sorry for being such a coward. I know you tried to reach out to me when you were a young student yourself. I received your messages when you arrived in Paris. I couldn't bring myself to reply. I didn't know how to find the words to tell you that, after returning to Paris without you that summer, your mother was so overcome with grief that, the following day, she slipped out of our hotel without telling me, and walked into the River Seine. Her body wasn't found until two days later . . .'

Chapter 55

TODAY – SUNDAY, 2.50 P.M.

I hold Amy until she stops crying, and for the second time in as many days, she reminds me of you – her frightened eyes and angry tears; the distraught sobs racking her body. Only now I know where the resemblance I've so fleetingly noticed comes from: you have always affectionately called her Aunty Amy, but in fact that's exactly what she is. More than that, she's my sister – and my heart breaks along with hers.

'*This* is what you found out. On the morning of Marley's birthday. Isn't it?'

'Yes. Luke sent the letter to your dad. *My* dad.' She pulls a face. 'Sorry, I'm never going to get used to calling him that. I'm surprised he passed it on to me. But he did.' Her mouth curls in disdain. 'Maybe he hoped I'd throw myself into his arms and call him *Daddy*.'

'But he definitely knew, though?' I say, determined to be absolutely clear. 'Dad knew, when he brought you to live with us, that you were his daughter. And my mum didn't.'

'Correct.'

'Jesus.'

287

'I'm sorry it's taken me so long to tell you. I . . . I wasn't even sure whether I should.'

'Well, at least it's only taken you eight weeks.' I nod at the letter, crumpled on the bed between us. 'Luke Jackson took more than twenty years. Why tell you now, anyway?'

'He's sick,' Amy says, wiping away more tears.

'Too right. To do what he did.' I shake my head.

'No, I mean he's ill. Cancer. That's why he wrote the letter. To clear his conscience, I guess.' She sighs. 'You know, it's funny because I haven't seen him for years. Or actually ever thought of him as my dad, really. Which he isn't, of course, but . . .'

'It still hurts.' I nod in understanding. 'It *all* hurts.' I think for a moment, picking up the letter. 'I presume he knows that's what killed Mum. Cancer.' I smooth out the crumpled paper, skimming the rest of the words, looking for my mum's name.

'He was too ashamed to come to the funeral. That's what he wrote, anyway.'

'Right.' I bite back a cynical response. However shocked I am, however much it changes my understanding of my own family, my parents and my childhood, I'm more concerned about Amy now. 'Everything's going to be OK,' I promise, squeezing her hand.

'I know.' She wipes her eyes. 'Well, I didn't for a while. But I do now. Thanks for not shooting the messenger.' She smiles crookedly. 'I was more worried about that than anything else. That it would hurt you, finding out the truth. Having me as a sister.' She laughs.

'You're not so bad. You have your moments, but I guess I can put up with you.' I give her a hug. 'Unless you really are planning to stay in Paris. Why would you go, anyway?'

'To say goodbye to my dad, of course. Well, the idea of him, anyway. I haven't thought of him that way in years. Like you said, family is as family does. Adam and Olivia brought me up. As far as I'm concerned, they've always been my parents. But I need to tell Luke that . . . that it's all OK. He's dying. I watched your mum . . .'

'You want his life to end more peacefully, yes?' Once again, I battle the pain of knowing that Mum's last moments were troubled. 'I wish I knew,' I whisper.

'If Olivia knew about me, you mean?' Amy says intuitively.

'Yes.' I search her eyes for the truth. 'What do *you* think?'

'I think she did. And I think the only way she could deal with it was by pretending she didn't. Which is exactly why I'm so mad at Adam.'

'Because he never told Mum?'

'Yep. Oh, I know he didn't want to hurt her. She couldn't have more kids. It would have been a tough conversation. But he should have had it. He shouldn't have let her go to her grave carrying that burden. Secrecy eats you up,' she says fiercely.

'So does worry,' I admit.

'Opposite sides of the same coin, hey?'

'The less we know, the more we worry.' Immediately, I'm reminded of you. 'I hope Marley is all right,' I say anxiously.

Amy frowns. 'You mean is she OK about me? The stuff she overheard with Jordan?'

'No. I explained all that to her. I think she understood. She's a clever girl. It all got mixed up in her head, that's all. Probably didn't help that you were in the middle of the lake.'

'Ha. Those bloody islands. Spooky as heck in the fog. I was a bag of nerves all day.'

'That day . . .' I picture the events of your birthday one more time. 'You came to the cottage looking like you'd seen a ghost. And Dad didn't come to the party at all.'

'He gave me the letter that morning. Dropped it off with a gift for Marley. In fairness, he was a wreck too. I made him wait while I read it. Then I gave him a piece of my mind.'

'I can imagine,' I say, wincing.

'He insisted he'd only been thinking of *you*. He said you'd always been jealous of me. He didn't want to make things worse by telling you the truth about me.'

'He was probably half-right,' I admit. 'I would have found it hard.'

'No, you wouldn't,' Amy says, surprising me. 'You'd have coped with it just like Olivia did. Because you're her daughter, and like her you're strong, and sweet, and bloody kind. Luke Jackson had that much right, at least. But it's the reason I can't forgive Adam. Because, in truth, I think the reason he kept quiet about everything wasn't to protect you, but himself. His prized reputation.' Her mouth twists. 'You know what village gossip is like.'

'I do.' *So did Mum*, and I wonder how many rumours about herself she had to ignore.

'That's really all I could think of that day. After I'd read the letter. How mad I was with Adam. And the more I drank, the madder I got. I kept thinking he was going to turn up at any moment. At the regatta. Marley's party. I wound myself up into a right state. Ridiculous, hey? Like I was a naughty child waiting for an angry parent to come home.'

'Parents hold all the power,' I muse, then look closely at Amy. 'What did you mean when you said "sometimes we have to take it back"?'

'I meant Paris. Adam doesn't want me to go. It's ridiculous! Even after all these years, with your mum and mine both dead, he's so bloody jealous of that man!'

'Or perhaps he's worried you'll decide you'd rather call him Dad after all.'

'Huh. I hadn't thought of that. You could be right. Maybe he's trying to cling on to his last bit of power over me. He pretty much smothered me, growing up.'

'Did it ever bother you?'

'Weird me out, you mean?' Amy says bluntly. 'Sometimes. He was always wanting to hang out with me. Go to London. Mini breaks when I was at college. In hindsight, obviously, I realise he was just thrilled to have this second daughter. At the time . . .'

'You wondered why he was so affectionate.'

'A bit. I guess it did freak me out sometimes. But I was needy, you know? Orphan Annie. Hungry for love.' She rolls her eyes. 'I took what I could get. Letting Adam bore on about his collections. Sneaking out to meet flirty Phil in the pub. Talk about a naughty girl!'

The words make me shudder. 'Dad must have known. But he never punished you.'

'He never even shouted at me. Your mum was gentle, but you always knew when she was cross, didn't you? I've never met anyone with as much self-control as Adam.'

'True,' I say thoughtfully. 'But like Luke said in his letter, people can be pushed too far. Especially if you're already wound up, it can take just one little thing to make you . . . snap.'

Amy and I exchange glances. Neither of us say a word, but I know we're each having the same thought. She strides to the door, checking the corridor outside, then looks around to find where Celia has left my clothes. I'm out of bed before she hands me my jeans.

'Fucking hospital car parks. This is daylight robbery,' Amy says, emptying the contents of her purse into a ticket machine. 'Take it easy, Holl,' she adds more gently, striding quickly around her car to open the passenger door for me.

'I'm so full of drugs, I can barely feel a thing,' I reassure her, even though my head is pounding and each step feels like I'm wading through mud. 'Can I borrow your phone?' I say, once I'm settled in the leather seat.

'Sure.' She taps in the passcode and hands me her iPhone. 'Although I've probably filled Jordan's voicemail.'

'Maybe he'll pick up this time.' He doesn't.

'Shit. There's Celia.' Wiping the steamed-up windscreen with her jacket sleeve, Amy nods towards the hospital canteen. 'She must be heading back to the ward after her break.'

'It's fine. Doctor Henry gave the OK for me to rest at home, remember?'

'Yeah, but we're not *going* home, are we?' Amy punches the ignition and grinds the Mini into gear.

'Not yet, anyway,' I say quietly. 'Not without my children.'

'Exactly. Now buckle up.' She drags her seatbelt into position, before stretching across me to help fasten mine. 'I want to get there before the light starts to fade. I hate driving on the motorway in the dark.'

I check my watch. 'God, look at the time, Amy. Your train . . . Paris?'

'Can wait. So can Luke Jackson. My family is here.' She leans sideways to bump shoulders with me, but her eyes are misty. '*You're* my family, Holl. And the kids, obviously. But mainly you. You're the only one who matters. The only one who's *ever* mattered to me.'

'Oh, Amy.' My eyes fill up too. 'You really mean that?'

'Why the hell do you think I've stuck around all these years? To keep an eye on you, of course, you noodle,' she says when I'm too choked up to speak. 'Sure, you're my sister. But more than that, you're my best – shit, probably my only true friend.'

'Amy . . .' I can see she's struggling, and I hate to see her upset.

'No, let me say it. I should have said it way before now. You're the centre of my world, Holl. No matter what I've thrown at you, you've always turned the other cheek.' She gives a watery smile. 'Ha, not to get all biblical about it, but you know what I mean.'

'I do,' I say, smiling through my tears.

'You've never turned your back on me, no matter what, and I want you to know that I'll always be here for you, too. We've both lost our mums, but we still have each other, yes? And right now, you need me more than a man who lied to me my whole fucking life.'

292

Chapter 56

TODAY – SUNDAY, 3.55 P.M.

The apartment building always smells the same: of beeswax and air freshener. Walking into the grey-carpet-tiled communal hallway, I realise that its soullessness is a big part of the reason I dislike visiting my dad here. Growing up, I never set foot in Sea View without being enveloped by the warm waft of baking, fresh laundry and the fragrance of cut flowers.

It was only in Dad's study that the smell was different, with pungent lingering traces of the chemicals he used to clean his 'curiosities'. As I make my way up the stairs towards the first-floor apartment where he's lived since selling Sea View, the acrid aroma of cleaning fluids catches more strongly at the back of my throat, and I have the sense that my dad brought all these smells with him, along with his collections.

'This one,' Amy announces, as though I've never been here before. 'Sorry,' she adds. 'Force of habit. Once a teacher, always a—'

'Bossy boots,' I cut in, smiling. 'You might be my big sister, but only by a month.'

'Big sister.' She grins. 'I like that.'

'I thought you would.' I roll my eyes, but the brief moment

293

of humour between us is swallowed a second later when I notice that the front door stands wide open. 'Hello? Dad?'

'There's no one here,' Amy says, after pushing past me to quickly search the small, modern, two-bedroomed flat. 'The heating isn't on, either.' She feels the radiators in the long, narrow living room, then pulls open the curtains to reveal a pretty view of the golf course.

'That's odd. Dad hates being cold. So does Marley.' I look around, searching for any clues that you've been there. The flat seems almost *too* tidy, with velvet cushions I remember from Sea View, handmade by my mum, arranged perfectly on the sofa. Various TV remotes are stacked in a neat pile on an empty bookcase that used to be stuffed full of books.

'Yeah. It's usually like a sauna in here,' Amy agrees. 'I can see my own breath. Look!' She puffs energetically in demonstration.

My own chest still feels too tight with anxiety to copy her. 'Where are they?' I whisper, trying hard not to panic. 'I can't see any of Marley's toys. And where are BB's things? I left a spare carry-cot here. Clothes and nappies, too.'

'I bet they've been out for the day,' Amy says logically. 'Adam's probably been trying to keep them occupied. To distract them.'

'He took them *hours* ago.' I rack my brains to think where he could have taken you on a cold, grey day in October, when he hates the beach and the local shops will be shut.

'Cinema?' Amy suggests, frowning.

'Not with BB. Dad likes absolute peace and quiet to watch films. Remember?'

'True. What about the golf club for hot chocolate?'

'Hmm. That does sound more likely. Can you phone—'

'It's practically over the road, Holl. I'll go check. You wait here.' She zips up her leather jacket and strides towards the door.

'No, I'm coming,' I say stubbornly, following her, even though I know she's right: I can barely walk.

'I'll be back before you know it.' She redirects me towards the sofa, urging me to sit down, before pulling a blanket around my shoulders. I'm still wearing the navy jacket and suede ankle boots Amy brought to the hospital for me, but it's freezing in the flat. 'Hopefully with the kids. Try not to worry about them. Or me.' She winks. 'I can handle Adam.'

'I don't doubt it for a second. In fact, it's him I'm worried about,' I try to joke, but the second she's left, I stand up and start pacing the flat in agitation.

The kitchen is compact and as spotlessly, almost clinically clean as the rest of the flat. I check the fridge, surprised to find it empty. There isn't so much as a loaf of bread, let alone a pizza or any of the snacks Dad usually buys for you. But it's only when I discover that there are no cartons of baby milk, or tins of Formula in the cupboard, that I really start to panic. BB is only two months old: if he isn't fed properly, he will dehydrate fast.

'Damn, damn, damn,' I mutter, striding through to the spare bedroom, hoping to find a stash of provisions in there, along with the travel cot Jordan set up for naps during visits. There's nothing. Even the books I know you left here on our last visit have been tidied away.

Opening the drawer in the cabinet by the bed, I rifle impatiently through old drawings and a scattering of pens, not quite sure what I'm looking for until my fingertips scrape something cold, hard and metallic.

'Oh, my God.' Shakily, I remove the awkward-shaped, weighty object and lay it carefully on the bed, sitting down next to it, staring at the familiar antique pistol in shock.

I recognise it immediately: it was a prized piece in Dad's collection. The black powder metal bears the patina of age, and there is a hairline crack in the ivory grip that I know was the reason he was able to buy it so cheaply at auction. 'It still fires true, Holly,' I remember Dad saying. 'Military weapons of this calibre were built to last.'

'No, no, *no*!' I leap off the bed, covering my ears with my hands, trying to silence the whispers at the back of my mind which are now a deafening roar, clamouring to be heard.

I stare at the barrel of the handgun, cursing as I realise I have no idea how to spot whether it has been recently discharged. 'Oh, Marley. I'm so *stupid*.' My eyes fill with tears as I remember your last note, creased and half-torn. Had there been part of a word missing?

I picture the crumpled piece of paper: *daddy wants to kill you*, it said, and my heart almost stops as it dawns on me that while you were clearly worried about *your* daddy, it could well have been mine that terrified you. For your own sake – but also mine . . .

He said you were too noisy, too messy – that you made me tired, 'just like your grandma', who died after she 'became broken' and no longer worked, and whose ghost you seemed convinced was still wandering the earth . . . Because she'd died in pain, having been punished for not coping with life? For being tired all the time, and ill? *Just like me.*

'If Daddy has a gun too . . .' That's what you said to me. If he has a gun *too*. Like my dad? 'Granddaddy wants to kill you,' I say, testing the words out loud. 'Is that what you wrote, Marley? Is that what you wanted to tell me?'

I leave the pistol on the bed and hurry back into the other bedroom, not sure what I'm looking for, but trying to convince myself there's no way my dad would have shown you this weapon, let alone planned to use it to hurt me – or you . . .

'Stop!' I cover my ears again, desperate to silence the tormenting voices in my head.

'Stop what?' a familiar clipped voice says behind me. 'I was just—'

'Jesus Christ, Dad!' I press a hand to my chest as I turn to face him.

'Sorry. The front door was open. I guess that's how you got in. I was just putting the recycling out.' He frowns. 'What are you doing here, anyway? You should be in—'

'Where are they?' I fly at him. 'Where are my *children*?'

'Whoa, steady on.' He reaches out with both hands. 'They're with their dad, of course. Jordan's taken them out for the day. I dropped them off with him earlier. Told him you needed a break. I, um, I didn't tell him you were in hospital, by the way. I know how he feels about that place. You've spent half your life in there. I didn't want to worry him.'

'You didn't *tell* him?' I stumble towards the bed, reaching for the phone on the bedside table. But my dad moves faster, putting out a hand to stop me.

'Please, come and sit down, Holly. We need to talk. But not . . . in here.'

He glances around the room with a frown, then turns and walks briskly back to the living room, smiling at me over his shoulder, for all the world as though I've just popped round for afternoon tea, rather than having spent the day in hospital, fighting for my life – and now being in fear for my *children's* lives.

Chapter 57

TODAY – SUNDAY, 4.15 P.M.

'The kids are fine, Holly.'

'What do you mean *fine*?' I snap, stalking after him. 'You snatch them off me, leaving me flat-out unconscious on the kitchen floor, covered in blood, I might add. And there's a . . . a gun in their bedroom.' My head is buzzing; I think I'm going to faint.

'Oh, *that's* where I put it.' Dad huffs. 'I haven't really got room for my collection here. I need to get a proper display cabinet. If you look in any of the wardrobes, you'll find all sorts. And as for snatching the kids, that's a slight exaggeration, pickle.'

'Excuse me?' I stare at him in disbelief.

'I called the ambulance, didn't I? I didn't want the children upset. Besides, Amy was with you. I knew she'd take care of you. I knew what she was telling you, too.' He sits awkwardly on the sofa, looking tired and suddenly much older.

'Everything *you* should have told me,' I say angrily. Even if I accept his explanation about the gun, which I'm not yet sure I do, it was deeply irresponsible of him to leave it in the room where you sleep. I take deep breaths, fighting to stay calm, to ask questions rather than hurl accusations. 'Why *didn't* you tell me about Amy? And don't say to protect me!'

'Why not?' He sits back, folding his arms across his chest. 'It's the truth.'

'Huh.' I roll my eyes. 'I'm not sure anyone in our family knows what that means.'

'I've never lied to you, Holly.'

'Oh, so hiding something really, really important isn't the same as lying?'

'Secrets aren't always bad. Some things are better off buried.'

The word instantly reminds me of your fear of the allotment. 'Burying secrets. You mean like about what happened to my friend Jane?' I say bluntly.

Dad sits up straighter. 'What do you know about that?'

'I know she died.' My hand drifts to my neck, feeling for the silver heart necklace Jane gave me all those years ago. I'm not wearing it – the doctors removed it at the hospital – but my fingers tingle as I imagine the smooth curves of the delicate trinket.

'It was an accident,' Dad says hoarsely.

I raise my eyebrows. 'So Amy told me.'

'Amy? What does *she* know about it? Or think she knows,' he scoffs.

The injustice rankles. 'Look, I know you and Amy have a lot to talk about. You can't blame her for being mad at you, though.' I turn back towards the living-room door, preparing to leave. 'But right now, all I'm concerned about is finding my children.'

'OK, fine. Have it your way. I've got nothing to lose now, anyway.' He sighs, then nods at the armchair. 'You may as well make yourself comfortable.'

I hesitate, then sit down, taking a moment to allow the dizziness to pass. Every little movement takes huge effort. Celia was right: I should still be in hospital. 'So?' I say sharply.

'Are you OK?' Dad half stands up. 'Do you need me to—'

'I need you to tell me the truth.' My head is pounding now;

I grit my teeth, ignoring the pain. 'And nothing but the truth. You're a lawyer. You must understand that.'

'Right, yes, of course.'

'So?' I prompt, suddenly having a flashback to being a child in his study, being interrogated for some misdemeanour. *How the tables are turned*, I think, recalling Amy's comment about taking back the power. I won't leave until I know everything.

'Yes, sadly, your friend Jane died. But it *was* an accident,' he insists. 'I'm surprised Amy didn't overhear that, too. That's how she found out, isn't it? Listening at doors. Poking through diaries.' He gives me a meaningful look, and I know he's referring to Mum's journal.

'If anyone had told her the truth, she wouldn't have had to,' I point out.

'And yet something tells me she still would have.' His lips twist. 'Oh, I know exactly what she's like. I always have. She's never changed, not since she was a little girl. I tried to turn a blind eye to her mistakes. I felt so damned guilty about the whole . . . situation.'

'About Amy being your daughter, you mean?' I refuse to skirt around the facts. 'About Mum having no idea that her best friend's little girl was also yours? Does Amy even *look* like Isabella?' I ask curiously, realising I've never seen any photos of her.

'Not so you'd notice. Unless you had reason to look more closely, of course.'

'But she has your dark hair. Your blue eyes. So there's a chance Mum guessed.' I realise I'm holding my breath, waiting for his answer – knowing it will change everything for me, and perhaps for Amy, too.

He sighs. 'Maybe.'

'Shit.' I take a moment to digest that – to imagine the impact it had on my mum. 'But she didn't know her best friend had died? No, *killed* herself. In despair at having her daughter stolen from her,' I add heatedly, remembering Luke Jackson's letter.

'No,' Dad says quietly, his face turning the colour of ash. 'At least, I don't think so.'

'Well, you know what? I hope she didn't!' Although as I think of that scorching bank holiday when Mum returned from the allotment so badly shaken, I wonder if Luke Jackson did speak to her then, after all – if she in fact knew the full, horrible truth and had to spend the rest of her life carrying it in silence . . . 'Poor Isabella. Poor Mum,' I sigh. 'Poor Amy, too. Growing up with no idea that her dad wasn't even her dad. And her mum was dead.'

'I had no idea about that, I swear.' Dad leans forward, gripping his knees. 'I tried to give Amy a good life. I bought her everything she wanted. Oh, I realise I spoiled her. She turned out wild. Out every night, lying about where she'd been. She's never *stopped* lying.'

'Sometimes it's easier than facing the truth,' I say quietly.

'The truth. Huh. People make up their own version of it, anyway, don't they? I know what the rumour mill says about me. All those wagging tongues in the village.'

'Amy has borne the brunt of it as much as you,' I remind him, thinking of Miss Shaw.

'Oh, I'm fully aware of my failings, believe you me.' Wearily, he rubs a hand over his face. 'And how others have paid the price for them.'

'Others.' I bite my lip, summoning up fresh courage. 'Like *Jane*?'

'Sorry?' He sits back, looking genuinely perplexed for a moment.

'Why did you ask Marley what happens to naughty girls, Dad? Was my friend *Jane* naughty?' I ask scathingly. 'Was she noisy and messy too? Did *she* need to be punished in some way?'

For a second, Dad looks furious, then he stands up and paces towards the window, staring out towards the golf course without saying a word. His shoulders hunch, and for a moment I wonder if he's crying. Then he turns to face me, arms folded, blue eyes sharp.

'I told you, Holly. There was an *accident*. Jane Price fell off the swing in your school playground. I know that for sure, because I was there.'

Chapter 58

Shock immobilises me for a few moments, before scepticism filters in; I glare at Dad. 'Mum collected us from school every single day without fail.' *Even when she was ill*, I reflect sadly.

'Yes, she did,' Dad agrees patiently. 'But it was the last day of term. I knew it would be crazy. Your mum was looking so tired, Holly. The forgetfulness was getting worse. Some days, she didn't know what year it was. We'd had the diagnosis by then, of course.' He rubs a hand across his short, now greying hair in a familiar gesture. 'I could see she was struggling.'

'So you offered to pick us up from school,' I surmise. 'Amy and me.'

'I waited for you in the playground. Jane was already out, playing on the swing. I went to talk to her. She was a sweet girl. Full of fun. Marley reminds me of her, in fact. Same bright eyes and curly hair. So inquisitive. So clever. Always laughing and chatting away.'

'Not lately,' I say tersely. 'In fact, she's been terrified, these last few weeks.'

'Oh?' Dad's eyes widen in surprise. 'Why?'

'Are you sure you don't know?' I give him a sharp look. 'I mean, for God's sake, there's a *gun* in the drawer next to her bed. She mentioned it. She must have *seen* it.'

'Impossible.'

'Are you sure about that? How long has it been there?'

'A few weeks. Couple of months, maybe.'

'So it was there before Marley's birthday?' I persist, already guessing the answer.

'Yes. Most likely. But it's not loaded. You see I—'

'Oh, spare me the excuses. Marley's been frightened out of her wits. Not just by the gun, which she obviously saw.' I give him another sharp look. 'But by things she overheard. She has that in common with her Aunty Amy, at least,' I say without humour. 'Listening to adult conversations. Trying to understand things that weren't meant for her ears.'

'Hang on, I didn't . . . I haven't . . . Marley hasn't been round here for *weeks*,' Dad blusters, stumbling over his words.

'You're right. She's refused to come here. She's refused to go to The Emporium, or any of the places she used to go with you. And why do you think that is? You *scared* her, Dad. Talking about Mum dying.'

'What?' He looks genuinely shocked. 'But I never said . . . I didn't tell her . . .'

'Kids hear far more than you realise. On Marley's birthday . . . she overheard Amy and Jordan talking. About Luke Jackson. About *you*.' I shake my head in despair. 'More people have paid the price for your secrets than I think you realise.'

'I'm sorry. Truly, I am.' He sighs, digging his hands in his pockets. 'All I've ever wanted is to protect my family. Your mother. *You*. And your children. Even Jordan.'

I roll my eyes. 'I thought you didn't like him.'

'Quite the contrary. Despite the fact that he reminds me of myself. When I was much younger, of course. All that energy, drive and ambition. Wanting to travel and see the world. I suppose I worried he wouldn't stay here. And I really wanted you to be settled, love. I knew you were going to lose your mum. I didn't know when, but I knew it was coming.'

I can feel tears welling up, but I fight to hold on to them. I refuse to let him distract me by playing on my sympathy. 'You were saying about Jane,' I prompt tersely.

'Right. Yes.' He pulls a handkerchief out of his pocket and blows his nose. 'Well, like I said, she was playing. *Happy*. It was the last day of primary school. I guess she got a bit reckless. She stood up on the swing, making it wobble. I made a silly joke about her flying.'

Look at me! I'm flying! I hear in my head, picturing you on your favourite swing in the park, imagining my friend, too . . . instinctively knowing what's coming next.

'The next thing I knew, Jane launched herself at me.' Dad starts pacing slowly up and down the room. 'It was all a blur. I reacted too slowly. I . . . couldn't catch her.'

'Oh, my God.' I picture Jane's bright eyes and pretty face, her chocolate curls flying up as she fell. 'What did you do?' I ask hoarsely.

'I helped her up. I gave her a hug. She smiled and started laughing. Then she ran off. I had no idea she wasn't OK. I swear it, Holly,' he pleads, coming to stand in front of me.

'Then what?' I say quietly.

'Then I took you and Amy home. I honestly never gave it a second thought. Not until Jane's uncle called me that evening to say she'd had a bleed on the brain. I was distraught. When she died, I was devastated. I couldn't tell you. I knew it would break your heart. It shocked *everyone*. For once, no one in the village even wanted to talk about it.'

'There was no inquest?' I frown, thinking of all my futile attempts over the years to find out the truth. Only Maria had any inkling of what had happened.

'Yes. But Jane's injuries were so obviously conducive with a fall. They also found her blood on the playground. Under the swing. It was an open and shut case.'

'And you offered to sue the LEA on behalf of her aunt and uncle,' I say, remembering what Amy told me.

'We settled out of court. I made sure they got sufficient compensation. Enough to move quietly away and start life afresh in London. I believe they had a child after that. I managed to keep it all out of the papers. Dave and Helen were worried that—'

'They never knew your part in it?' I cut in, aghast at how he's managed to keep such a dreadful secret, feeling a spike of annoyance at his hypocrisy as I remember him lecturing me as a child to 'own up and take responsibility' for my mistakes.

'It was an accident. Jane was dead,' Dad says bluntly. 'I didn't see the point of risking my family by revealing the circumstances. You may call that cowardly, but I had a decision to make, and I took it. Parents do that. They make choices, and they have to stand by them. I'm not a bad man, sweetheart. I'm just a man. A husband. A father.'

I think of the choice Luke Jackson made. He regretted it for the rest of his life; he'll no doubt die wishing he made a different one. Then again, he wasn't Amy's father, and he was never even her parent. He abandoned her completely, and despite his remorse at the eleventh hour, it all smacks of too little, too late.

Then I remember Amy's comment that my dad is only human. If she can find it in her heart to pardon Luke, surely I can forgive my own father? I try my hardest to feel the understanding he obviously wants from me, but my thoughts go around and around. Before I can make up my mind, he stands up and strides towards the sideboard, pulling open a drawer and taking out a long white envelope, exactly like the one you left for me.

'There's only one thing I've ever done in my life that I truly, bitterly regret. It's been preying on my mind a lot, lately. It's the reason I couldn't face Marley's birthday party. I can barely face myself in the mirror,' he admits, sinking down onto the sofa again.

I sigh. 'I can imagine. But . . . thank you for telling me the truth,' I add reluctantly.

'I've wanted to a million times. But you'd already lost your mum, Holly. I didn't want you to lose your dad, too. Oh, I don't mean prison. I didn't commit any crime.'

'Except lying by omission.'

'I'm so sorry. I wish I could make it up to you. I wanted to make it up to *Marley*. For missing her birthday. I'm the only grandparent she has in her life. I know that. I've always felt sad that she never met Olivia. I guess I've talked about your mum more than I realised.'

'I *want* Marley to know about her grandma, Dad. I just don't want her being scared.'

'I wanted to show her Sea View, as well,' he continues as though I haven't spoken, clearly locked into his own thoughts. 'I came to see you this morning to ask if that would be OK. Then Amy turned up. I guessed straightaway she'd told you everything. I panicked, I suppose. I knew my mistakes had finally come back to haunt me.'

'We never truly escape our past.' I glance at the door as I quote Amy, suddenly wondering what's keeping her, why she hasn't returned yet.

'Exactly. Which is why, in the end, I took the children to be with their daddy. I needed space to think. To decide what to do about . . . what I did.'

An image of the gun flashes in my head, and I glance around the immaculate flat. Dad has always been fastidiously tidy, but I can see now that all his personal possessions have been packed up, as though it's a hotel room and he's checking out.

'Dad, you're scaring me,' I whisper breathlessly.

He laughs, but there are tears in his eyes. 'You're far, far braver than I am, pickle. But you know what? It's not my own pain that scares me. It's other people's. The people I love. I can't bear to see them suffer. Which is why I've written it all down. A blank sheet of paper can't judge you, can it? You can't hurt it. Or disappoint it. Same goes for a diary.'

'Mum's journal. So you *did* take it.'

'Olivia was brave, too. She endured more pain than anyone should have to, with more grace than I could believe. Your mum hid her feelings to protect others. Me, I'm a coward. Just like my so-called friend Luke Jackson.' He holds up the envelope. 'That's the beauty of a letter. You can spill out your deepest, darkest secrets and shove them in a letterbox.' His mouth twists wryly. 'Or you can fold up them up and tuck them away in a drawer.'

Or a worry box, I think, torn between anger and sadness that the man who always preached about lies has told so many of his own; that he lectured me about taking responsibility for mistakes, while he buried his. Most of all, as I stare at the envelope in his hands, I'm struck by the irony that the notes you left for me ultimately led me to your fear of this one man: my dad, your grandfather, who now stands before me with a note of his own.

I feel hysterical laughter bubble inside me, until I look up at his familiar face, the proud, still handsome features softened now by grief, guilt and something more . . . *Fear?* Of what, though? 'Please, just *tell* me,' I say, as I should have said so many times over the years.

'I wish I could, Holly. But I can't. I'm the parent. I'm supposed to be strong. Only I'm not, and I can't bear to see the look on my little girl's face when you find out . . .'

'When I find out *what?*' I snap desperately.

Dad takes faltering steps towards me. 'Here.' He places the envelope in my hands, and as his fingers brush mine I can feel them trembling. 'I hope . . . I trust it answers all your questions.' Before I can open the envelope, he turns and walks towards the door, pausing at the last moment to add softly: 'And that you can forgive me. For everything.'

Chapter 59

TODAY – SUNDAY, 10.45 P.M.

'Wow. As secrets go, that's a humdinger. It definitely knocks Amy's into the long grass.' Jordan wraps his arms around me, and I lean into him, needing his strength, not just physically, but also to help me come to terms with by far the biggest shock of my life.

Jordan was shocked, too, when I showed him Dad's letter. But he hadn't spent every sleepless night of his childhood worrying about what was happening behind closed doors, and every waking moment since racked by unanswered questions. Now I finally know the whole truth and I feel numb, lost – and strangely alone.

I turn my head to stare across the sea, watching moonlight paint it silver, listening to the sound that's as familiar to me as Jordan's strong heartbeat, and my own faulty one. 'Mum loved this place,' I whisper, choked with yearning for her, aching with desperation to hold her hand one last time and hear the soft, soothing voice that always made everything better.

'And your dad loved *her*. Whatever he once felt about Amy's mum, it was obvious how much he adored yours. People do strange things when they love someone that much. Irrational things. OK, idiotic.' Jordan's arms tighten around me. 'I can vouch for that.'

'Hmm.' I pull back to look up at him. 'I won't deny you've been acting rather peculiar, these last few weeks.' It's a relief to change the subject for a moment. I need time and space to process my dad's confession, but right now I need to focus on my own little family – and the marriage I thought I'd lost.

'I hope you understand why now. I'm so sorry I didn't tell you, babe. I *wanted* to, but I've been so damned worried about you. You've been so anxious, looking so tired. I was scared your heart . . .' Jordan drags in a breath so deep, I feel it working up through his chest.

'It's OK. I know. I get it. Finally.' I crook a smile at him.

'I *hated* keeping secrets from you. It was so bloody hard, for one thing. Every time I opened my mouth, I was tempted to say something. It was just easier to stay away.'

'It upset me, I won't lie.' I slip my hands inside his jacket, savouring our renewed closeness. 'But you were right. It was Amy's story. She just had to bite the bullet and tell it. And it *did* almost kill me.' I sigh, remembering the ill-fated conversation you overheard.

'God, I'm so sorry, Holl.'

'I'm just glad she found the strength to do so before she left for Paris.' Another wave of loneliness sweeps through me. 'Do you think she'll ever come back?'

'Absolutely. Oh, Amy bitches about this place, but it's home. And she adores you.'

'I had no idea,' I say huskily, recalling Amy's unexpected, uncharacteristically emotional declaration in the hospital car park. 'I truly didn't.'

'I'm not surprised. She's always played her cards close to her chest.'

'Self-preservation,' I sigh. 'A lifetime of secrecy taught her that, I guess.'

'Exactly. But that afternoon on the boat . . . she was crazy with worry about you.'

'Yes, Marley told me. Well, her version of it, anyway.'

Jordan winces. 'I'm so sorry,' he says again.

'I know. Honestly. You don't need to keep saying it.'

'I do. I messed up. I got overexcited about the regatta. And Marley's party. I wanted her to have a great time. I was too loud, too thoughtless. I didn't realise how much she overheard. How badly she misunderstood it.' He tips his head back and groans loudly. 'I genuinely thought she was just going through a quiet phase. I'm such an idiot!'

'You're an amazing dad, Jordan. I know what it's like to grow up with parents who bottle everything up. That's not you.' I sigh again, regretting the doubts I've had. 'Marley is just like you, you know? A chatterbox. It's why I knew something was so badly wrong.'

'You're a good mum, Holly. The best.'

Gently, Jordan strokes back my hair, letting his fingers tangle in the curls I haven't had time to straighten. The last few hours have been the most intense I have ever known – worse than being rushed into hospital for an emergency delivery when BB was born; close, even, to the devastating hours, days and weeks after my mum died.

'A good mum. Amy said that.' I pause, remembering. 'I just feel so sorry for her. For the baby she lost. For growing up feeling like she never really belonged anywhere.'

'You see? That's what I love about you.' Jordan cups my face in his hands, wiping away my tears. 'You always worry about everyone else, never yourself.'

'Trust me, I've felt plenty sorry for myself,' I admit. 'I thought you were leaving me.'

Briefly, I close my eyes, giving silent thanks that Jordan finally picked up my phone call and drove straight over to my dad's flat, with you and BB safely in the back of his car. 'We're a team, babe,' he insisted, when I expressed frustration at how little I was able to do practically – not just because of physical weakness, but also the trauma of reading my dad's painful recounting of the devastating secret he'd carried for eight years.

I'd wanted Dad to tell me in person, but as soon as I opened his letter, I was glad he'd left me to read it alone. Rage had burned through me at every word, followed by shock, bewilderment and overwhelming grief that almost put me straight back in hospital.

'I'll *never* leave you, Holly,' Jordan says seriously, linking his hands behind my back and pulling me closer against him. 'Forever-together-whatever, remember?'

'I do.' I manage to smile up at him. 'That was the happiest day of my life. But also the saddest. Such a perfect wedding, but without Mum . . . She'd have loved it, wouldn't she?'

'She'd have thrown the biggest and best party ever, you mean.' Jordan grins.

'Like she did the first time I took you to Sea View. You know, I think she wanted to tell me then. About Amy. Luke and Isabella. But then Dad . . .' I break off, my chest tightening as I think of my dad's letter and recall exactly what happened that night.

'Do you forgive him?' Jordan asks quietly.

'No,' I snap, then bite my lip. 'I mean, I need time to think.'

'Take as long as you need, sweetheart.' Jordan steps back, turning to look across the moonlit, shimmering pebble beach, towards our little terraced row of cottages, now shrouded in darkness. 'Maria's got the kids. They're safe. *You're* safe.'

'And my dad? The gun . . .' Panic flutters in my chest.

'Gone,' Jordan reassures me. 'He made a bloody stupid mistake leaving it in his flat.'

'He wasn't thinking straight. Oh, I'm not excusing him,' I say quickly. 'But maybe I understand his pain. You know, I don't think Dad actually wanted to die. He just wanted the guilt to stop,' I acknowledge, still thinking of the brutally honest confession he'd originally intended for me to read after his death.

'Thank God he let me take the gun. Although, your dad being your dad, he told me to make sure I get a good price for it. Huh. I'll use it to buy Amy a thirtieth birthday present, hey? I reckon Adam owes her a bloody good one.'

'As does Luke Jackson.' I shake my head. 'I know he's sick, and I feel sorry for him. But I hope he spends the next few days grovelling at Amy's feet. He's hurt her so much, and now she has to cope with . . . this.' I reach into my pocket and take out Dad's letter.

Jordan looks surprised. 'You showed it to her?'

I nod. 'I had to see Amy's reaction with my own eyes. It was the only way I could be sure whether she knew. If she'd ever guessed.'

'And? Had she? How *did* she react?'

I recall Amy's howls of anger, her anguished wails of despair. She was as devastated by Dad's confession as I had been, but I suspected she wouldn't want Jordan to know that. Sisterly loyalty kicks in. 'She was shocked, of course. But, no, she'd never guessed.'

'Thank God. I can forgive Amy for many things, but if she'd kept that from you . . .'

'Amy doesn't always go about things the right way, but I know she only wants the best for me. And now she's gone. To Paris. With barely a goodbye.' I thought I was all cried out, but I have to fight back yet more tears as I recall Amy's final text:

Love you, sis. Always. But it's finally time for me to fly away.

Chapter 60

'You know what? Amy Jackson has totally missed her vocation,' Jordan says dryly. 'She should be on the stage. She *never* misses the chance for a dramatic entrance. Or exit.'

I try to smile, but there's a huge lump in my throat. 'I guess she needs time to come to terms with everything, too. She thought *she* was the only one keepings secrets. Poor Amy.'

'Not so perfect Amy, hey?' Jordan teases gently.

'I guess none of us are. It's just hard to admit our flaws. Or worries.' I reach into my other pocket and take out a handful of colourful, mismatched scraps of paper.

'Are those Marley's notes?'

'All seven of them.' I curl my fingers around the precious clues you gave me.

Jordan tuts, shaking his head. 'I'm amazed you figured them out.'

'I didn't really,' I admit. 'Well, I got close. But I needed to hear the words in Marley's own voice, from her own mouth.'

'Like she heard them from mine. Huh. Only they were the wrong words.'

I take hold of his hands. 'It's the worst thing we learn as we grow up, isn't it? How to say one thing and mean another. How to hide our true feelings behind silly sayings. Children just say things as they see them. Marley took everything she overheard *literally*.'

'Me acting like some kind of half-arsed double agent, you mean. Leaping onto Pirate Island.' Jordan groans. 'I still feel so damned bad about her birthday. Not only that I scared her, but that she didn't feel able to *tell* me. What kind of monster must I be?'

'It wasn't that, Jordan. It wasn't even you she was scared of. It was my dad. He's been talking obsessively about what happened to Mum. Not directly to Marley, but around her. Muttering to himself, like he's stuck in the past. Reliving it. Trying to *rewrite* it, maybe.'

'He's certainly a changed man.' Jordan's usually mellow voice is gruff, and his hands squeeze mine. 'Your dad is—'

'Broken, actually,' I say sadly. 'I think Marley saw that, and it scared her. She also heard him muttering about her Grandma Olivia getting so tired that she went to sleep and never woke up. Then she saw Dad's gun, put two and two together and—'

'Made ten,' Jordan finishes for me. 'Our little girl's always had a vivid imagination. I wonder where she gets it from,' he adds, lifting my hands to press them against his chest.

'She does – and she was terrified that what happened to Mum would happen to me. And that it would be her fault. Because she's so messy, so noisy.' I shake my head. 'If only she knew how much I love that about her. How I've *missed* it. She thought – and I know it sounds silly to us, but it was very real to Marley – she thought you were spying on her, Jordan. About how well she behaved.'

'Seriously? Oh, God. Because Amy and I were joking around about James Bond?'

'Exactly. That's when her nightmare really started to take shape in her mind. As you say, she has a vivid imagination. Stories are real to Marley. That's why she stopped wanting to read them. Or write them. They made the scary pictures in her head come alive. Of me being hurt. You and Amy sailing off on your boat with BB.'

'Huh. That was Amy's flight of fantasy. She didn't mean it, babe. She was desperate.'

'I know. And if it's any consolation, Marley was worried the police would catch you.'

I remember your anxiety about Sergeant Robins, the question you never got to ask about him. I think I know what it was now: you wanted to know if he had a gun too. Because you'd seen my dad's, and instinctively you associated the police with punishment. As scared as you were for my safety, you didn't want your daddy to get hurt, either.

'If only she'd told me. If only I'd stopped to *listen*,' Jordan berates himself.

'She thought she was doing the right thing by *not* telling us. About anything. Like bruising her knees when she slipped on the rocks, that morning you took her to the beach.' A shiver works through me as I recall finding those bruises – the sickening fear that took hold when I heard you say: 'Daddy said it was a secret.'

Jordan sighs. 'I only meant that I didn't want you worrying.'

'I know that now. I should have realised *before*, only I was so overwrought. I'm so used to Marley telling me everything. Then, all of a sudden, she clammed up. The same thing happened with Leah, when she gave her that nasty scratch.'

Jordan frowns. 'Leah did *what*?'

'Oh, it wasn't serious. I just worried it might be. Leah's been going through a tough time, too. She's taken it out on Marley a bit, I'm afraid. Telling stories. Lashing out.'

Instantly, I'm reminded of Amy: the angry fights and hard-won forgiveness; our enduring friendship beyond being sisters. I pray that bond will survive my dad's confession; I wonder if you and Leah will become lifelong friends, too.

Then I think of my first ever friend, Jane, and I know I'll always regret that her childhood wish on a shooting star never came true. But I won't ever forget her. True friendship doesn't die; it just changes with time.

'That doesn't sound good.' Jordan pulls away from me and paces to and fro, his trainers crunching on the damp shingle. 'Leah hurting Marley? What the heck? Marley really should have told us about that.'

'She didn't want her best friend to get into trouble,' I say simply. 'Leah told her secrets, and Marley kept them. It made her sad—' I pause, thinking of your note '—but she felt stuck. After all, it's what we teach kids, isn't it? *Don't be a tell-tale.*'

'I guess there's a little kid inside all of us,' Jordan muses. 'Holding on to worry. Too scared to say what frightens us. Hmm. Maybe we should keep that damned worry box, after all.' He chuckles, gently grabbing the lapels of my jacket and pulling me close again.

'Some fears are too big to put into words. But we have to try, don't we? Be brave. Tell the truth. Before the chance is taken away from us,' I whisper, knowing I'll always regret that last unfinished conversation with my mum, before her life ended so prematurely – that I'll forever imagine and reimagine it in my head, for the rest of *my* life.

'I'll kick this off, then, shall I?' Jordan's head dips lower, his mouth inches from mine, his breath warm on my face as his lean body presses against me, strong and familiar. 'I love you, Holly Mayhew. I'm sorry I ever let you doubt it. And I promise to keep on trying. To be a better husband. A better dad. Heck, even a better brother-in-law.'

I smile up at him. 'I'm sure Amy won't have any trouble letting you know when you slip up. Which reminds me. I'm sorry too. For ever thinking that you . . . and she . . .'

'It never entered my head for a second. You, me and the kids. That's the real deal, Holly. You feel the same, don't you?' he says, suddenly hesitant. 'You still love me?'

'Till the seas run dry,' I agree, and this time I kiss him first.

Chapter 61

The moon slips out from behind a cloud, breaking the spell, and I look up at the night sky, spotting a shooting star streaking towards the horizon. Pulling away from Jordan, I keep my eyes fixed on the bright tail, waiting to see where it lands, following the sound of the sea towards the foaming shore.

As my feet encounter the first shock of cold, I shiver, feeling water soak into my ankle boots, followed by the hem of my jeans. I pause, giving my body temperature time to adjust, then I take two steps forward. And then another two, and another . . .

I think of Isabella, imagining her heartache as she walked into the River Seine, desperate to escape the mental torment of having lost her daughter; I picture my mum, her gentle brown eyes filling with tears as she clung trustingly to my dad's hand as he helped her take the pills that finally put an end to the physical pain that was making life unbearable.

Reaching into my coat pocket, I pull out Dad's letter and stare once more at the neatly handwritten words. I can't read them; there is no darkness like the beach at night. It's almost like being back inside the womb: cocooned in pitch-blackness; lulled by the rhythmic sound of water. But it doesn't matter: I have memorised every word . . .

My dearest, darling Holly – for that is what you have always been, and will be for ever, even when I'm no longer here to tell you. If you are reading this letter, I know that time has come, and I only hope you are not alone, that Jordan is right by your side, where I know he will always be. He's lucky to have you, and I have been blessed to have you as my daughter.

I wish I'd told you that more often; there are so many things I wish I'd told you. About my life, about Amy. When she came along, I was twice blessed. She has her own story to tell, and knowing Amy I'm sure she will – but, while there's still breath in my body, there is one last thing I need to tell you . . . Coward soul that I am, I've waited until now.

My weakness shames me, Holly. I hope I haven't been a bad father, but I know I could have been a better one – a better grandfather to Marley and Benjamin. I love them both dearly, and it hurts unbearably not to see them grow up.

But I won't indulge in self-pity. I have brought this on myself, and I deserve every ounce of the torment I've suffered and can endure no longer. I'm so sorry, pickle. Please, forgive me: for the hurt I know I'm inflicting on you now, and for what I have to tell you before I leave this world to be with my own dear sweet Olivia.

I promise you I never let go of her hand until she drew her last breath; I held her, comforted her and talked of happier days. It was her own choice, Holly – I tell you that not to exonerate my guilt, but to try, in some small way, to ease your mind. Beyond all things, your mum never wanted you to suffer; in ending her own life, she sought to put an end not to her pain, but yours.

319

Believe me, she wanted to tell you herself – she wrote so many letters, then asked me to destroy them all, along with her diary. The thought of leaving you broke Olivia's heart, you see; she couldn't bear to say goodbye to you, and she was desperate for you to remember her at her best, her happiest. That's why she chose to leave us that night – the night of the party, after she'd seen you safe and happy with Jordan.

All these years, I've respected Olivia's wish for silence, but now the time has come for my own goodbye, and I want you to know that, in her final moments, your mum was at peace – thinking and talking only of you. The last word she spoke was your name. Her darling Holly . . .

I close my eyes, once again remembering that night, how Dad hadn't dressed up for the party, how he didn't seem to get into the spirit of it at all. If only I'd guessed what he was about to do; if only I'd guessed what Mum had asked him to do *for* her . . .

I realise now that Dr Henry must have known: his frequent visits and hushed conversations. He was there that night, too – and he reassured me Mum was *fine*, I recall bitterly. Later, he changed his story to say she'd probably had a stroke, but the post-mortem was inconclusive, the coroner recording a narrative verdict that began with terminal cancer and ended with an accidental overdose of morphine tablets.

I know Dr Henry prescribed those tablets, and anger rises up again. I feel like he stole something from me – Dad, too. Whatever their good intentions, they stole the truth; they stole my last chance to say goodbye to my mum.

Neither of them benefited from Mum's will, and everything I know points to assisted suicide rather than murder. But Dad covered his tracks well; the police would never be able to prove his actions, and it weighs heavily on my mind that, without Mum's letters, I only have his word that it was really her choice . . .

Jordan asked me if I've forgiven my dad, and the honest answer is, I don't know; my trust in him has been badly shaken. I understand now why he sold Sea View; the memories must have been unbearable. I *don't* understand why he never told me.

Maybe time will heal the rift between us – heal *him*, too, after his dark thoughts about ending his own life. I know the counsellor he's agreed to see will help him; perhaps, at some point, we might even see her together, and get the help we need to speak to each other.

At least that possibility still exists: to talk to Dad, ask the questions Mum never had the chance to answer – or chose not to. I wish so much that she'd made a different choice; I wish I could wind back time and finish that last conversation with her: beg her to stay, hold on just a little longer . . . spend a few more precious days, hours, moments with me.

I understand that she wanted to spare me pain; the very beating of my heart reminds me of her protectiveness. Every time I had an attack, I saw fear on her face – fear she tried to hide. *Bury.* Like Jane's lost doll, with its broken eyes and battered body. I feel battered, too. 'But I'm still here, Mum! I survived!' I cry out, the wind carrying my voice into the darkness. 'I was strong enough to hear the truth,' I whisper, shivering in the cool, silent air.

In the end, hard as it is, I have to respect that my mum wanted to slip away on her own terms. She lived for her family, always putting us first; she had the right to make that final difficult choice about her own life – even though it broke my heart.

As Amy said: *parents hold all the power*. But Mum wielded it with a gentle, loving hand. And I forgive her.

My mum was the secret keeper – and I am her daughter. But I want her legacy to be so much more than the money she left to always keep me safe. I want to learn from her life, and pass on her love; I'm determined to break the pattern that broke her, and that has haunted me . . .

I want no more secrets with you, my own daughter. I want to tell you every day that I love you; I want us to share our worries, and solve them together. Your grandma was a gardener, Marley; she knew better than anyone that flowers can't bloom in the dark. I wish she'd had the chance to share her passions with you, just as I wish she had shared her secrets with me. I promise you that, from this moment on, I will do both.

Holding out my arms, I let the wind carry away your notes, and my dad's letter, and as I watch the fragments of paper float across the North Sea, I smile, imagining them mingling with Mum's ashes. Icy waves rush up at me, but suddenly I feel no fear, not of drowning, or death . . . or a life without the woman I loved so much but who never felt able to share her truth with me.

Mum kept her husband's secrets to protect him; she kept her own to protect me . . . because she loved me more than her own life, just as I do you. It's not easy sharing our deepest feelings; your notes taught me that. But, in the end, I think I understand that my mum's silence said more than words.

After one last look at the scraps of paper already beginning to disintegrate around me, I turn back and forge my way purposefully towards the shore. As the gritty stones of the pebble beach finally crunch beneath my boots, I glance upwards and imagine I can see the bright lights of Sea View beckoning me home. I smile, then close my eyes and answer the gentle siren call I will forever hear in my heart: 'Goodbye, Mum. I love you, too.'

Author's Note

Eagle-eyed readers will spot that this book is set during the time of COVID-19 – a term blessedly unknown to me when I first started writing Holly's story. In order to do justice to my characters, I've claimed the privilege of dramatic license to pretend that the world they inhabit is similarly untouched by the distressing impact of a global pandemic. I hope you'll forgive this creative trickery; I used it with the best of intentions – to allow Holly and her family to live and breathe on the page, unfettered by masks, constant handwashing, school closures and multiple other daily restrictions! Not to mention the all-consuming worry of coronavirus that has plagued us all. Indeed, I think the challenges I have set my characters are sufficient for them to contend with . . .

We all wonder what our loved ones are thinking – especially if their mood or behaviour changes unexpectedly. But opening up about our fears can be tough, even more so for children. I learned this while previously practising as a psychotherapist, and as a parent it's become one of my most pressing concerns: *How do I know what my children are worrying about?*

The answer might seem simple: *talk* to them; ask them what's on their mind. Not so easy when children are very young and haven't yet developed the cognitive skills to understand and articulate their feelings ... even harder as they grow up and learn to be wary of sharing their worries, either for fear of exposing themselves or upsetting others.

I experienced exactly this situation with my own children, and one strategy I used to help them express their anxieties was to make a worry box where they could post little notes. Of course, the plan was to help *them*, but *I* needed help, too! The more I wondered about my children's fears, the bigger my own grew, my imagination running riot with terrifying possibilities ...

Monsters live in darkness – in secrecy and lies – yet as much as every parent torments themselves conjuring up nightmare scenarios, sadly, the real truth can sometimes be even more painful. As I contemplated this, the idea for *The Secret Keeper's Daughter* was born. In the story, Holly uses a worry box to unlock her daughter's anxiety, but at the same time she unearths her own deeply buried childhood fears – along with a devastating family secret.

Holly's journey towards discovering her inner strength begins with finding out the truth; after all, it's only in facing our fears that we can overcome them. I wish you courage in conquering yours ... with or without a worry box!

Samantha King

Acknowledgements

The setting for this book is a special place, very close to my heart – one I have visited with my family every year, since my children were tiny – and I would never have known about it were it not for a chance recommendation by Kate Mills. It feels like serendipity, therefore, that Kate should be the publisher to invite me to join the fabulous list at HQ Stories, and for that I am truly grateful.

Having the opportunity to keep writing, and for my books to reach readers all around the world, is a privilege I value beyond words; working with the hugely creative, dynamic publishing team of HQ is a pure joy. I especially want to thank my clever, insightful, wonderful editor Belinda Toor, whose enthusiasm for this story has spurred me on to tell it, and whose kind supportiveness has made writing it such a happy experience.

Publishing a book involves a great many people, and I owe several big bundles of gratitude to: Eugenie Furniss, my brilliant agent, for her enduring faith in me; Emily MacDonald, for her fabulous early editorial critiques; Audrey Linton, for smoothly guiding my manuscript through its publication journey; copy editor extraordinaire Helena Newton, and eagle-eyed proofreader Michelle

Bullock, for taking such good care of my words – and everyone at HQ and HarperCollins involved in publishing, marketing, promoting and selling them!

As ever, I'm super thankful for the encouragement of other authors, and the enthusiastic cheerleading of my family and lovely friends far and wide. The idea for *The Secret Keeper's Daughter* was born out of my own experiences as a mum, and for that I can never thank my children enough. Hani and Rafi: you are the heartbeat of my writing; without you, and the never-wavering love and championing of your amazing dad, I would never have written a single word. Paul, it's all about our love, and so shall it be for ever.

Dear Reader,

We hope you enjoyed reading this book. If you did, we'd be so appreciative if you left a review. It really helps us and the author to bring more books like this to you.

Here at HQ Digital we are dedicated to publishing fiction that will keep you turning the pages into the early hours. Don't want to miss a thing? To find out more about our books, promotions, discover exclusive content and enter competitions you can keep in touch in the following ways:

JOIN OUR COMMUNITY:

Sign up to our new email newsletter:
http://smarturl.it/SignUpHQ

Read our new blog www.hqstories.co.uk

 https://twitter.com/HQStories

 www.facebook.com/HQStories

BUDDING WRITER?

We're also looking for authors to join the HQ Digital family!
Find out more here:

https://www.hqstories.co.uk/want-to-write-for-us/

Thanks for reading, from the HQ Digital team

**If you enjoyed *The Secret Keeper's Daughter*,
then why not try another gripping page-turner
from HQ Digital?**